**Outstanding praise for Michael Hiebert
and *Dream with Little Angels***

"Hiebert has an authentic Southern voice and his protagonist is as
engaging as Harper Lee's Scout.
A masterful coming-of-age gem."

"Gorge   , with
attention   s debut
delivers   with a
heart   nd

"A trip to   d with
that elusi   often
settles   ."

"*Dream wi*   g plot,
and pacir   t's a
marvelous   gling
to come   ."

"*Dream with Little Angels* is quality storytelling sure to keep
readers enthralled."
—*Kane County Chronicle*

Books by Michael Hiebert

DREAM WITH LITTLE ANGELS

CLOSE TO THE BROKEN HEARTED

Published by Kensington Publishing Corporation

CLOSE TO

The

BROKEN HEARTED

MICHAEL HIEBERT

KENSINGTON BOOKS
www.kensingtonbooks.com

KENSINGTON BOOKS are published by

Kensington Publishing Corp.
119 West 40th Street
New York, NY 10018

All Kensington titles, imprints, and distributed lines are available at special quantity discounts for bulk purchases for sales promotion, premiums, fund-raising, and educational or institutional use.

Special book excerpts or customized printings can also be created to fit specific needs. For details, write or phone the office of the Kensington Special Sales Manager: Kensington Publishing Corp., 119 West 40th Street, New York, NY 10018. Attn. Special Sales Department. Phone: 1-800-221-2647.

Kensington and the K logo Reg. U.S. Pat. & TM Off.

eISBN-13: 978-0-7582-9427-2
eISBN-10: 0-7582-9427-1
First Kensington Electronic Edition: July 2014

ISBN-13: 978-0-7582-9426-5
ISBN-10: 0-7582-9426-3
First Kensington Trade Paperback Printing: July 2014

10 9 8 7 6 5 4 3 2 1

Printed in the United States of America

For Sagan
with the heart of a warrior . . .

ACKNOWLEDGMENTS

A debt of gratitude to my agent, Adrienne Rosado, for selling this book and its predecessor, *Dream with Little Angels*.

To my incomparable editor, John Scognamiglio, along with the rest of my friends at Kensington for their ongoing support and ability to surprise me with how much they really do stand behind their authors.

To Vida Engstrand, publicity director extraordinaire, for knowing when to give me a kick in the pants and knowing when to let me try the tightrope without a net.

To my girlfriend, Shannon Mairs, for putting up with my late-night write-a-thons and hardly ever complaining about it.

To my dearest friend, Julianna Hinckley, for providing me with answers to my infinite questions about life in the South.

To Yvonne Rupert for giving me a shoulder to cry on and an endless fountain of encouragement when things got overwhelming.

To Ken Loomes for reading a very rough draft of *Close to the Broken Hearted* and pointing out all my discrepancies, especially in the area of weaponry. Sometimes you scare me, Ken.

To the Chilliwack Writers' Group: Garth Pettersen, Mary Keane, Fran Brown, Lori Christine, and Terri McKee, for giving me an audience for parts of this book and providing fantastic feedback and critique.

To my three children, Valentine, Sagan, and Legend. They continue to be my ongoing inspiration for the relationship between Abe and Carry.

And to my parents, Abe and Ann Hiebert, for providing me with everything I needed to finish this book, including the very roof over my head, not including everything else in my life. I doubt the scales will ever be balanced again.

Thanks to Mark Leland for taking time to help me find

answers to all my questions regarding police work that I couldn't find anywhere else.

And to Pastor Badwell of the Parkway Baptist Church in Alabama for giving me guidance involving the Baptist faith.

Thanks also to the Mobile, Alabama, Police Department and their openness to answering my questions about Southern police work.

Finally, a shout-out to Writers' Village University (www.writers village.com); National Public Radio; Joshua Graham and his online radio show, *Between the Lines*; the Chilliwack Book Man; and the Chilliwack Library.

PROLOGUE

Alvin, Alabama—1971

The spring sun is low in the sky outside the single-paned windows of the kitchen in the small farmhouse where the family has gathered to eat. Upon the table sits a roast chicken ready to be carved, a plate of mashed potatoes, and a bowl of peas and corn, both harvested last year but kept frozen through the winter months. The light falling in through the windows is a deep orange, almost red, as the father, Tom Carson, stands to say grace. His hat sits on the top newel of the short run of stairs that separates this room from the living room below.

The table, like the house, was built by his father. The chicken and the vegetables came from the farm. Unlike the house, the rest of the farm had once all belonged to his father's father. Tom Carson is a proud man even though he lives a modest life. He is proud of his work in the fields that starts at daybreak and ends at supper. He is proud of his two children: Caleb, barely three, with black hair and fair skin like his father, and Sylvie, five and a half, with blond hair like her mother used to have. They are good kids. Respectful kids. Long ago they learned not to make noise or fuss about while their father says grace. Soon Caleb will start working with his father little by little out on the farm. Sylvie already does some jobs with her mother around the home.

Each of the kids clutches their mother's hands. Mother closes her eyes. She is a good woman. Tom is lucky to have all he has. There're wrinkles around his wife's eyes he hasn't noticed before, and he wonders how hard this life has been on her. It's a thought that hasn't occurred to him until now.

In his cracked voice, he delivers the blessing, thanking the Lord Jesus for this wonderful bounty He has bestowed upon their family. The Lord Jesus has been good to Tom Carson.

Tom finishes and takes his chair at the table, folding his napkin onto his lap. Mother's fingers let go of the children's hands. Her gray eyes open and she smiles across the table at Tom. Tom reaches for the platter of chicken so that he may start to carve.

Across the room, there's a loud knock at the door.

Mother jumps. "Who would be knockin' aroun' here at suppertime?" she asks.

"Dunno," Tom Carson says gruffly. He gently lifts the napkin from his lap and begins to rise from the table when the door swings open with a squeak. It wasn't locked. Tom and his family never lock their doors. Nobody around these parts ever locks their doors.

Tom freezes, half out of his chair, as Preacher Eli Brown steps into his home. The preacher man is dressed in a white shirt with black trousers and vest. Muddy boots cover his feet. His thin face is fixed and stern, but what's caught Tom's attention is the gun the preacher holds in his right hand. It is pointed at the floor, being held as though it wasn't there at all.

"Preacher Eli," Tom says, trying to keep his voice calm. "What brings you round here? We's just 'bout to sit down to supper, as you can see." He sits back down.

The preacher says nothing, just stomps across Tom's living room leaving a trail of dried mud on the wooden floor. He comes up the few stairs toward the small kitchen where the family squeezes around the table. With each of the man's footsteps, Caleb wiggles out of his chair and crawls under the table where he seeks out the safety of his father's legs.

Preacher Eli dangles over the rail along the top of the stairs, the gun hand waving conspicuously in the air as he speaks with a low, slow drawl. "Tom, you and I have quite a land dispute goin' on.

This thing oughta be worked out soon or there could be some trouble comin'."

Tom Carson looks down at his empty plate. "There ain't no dispute, Eli. The land's mine. It belonged to my father, just as it belonged to his father. Been in my family at least three generations. Maybe even more."

"The church disagrees with you."

Tom turned back to the preacher, his face red. "The church has no jurisdiction here, Preacher. If the land belonged to you, you'd have a title to it. If you got a title, produce it. But you can't do that cuz you ain't got one, and since you ain't got no title, you ain't got no land."

"The title is *missing*. You can't produce one either."

"Yes, well, the title seems to have *gone* missing." Tom clears his throat. "I'd say you had somethin' to do with that. Doesn't matter, Eli. Everyone knows the land belongs to me."

"You wanna start asking folk?"

"No. Folk is 'fraid of you."

Preacher Eli Brown's teeth form a thin V of a smile. They are more brown than white and less than straight.

"That how the church doin' things these days, Eli? Bit of a step backward ain't it?" Tom nods at the gun. "That why you here? To scare me into giving you my land so you can build your new 'facility' on it? I got news for you, Eli. I ain't afraid of you or your 'church.' "

This time it's Preacher Eli who reddens. "Well, you oughta be. You oughta be very 'fraid. It is a spiteful and vengeful God you forsake. One does not just turn his back on the will of the Lord Jesus without severe repercussions." His bony voice grows in anger and volume. From under the table, Caleb climbs up onto his father's lap.

For a minute, Tom Carson says nothing, just stares pathetically back at the tall preacher who looks somehow scarecrowlike bathed in the red-orange light of dusk. "You are a fool, Eli. Who said anything about forsakin' God? I ain't turned my back on the Lord Jesus. Your church has nothing to do with neither God nor Jesus. Least if it does, it sure ain't my Jesus. If it were, heaven help us all.

There is absolutely nothing holy about your affairs, Eli. You oughta be ashamed of callin' yourself a man of the cloth. You've made a mockery of everything folk hold sacred."

Tom turns back to the chicken. He's done talking to the preacher. He's given this man too much time in his house already. But as soon as he picks up the knife to begin carving the bird, a strange feeling comes over him, and he hesitates, glancing back at the man with the gun.

Preacher Eli's eye twitches. His facial muscles tighten. When he talks again, it's with the same commanding voice he uses from the pulpit. "How dare you speak to me with such irreverence? It is *you* . . ." His hand holding the gun shakes. "*You*, Tom Carson. You who must . . . who *will* answer for your sins."

Something flashes in the preacher man's eyes: a flicker of insanity.

Tom Carson has never been much of a gambler, but in that instant when he sees that look in Preacher Eli's eyes, he knows he's made a grave mistake. Until now, Tom had thought Eli Brown was many things, but a killer was definitely not one of them. Sure, the man had brought a gun into his home, but Tom had never really been scared. At no time did he think he or his family were in jeopardy of being hurt. Tom had chalked up the weapon to being part of the preacher's game—part of his ploy to scare him into giving up what was rightfully his. Tom had decided almost immediately after the man entered that he wouldn't let himself be so easily duped.

Only now, in this split second, Tom knows he's played his cards all wrong. Everything is over. It's all about to come to an end at the hands of a madman he grossly underestimated.

That thought's the last thing to go through Tom's mind as Eli raises the gun and pulls the trigger.

The small room, suddenly gone dark, fills with the smell and the sound of a gunshot. It echoes off the wooden walls and floor like a thunderous death knell. Tom hears nothing else, only that deadly explosion. It seems to last an eternity and fills everything, even his mind.

In fact, Tom has been so focused on Preacher Eli, he hadn't

noticed when Caleb made his way up his pant legs onto his lap minutes ago.

Now, as the sound dies away, leaving only the smell of gunpowder in its wake, Tom looks down, expecting to see his own stomach blown open, expecting to see himself dying.

What he sees is far, far worse.

There in his lap lies what remains of his little boy.

His perfect little man who just turned three years old barely two weeks ago lies with half his head on Tom's leg and one arm wrapped around his papa's waist.

Tom's eyes fill with tears as he takes in the blood splattered across the table, the floor, the counters, and most of this side of the kitchen. Tom himself is covered in it. He begins to shake. He rubs his son's arm as the world grows very small, and he looks back up to the preacher. It takes a minute for the words to come. When they do, they barely escape his lips. "What . . . what have you done?" he asks quietly.

The preacher's eyes widen in surprise as he steps slowly back down the stairs. His hand holding the gun falls to his side, the weapon slipping off his fingers and falling to the floor. His head shakes. "No . . . ," he says. "No."

Across the table, Mother begins screaming, "My baby! My baby!" She comes around to where Caleb lies dead in a bundle in his father's lap. "My poor sweet baby."

Their daughter, Sylvie, remains quiet. She just pulls her feet up onto her chair and, wrapping her arms around her knees, tries to make herself as small as possible. She watches her mother and father cry over their dead son. She sees the preacher man who came in right before supper and killed her baby brother in the name of Jesus leave by the same door he came in through. She watches it all like a movie, unable to really comprehend what it means. It's so emotionally confusing, she feels almost nothing.

Just an emptiness inside. All empty and hollow.

She begins rocking back and forth on the wooden chair, her long blond pigtails swinging against her face. In her mind, a voice screams, "No! No! No!" over and over, but it's only in her head. On the outside, she's quiet. In fact, she doesn't even hear her parents crying anymore. She sees them, but she doesn't really process what she's looking at.

Nothing makes any sense.

When she woke up this morning, she had been a happy five-year-old girl with a good family and a good life. For the last year, she always told her mom her biggest wish was to raise horses and have babies when she grew up. Three babies.

Those had been her dreams. Horses and babies.

Now, sitting in that kitchen of death, Sylvie Carson no longer cares about the horses or the babies. She no longer cares about life. Preacher Eli killed her baby brother and he also killed her dreams. And none of it made any sense.

What Sylvie doesn't know is that this is only the beginning.

Because for her, the world will never make sense ever again.

CHAPTER 1

Seventeen Years Later

"Dewey," I said, "if I say it was blue, it was blue. Why the heck would I say it was blue if it was some other color? It's not like the important part of the story has anything to do with it bein' blue."

"I just ain't never seen one that's blue," Dewey said. "That's all, Abe."

"You ever seen one any other color?" I asked.

"What do you mean?"

"I mean, have you ever even seen one at all, blue or not? This one was the first one *I'd* ever seen. I mean other than in movies and on TV an' all that. It's not like you see 'em every day."

This question seemed to stump Dewey for a bit as he thought it over. Least, I think he was thinking about it. He may have been pondering the aluminum foil he was unrolling around my mother's living room floor. "Not sure," he said. "Not that I can remember."

"I think that's enough aluminum foil, don't you?" I asked. "How much is in a roll?"

He read the side of the box. "Fifty feet."

"And you had four boxes? That's two hundred feet, Dewey."

"I know, but when I paced off your livin' room, it was ten by twelve. Right there we have a hundred and twenty feet. And it ain't like the foil's gonna be laid down flat. And I reckon for this to work, Abe, we're gonna need to go into your dinin' room, too."

"Well, there ain't no more foil," I said. "My mom's already gonna be mad we used up two brand-new rolls."

"I took two from my house, too," he said. "At least we're sharin' responsibility."

"But the difference is that you reckon this is gonna work. I don't."

"It'll work."

I sighed.

"We need two more rolls," he said.

"We ain't got two more rolls, Dewey. I reckon if two hundred feet don't do it, two thousand feet ain't gonna make no difference."

He thought this over. "You might have a point. At the very least we should see some indication of it workin'. Then we can show your mom and she'll gladly buy us two more rolls."

"My mom ain't gonna want aluminum foil runnin' around the inside of her house, Dewey."

"She is when she sees what it does for her television reception," he said. "Think of how much money we're savin' her."

"How do you figure?" I asked.

"On a satellite dish."

"She ain't buyin' no satellite dish."

"Exactly."

"*Why* aren't we doing this at your place?" I asked him.

"Abe, my mom's *home*. It's hard enough to do anythin' at my place when my mom *ain't* home," he said. "You're lucky your mom works all day shootin' people."

"She don't shoot people all day," I said. "I don't reckon she's ever actually shot *anyone*." My mother was the only detective the Alvin Police Department had, and, if she had shot anyone, she certainly hadn't told me about it. And it seemed like the sort of thing she'd probably mention.

"I reckon she has."

"She hasn't," I assured him.

"I bet she thinks about it, though," Dewey said. "A lot."

"Can we just get this finished so I can have it cleaned up 'fore she gets home?" I asked him.

Dewey was taking the aluminum foil and rolling it into a sort of shiny rope. He made sure all the new pieces fit tightly against the old ones, making one solid snake that ran around the inside of my living room, starting and ending at the back of the television set.

"So why was they *all* blue?" Dewey asked. "The knights, I mean. Or was there other colors, too? They can't *all* be on the same side. Be awful confusin' if they was all blue."

"The other ones were red. I saw one of them later."

"Which ones were the good guys?" Dewey asked.

"How do you mean?"

"There's always a good side and a bad side, Abe. Were the blue ones the good ones or the bad ones? These colors make it hard to know. Usually they use somethin' obvious like black and white. Then you know who you should be rootin' for."

"Do you root for the good guys or the bad guys?" I asked.

Dewey stopped laying down his aluminum foil pipeline and considered this. "That depends on when in my life you had asked me. When I was little I always wanted the good guys to win. Then I went through a phase where I secretly hoped for the bad guys."

"And?" I asked. "What about now?"

"Now I guess I just want to see a fair fight," he said. "Did the blues and the reds both have swords?"

I started to get excited. The swords had been the best part. "You shoulda seen the swords," I said. "The red blades actually glowed the same color as the knights, and they were huge. They looked so big I doubt I coulda lifted one off the ground. And each sword had a different gem in its pommel and smaller ones all over its hilt. They actually had *real* swords for sale in Sleeping Beauty's Castle, but Mom refused to buy me one. She told me I'd wind up takin' somebody's eye out with it or somethin'."

"Wow," Dewey said, looking off into the distance and seemingly speaking to himself. "A *real* sword. That would be somethin'." His attention came back to the living room and all the foil. He looked me straight in the eyes. "Especially if we *both* had one. We could have sword fights."

"Are you even listenin' to a word I'm sayin'?" I asked him. "These were *real* swords, Dewey. We couldn't have sword fights with 'em. We'd wind up killin' each other."

"Still, it's fun to think about."

I hesitated. "You're right. It *is* fun to think about."

Dewey's aluminum foil rope ran along the walls of the entire living room, running behind the big stuffed chair and coming right up to the back of the TV. We'd even pushed the sofa away from the wall so that we could make sure it was as long as possible.

"Okay," I said, just in case Dewey had other ideas, "I think we've done as much as we're doin' with the foil. Now what?"

"Now I unhook the cable from your TV and attach the foil antenna with these alligator clips," he said.

"Can I ask where you got this idea?"

He shrugged. "While you was at Disney World I started an inventor's notebook. Turns out I'm pretty smart. I got lots of great ideas. They're probably worth a million dollars."

I glanced around the room. My mother was going to have a conniption when she saw what we'd done to it, and especially when she found out we'd used up two brand-new rolls of her aluminum foil. "Probably," I said. "You give off a glow of genius, that's for certain."

The light falling in through the window above the sofa was starting to turn purple and orange, which meant it was getting late. This further meant my mother would probably be home soon—unless she wound up working late like she sometimes did. I took another look at Dewey's tinfoil snake and hoped this was going to be a late night for her.

Dewey hooked up the alligator clips to the screws attached to the electronic box where the Cable Vision wire normally attached to the television. "That should do it," he said.

"So now what?"

"Now we turn on the TV and enjoy havin' all the stations folks get with satellite dishes without payin' a cent. All it cost us was the price of four rolls of aluminum foil."

"It didn't cost us nothin'," I reminded him. "We *stole* the foil from our moms, remember?"

"Even better," he said, rubbing his hands together. He pulled the button on the television that turned the set on. For a minute the screen stayed dark, then it slowly grew into a picture of white static.

"Works well," I said sarcastically. I snuck another glance out the window. The weather had cleared up considerably from this morning. It had been four days since we'd gotten back from Disney World, and every day since we'd returned had been full of pouring rain, including the beginning of this one. This afternoon, though, the sun had finally broken through the clouds and cleaned up the sky.

Dewey changed the channel to more static. "Somethin's wrong. We didn't hook somethin' up properly."

"You know what's wrong?" I asked. "You're tryin' to get satellite TV with aluminum foil."

"Wait, this *has* to work. I had it all figured out." He started rapidly switching channels. Then he came to a channel that was clear as Mount Bell on a brisk autumn morning, as my mother would say. "Look!" he said, nearly screaming it. "It works! Look how clear it is!"

I had to admit it was clear.

"Told you it would work!" He went around the dial the entire way and found three more channels we could get. All tremendously clear. This seemed to satisfy him immensely.

"So you're happy with your invention?" I asked.

"I'll say."

I looked at him and blinked. "I'm a little confused."

"About what?"

"Who exactly you'll be marketin' this to."

"What do you mean?"

"I mean, is this for folk who can't afford Cable Vision but happen to have a surplus of aluminum foil and one or two favorite channels they simply cannot live without?" I once again looked at the foil running along the edge of the floor everywhere. "Or will you try and make it some sort of home décor product? Not to mention the fact that you can't really charge more than the price of four rolls of aluminum foil for it or people will just go out and buy their own and set everythin' up for themselves."

Dewey frowned, perplexed by my complex questions. "It's a

start, okay? I have many inventions. I've already filled half a notebook," he said. "You may have been wastin' time in Disney World with blue and red knights, but at least *I* was doing somethin' productive."

Nodding, I said, "Okay. Now, do you mind if we try to get all this put away and see if we can make the television work properly again 'fore my mom gets home from work?"

Dewey glared at me. "You just don't know genius when you see it."

"You're probably right. I don't. I've never really been much of a noticer of brilliance."

He unhooked the alligator clips. I began to roll up the two hundred feet of foil.

Just then my sister, Carry, came into the living room. She'd been out with some friends all day and I hadn't even heard her come home. "Abe?" she asked quietly. I looked up into her blue eyes. Her blond curls swayed on either side of her face. "What the hell are you two doin'?" she asked.

"Preparin' ourselves for the future," I said. "It's comin'. And it's full of aluminum foil."

"And other inventions!" Dewey said. "Wanna see my notebook?"

"Mom's gonna kill you," Carry said.

"I know," I said.

CHAPTER 2

Leah Teal pulled her squad car into the driveway of the home of Sylvie Carson. She was attending because of a call Sylvie made to the station saying something about somebody illegally trespassing on her property. Leah wasn't entirely sure of the report that was taken because she hadn't taken it. Her partner, Officer Christopher Jackson, had. Like most times when Sylvie Carson called, Officer Jackson laughed after hanging up the phone.

"Guess who that was . . . *again,*" he had said.

It bothered Leah when Sylvie was made fun of, especially when it was by Chris. She had a pretty good hunch as to why it irked her so much, too.

"You know," she had told Chris, "it wasn't so long ago that I can remember folks makin' all sorts of a ruckus 'bout you bein' hired by the department."

"Yeah, well, those folks were wrong. They just like to hate people," Chris said. "Especially black people. This is different. The woman is nuts. She calls the station every week."

"This *isn't* much different, Chris. Sylvie can't help the way she is no more than you can help the color you is."

"What's wrong with the color I am?"

"That's not what I meant and you know it." Leah looked back at Police Chief Ethan Montgomery's office for a little backup but his door was closed. She could see through the partially opened blinds hanging down over the window in his door that the chief was sitting back in his chair with his hands behind his head watching the television that hung from the ceiling in the corner of the room. The chief loved to watch his sports.

Chris wouldn't let things go. "Leah, most people get better over time. But Sylvie's gotten worse, far as I can tell. Her calls are coming in at an all-time high." That was likely true. Leah had at least noticed them more, and she was the one who usually ended up attending to them.

"And every single one turns out to be some sort of false alarm," Chris said. "I don't know why you even bother showin' up. I stopped takin' her seriously a long time ago."

"Because it's our job to show up, Chris. Because for every hundred or so false alarms, there might actually be one real emergency and it's for *that* real emergency I attend to the ninety-nine others. Besides, what else do I have to do? We live in a town of barely two thousand people; it's not like our phone's ringin' off the desk."

"I'd rather do the crossword than deal with Sylvie," he said. Leah couldn't believe how heartless he was being. She was about to tell him that when he started talking again. "I'm sorry," he said, "but I've just reached the end of my wits with her. I think it's on account of the baby. I think she must be all hormonal or somethin'."

Okay, Leah knew then it was time to end her conversation with Officer Christopher Jackson, or she would say something she definitely would regret.

Grabbing her pistol from her desk, she headed for the door. "Well, I'm gonna go see what she needs. At least one of us is gonna represent this department."

Chris laughed behind her. "Have fun."

It was the part about the baby that had almost pushed Leah over the edge. Even now, sitting in her car in front of Sylvie's house, thinking about that baby kept Leah worked up to a degree that wasn't healthy for nobody.

Generally, Leah tried not to think about Sylvie's baby, especially when she was off shift. It was the sort of thing that would lodge itself into her head and wouldn't get unstuck for hours while she lay in bed trying to fall asleep. To make matters worse, she couldn't even refer to it as anything but "The Baby" because Sylvie Carson hadn't given it a name yet. It had been three months now, and the girl still called her daughter "The Baby." Whenever Leah asked her why she hadn't named her, Sylvie told her, "It's so much responsibility. I get too overwhelmed thinkin' that whatever I come up with is gonna be with this girl for the rest of her life. It's a huge decision that's gonna affect everything. Nothin' I think of is good enough. Not for my daughter. Not for her whole life."

Leah couldn't argue with her. It was pointless telling Sylvie that anything was better than "The Baby." So Leah just let it lie as best she could. But her brain wouldn't let go of it quite so easily. It hung on to things like the baby not having a name and how *that* might affect the rest of her life. Or what effect having a mother who could barely manage to keep herself together an entire day might have.

Some babies come into the world with better chances than others right from the start. This one seemed to come in with a pretty bad poker hand, at least in Leah's eyes, which was probably one of the big reasons Leah felt compelled to take Sylvie's calls seriously.

Leah also suspected she had a soft spot for Sylvie because deep down she felt they weren't so different. If fate had changed up some of the pitches Leah had been thrown, her life might have turned out very similar to Sylvie's. In some ways it had.

They were both single mothers. Sylvie had The Baby and Leah had two children: a fifteen-year-old daughter named Carry, and a twelve-year-old boy named Abe.

Both Leah and Sylvie had lost the fathers to their children unexpectedly. Sylvie's was named Orwin Thomas and he had been barely an adult when Sylvie got pregnant. He just up and disappeared one night without even leaving so much as a note. There was no indication the day before that anything was wrong. He took Sylvie's car, a few dollars cash they'd kept in a jar, and some clothing. He left her three months along in a pregnancy she then had to face all alone.

Leah's husband, Billy, coming home from work after pulling an overnight shift, had accidentally run his car—headlights first—into an oncoming car while passing an eighteen-wheeler. Abe had only been two. Those had been very hard times for Leah. She didn't like to think about them, even now.

Neither Leah nor Sylvie had living parents. Sylvie's had died tragically when she was in her teens; her mother was murdered and her pa took his own life shortly thereafter. Leah had lost her parents when they were older; her ma from a stroke a year after Leah had lost her husband, and her pa to cancer three years later.

But that was where the similarities ended, because at least Leah could cope with life. Sylvie was a different story. Sure, she had emotional problems (yet another reason for Leah being upset at Chris. Although, comparing her disorder to him being black would probably not be a good idea on Leah's part). Possibly it was post-traumatic stress disorder brought on from what happened when Sylvie was a kid. She'd actually seen her baby brother get murdered just a few feet away from her. It happened long before Leah became detective, back when she was only fourteen. But Leah's father had been on the force then, and he had handled the case, so Leah knew a lot about it.

After Leah's husband, Billy, died, there were times Leah didn't think she would make it. And she hadn't had to deal with any of the psychological trauma Sylvie faced. Leah tried not to forget that. No matter what it looked like from the outside, this girl was rising above herself—or at least trying to—and that was something to be applauded, not laughed at.

Leah couldn't imagine what her own life would've been like had she been in the same shoes Sylvie was during her childhood. Leah tried to picture what it would be like watching her own uncle, Hank, get shot to death right in front of her when, not ten minutes earlier, she had been ready to enjoy a happy supper with her family.

She shivered. It was so horrific, she couldn't even think about it.

Yet it was something Sylvie had to live with every single day of her life. And everyone seemed so surprised the girl was a little messed up. Something like that had to do strange things to your mind. It had to haunt you in unimaginable ways.

Sylvie was a lost soul trying to navigate in a world she always seemed to be trying to catch up with.

Leah got out of her squad car and headed for the few wooden steps that rose to the landing in front of Sylvie's front door.

Sylvie's house was small and old. It would be considered a shotgun shack if it weren't for the hallway and bedroom someone had added on some time ago. Shotgun shacks were normally fewer than twelve feet wide with no more than three to five rooms, all arranged one behind the other.

The outside had once been painted white, but most of the paint was flaking off the siding, leaving the bare wood showing underneath. The picture window that looked out of the living room beside the front door had the drapes pulled shut, but Leah could see the yellow light of a lamp through the crack between them. Leah had been inside enough times to know that was the only light in that room. At times like this, after the sun was down, that light cast everything inside with an amber glow that threw long, eerie shadows.

It certainly didn't help the atmosphere any.

Leah stepped up and knocked on the wooden door. Like the siding, the paint on the door was also starting to peel. "Sylvie?" she called out. "Sylvie, it's Detective Teal. Alvin Police."

It didn't take long before she heard the chain slide and the dead bolt shoot. Like always, Leah waited while Sylvie opened the door a few inches and made sure Leah was who she said she was. Leah didn't really mind this behavior. She would rather see somebody overly protective than the other way around, although Sylvie's protectiveness crossed the line well into paranoia.

"Hi," Sylvie said. Her dirty blond hair hung straight down over her eyes. For a brief moment, those eyes caught the moon, and Leah saw its reflection in their speckled blue pools.

Sylvie Carson looked and dressed like a homeless person. She'd gotten worse since Orwin took off. It was funny, because Leah could tell if the girl dressed in nice clothes and wore proper makeup she could be really pretty. Maybe she looked this way intentionally. Like a victim.

Yet the baby seemed clean enough. That had been a huge worry of Leah's when Sylvie first brought her home from the hospital. Leah really hadn't wanted to involve the state with the child's care, but part of her suspected she would eventually have to step in given the way Sylvie was.

So Leah had kept a close eye on the baby for the past three months. Sylvie had given her many opportunities to do so with all her calls. Every time Sylvie called into the station, Leah just chalked it up as another chance to check on the welfare of the baby.

Leah heard Sylvie slide the chain again. Then the door opened completely. "Thanks for comin' out," Sylvie said.

"Not a problem," Leah said stepping inside. "Glad to see you're okay."

Sylvie immediately locked the door again behind Leah. "Yeah," she mumbled. She was always very quiet when she talked. Quiet, pensive, and uncertain. It was very much like dealing with a child.

Which, Leah assumed, Sylvie probably still was. Chronologically, she wasn't much older than a teenager. What had she turned on her last birthday? Twenty-two? And hadn't Leah read somewhere that when something traumatic happens in childhood the person emotionally stays at whatever age they were at when the event took place?

Leah was pretty sure wherever she had read that fact they'd gotten it right because Sylvie had been five when she lost her brother and, in many ways, Sylvie still seemed like a five-year-old trapped in a twenty-two-year-old girl's body.

Surprisingly, given her appearance, Sylvie's home always had that just-tidied-up-in-a-rush look when Leah showed up. That might be because she just had tidied it after calling the station—Leah had no way of knowing. But at least she kept it fairly neat.

Each of these little things—the clean house, the clean baby, and other little changes—gave Leah some hope that Sylvie might have it together enough to actually be a proper mother. God knew she appeared to love the child enough. If love was all you needed (like that Beatles song said) then Sylvie was like a billionaire.

Unfortunately, Leah didn't think John Lennon had taken everything into account when he wrote that song. He'd probably never met anyone like Sylvie Carson.

"So what's the problem?" Leah asked.

"Someone's been in the yard," Sylvie said.

Leah sighed. This wasn't a surprise. The girl always thought someone was in her yard, or spying on her, or something.

"Place looks nice," Leah said, for now tabling the "someone's been in the yard" discussion.

"Thanks."

"Baby okay?"

"Yeah, she's fine. A bit colicky, I reckon."

"That'll go away," Leah said.

"I think so," Sylvie said.

"You okay? You look pale," Leah said.

"I'm fine."

"So," Leah asked, "what exactly makes you think someone's been trespassing on your property? Who's been where?"

"The yard," Sylvie said. "Someone's been in the backyard." She was wearing an old oversized LSU Tigers T-shirt that hung untucked over gray sweatpants. Her hands trembled as she wrung them together while speaking. Leah could tell she was scared. She was hoping her little conversation diversion might settle Sylvie down.

Leah knew enough about Sylvie and her calls to know this would undoubtedly turn out to be another false alarm.

The living room had a dark hardwood floor that creaked when you walked across it. The drapes in the window were missing some hooks, and that made them hang awkwardly from the inside. They were once white, but now they looked a more pale washed-out yellow than anything else. Dark stains covered one.

Tattered magazines were stacked on the oval glass coffee table in the room's center. An old TV with wood panel trim sat on some plastic crates on one side of the table. Two paintings of clowns hung crookedly on the chestnut-paneled wall behind the TV.

"Been cleanin', I see," Leah said.

"I like it clean for The Baby."

"That's good. Babies need things clean. You should clean yourself up, too."

"What do you mean?"

Leah pointed to the oversized LSU shirt with the ripped holes in it. "Don't you have any clothes of your own? Orwin's stuff's gettin' a mite old."

"These are comfortable. Besides, my money goes to The Baby."

The Baby. It made Leah cringe every time Sylvie said it.

A small white cat came in and brushed up against Leah's leg, purring.

"Snowflake," Sylvie said. "Get outta here. Leave Officer Teal alone."

"Oh, she's all right," Leah said, bending down and lifting up the cat. She'd come here enough times that she knew the animal well. It was an indoor/outdoor cat that had surprised Leah by lasting as long as it had. Sylvie had gotten the cat as a kitten after Orwin left her. Normally, cats allowed to go outdoors in these parts became prey to other animals pretty quickly.

There were two small unmatched sofas in the room: one was green and threadbare, the other was taupe, with silver duct tape covering up tears in the upholstery. The only light in the room—a black metal floor lamp—stood beside the sofa. Its bulb shined a circular pattern on the white textured ceiling.

"You know, this place would look a lot better if you had more light," Leah said.

"I only have one lamp."

"I'll see if I can dig up somethin' for you."

"That would be nice."

"This one makes the room too dark."

"I don't mind it," Sylvie said.

The baby was asleep on a small blanket on the green sofa. She was wearing pink pajamas that appeared to be as clean as she was. So clean, they didn't even look like they'd ever been washed. The baby's brown skin shone in contrast to those pajamas. She'd inherited that skin color from her daddy.

Leah walked over with Snowflake in her arms and looked down on her. She appeared healthy. Leah hoped to God she was doing the right thing leaving this baby with this girl. "New PJs?" she asked Sylvie.

"Salvation Army," Sylvie said.

The living room looked into the kitchen. The kitchen lights were off, making it appear creepy by the light of this single lamp with the yellowish bulb. An old kitchen table with a brown Formica top stood in the darkness with three chairs around it in various states of disrepair. Behind it, the kitchen window allowed a view into the backyard, but from where she stood, Leah could only make out shadows. Living here alone with just a baby and this creepy lamp, it was no wonder Sylvie was seeing things in the backyard. Even if it *was* clean, this house was old and ghostly. It felt off, somehow.

Leah rubbed the cat under its neck, listening to it purr louder. She wondered how Sylvie ever managed to give *it* a name. She just hoped her daughter didn't end up with a name like Snowflake. But then, she figured even Snowflake would be better than growing up with no name at all. "What makes you think someone's been in your backyard?"

"Things have been moved," Sylvie said. "An' there's footprints."

Leah sighed. This was obviously turning out to be another false alarm. She wanted to take Sylvie's mind off the immediate problem. Deciding to try to put it somewhere else, she asked a different question: "Found a name for your daughter yet?"

A pause followed. Then, "Not yet."

"You gotta name her soon, Sylvie. It's not good for a baby not to have a name."

Another pause. "I know. I will."

They stood there in silence a minute or two, then Leah said, "Why don't you show me what's been moved?"

She followed Sylvie through the kitchen to the back door, noticing the dishes in the sink had been recently washed but not dried. Sylvie didn't turn on any lights, but Leah could tell the house was cleaner than ever. Every time she came to Sylvie's there appeared to be some improvement in some way. The only thing that didn't seem to improve were the number of calls into the station.

A shotgun stood beside the back door, propped up against the wall. Leah knew the answer to the question she was about to ask before even asking it.

"That thing loaded?"

"You betcha. No point in keepin' an unloaded shotgun around now, is there?" Sylvie said.

"You do realize how dangerous it is, right?"

"You guys tell me that every time you come in here and every time I tell you the same thing. You won't take me seriously, so that shotgun's the only recourse I have. I ain't livin' with my baby and bein' unable to defend myself. Not when someone's after me."

Leah let out a big breath. There was no point in arguing with her. Not while she was like this.

Sylvie fumbled with the dead bolt on the back door until she finally opened it.

"You got a light out here?" Leah asked.

"Burned out a few weeks ago."

"Should replace it."

"I will," Sylvie said. "Haven't had time."

Leah pulled out her pocket flashlight. She wasn't in uniform because she didn't wear one, but she had a pack snapped around her waist containing small items she commonly used. Her major gear was in her car, packed in her "go bag."

"You see that you do. Not safe having no light back here," Leah said, coming down the steps that led to the backyard. Sylvie followed behind her in shoes that had holes bigger than golf balls. "Those the only shoes you have, girl?" Leah asked.

"Yeah."

"Get some new shoes, too."

"Can't afford new shoes. The Baby takes all my money."

Once again, Leah felt something pull inside her. She liked this girl. Deep inside, she was rooting for her to win a war she never should have been involved in to begin with. A war that enlisted her without any permission.

What Sylvie had improved upon inside the house was more than compensated for by the state of the backyard. It looked like it hadn't seen any attention for a long time. Car engine parts littered the long grass and wildflowers that fought to choke each other back from existence. It had rained the past few days. That morning there were spotty showers, but the sky had started to completely clear just as the sun began to set. Still, everything had that wet smell to it. Even though it was a bright night (now that Leah's eyes had adjusted to being outside and seeing by the stars and moon), it still *felt* wet. Rainwater pooled in everything around her. There were jars, stacks of old newspapers, tires, even an old, broken kitchen sink. The yard was maybe a quarter acre before the surrounding forest choked it in, yet somehow it held a treasure trove of junk so well hidden that, until now, Leah hadn't even realized Sylvie had so much crap out here.

She followed as Sylvie walked slowly over to some small flowerpots that stood on top of a wooden box laid on its side against the back of the house. "Here," she said, gesturing to the pots. "These."

"The flowerpots?" Leah asked. She had pulled out a notepad and had her pen poised over it, ready to start a report.

"Yeah."

"What about them?" Leah asked.

"They was moved," Sylvie said. "They used to be inside the box. Now they're on top."

"When were they inside?"

"Yesterday."

"How do you know?" Leah wondered what kind of person notices something like clay flowerpots. She never would. She doubted many other people would, either.

"I saw 'em," Sylvie said.

"How can you remember somethin' like that?"

"I just do. I noticed 'em."

"I'm sure they were where they are now and you just reckon you saw 'em inside," Leah said, trying to placate the girl.

"No," Sylvie said. Leah heard the frustration in her voice. She'd heard it many times before. "They were *inside*. I'm *sure*. Somebody moved 'em last night. Or during the day today."

"Why would somebody move your flowerpots?" This was the rational question that Sylvie Carson's mind seemed incapable of asking itself.

"I don't know."

"What else was moved?" Leah asked.

Sylvie hesitated. "Nothin'. Just the pots."

Now it was Leah's turn to pause. "That's it?" She realized she hadn't written anything down and was probably making the girl feel bad. She quickly wrote on her pad: *Flowerpots moved. From inside to top of wooden box.* "You say you have footprints?" Leah asked, glancing up.

"In the vegetable garden."

"Show me."

Sylvie led her to a patch of dirt that could only be a vegetable garden by mere designation. If it ever had been such a thing, many years had passed since then. Now it was a patch of ground with spotty grass and weeds that had grown in not quite as dense as the rest of the yard. Some of it was bare of any growth. Those areas were a gray color, and Leah suspected the ground was clay there. The clay looked moist and soft on account of all the rain.

Sylvie brought Leah's attention to one of these patches of clay. "Here. There's one here," she said. She moved over about two feet, straining to see in the night's light. "And here."

Leah shined her flashlight on the spots. Sure enough, the imprints in the clay could've very well been footprints. They might also just have been natural indentations made by the weather. They were pretty formless. Any detail they had—*if* they ever had any—had been washed away by the rain. "They don't necessarily look like footprints to me," Leah said. "I can't make out any details."

"They were detailed earlier," Sylvie said. "I *saw* them. They *were* footprints."

"Maybe you made them?" Leah asked.

Sylvie looked at her. "They're this big," she said, holding her hands almost a foot apart. "I'm a seven. They ain't mine."

"They don't look like anythin' to me," Leah said.

"Not anymore. But they did."

"I believe you."

"No you don't."

No I don't, Leah thought. "Okay," she said. "Let's say they *are* footprints. So somebody came into your backyard and moved your pots up to the top of your box and left footprints. So what?"

"I don't like strangers near my home. I have a baby."

Good girl. Too bad her worries were so misplaced. "I understand that," Leah said. "But I don't reckon this would be the kind of person you'd have to worry much 'bout, do you?"

"I would be worried 'bout anyone comin' into my yard," Sylvie said.

Leah thought about this. She didn't know what to say to the girl. All she could really do was tell her the truth. "I'm sorry, Sylvie. There ain't nothin' I can do with what you showed me. I'm afraid I need more to go on than some pots that may or may not have been moved and some spots in the clay that might possibly be footprints."

"They *was* footprints," Sylvie said. Leah could tell she was almost angry now, she was getting so frustrated.

"Okay, they was footprints. Listen, Sylvie. Think about this: Say they still was *perfect* footprints. And say the pots were obviously moved. Even then, *what would you expect me to do?*"

"Figure out who moved 'em?" Sylvie replied, forming it more like a question than an answer.

"And do what then?" Leah asked. "Nobody's really broken any laws now, have they? *Maybe* trespassin'. But it ain't like I'm 'bout to arrest someone for movin' a few pots."

Sylvie took a deep breath. Leah could tell the girl was shaky. "So what're you sayin'?" Sylvie asked, her voice quivering. "I'm supposed to just stay here with my baby while people come into my backyard just as merrily as they please?"

Leah held up her hand. "I can tell you're upset and worried. How about this?" Everything in Leah's head was telling her not to do what she was about to do, but she didn't listen. She already knew she was going to do it. It was the only way she could come up with of getting out of here and still making Sylvie happy in the process. "I'll give you my home number. You have any problems, you can call me. *Any* time, day or night." The quarter moon rose in the night sky like a tipped grin. "Try the station first, of course. If I'm not there, try me at home. How does that sound?"

Sylvie thought this over. "Okay, I suppose. I guess it might help if somethin' else happens. You're the only one whoever comes right away anymore."

Ouch. That last one stung. Leah immediately tried to cover with an excuse. "Things get really busy sometimes, Sylvie," she said. But as soon as it came out, she realized both of them knew it was a lie.

They went back inside and Leah wrote her home phone number on a blank page of her report pad. Ripping out the page, she handed it to Sylvie, regretting the action the moment she felt the paper leave her fingertips. "Remember," she said. "This is only for emergencies, and *only* after tryin' the station first. Deal?"

"Deal," Sylvie said. She seemed a lot better. Being inside probably took the edge off. Leah couldn't imagine what it was like to be as paranoid as Sylvie, but being paranoid like that *and* being outside at night had to be even worse.

"Thanks for comin' out," Sylvie mumbled.

"You don't have to thank me," Leah said. "It's my duty to come out. It's my job. Just like your job's to look after your daughter. You just do me a big ol' favor, okay? Find her a name nice and quick?"

"I'm tryin'," Sylvie said. "I really am tryin' hard."

"Try a little harder. I don't think it matters as much as you go on about it matterin'."

"Wish I thought same as you," Sylvie said.

Leah walked to the front door. "Just take care of yourself, all right? And look after your girl." She unlocked the door, opened it, and stepped out onto the porch. "Don't forget to lock up behind me."

Leah walked down the stairs, hearing the door shut and the dead bolt shoot in her wake. She thought she probably didn't need to add that last bit. She doubted locking up her doors was something Sylvie Carson ever forgot to do.

CHAPTER 3

My mother actually did turn out to work late the afternoon Dewey talked me into wrapping aluminum foil all around our living room. I doubt I would have gotten into much trouble for it anyway—my mother knew a Dewey scheme when she saw one. But it definitely saved me from having to come up with a whole bunch of explaining about why I didn't think for myself before I did stupid things conjured up by other people. It was a conversation I'd had enough times that I didn't really relish the thought of having to go through it yet again.

When she finally did get home, it was late enough that I had already gone to bed. Carry was up watching something on television, but I was exhausted. I guess running tinfoil in a big circle around your house was a harder job than I thought.

I managed to still be awake when my mother came in to check on me.

"How was your day, Abe?" she asked.

"Not bad," I said, sitting up in my bed. "How 'bout you?"

She let out a little sigh. "Oh, I suppose it was all right. Had to go see Miss Sylvie again."

I knew all about Miss Sylvie. My mother was called to her home at least every other week it seemed for one thing or another. I didn't really understand why Miss Sylvie couldn't get along without always calling the police. Everyone else in town seemed to manage to do all right.

"Again?" I asked. "What's wrong with her, anyway?"

My mother shot me a look and I immediately knew I'd said something wrong. She had a way of just glancing at you that made you wish you could go back in time thirty seconds and completely change what you just said.

"There's nothin' *wrong* with her, Abe. She's just . . . *different*. She's got problems."

"Aren't problems something that's wrong?" I asked. I figured I already got the look, I might as well keep going and see where my line of reasoning took me.

"Well, yes and no, I suppose. You know what happened when she was little, right?"

"You mean 'bout her brother bein' shot by that preacher man and it happenin' right in front of her?" I asked. I looked down at my comforter. "Yeah, I know."

"Just imagine if you was her and that had happened to Caroline. How would you feel?"

I thought it over and realized I didn't rightly know exactly how I'd feel. "Probably sad?" I asked.

"Probably," she agreed.

"But I don't think that would make me keep callin' the police all the time when I grew up, would it?"

"You don't know what it would do, Abe. When things happen in your childhood, they change you. They affect you emotionally in unpredictable ways. Miss Sylvie can't help how she is. Do you think she likes bein' this way?"

"I ain't never thought 'bout it 'fore," I said. "I guess not. I guess you're right. I don't reckon anybody'd want to be callin' the police all the time."

"Anyway," my mother said, "you get back to sleep. Oh, and she might be callin' the house. I gave her our number to set her mind at ease."

"You gave her our *home* number?" Even to me, a twelve-year-old, this seemed like a ridiculous thing for my mother to have done.

"She needs to know she has access to someone she can count on, Abe."

"Will she be callin' all night?"

"What does it matter to you? You won't be answerin' it."

"I'm just askin'."

"I don't know if she'll call."

I hesitated, then asked, "Do you know what you're doin'?"

"Just go to sleep."

She got up off the edge of my bed where she'd been sitting and walked to my door as I lay back down. She stopped in the doorway and turned. "Oh," she said, "and in the mornin' we can talk about the oodles of aluminum foil I found spillin' outta the trash can outside."

I swallowed. "It was—"

"I know, Abe," she said. "It was Dewey's idea. That's what I want to talk about. The blind leading the stupid."

She walked out of the room, leaving me staring up at my ceiling wondering what Dewey was doing right now. Most likely he was lying in his own bed, dreaming up some ridiculous new invention that made no sense other than as a tool to show off my ability to be led by an moron.

The more I hung out with Dewey, the more my mother thought I was an idiot.

Dewey came over the next morning and asked if I wanted to ride my bike down to the grocery store to get his mom some more aluminum foil.

"I bet you got in some serious trouble when she saw you'd taken it all," I said.

"She never suspected a thing," Dewey said smugly. "She just told me, 'You know, I coulda swore I bought some last time I went grocery shoppin'.' " Dewey smiled. "Took all I had not to laugh." The way he said it made him sound just like her.

Sometimes I think some of Dewey's traits run through his family.

It was pretty early in the morning, having just gone on seven thirty. My own mother was still asleep, but I woke her to ask if it was okay if I went along with Dewey. Experience had taught me that my mother's sleep wasn't as valuable as me getting permission to do stuff, especially where Dewey was concerned.

She told me it was okay if I went, so I threw on my sneakers, grabbed my bike, and we headed off into what felt like a fine summer morning. The sun had already started beating down something fierce, making the world extremely bright. Sunlight bounced off the windows of the houses and stores along the sides of the street, and it reflected off the chrome of the cars parked along it, but there was a slight breeze that would pick itself up every so often and blow over us, keeping things tolerable.

Normally, for something like a couple rolls of aluminum foil, we'd just go to the Mercantile or what my mother referred to as Mr. Harrison's five and dime. But, it being so early on a Saturday, I was pretty sure the Mercantile wasn't going to be open. "I think we're gonna have to go all the way to Applesmart's," I told Dewey. Applesmart's Grocery was halfway up Main Street. Almost twice as far as Mr. Harrison's place.

"You don't think the Mercantile will be open?"

"I doubt Mr. Harrison gets up as early as Mr. Wyatt Edward Farrow," I said, referring to my neighbor across the street, who I knew liked to go on early-morning walks every Saturday. I also knew the grocery store opened at seven in the morning every day on account of my mother sometimes took me shopping early in the mornings. "Besides, it will be cheaper at Applesmart's," I said.

Dewey looked at me strangely. "Now you sound like my ma."

"Yeah, I don't know why I said that, to be right honest. Must be my own mom comin' out in me." I felt a little shiver run up my legs and through my arms.

We rode down Hunter Road and passed the Mercantile, which was indeed closed. "It doesn't open until eleven!" Dewey yelled out, riding up on the sidewalk so he could get a close look at the sign in the door. "Mr. Harrison must really like his sleep."

"Oh, well," I said. "It's a nice day for a ride."

And it was. It was an enjoyable ride all the way to Main Street.

Then things changed.

Because that's when I noticed something strange happening while we were on that bike ride.

A car was following me and Dewey. I'm not sure where it started, but at some point I noticed somebody was driving slowly behind us. Even though we kept going to the side of the road to let the car pass, it wouldn't. It was like whoever was driving wanted to keep on our tail and see where we were headed.

I didn't like it one bit. It gave me a sick feeling in my stomach.

At first I kept the fact about the car to myself, but after a while I figured it was only fair to let Dewey in on it. After all, he was being followed, too.

So I told him. I couldn't tell if he got the same sick feeling as me. It's hard to tell things like that with Dewey sometimes.

"This is creepy," Dewey said, sounding oddly excited.

"Just ignore it. It's probably one of the high school kids bein' a goof." I think I was trying to make myself feel better about the whole thing by saying that.

I kept trying to glance back and get a look at the car, but I couldn't see who was driving on account of the sun reflecting off the windshield. I hoped my guess was going to turn out to be pretty close. I tried to tell myself to relax. Who else would be following us on a bright and sunny Saturday morning in Alvin? It's not like me and Dewey were fugitives or anything. But then, what kind of teenager woke up before noon during the summer holidays? Sometimes Carry didn't roll out of bed before three.

From what I could tell, the car was a dark gray sedan that looked quite new. It may have even been black—it was hard to tell in all this sunlight. It looked pretty nice, and probably expensive. This didn't help the feeling in my stomach one bit. High school kids didn't drive nice, expensive cars. They drove old broken-down beaters they used to get them to and from school in Satsuma because they were lucky enough to not have to take the bus.

The car continued following us all the way to Applesmart's. We leaned our bikes up against the front window that said APPLESMART'S GROCERY in big arched lettering. I was considerably relieved when the car picked up speed and headed right past us. If it had been following us, it obviously decided we weren't worth stopping for. Thank goodness for that. Because, as I said before, it certainly didn't look like a car that belonged to one of the high school kids.

The town of Alvin was too small to have its own high school. All we had was an elementary school, so for anything above seventh grade you had to go all the way to Satsuma for school.

Even me and Dewey would be going to Satsuma after summer break was over, but we wouldn't have the luxury of driving. For one thing, we were still too young to get our licenses and for another thing, neither of us could ever afford to buy a car. Not even one of those lousy ones you always saw the high school kids pulled over in on the side of the road with their hoods up, trying to pretend they knew anything about fixing cars. Besides, there was no way my mother was about to put out that kind of money.

My sister, Carry, had been going to school in Satsuma for three years and she *still* had to take the bus back and forth. It took more than two hours total if you counted both ways. It seemed like a colossal waste of time to me. Especially compared to how good we had it here in Alvin for elementary school. Just a fifteen-minute walk, sixteen if there was a headwind.

No, I certainly wasn't looking forward to the end of this summer. Me and Dewey had better make the best of this one, that was for certain. It was almost like this summer marked the end of something special, like these days were a countdown of our final days of childhood before we moved on to a new part of our lives.

It turned out Dewey's mom had given him a bit of extra money for candy (which was increased by the fact that we probably saved an extra twenty cents coming to Applesmart's instead of going to the Mercantile), so that was a nice surprise. He hadn't told me until we got to the store. So we managed to get a grab bag each from old man Eakins, the guy who owned the store. I remembered his name on account of my mother tried to make me remember the names of adults I met so that I could be polite and say hello next time I saw them. She liked to say, "If you remember someone's name it impresses upon them that you're worth listening to." I wasn't quite sure what that meant, as I really didn't have much to say to anyone that was worth listening to, but I tried to do as she told me. So I remembered as many names as I could.

The part I couldn't believe is that Mr. Eakins remembered *my* name. Or at least he remembered me. As soon as he saw me and Dewey, he said, "You're the boy with the mother who's a detective, that right?"

"I sure am, Mr. Eakins, sir!" I said with a big smile. I'd always found big smiles worked in your favor at times like this. And I used his name so he'd know I was someone worth listening to.

It turned out, using his name got me more than that. With a grin, he quickly threw some extra gummies into my and Dewey's grab bags after asking us what our favorite candies were. Of course we said gummies were our favorites. I didn't understand why gummies weren't everybody's favorites.

I had forgotten all about the car that had been tailing us on our way here.

We were laughing and joking with Mr. Eakins about all sorts of stuff—nothing in particular, just the kind of mindless stuff you talk to guys who own stores about, you know.

That's when I happened to look outside.

Well, let me tell you, I stopped talking immediately. My mouth hung open, and my eyes grew wide. The car that had been following us, the nice black one (and it *was* black, I could tell now) was parked across the street from the general store and the driver was watching us through the window. The car was parked in the shade of a line of maple trees, so the sunlight was blocked from reflecting off the glass and the chrome, allowing me to see the driver. It was a woman, not a high school kid—a woman who must've been at least as old as my mom. Or maybe not quite that old, I don't know. I wasn't a very good judge of age when it came to anyone over twenty.

I heard Dewey and Mr. Eakins still jabbering away behind me. "Dewey?" I said quietly. But he didn't hear, he just kept laughing and filling his face with gummies.

"Dewey," I said louder.

"What?" he asked. "What's wrong with you?" He was near on

impossible to understand since his mouth was stuffed with gummies.

I continued staring out the window. "Look. It's . . ."

"The car," he said, astonished, as he came up beside me. "She really *was* followin' us." Only he didn't sound scared like I was. He sounded . . . *excited.*

I looked at him. "What the hell's the matter with you?"

He swallowed. "What?"

"Aren't you pissin'-your-pants scared right now?"

He shrugged. "Not really. I think it's like a movie."

"You're so weird." Then, quietly, I added, "I'm really worried. What do we do?" Behind us, Mr. Eakins hadn't even noticed we'd moved on from our conversation with him. He was busy now helping some old lady find a bag of biscuits for her dog.

"I dunno," Dewey said. "Nobody ever wanted to follow me before." Then it was like all the shutter blinds opened up in his head. I heard him gasp and his hand came to his mouth.

"What is it?" I asked, looking at him again.

"What if," he said, "she's after my inventions?"

Oh my God, this guy lived in a fantasy world. "Are you serious?"

"I think it's a strange coincidence that she shows up right when I've decided to start puttin' them in a book, is all."

"I think you have mental problems."

"What are we gonna do?" he asked.

"Not much choice," I said. "I guess we get back on our bikes and head home."

"And what if she follows us?"

"Then I get my mom."

"And what if she *doesn't* follow us?"

I stopped and thought about this. "Then . . . then there's no problem."

"Oh." Dewey sounded disappointed. "What if she does somethin' else?"

"Like what?"

"I dunno," he said. "Shoots us?"

I let out a big sigh. "I don't think she's gonna shoot us. Besides, she had the whole ride here to do somethin' and she didn't. That's the weird part. It's almost like she wanted to see where we was headed."

"I know!" Dewey said. "Maybe she's after our candy."

"Or our aluminum foil!" I offered sarcastically.

"You think maybe?" Dewey asked, not getting the sarcasm.

"No," I said. "I don't. Come on."

We went outside and I kept glancing over at her as we got back on our bikes. The driver's side window of her car was rolled down, so it was easy to see her. She had blondy-brown hair that was tied up, and she wore a lot of makeup. She was probably older than she looked, I guess. Her face was thin. She had big blue earrings on.

We began riding back the way we had come. At first it looked like she was just going to sit in her car, but then I heard it start up. I looked back to see her slowly start moving and go back to following us down Main Street.

"So much for there not bein' a problem," Dewey said.

I didn't reply. Instead, I just tried not to notice the stone turning over inside my stomach.

A couple blocks later, I heard her car getting closer. Then closer.

Then closer still.

Then I realized she was pulling up beside us.

Part of my brain remembered what Dewey had said in the store. I hoped she wasn't about to shoot us.

"Hey!" she called out through the open passenger window. Her voice had a strange kind of nasally accent.

I ignored her and kept riding. My mother always said never talk to strangers and all that. I was sure it included stalkers.

"Hey," she said again. "Is your name Abe?" she asked.

That caught me off guard. Now I wasn't sure what to do. Was she a stranger if she knew my name?

"She knows who you are," Dewey said from the other side.

I decided to answer her. I looked up. "Yes."

"I need to talk to you," she said.

What? Why did this strange woman need to talk to me? I

didn't know what to do. I had no idea who she was. "I don't know who you are," I said honestly.

"I'm . . . I'm your aunt."

I paused. Then I said, "I don't have an aunt."

"Yes you do. On your dad's side. I'm your daddy's sister."

Suddenly, it was as if a burst of sparrows sprang into my mind like they were flying from the treetops after a gunshot. I had never known my pa. He died when I was two. I didn't know very much about him. My mother never wanted to talk about him, and whenever I asked anything, she always kept her answers as short and to the point as possible. I certainly had no idea he had a sister.

Wouldn't my mother have told me if he had? Did she even know if he had?

I decided this was too important not to find out.

I hit my brakes.

"What are you doin'?" Dewey asked.

"I need to talk to this woman," I said.

"You don't know her from Adam," Dewey said, then stumbled. "—er, or Eve. She could be makin' this all up. She could be one of those child abductors or somethin'."

"You don't have to hang round here," I said to him. "You're free to go home and tell my mom where I am, if you like."

"Hell no," he said. "If you're stayin', I'm stayin'."

"Where's a good place to talk?" the woman in the car asked.

We wound up sitting with her on the outside steps of the library, the same steps Robert Lee Garner had stood on last fall when Mary Ann Dailey went missing—a time of my life I will probably never forget.

That day, it had been pouring rain, and Dewey had been wearing galoshes ten times too big for him. Today it was so hot I didn't know how long I could survive out here before I fainted. The wind that had been making the ride tolerable on our way into town seemed to have given in to the pounding sun as the day continued into the early morning.

"How come I ain't never heard of you?" I asked the woman as we took our seats.

"I don't know. I guess nobody ever thought to tell you . . ." She sort of drifted off. "I'm sure they had their reasons."

I kept waiting for reasons that never came. Instead, she held out her hand and said, "My name's Addison, by the way."

"I'm Abe," I said, shaking her hand, "which you already seem to know. This here's Dewey."

Dewey shook her hand, too. "Mighty pleased," he said.

"I would've just come straight to your house," she said, "but I'm worried about your mom's reaction to me just showing up like that. I was hoping you might tell her you met me and give her my phone number. I have some important things I need to talk with her about. You know what I mean?"

I had no idea what she meant. I thought this over. It was weird that this woman seemed to know so much about me and my family. "You *do* know my pa died, right?" I asked.

She smiled sadly. "Yes, Abe. I do. I'm really sorry about your loss."

The steps were white marble and had recently been cleaned. They looked extremely bright today. "I didn't really know him much," I said. "Carry knew him better than me." Then something occurred to me. This woman—Addison—had mentioned my mother and followed me, but hadn't said a thing about my sister. "You know about Carry?"

"Yes, I know quite a bit about you and your sister, actually. My mom and dad have pictures of both of you growing up. Lots of pictures."

"Your ma and pa?" I asked, trying to figure out how that fit. "You mean—"

"Your grandma and grandpa," she said.

"I have a granddaddy and grandma?" I asked.

She laughed. "Of course. You think the stork brought your dad? How old are you, again?"

"They still alive?" asked Dewey.

I elbowed him. "Don't be so rude," I said. Then I looked at Addison and quietly asked, "Is they?"

She nodded. "Sure are. That's kind of what brought me here to meet you."

"What do you mean?"

She sat there as though thinking about whether or not she should answer my question. I suppose she decided not to because the next thing she said was, "I really should be talking to your mother about all of this."

"How come you know so much about 'em all?" Dewey asked suspiciously, his eyes squinting at her on account of the sun.

She looked over at the other side of the street as if once again contemplating whether she should give out some important information or not. Her eyes came back to mine. "Just get your mom to call me. Then we can figure this whole thing out. I promise it will all become clear soon enough. Okay?"

"Okay," I said, disappointed in her answer.

She pulled a piece of paper and a pen from her purse and wrote a telephone number on it. Folding the paper once, she handed it to me.

I unfolded it, and read the number. "You don't live in Alvin?"

She laughed. "No, I'm from up in Boston. Can't you tell? Most people know immediately by the way I talk."

"I just thought you talked strange," Dewey said. "Some kind of weird accent."

I shushed him. "Don't be so rude."

She laughed again. "It's okay. Lots of people think I talk strange. Lots of people where I live would think *you* talk strange." A starling caught her attention. "A whole bunch of people . . ." she said, trailing off.

"You came all the way from Boston to give me this number?" I asked.

She paused again. "Yes and no. There were a few reasons I came down here. Again, I need to talk to your mom about this. Please get her to call me. But make sure you explain that I won't be back in Boston until the day after tomorrow, so she should wait at least two days before calling. You know what I mean?" She sounded especially funny when she said words like *again* and *about*. I almost expected Dewey to say something. I was glad when he didn't.

"I'll give it to her," I said, blocking the sunlight with the back of my hand as Addison stood up.

"Thanks, Abe, and let me tell you what a nice experience it's been to finally meet you. You too, Dewey. You seem like very nice boys."

She walked back down the street to her car and got inside. A moment later she drove off. We watched her go in silence until she was out of sight.

"She seems like a psycho to me," Dewey said.

"I thought she seemed nice enough."

"She hunted you down from Boston."

"Yeah, somethin' weird's going on."

"Think she's really your aunt?" Dewey asked.

"Dunno."

"She looks nothin' like you."

I didn't respond. I just wondered about all the questions she kept refusing to answer. And what did she mean by it's been nice to *finally* meet me? One thing was for sure: She did seem a little bit creepy.

Something was definitely not right.

CHAPTER 4

My mother was just getting out of bed when me and Dewey made it back home from the grocery store. We didn't even bother going to Dewey's first to drop off the aluminum foil before heading straight to my place so I could tell my mother about this strange woman who called herself my "aunt."

My mother met us in the kitchen.

Quickly, I told my mother everything that had happened, the words fighting their way out of my mouth.

"And she wanted me to give you this," I said when I had finished relaying the story. I handed my mother the piece of paper with the telephone number written on it.

"Abe, what have I told you 'bout talkin' to strangers?" my mother asked.

I looked down at my sneakers, which I had forgotten to take off at the door in my mad rush to come inside and tell the story. "I know," I said, "but this woman seemed to know who I was. She told me I was her blood."

"People can tell you a lot of things, Abe."

My eyes turned up to hers. "So she's not my aunt?" I felt strangely disappointed.

"To the best of my knowledge, your pa never had no siblings," she said. "Would've been strange for him not to have mentioned 'em to me. We were married five years 'fore he . . ." She trailed off and I knew bad memories had started swooping in like hawks going after field mice.

My pa had married my mother when my mother was just a kid, not much older than Carry. I think the reason they even got married in the first place was all on account of my mother getting pregnant with Carry, but from what I've come to understand they *were* in love. But then, when I was two years old, my pa died.

I never really got to know him. It made me sad that I barely remembered him. When I was older, I found a picture of him in my mother's closet that I kept. I still carried it around with me all the time. I don't think my mother knew that I had it. I found it in a box in her closet with a whole bunch of other pictures of my pa and my mother. They were the only pictures of my pa I'd ever remembered seeing on account of my mother getting rid of all the ones around the house after him dying.

She didn't like to talk about my pa much. Even now, she still seemed very uncomfortable when topics spilled over into anything regarding him. I didn't think she'd dealt with his death properly.

That was something I got from watching the TV, that you had to go through a certain grieving process. And, until you got through it, you couldn't get over the person you lost.

I think my mother was stuck somewhere in the middle, just going round and round.

"Well, how did this woman know so much about Abe and Carry if she's not their aunt?" Dewey asked.

"I don't know," my mother answered after thinking about it, "but if she tries to talk to you again, you come and find me or go to the station and get Chief Montgomery to talk to her, you understand?" It was funny how Dewey had asked the question, but her answer had been directed straight at me.

"Yes, ma'am," I said, watching the toe of my sneaker outline one of the checkered squares of our kitchen floor.

My mother seemed upset by our news, and I hadn't wanted to upset her. I thought she'd be happy, or at least interested in knowing more about what was going on, the same way me and

Dewey were. Instead, she seemed almost angry, or maybe it was scared I was looking at. I couldn't tell.

"I think she's a nice lady," I said. "I don't think she means to hurt anyone."

"She seemed like a psycho to me," Dewey said. "She hunted Abe down from Boston."

"You don't know nothin'," I said to Dewey.

"You're too young to know if someone's nice or not," my mother told me.

"What do you mean?" I asked. I thought this was a ridiculous statement.

"I mean you're naïve, Abe. Anyone can make you think they're nice when really they have ulterior motives."

"That's not true," I said. "If anythin' it's the opposite. I tend to think people ain't nice when they really are. Remember what happened with Mr. Wyatt Edward Farrow?"

Mr. Wyatt Edward Farrow had moved in across the street near on a year ago and, at the time, Dewey and I thought for sure he had been up to no good. Little girls were disappearing around Alvin and my mother was trying to figure out who was nabbing them and I thought with all my heart that Mr. Wyatt Edward Farrow had something to do with it. He just seemed so suspicious. Dewey and me even followed him one morning all the way into town to see what he was up to.

In the end, he turned out to be one of the nicest fellers I'd ever met. He was a carpenter, and he made Dewey and me biplanes— real big ones—that we played with all through the winter. We were *still* playing with them. When we weren't, mine hung from fishing line right above my bed. I loved it.

My mother still hadn't answered my question. Maybe she was thinking about something else and hadn't heard me ask it. At any rate, I decided to drop it. It didn't matter what she said, I *knew* I was able to tell bad people from nice ones. It was something I was good at. Like I said, it was the other way around I sometimes had problems with.

"You gonna call the number?" Dewey asked her.

She let out a long sigh. "I dunno."

What I didn't know was why Dewey's questions were getting answered and mine weren't. "Why wouldn't you call?" I asked. "What's the worst thing that could happen? And even if he didn't talk 'bout them, surely Pa must've had a mom and a pa. So that part's probably true, don't you think?"

Another sigh came to her lips. "Your pa never spoke of his folks," she said. "I don't *know* why. But—" She stopped as if in deep thought about all this.

"I don't see what callin' the number can possibly hurt," I said.

"I don't know who this person is, Abe," she said. "I don't want to call someone I don't know."

"You gave Miss Sylvie your home number and you're afraid of talkin' to a stranger?" I laughed. "Whoever this number belongs to, she's gotta be more normal than Miss Sylvie." I regretted saying it as soon as it came out.

Then Dewey followed with, "You *really* gave Miss Sylvie your home number? Are you *crazy?*" And then *he* laughed, and everything got even worse. A *lot* worse.

My mother's eyes narrowed, and if laser beams could've shot right out of them, we'd both have been fried all over the fridge and stove. "I'll hear none of that from either of you!" she said. "Miss Sylvie is *not* to be made fun of. Especially not by *you* two. Especially not in *this* house. Am I clear?"

Dewey's hands went into his pockets. "Yes, ma'am," he said quietly.

I hung my head and just nodded.

"Good. Now, Dewey, I reckon you oughta get home with that aluminum foil 'fore your ma starts figurin' out she didn't go through two rolls on her own in a single day, don't you?"

Dewey had set the foil, which was sticking out of the top of a brown paper bag, on the counter when he came into the kitchen. "Yes, ma'am," he said again.

I was about to tag along with him when my mother said. "And, Abe . . ."

I stopped and turned.

"I want your room cleaned."

"But—" It wasn't even messy.

"No buts. You're stayin' in today. Go take off your shoes."

"Yes, ma'am," I said. She was in one of her moods. I knew there was no point in even trying to post a disagreement.

Dewey was barely out the door and my sneakers had just been kicked off my feet when the phone rang. I raced from the back door through the dining room back toward the kitchen to grab it when my mother picked up the receiver right in front of me. I could tell she was still upset; I just wasn't sure what she was upset about. I think it was a number of different things, some of which made sense to me, some of which did not. My giving her the phone number of this woman who called herself my aunt seemed to really have knocked her for a loop.

I stood in the kitchen beside the sink listening to my mother's side of the telephone conversation. The sun was higher in the sky now and just edged the top of the window looking outside over the backyard where the cherries hung from the two trees, just waiting to be picked. Their dark red skin glistened under the hot sun.

"Hello?" she answered. "Oh, hi, Ethan. How are you this mornin'?"

Ethan was Ethan Montgomery, the police chief of the Alvin Police Department, my mother's boss.

"What do you mean?" she asked, suddenly on the defensive.

"No, I didn't do it so she could threaten you. I—" Whatever Chief Montgomery was saying to her was making her even more agitated than before. This was definitely not a good day to be stuck inside with my mother. I wished more than ever I had been able to escape with Dewey.

"No, Ethan, listen. I told her she could call me if she *needed* to, but only for emergencies. And I emphasized that she had to call the station *first*."

I was guessing this had to do with my mother giving Miss Sylvie her home phone number. I don't think anybody would think that was a good idea. I still wasn't quite sure why *she* did.

"Well, I certainly didn't mean for her to use it as leverage." There was a brief pause and then, "Yes, I'll talk to her. I'll let her know."

Another pause and, "Ethan, before you go, do you mind if I ask you something about an unrelated issue? It concerns an encounter Abe had with a woman on Main Street this morning."

And my mother told Chief Montgomery the whole story about the woman claiming to be my aunt. She got most of the details surprisingly accurate. I guessed that's what made her a good detective. When I had told her about it, I hadn't thought she'd been paying that much attention, but I suppose she actually had been.

When she was finished, she fell silent while Chief Montgomery spoke. Then my mother said, "Well, I guess I just wanted your opinion. Do you think it's *possible* this woman might actually be Billy's sister? Could Billy have had siblings and not mentioned them the entire six years we were together?"

Billy was the name of my pa.

Another pause and then, "I don't know. Do you think I should? That seems a bit like using the system for my own personal agenda. And I feel somehow like I'm being disloyal to Billy's memory. Like I'm spyin' on him or somethin'." She turned a thing over in her mind and then said, "Okay, go ahead and do a background check on Billy." She let out a deep breath "I don't know how I feel about this, but at least I'll know whether or not to trust this woman. Oh, and she says she's from Boston. Abe said she sounded funny, so she's probably got the accent to go with the claim. Thanks, Ethan. I owe you one. And don't worry 'bout Sylvie; I'll talk to her right away. It won't happen again."

My mother hung up the phone.

"Why you doin' a background check on Pa?" I asked.

"To see if it turns up any brothers or sisters."

"Why don't you just call the number?" I asked. "Wouldn't that be easier?"

"Because I don't trust people I don't know, Abe. I'd rather not go into this blind. It's too strange, her showin' up after all this time. It just strikes me odd."

"Everythin' 'bout Pa strikes you odd."

"Now what's that supposed to mean?"

"I dunno."

She searched my face, as though trying to decide if I had

insulted her and deserved a good talking to. "I reckon you think too much."

I had no idea what she meant by that. "What did Chief Montgomery say 'bout Miss Sylvie?" I asked, figuring she'd answer my question by telling me to mind my business.

She surprised me. "Oh, apparently she called the station again with another problem and asked Chris to put her through to Ethan. When Ethan took the call, she immediately threatened him by sayin' if he didn't take her seriously, she would just call me at home. So now I got Ethan thinkin' I'm in cahoots with Miss Sylvie, givin' her ammunition to blackmail the department into attendin' to her."

"Why would they think that?"

She took another deep breath. "Because apparently you're not the only one who reckons givin' out my home number to Miss Sylvie was a bad idea. And they all know how I feel about the way her calls are treated at the station. I don't keep it a big secret. I think the girl is treated unfairly. I hate injustice, Abe. You, of all people, should know that."

I thought about it. I reckoned I did know it and it was something I admired about my mother very much. "I hate injustice, too," I said.

She held out her arms and I moved in close. Pulling me into her chest with a warm hug, she said, "Now you're just tryin' to suck up."

"Mom?" I asked, while her arms were still wrapped tightly around me. "Did I really do something wrong today by talking to that woman?"

"You did what you thought was right," she said. "I just wish you hadn't talked to a stranger. At least you did it in a public place. This time it turned out okay. You got home safe. But next time you might not be so lucky. I just don't want anythin' bad to ever happen to you."

"I don't want anythin' bad to ever happen to you, either," I said.

She let go of me. I could see a tear standing in her eye. "All right. I reckon it's time for you to go start cleanin' up your bedroom."

"Okay," I said reluctantly, and slunk down the hall, wondering what all might show up in that background check Chief Montgomery was doing on my pa. There were sure a lot of things about him that *I* didn't know. I would *love* to find out more.

That night, Leah Teal went to bed with a lot on her mind. She left the drapes of her bedroom window open, and outside heavy clouds had started moving in. Somehow, the moonlight still managed to find gaps between them to shine through and, once Leah turned off the lamp on her nightstand, a pale gray light fell into the room. It was enough to cast small shadows on her sprayed white ceiling. She stared up at that ceiling, unable to stop thinking about poor Sylvie Carson all holed up in that little house with that newborn. The times Leah managed to release those thoughts, her brain just switched over to ciphering about this woman who had suddenly appeared into her little Abe's life claiming to be his aunt.

Could Billy have had a sister? Was it *possible* he kept that sort of information private all those years? Do you keep that sort of thing hidden from your wife? Then she started second-guessing herself—wondering if it's really a lie if you just don't mention it. Because deep down, Leah didn't want to believe Billy was capable of ever lying to her.

But *could* it all be true? And *parents*. New grandparents for Abe. That idea both excited and scared Leah. The last thing she wanted to do was see her boy get attached to someone only to lose them. The first time that had happened was almost too tragic to survive. She doubted she could manage it a second time around.

But Billy certainly *did* have a ma and a pa; he just rarely mentioned them. Not that he was one for being too outspoken. She used to tell him he could keep the devil's secrets in a poker game with Jesus if he'd wanted to.

Did he lie to her?

She couldn't figure it out.

One thing was for sure. She wasn't getting any sleep tonight. It didn't help that she went to bed so early. The room grew darker. The cherrywood of the dresser across the room became lost in the shadows of the waning light, but she could still make out the bright white face of the clock set on its top. It was barely ten. She'd only tucked Abe in a half hour ago. From the living room, she heard the sound of canned laughter coming from the television. Caroline was still up, no doubt cuddled in a blanket on the sofa. That girl was a night owl during the summer, and she always had that damn television set so loud it was a wonder Leah ever managed any sleep.

That's when the phone rang and Leah nearly jumped out of her pajama bottoms. Her head and pillow had been right beside the nightstand where the phone sat between the bed and the lamp.

Figuring it was likely Sylvie, she quickly answered it. The last thing she needed was a reason for Abe to give her any more back talk about handing out her home phone number than he already had.

She was surprised, though, when the voice on the other end didn't belong to Sylvie Carson at all, but to Police Chief Ethan Montgomery whom she'd just spoken to barely four hours earlier.

"Ethan, what is it?" She hoped it wasn't Sylvie blackmailing him at the station again. She hadn't had a chance to talk to the girl about it yet. She figured that was a conversation best done in person when it came to someone like Sylvie Carson.

"Leah, we got ourselves a problem."

"I figured that. Otherwise, why else would you be callin' me at all hours of the night?"

"Since when is ten all hours of the night?"

"Since I got a boy comin' home tellin' me he met his auntie in the street today. Can we just move past this part of the conversation?"

"You know what tomorrow is, don't you?" Ethan asked.

"Sunday."

"I know it's goddamn Sunday. You know what *else* it is?"

"Why don't you just assume I don't and tell me and save a whole bunch of time?"

"Tomorrow is the day our old preacher man gets released."

Oh dear Lord Jesus, how did Leah forget *that*? She'd marked it on her calendar at work barely two weeks ago. Eli Brown finished his sentence tomorrow after spending over seventeen years in jail. Twelve of them in the Federal Correctional Institution in Talladega, the rest up in Birmingham at the Work Release Center. He was being let out just under three years of the full twenty he got handed down for manslaughter after killing little three-year-old Caleb Carson.

After a period of silenced panic while Leah's mind raced over ideas about how to handle damage control on this event, she finally came to a realization. "Sylvie doesn't know," she said. "Does she?"

"Well, she's not *supposed* to," Ethan said.

That was an odd thing to say, Leah thought. "I don't see this as bein' a huge problem, to be right honest, Ethan," she said. "Sylvie doesn't know, and the man's done his time. In the eyes of the law, he's no longer a criminal. Besides, she might never find out. He probably won't ever return to Alvin. After all that happened it's the last place I'd think of headin' back to if I were him."

There was a slight chuckle in Ethan Montgomery's voice when he responded that Leah didn't like one bit. "Go turn your television set on," he said.

"What?"

"Turn on your TV, Leah. Channel six. The ten o'clock news."

"Caroline's watching the goddamn TV," she said. "Just tell me."

"Go turn the channel," he said and hung up.

"Oh dear Christ." She set down the receiver. Pulling back the covers of her bed, she swung her legs over her mattress and slid her feet into her slippers. Even though it was July, the hardwood floors of the bedrooms still managed to somehow get cold at night.

She padded down the hallway, through the kitchen and dining room, and into the living room where Caroline sat curled up on the sofa just as Leah had expected, wrapped in the yellow blanket she'd had since she was about ten years old. The thing was ridiculously worn, with tattered corners and even holes in some places, but Caroline refused to give it up, even when Leah offered to replace it with a new one.

She was watching some situational comedy Leah hadn't ever seen. Before Caroline even had a chance to complain, Leah walked over to the television and started turning the dial.

"Hey!" Caroline yelled. "What are you doin'? I was watchin' that!"

"Police business," Leah said. "Now shush."

Leah got to channel six and stopped turning the dial. On the screen, a reporter was at the Birmingham Penitentiary interviewing a very old-looking Eli Brown. His face was even more creased than it had been the last time Leah had seen the man, when he was transferred up to Birmingham. He had less hair and what little he had was pure white.

"Mother," Caroline whined from the sofa. "Please turn it back to my show?"

Leah shushed her again and turned up the volume. "So," the reporter asked the old preacher man, "after seventeen years, how do you go about stepping back into your life?" The reporter was a young dark-haired kid in a gray blazer.

Eli Brown was wearing an orange prison outfit. Leah couldn't help but think it kind of suited him. "Just the way I left it, I s'pose," Eli said, his voice more hollow and broken than ever. "I'll find my way back to God and back home to Alvin. For me it's really about picking up the thread right where it started to unwind."

The phone immediately rang again. And this time, Leah had no doubt when she picked it up whose voice she was going to hear at the other end. It certainly wouldn't be Police Chief Montgomery. Not *this* time.

Staring at the screen, she let the phone ring once more as two words came out of her mouth. One was "Oh." The other was "Shit."

CHAPTER 5

As Leah had imagined, the telephone call was a disaster. It was Sylvie, of course, and she'd been watching the same channel six news program. Until now, nobody had told her that Eli Brown's parole was coming up two and a half years early. Far as Leah knew, the girl didn't even know the man had been moved from Talladega into the work release program in Birmingham. Apparently, old Preacher Eli was as good as gold behind bars. Nobody wanted to see him spend any more time there than he had to.

Obviously, Sylvie Carson didn't feel the same way about the man.

"What are you gonna do 'bout this?" she asked Leah, although it was more like she screamed it into her phone than so much as asked a question. Leah could barely understand a word the girl was saying she was talking so loud and fast.

"What do you mean, what am I gonna do?" Leah asked back. She tried to keep her own voice as quiet and slow as possible, hoping to calm Sylvie down, but she knew in her mind there was no calming this girl down. She'd been jumping at boogeymen hiding in corners too many years. Now, suddenly, she felt she had a real boogeyman to jump at and seeing him on the television screen made the danger more real than ever.

"I mean you *can't* just let him walk out free! You *know* what he did to little Caleb!" Leah heard Sylvie begin to wail. "He don't deserve to ever be free. He don't deserve to be alive. He shoulda been sentenced to die!"

Leah stayed quiet. It was the only thing she could think of to do. Nothing she could say would placate Sylvie when she was this upset. Preacher Eli Brown had been convicted of manslaughter in the first degree, a class B felony in the state of Alabama. "He got the maximum prison time the judge could sentence him to, Sylvie," Leah said. "The minimum was ten years. Eli got twenty. You should be happy 'bout that. Justice was served."

Sylvie's voice suddenly grew eerily quiet as the sobbing stopped. It almost sounded scary from Leah's end of the phone. "Justice was served?" Sylvie asked, now speaking slowly. "Justice was served?" Her voice slowly rose in volume. "You didn't see your little brother get blown apart four feet in front of you at the supper table when you was five. Don't *you* tell *me* that justice was served when the murderin' son of a bitch who done it is about to walk out of prison a free man tomorrow."

"You're right," Leah said, remaining calm. "I can't possibly know how it feels to be you. It must be horrible. But Eli Brown has done his time. By the laws of this state, he's no longer a criminal."

"Yeah? Well, by the laws of me, he's still a murderin' son of a bitch who better not show his face anywhere near round here on account of I got a loaded shotgun with his name on it just waitin' for a chance to have its trigger pulled."

Leah sighed. "Now don't you go doin' nothin' stupid. You just go on pretendin' things are the same as al—"

"I will *not* pretend things are the same as anythin'," Sylvie said. "If I have to, I will hunt that man down, but he will get what he has comin'. Because the law might not think he deserves to serve his full sentence, but I'm gonna make certain he is fully punished for the crime he committed. I don't think the *law* completely understands real life. Things might look good to all them fancy lawyers, but all them fancy lawyers ain't livin' with pictures in their heads of their baby brother bein' blown to bits. They're just sittin' round big tables makin' chitchat and decidin' on things they have no right decidin' on." She kept talking and Leah wondered if she was even going to stop to take a breath. "But I'm gonna make the decisions regardin' what's adequate punishment for Preacher Eli from now on because I'm someone who *does* live with those pictures in my mind. I'm someone *affected* by all this. I can make the *right* decision."

Leah heard something in Sylvie's voice she didn't like. Maybe it was on account of the fact that the panic seemed to have gone. It was replaced with something more like determination. Sylvie meant what she was saying, and that scared Leah. The last thing she wanted was Sylvie becoming a vigilante and going on a manhunt, trying to kill someone who had just finished serving his time.

Leah decided this was something too important to just shrug off or even to leave until tomorrow to deal with. By tomorrow, Sylvie could have disappeared and be fully engaged in some or other creative plan.

Leah had to change Sylvie's mind. And she had to do it tonight.

"I'm comin' to your house," she said.

"Why's that?" Sylvie asked. She sounded genuinely surprised.

"To talk."

"We's talkin' now."

"I want to talk face-to-face."

"Ain't gonna make no difference," Sylvie said. In the background, Leah heard the baby crying. "Oh, damn it, The Baby just woke up."

"Well, you go put her back down and listen to me, Sylvie. I want you to be there when I arrive, you understand? And you'll let me in. And you're gonna talk to me."

There was a long pause and Leah thought Sylvie might have gone to get the baby, but then she heard her breathing on the other end. Finally, Sylvie said, "Okay, but I might not listen too close."

"That's okay," Leah said. "I can't control how much you listen. Just do me a favor and put the kettle on? It's been a long day already. You *do* have coffee, right? If not, I can bring some."

"I got coffee," Sylvie said. "But I ain't got no milk. Well," she laughed, " 'cept for my breast milk. You better bring some of your own milk."

"I'll take it black," Leah said. "Just make sure it's strong." Leah dug her forefinger and thumb into her temples. The day had given her a headache. Now, instead of letting her go to bed early, it was continuing on into the night, giving Leah a second act.

"How long will you be?" Sylvie asked. "I wanna know it's you when you come to the door. I don't like people comin' to the door after dark."

Leah already knew that. "I'll leave in ten minutes. Probably be there in twenty-five. Don't worry, I'll call out from the other side of the door and let you know it's me. Don't ever open the door for anyone you don't know. Understand?"

"What you think I am? Stupid?"

"No, Sylvie. Just young."

"I ain't so young."

Leah's fingers dug harder into the side of her head. "Maybe not. But you're a lot younger than me."

Sylvie Carson lived up on Old Mill Road in the northeast part of town. The road should have been called Old Mill River Road, as it almost exactly followed the Old Mill River, although the river ran all the way down to the Anikawa and the road started where the old railroad tracks crossed Main Street at Finley's Crossing.

It was one of the oldest roads in town, and most of the houses along it were spaced far apart, giving it a very desolate feeling as you drove along, especially at night. In a way, it was much like the area on the exact other side of town called Cloverdale where a lot of the black people lived. Both Cloverdale and Old Mill Road were probably built around the same time.

Alvin had the distinct look and feel of a town that was originally built from the outside in. Leah hadn't noticed this in other small Alabama towns. When you came into Alvin from the west side by Highway Seventeen or from the east side through Finley's Crossing, you came through the oldest farms and ranches first. Once you got off the main highways, the roads on the outskirts were all gravel. It wasn't until you started getting past the perimeter that things became paved and houses started looking newer.

This was opposite to how she thought it should be. In her mind she thought a town would start with a single building, maybe a Town Hall, and then grow around that building. Start with a central street, such as Main Street, and grow around that street. Alvin had a Town Hall and a Main Street, but it all seemed in much better repair than the buildings and streets on the outskirts.

This was a question she would one day ask her uncle Hank about. Hank knew lots about everything, and even if he didn't have the right answer, he'd give her an answer that she would be satisfied with. That was the way Hank worked.

Earlier, when the sun had gone down, the sky had only been partially cloudy with a waxing moon. Before going to bed, the sunset had been quite pretty, even with the clouds stretched across it. It was one of those late afternoons when the sun and the moon were in the sky at the same time, something Leah had once thought impossible when she was a kid. It wasn't until she was well into her teens that she realized the moon didn't only come out at night.

But since sunset, a layer of thick clouds had rolled in, and now there was no moon and no stars whatsoever. To make matters worse, the few streetlights along Old Mill Road were sparsely strung while it curved and twisted its way along the edge of the river. The road felt even more desolate, cold, and lonely as it began to climb upward into thicker forest. And, as she came up on Sylvie's old house with the peeling paint, things felt more desolate, colder, and lonelier still. Even though it wasn't actually cold at all, this road just brought with it a chill Leah didn't like at all.

Leah parked in the drive and walked the few steps to the door, hoping Sylvie had that coffee ready. Leah's eyes were barely staying open on their own. She knocked on the door and called out, "Sylvie? It's Leah." Then she caught herself. She was being much too friendly and informal. Normally, she would never act so casual. Quickly, she knocked again and corrected the mistake. "Sylvie? It's Detective Teal, Alvin Police Department."

Surprisingly, Sylvie didn't go through her usual routine of sliding the chain over and peering through the crack to verify Leah was who she said she was before opening the door. She just shot the dead bolts, opened the door, and welcomed her in. This was so unprecedented that, for a moment, Leah just stood there, stunned.

"Well, you comin' in or what?" Sylvie asked. "You said you wanted to talk, let's talk. I've had your coffee ready for ten minutes. It's probably not even hot no more."

Blinking her eyes wider open, Leah stepped across the threshold into Sylvie's place. Once again, the ugly living room lamp was on, but this time the light over the kitchen table was on too, so things didn't look quite so much like death.

The living room wasn't as tidy as it had been on Leah's last visit. The magazines were no longer neatly stacked, and there were a few plates with leftover food sitting on the old coffee table. But Leah had come unexpectedly. She had to remind herself that there were times her place looked like a hurricane had hit it. *Having kids will do that. Kids of any age. Speaking of which—*

"Did you get the baby down again?"

Sylvie smiled. One of her front teeth was crooked. Leah hadn't noticed this before and wondered if maybe that was on account of this possibly being the first time she'd ever actually seen the girl's teeth. Could she really have never seen Sylvie smile before?

"Yeah," Sylvie said, "she fell right back to sleep after I fed her for a bit. Come on in. Never mind the mess. Coffee's in the kitchen."

As soon as they walked into the kitchen, Leah's eyes locked on the shotgun still leaning against the wall beside the back door. She knew it would be loaded. There was no point in even asking anymore. She'd asked so many times she'd lost count, and the answer never changed. There was no way it would be any different *now,* of *all* times.

They sat at the table. Leah instinctively took the chair facing out into the room.

"So what brings you here so late?" Sylvie asked. Her voice was pleasant. She even smiled again. It felt so strange to Leah. It was as if she was talking to somebody normal. And, really, she should be very happy about that, but something inside her wouldn't let it settle right, because she knew very well that Sylvie wasn't normal.

Sylvie shouldn't be acting normal. She shouldn't be happy. A half hour ago, she was yelling on the phone that she was going to hunt down and kill a man tomorrow, and now it was as though she had turned into Miss Congeniality.

Leah took a sip of her coffee. Sylvie was right, it had gotten a bit cold, but at least the girl had listened to her and made it strong. It tasted like the old campfire coffee she used to make when she and Billy would drive up into Mississippi for the weekends. That was back before their marriage. She'd been seven years younger than Sylvie. "I wanna talk about Eli, Sylvie," Leah said. "I wanna finish what we was talkin' 'bout on the phone."

"Oh." Sylvie looked away and, for a moment, her face fell. Leah watched it very closely. The girl was being very guarded with her emotions, and that scared Leah, because it meant she really did have a plan. This wasn't just some displaced reaction; this was something cold and calculated.

The smile came back, as though by magic. "Would you like to try some oatmeal raisin cookies I made? They aren't too good. I'm not much of a baker, but I thought I'd give 'em a try. I watched this woman on the TV make 'em? And she said they was easy as pie. So I tried to follow step by step, only she started going too fast, and I think maybe I—"

"Sylvie," Leah said, reaching out and touching the girl's hand, which was grasping the side of her coffee cup. "I didn't come here for cookies. I came to talk about Preacher Eli. He's bein' released tomorrow and he says he's movin' back to Alvin. Now, that probably bothers you a mite. I know if I were you, I'd probably be bothered a mite by it, too."

Concern fell over Sylvie's face. "You think I should be worried?"

"That's not what I said. I said I think it bothers you. Which means I think *I* maybe should be worried. Tell me how it makes you feel."

Sylvie looked at her cup. "Mad. Sad. I dunno. Kinda like it hurts and I can't do nothin' 'bout it." Turning her face back up, Sylvie revealed tears pooling in her eyes. "How do you think it makes me feel? I want the man dead, Miss Teal. I can't rest without him bein' dead."

"Please call me *Officer* Teal, Sylvie. And him bein' dead won't help your rest any. I agree you need closure, but not the kind of closure you think you need. That kind of closure never actually closes anythin'. You'd wind up with his ghost hauntin' you the rest of your life."

"What do I do then?"

"I reckon you need to find a way to forgive him for what happened all them years ago."

Anger flashed in Sylvie's eyes, and for a brief second Leah thought things were going to blow out of control. But the anger was washed away by more tears. They still just stood there, tiny pools reflecting the light overhead like small blue moons.

"I can never forgive him for what he did. Not to Caleb. Or to me. He took away everything I ever had." As she said this, her voice broke, betraying the control she'd been exhibiting since Leah had arrived.

Leah sighed. She remembered what she'd heard about Sylvie still being emotionally five years old. She had to talk to her like she was a five-year-old and this was a concept far beyond a five-year-old's understanding.

"No, Sylvie, he didn't. He accidentally shot your brother. Caleb wasn't meant to die. What happened to him happened because the Lord saw fit for it to happen. For whatever reason, it makes sense in some way or another. That's why Eli only got sentenced to manslaughter. To be honest, I don't think he meant to pull that trigger at all. I don't think he even meant to shoot your daddy."

Sylvie just sat there quietly as Leah took a long sip of her coffee before continuing. The girl actually seemed to be listening.

"My own daddy was the police officer assigned to that case," Leah said, "and he would come home at night and tell me 'bout it. I was only a kid then, but I remember him sayin' how remorseful Eli was about what happened, and my daddy felt sorry for him on account of him feelin' so bad. What happened to your brother was terrible, don't ever get me wrong."

With another gulp, three quarters of Leah's coffee was done. She was trying to time it so she'd be done just in time to leave.

She continued talking, grateful Sylvie hadn't tried stepping into the conversation. Instead, she just sat there with her hands folded in her lap like a little girl. Occasionally, she would lift one hand to the table to take a small sip of her coffee, but then her hand would go right back to her lap.

"But all the hate you're carryin' for Eli?" Leah said. "It ain't hurtin' Eli none, Sylvie. It's hurtin' you. You're carryin' it round with you like a bucket o' poison. And every time you think 'bout how much you hate him, you drink a little bit more of that poison. Eli don't drink any of it, you do. And that poison eats away at you from the inside. It makes you see the world as a dark, scary place where people are out to get you."

Sylvie looked down at the table.

"And the only way you can heal the wounds you've got from drinkin' all that poison is by learnin' how to forgive," Leah continued on. "And when you forgive, you're not givin' anything to Eli either. He ain't the one gettin' the forgiveness, *you* are. If someone gives you a gift and you don't take it, who does it belong to?"

Leah wasn't sure if Sylvie was even listening to her anymore. She was just staring at a spot on the table directly in front of her. The light above the table began to flicker and buzz for several seconds before settling back to normal. Leah sat there, waiting for a response. Finally, Sylvie looked up and answered her question. "I guess it still belongs to the person givin' it?" she offered.

Leah was happy to hear her sounding like her old self again, even if that old self was the scared, paranoid Sylvie who called the police every time a car so much as backfired in the neighborhood. The way Sylvie had been acting when Leah got here had scared Leah into thinking Sylvie was well on her way to making some really bad decisions. Now Leah thought that just maybe she might have turned things around.

"Exactly," Leah said. "Eli's not acceptin' your gift of hate, and he ain't gonna accept your gift of forgiveness, neither. Besides, these gifts ain't *for* him. Both of these things belong to you. One of them tears you up and hurts you inside, and one of them will heal you. Do you understand any of what I'm sayin' to you?"

Sylvie sniffled. "A little, I guess."

"Can you do some thinkin' on it?"

Sylvie blinked away some tears. "Guess so."

"Can you stop talkin' 'bout killin' Eli? Because all that's gonna do is put you in prison, and you won't even get manslaughter. You'll get murder one. And then there really *will* be no justice in the world. And who would raise that little girl of yours? Who would be left to give her a name?"

Sylvie wiped her eyes with the back of her sleeve. When she spoke, there were tears in her voice. "No one."

With a drink of her coffee, Leah nodded. "No one. That baby needs you more than you need to drink any more poison from that bucket you's carryin' round with you. So I want you to just relax for the next few days and let things settle. If you need me, or get anxious at all, you call me. You don't even need to call the station first. Do we have a deal?"

Sylvie was crying. "Okay."

Leah rose from her chair. "Now stand up and give me a hug."

She did. And Leah felt the girl tremble in her arms.

With a look back at the shotgun, Leah asked, "I don't suppose there's any chance I can convince you to take the shells out of that 'fore I leave, is there?"

Still crying, Sylvie shook her head.

"Didn't think so. Just be careful. And call me if *anything* happens, you understand? Do not pick up that shotgun. Pick up the phone. Am I clear?"

Sylvie nodded.

Leah kissed her forehead. "You'll be okay. Just take care of that baby. And get some sleep." Reaching down, she lifted her cup to her lips and finished her coffee. "Tell you what I'll do. Once Eli Brown's moved back here, I'll pay him a little visit and just get a feel for the man—make sure he's as safe as I believe he is. Then I'll come back here and tell you everything me and him talked about. Does that sound like a good plan to you?"

Sylvie nodded. "I'd appreciate that." Her words were broken.

"Okay. I've gotta leave now." Leah stepped into the living room. "Don't forget to lock the door behind me."

Once again, it was probably something that didn't need saying.

CHAPTER 6

On Monday afternoon I came up with a brilliant plan.

It was too late to get a real sword; they were back at Disney World, and my mother wasn't about to buy me one anyway, but she couldn't stop me from making my own. Sure, it wouldn't look as impressive as the ones I saw while on vacation, with the steel blades and the hilts full of gems, but at least I'd have a sword. And if I made it out of wood, I could use it to play fight with Dewey, which would mean I'd have to make two of them.

Problem was, I wasn't so good with building stuff when it came to wood. Not that I was all that bad; I just didn't have any experience. But I knew somebody who did. My sister, Carry. And Carry was home right now, in the living room, watching television. And my mother was at work, so the timing was pretty near perfect.

All that remained to my plan was to come up with another plan on how to get Carry to help me.

I decided the direct approach was the best. So I walked into the living room where she was sprawled all over the sofa and just asked her straight out if she'd do me a favor,

"Well, I guess that depends now, don't it?" she said smugly.

"On what?"

"On what the favor is, dork."

I didn't feel we were off to great start with her calling me a dork already, but I decided to press on. "Will you help me build a couple swords from some of the wood Pa left in the garage?"

She didn't even look at me. Her eyes were glued to that television screen. "What are you talking 'bout?"

"I wanna make two swords so me an' Dewey can pretend sword fight with 'em, but I need your help on account of I ain't no good at woodwork and stuff."

She laughed. "And you think I *am?* You *do* remember the non-tree tree fort we made when you was little, don't you? That thing didn't last through the night."

The drapes above the sofa were open and sunlight was pouring into the room, casting my sister in the shadow of the sofa cushions. It made it hard for me to see her properly. "Yeah, but we was just kids then. You're almost an adult now."

"Tell Mom that. She still thinks I'm twelve." She hesitated and added, "No offense."

"None taken," I said honestly.

"Anyway," I said, "I'm thinkin' swords might be easier to make than forts. They don't seem to me like they'd be all that complicated."

I stood there, waiting for her to reply, but a response never came. She just kept watching her television show. After what felt like at least five whole minutes of waiting, I asked again. "So?"

"So, what?" she asked back.

"So will you help me?"

"I'm watching *The Facts of Life* right now. Maybe later."

I looked at the television. "This is a rerun. You've seen this one at least a hundred times. I think I've seen it more than half a dozen, and I can't even stand this show."

"So what? They're all reruns. The show ended in May. I wanna watch it again, ass face."

"Hey! Mom told you to stop callin' me that!"

"Oh, you gonna tattle on me?"

I kicked at the gold shag carpet with the toe of my sock. "No. I just really want you to help me make a couple swords so me and Dewey can pretend sword fight. Please? It'll only take an hour."

She turned her head and stared at me. "An *hour?* You think I have an hour to stand around and make stupid swords with you? *Please.*"

I sighed. "Okay, then a *half* hour. It won't take long, I promise. They can be real simple."

Lying there with her head on the rise of the sofa's arm and one leg thrown over the top and the other askew along the cushions, I could tell she was considering it. Finally, she pushed herself into a sitting position. The sunlight from the window lit her blond hair from behind, making her look almost like an angel. "Fine! I'll help you make simple swords," she snapped. "But they're gonna be *real* simple. And you're gonna owe me somethin' for this. Don't you forget it."

My heart flipped over in my chest. "I won't," I said, smiling. "I promise. Cross my heart."

Crossing your heart and promising your sister you owe her one is like signing a pact with the devil. Especially if your sister is Caroline Josephine Teal. Oh, she helped me make the swords, all right, and they turned out not half bad. We made them from two pieces of narrow pine. One piece was about two feet long and it made the handle and blade. The other was maybe six inches and we nailed it across the other maybe six inches from the bottom to form the cross guard of the hilt. Carry figured out how to use my pa's old belt sander to taper the long piece down into a point. When we were done, they looked pretty good. Even better than I'd hoped.

"There," Carry said, as I inspected our handiwork, one sword in each of my hands. "You happy with 'em?"

I beamed back at her. "I sure am. Dewey's gonna love 'em." The garage smelled like old car oil, which was strange because there hadn't been a car parked in here for as long as I could remember. It was too full of wood and tools and other junk left over from my pa after he died that my mother had never bothered cleaning up or getting rid of. We had the garage door open for light and the sun picked out specks of dust scattering through the air.

"How long we been out here?" Carry asked.

I checked my watch. Uncle Henry had bought it for me last fall—it was a Timex, just like his. Except for when I had baths, I always wore it. "Just over half an hour."

"That's a lot of my time. You remember our deal?"

I fell silent, trying to figure out what she was talking about. I didn't rightly have any idea what she meant.

"We had a deal, ass face. You promised if I made you your swords that you'd owe me one."

"Oh, yeah," I said. "What do I owe you exactly?" I realized now that I'd been so excited at the prospect of getting my swords made that I never confirmed what the "one" was that I owed her and that the whole deal was probably a mistake.

"That's for me to decide. But when the time comes, I'll let you know."

"Okay," I said hesitantly. The way she said it made me wonder if she was going to get me to kill someone for her or something.

Oh, well, there was no point in worrying about my deal with Carry until the time came for me to fulfill whatever she came up with. I decided to just ignore it for now and be happy I had swords.

I was just about to rush inside and call Dewey when my mother drove into the driveway. Unsure of how she'd feel about us being in the garage and playing with Pa's tools, I nearly raced over to close the door, but realized she'd see me do it, and that would just make me look guiltier. Besides, way back when Carry helped me build the non-tree tree fort, my mother hadn't been upset at all. She'd been right happy about it, in fact.

As I mostly do—at least more times than not—I decided honesty was the best policy and walked out of the garage into the afternoon sun with my swords in my hands to show her my and Carry's handiwork.

"What're you kids doin' in the garage?" she asked, getting out of her car.

"Carry helped me make some swords so me and Dewey can pretend sword fight." I held up the one in my right hand, pretending the sunlight was glinting off its hardened steel blade. It actually looked more like sun shining on dull wood with rounded corners that Carry had sanded so we wouldn't hurt ourselves, but I had a pretty good imagination.

"Did I say you're allowed to play in the garage?"

"I—" I started, but changed to "You didn't say we *wasn't* allowed to."

"Don't be smart with me, Abe."

"Should we not have made them?" I asked, wondering why this was different than the fort had been.

For a moment she seemed at a loss for words. I think her mind was somewhere else and she wasn't really sure what she was angry about. "You just should've asked first. Did you clean up after yourselves?"

I nearly laughed. That garage was such a mess, you couldn't find an elephant in there with a magnifying glass. We *had* to clean up just to be able to get at things. So, "Yes," I said, quite honestly.

"Good." She still hadn't really looked at my and Carry's woodworking projects as she closed her car door and started toward the house. In her hand was a file folder.

"You never said if you liked my swords," I said from behind her, still raising the one majestically. A slight breeze picked up, swirling leaves around my feet. They had fallen from the shrubs planted around the driveway.

"They're fine. Just don't play with 'em in the house."

She walked up the front steps and was just about to open the door when I asked, "Somethin' wrong?"

Stopping, she rested her forehead against the door. After a minute she said, "Listen, Abe, I'm sorry. It's not you. Here, let me see your swords."

I walked over and showed them to her.

"Oh, these are nice. Did Carry help you make them come to a point like this?"

I nodded. I decided not to tell her that I had to sign a pact with my sister in order to engage her services. "I think Dewey will like 'em," I said with a grin. "We can pretend sword fight."

"Just be careful. Just because they're not metal doesn't make them not dangerous. You could still poke out an eye with one of these."

"I'll be careful. We rounded the corners and made the ends blunt, see?" Then I nodded to the file folder in her hand. "What's that?"

She looked at it and her expression fell. "Oh." She took a breath. "It's the background check Chief Montgomery ran on your pa."

Suddenly, my swords were no longer important to me. Excitement frizzled through my body. It was like an electric bolt of lightning had erupted at my heart and quickly spread throughout my entire insides. "What's it say? Can I read it?"

Looking down at me standing there expectantly, she exhaled so hard her shoulders heaved. "Come in the house. We'll sit at the kitchen table and go through it together."

I couldn't get inside the house fast enough. Leaning my swords up against the wall beside the door outside on the porch, I went in and took off my shoes. It seemed to take her forever to get to the kitchen table where I was already anxiously seated and waiting. I could tell there was something inside that folder that my mother obviously didn't like. Still, I was filled with anticipation. I never really got to know my pa. I barely even remembered him. Mostly I remembered the picture I carried around in my pocket that I found in my mother's closet. And it seemed nobody would ever give me any details about him when I asked anything either. But now, here was a file folder, full of real information concerning my pa. And it was only a few feet from my hands.

We sat there, our chairs almost touching, and my mother laid the folder in front of her. "There's not a lot of information here," she told me. "Your pa never got in trouble with the law or nothin' like that, thank the Lord"—she said "thank the Lord" in a way that made it sound like that was a potential possibility, given something else she found—"so it's really limited to things like employment, family history, stuff like that. It's really quite boring."

"Then why are you so worked up over it?" I asked.

"I'm not worked up."

"Seems like it to me."

"Okay, maybe a little. But it's for something dumb."

"What?" I figured if she was worked up about it, it couldn't rightly be so dumb.

"Well, in a way, I think your daddy lied to me, and that don't sit very well is all."

"Pa was a liar?" I didn't know much about him, but this was the last thing I thought about my pa.

"Now I didn't call him a liar. I said *in a way* he sorta lied to me."

"What do you mean by sorta?"

"I mean he didn't rightly tell me the truth."

I couldn't figure out the difference between that being just a "sorta lie" and a real lie, so I asked her.

With yet another sigh, she flipped open the folder. Inside was a document on blue paper with a staple in the corner. It turned out to have three pages to it.

"He didn't *not* tell me the truth, I suppose, better explains it," she said.

I scrunched up my forehead. "Huh?" I asked. "What does that mean? I don't get it."

"Your pa had a family he never told me 'bout. In fact, he had an entire past he seemed to have neglected mentionin'."

"Doesn't everyone have a past?"

"Yeah, but usually bits and pieces of it come up from time to time in casual conversation. Your pa kept things all to himself. He didn't so much as even hint at any of this." She was flipping through the pages. I still hadn't heard a word of what any of "this" was.

"So he lied to you by not tellin' you what he was lyin' 'bout?" That question didn't even make sense to me.

"This is why it's not sittin' so well, Abe. Part of me thinks I'm bein' a fool for caring 'bout this at all. I mean, of *course* he had a past. Everyone has a past. Why did I expect anythin' different from him? But for some reason, I never thought of his life before we met, and since he never mentioned it, it was like it never existed. And that life led into the life we spent together. So, in a way, to me, he had no life before our marriage. Our marriage was his life. Now I find out about all this stuff and that he really did have a life that led into our life together, and so it changes our marriage in a way. It's sort of like our whole life together was a lie."

She was sounding crazy, but I wasn't sure I should tell her that. "Maybe Pa just didn't think the stuff that happened to him 'fore he met you was important. Maybe in a way he liked pretendin' his life didn't really start until he met you."

Her head jerked up and her eyes met mine. There were tears in hers, but they looked surprised.

"Did I say somethin' wrong?" I asked, worried I was about to get in trouble.

She took me in her arms. "No, Abe. You just said possibly the single most right thing you've ever said."

"I did?" I asked, my voice muffled by her shirt. I wasn't even sure what I'd said. This conversation had stopped making total sense to me a while back.

When she let go, I asked, "Will you tell me what it says about Pa now?"

"Well, for one thing, the woman you met? Addison? She probably really is your aunt."

I couldn't help but smile. I'd met family. "Really? Is her last name Teal like mine?"

"Yup. Least it was last time these records were updated. Unless she got married since. And you do have two grandparents livin' in Georgia. I *knew* he had parents. He *had* mentioned them from time to time, but only in passing. He told me he didn't get along with them and sort of left it at that. From what little information I gathered from your pa, your grandpa ran the house like some sort of military sergeant. I never dreamed they was livin' barely three hours away the whole time. The way your pa talked, it was like they was clear across the country or somethin'."

"I have another granddaddy!" I said.

"And a grandma," my mother said.

"Wow! This is really great! I can't wait to tell Dewey! Are we gonna meet 'em?"

She looked at me sternly. "I dunno yet. That waits to be seen."

"Waits for what?"

"For me to decide."

I looked down at the table. "Oh."

My mother flipped to the last page. I could tell there was something on that page she really didn't like.

"What else does it say?" I asked.

"Nothin' that concerns you."

"Please? He was my pa and I don't know nothin' 'bout him."

She looked into my eyes for a second.

"Please?" I asked again.

"Fine, I guess." I watched her swallow hard before she continued. When she did, her voice was much quieter than before and it sounded like she might be holding back tears. "Says here your pa was married once before. Can you believe it? You know how young he was when he married me? He'd barely turned twenty. Well, he was even younger when he married her. He was only eighteen. They lasted two months."

"That makes you mad?"

"He shoulda told me."

"So you could get mad at him?"

"So I would know."

"What would you have done?"

"Gotten mad at him."

"I'm bettin' that's likely why he never told you," I said. Why did this all seem so easy for me to understand and yet my mother seemed to be having such a hard time with it?

"He *still* shoulda told me. For better or worse. We vowed that. I'm supposed to know all the 'for worse' parts."

"But this was before your weddin'."

She glared at me. "Why don't you run along and play with your swords? I want to be angry some more and you're just makin' it tough."

"There anythin' else in there about Pa?"

"Nothin' interestin'."

"You sure? You said that 'fore and then you tol' me he was married once before."

She lifted the papers off the table and snapped them in the air. "Well, let's see. You wanna know his fishing license number? His driver's license number? How about his Social Security information? I can give you some of his tax records if you'd like. Any of this sound like somethin' you'd like to be let in on, Abe?"

I pushed myself off the chair. I could tell she was done showing me the file. "No," I said. "Thanks for letting me know 'bout the family stuff."

"You're welcome."

"I'd really like to meet 'em," I said.

"I know you would."

"And I know you're scared to," I told her.

"I know you know. Now take off. You're too old for your own good."

"I know," I said, and left the kitchen.

Leah watched her little Abe leave, wondering how in the world she'd managed to raise him all by herself and still have him turn out so well.

Then she thought of Miss Sylvie and realized she was going to turn out okay, too. It was just going to take some time, was all. Eli Brown had moved back to Alvin already and, even though Leah hadn't yet paid him her little visit that she promised Sylvie she would, Sylvie seemed to be handling the situation just fine. Leah would go see Eli sometime in the coming week. She wasn't worried. The man was harmless. She'd seen him when he'd been moved from Talladega to the Birmingham Work Release Center and the man she'd seen was a kind and gentle man, not a man worth being a mite scared of.

Sylvie was just afraid of her memories. And they were memories being amplified because they were coming from a five-year-old girl.

No, Leah wasn't worried one bit about Eli Brown. That's why she hadn't *bothered* going to see him yet.

Despite Sylvie's fears, nothing bad was about to happen.

Or so Leah thought.

Then, four days later, Sylvie found her cat, Snowflake, lying dead on her back porch.

CHAPTER 7

Leah was at the station when the call came in. Chris had picked up the phone and immediately Leah knew it was Sylvie by the way he rolled his eyes. "Yes, Miss Carson," he said in that condescending voice that made Leah want to pistol-whip him. "And what can we do for you today?"

Sitting at her desk, Leah tried to keep looking busy, as though she wasn't interested in listening to Chris's side of the conversation, but the truth was that she was eavesdropping because if she didn't take an interest she knew nobody else would. So, while she pretended to be going through files and looking things up on her computer terminal, she was actually on autopilot, eavesdropping on Chris sitting at the desk beside her.

It was probably pretty obvious to Chris. The station had only switched over to computers in the last year and Leah still wasn't really sure how to use hers properly. Chief Montgomery liked to go on about how one day all the computers in all the police departments across the country would be connected and share a central repository of information, but that all sounded like science fiction to Leah. Right now, any data they wanted in the system, they had to put there and store on floppy discs that they kept in a cabinet. They had probably five hundred such discs and, once the data was inputted, it was easier to work with. But inputting it was a big job. This was why the only data Leah had access to was recent events that happened in and around Alvin. For anything else, they still had to order background checks or reports, usually from places like Mobile.

She knew just enough about her computer to get by. She wished she knew as much about it as her son did. Sometimes, after hours, when it was just her and Abe (and occasionally his friend Dewey), she'd let them go on the terminal. They were much better at it than her and even discovered a game they liked playing on it called *Super Slither.* Leah had no idea the computer even had games. She still didn't understand why it does.

But for now, while she listened, she pretended she knew what she was doing. Even if what she was doing was only scrolling the bright green text of her contact list of other stations and emergency numbers up and down the dark green screen.

"Is that so?" Chris asked. "And how long do you figure he's been dead?"

Dead? Who's dead? This immediately grabbed Leah's attention. She no longer pretended to be playing with her contact list or shuffling around papers. Now she was just in her seat, obviously paying attention to what Chris was saying to Sylvie.

"I'm sorry," he said. "*She.* How long do you figure *she's* been dead?" He wrote something down on the pad in front of him. "And what was the cause of death?" He wrote a bit more and said, "I see."

She? Well, for someone being dead, Chris was remaining awfully calm. It better not be the baby, or there'd be hell to pay. In fact, she couldn't think of anyone it could be that would allow for his demeanor to be so inappropriate at such news.

"Yes," he said finally, still remaining calm as a salamander sunning himself atop a rock in mid-July, "of course we'll send an officer out right away." He sat back in his chair, half turned, and gave Leah a smile and a wink. "Yes, I'm aware of the severity of the situation. You just sit tight now, all right? Okay. Bye, Miss Sylvie."

Reaching over, Chris dropped the receiver onto the telephone and said, "And now the community tax dollars shall once again be spent on yet another crazy quest for that woman."

Leah didn't share Chris's lackadaisical attitude. She was anxious to find out about the details of the call. "What was that about? Who's dead?"

Chris laughed. "You're not gonna believe it. It's her damn cat. She found it dead on her back porch. Now she wants to file a police report. I guess she suspects murder?" He made a gun out of his forefinger and thumb and pointed it at the floor. "Pow!" he said, lifting the barrel of his finger-weapon. "That'll show *you,* you mangy cat. Next time you'll know better than to mess with us." He laughed even louder this time.

Still Leah felt anxious. "What did she say happened to it? What killed her?"

With a shrug, Chris said, "Damned if she knows. She said she can't see no reason why the cat should be dead. It isn't like it's very old or nothin'. She sounded a bit loopy, if you ask me. I think she was pretty messed up about it."

"You think?" Leah asked, standing from her seat.

"Where you goin' so fast?" Chris asked.

"To Sylvie's. To check out what happened to her damn cat. Some of us have to take our jobs a little more seriously." Grabbing the keys to her car, Leah headed straight for the doors.

"It's just a goddamn cat!" Chris yelled in her wake, his sentence getting cut off by the sound of the door slamming shut behind her.

Leah had been getting more and more annoyed with Chris's attitude at work lately. It had gotten progressively worse since he single-handedly made what could've been called "Alvin's biggest bust" (and *was* in some papers even as far up as Birmingham).

Chris had brought down a cocaine deal that went bad for the people involved, and he did it pretty near all by himself (although a lot of it happened by utter good fortune) and seized over one and a half million dollars' worth of coke off the street, according to the values the feds in Mobile came back with.

Stories of exactly what happened that night tended to vary. Some said the deal was in progress, some said Chris caught them by surprise as they were leaving their hotel room with the drugs to make the deal. Some said both they and Chris caught each other by surprise. There were stories involving civilian passersby getting involved and helping Chris take down the gang. Some reports said Chris was responsible for two of the men. Chris said that he nabbed all four men, and had planned his entire takedown well ahead of time. At any rate, four men did go into custody. Ethan was just happy Chris was still alive.

What that amount of drugs had been doing passing through Alvin was anybody's guess. Chris only got wind of it from a last-minute tip. Then he did a one-man stakeout, which Leah thought was incredibly irresponsible of him, not bringing her into the loop. He could've easily been killed. Drug dealers don't carry around product worth millions of dollars without also carrying around weapons.

But it all worked out in the end. Chris rounded up the two or four men (depending on who you listened to) and got the coke. He even made all the papers right across the state and, for five or six days, Alvin was actually put on the map, so to speak.

Leah found it funny that she could solve crimes of girls going missing and turning up murdered and raped and that didn't make nothing but the local news, but when cocaine was involved, everyone was suddenly interested.

Anyway, the bust happened, oh, must be going on nine or ten months or so ago now, and Chris seemed to have been resting on his laurels ever since. It wasn't that he didn't do *anything;* it was just that his work lacked its usual dedication, commitment, and luster. If it stayed like this much longer, Leah was going to have to say something to Ethan about it. She hoped Chris would figure it out and work things through on his own, though. She hated going above people's heads, or behind their backs, or around any other body part. It all just sounded so sneaky.

Chris did know his stuff, and he was dead on with a bull's-eye when Leah arrived at Sylvie's. Miss Sylvie was truly messed up by what had happened to her cat. "Thank God you got here so fast," she said, opening the door before Leah was even fully out of her car. "I didn't know what to do. The cat—she's . . ."

Leah tried to calm her down. "It's okay, honey. I'll take care of it."

Sylvie let Leah into the house. She had the baby on her shoulder. The baby was awake but quiet. The moment Leah was inside with the door closed and locked behind her, Sylvie started pacing the floor, rubbing the baby's back. Leah got the impression she'd been doing this ever since calling the station.

"Where's the cat?" Leah asked.

"Right outside the back door."

Opening the door, Leah found the animal lying lifeless right on the back step. It looked as though it just fell over and died. Putting on blue latex gloves, she squatted down and, touching the body as little as possible, turned it different ways looking for any sort of mark that might indicate a cause of death. She expected to find some blood somewhere. Maybe the cat caught itself on some barbed wire or a piece of sharp metal. God knew there was enough garbage lying around this backyard for anything to kill itself on if it tried hard enough.

But there was nothing. No puncture wounds. No blood. Not a mark on its body. Rigor mortis had begun setting in, so the body was stiff. Leah didn't have the background needed to discern any time frame as to when death might have occurred.

But the lack of obvious means of death niggled at the back of her mind. *Something* killed this cat. Normally, the first thing Leah would suspect would be a coyote. But if it had been a coyote, there'd be no body left here for Leah to be examining. Whatever it was that took this animal's life did so without leaving a single mark. Not even a scar. And, like Sylvie told Chris on the phone, it wasn't like Snowflake was old. She wasn't even a year yet, by Leah's calculations.

Something wasn't right. Leah could feel it. She hated that feeling, that gut feeling she got all the time when something "wasn't right." Her own daddy and Police Chief Montgomery always said it separated the good detectives from the bad ones. She hated it because it meant she had to follow it, even though, rationally, she knew it was crazy.

But she wouldn't be a good detective if she didn't. So, turning around, she started back for her car.

"What're you doin'?" Sylvie asked, a slight panic in her voice. Leah suspected she thought Leah might just be leaving her alone again to have to deal with the dead cat by herself.

"I left my radio in the car. I'm going to call Chris. I want him to come out here, too."

"So you suspect somethin's up?"

Leah looked into Sylvie's eyes, searching them for any emotion. It was uncanny how much she could feel that five-year-old girl staring back at her. "I don't know what I suspect, Sylvie. I just don't want to leave any stone unturned is all."

Leah got into her car and radioed Chris back at the station, telling him to come by Sylvie's and bring the cruiser with the CSI kit in the trunk. Even though she could tell he was trying to contain it, Chris couldn't help cracking up. "Backup?" he asked, his laughter breaking up a bit over the radio. "For a dead cat?"

She steeled her voice and said loudly, "Chris. Get your ass over here, now."

That got rid of his giggles but fast. "I'm comin'," was his only reply.

When Leah returned to the backyard, Sylvie was standing in the frame of the back door, purposely looking anywhere but down where the cat was lying basically at her feet. She still held the baby in her arms, but Leah was quite sure the baby had fallen asleep.

"You think same as I do, don't ya?" Sylvie said, whispering now, so as not to wake her daughter. "That someone killed Snowflake? That someone came into my yard and killed my poor kitty?" The poor girl was on the brink of breaking down. Leah didn't need that right now.

"I don't reckon I know *what* I think right now, Sylvie. I just reckon we gotta check this out as thoroughly as possible. Now I promised you I'd take your calls seriously, so I'm takin' this one as seriously as I can. That's why I called for Chris, understand? That's the *only* reason. Don't go readin' anythin' into this that ain't there."

"You talk to Preacher Eli yet?"

That was a question Leah had hoped Sylvie wouldn't ask. "Not yet."

"How come? You promised me that you would do that, too. He's been back in town over a week now, and here my cat winds up dead on my back porch. I'd say that's a mite coincidental, wouldn't you?"

"Now, Sylvie, I don't think Eli killed your cat."

"Why not?"

"Because what would his motive be?"

"Just that he likes killin' things smaller than him. He killed my baby brother."

Leah rubbed her eyes in exhaustion. She hoped Chris wasn't taking his time getting here. The last thing she wanted was to keep up this line of conversation with Sylvie any longer than she had to. "I will go talk to Eli Brown tomorrow. Hell, I'll go do it today if we get done here in time. You have my word."

"I've had your word before. It's suddenly not meanin' so much no more."

Wow. The girl knew how to make things sting, that was for certain. But guilt trips were something Leah was used to. She had two kids at home and one was a fifteen-year-old daughter who made Sylvie look like a rank amateur when it came to laying on the guilt.

"My word is my word, Sylvie. You take it any way you like. Folks around town know what it's worth. Main thing is that *I* know what it's worth."

Fifteen minutes later Chris showed up, but the time seemed to go by so slowly that it could've been hours. He took one look at Snowflake on the porch out back and said, "Hmm. Dead cat. Yep. Dead." Then he saw the look in Leah's eyes and his demeanor instantly changed. For the rest of the time he spent there, he was very professional and polite to Miss Sylvie, which made Leah quite happy. If he hadn't gotten rid of the attitude, she was ready to tear a side off him something fierce when they got back to the station. Leah could shout louder than Chris could. Besides, she had seniority. And her pa and Ethan Montgomery went way back. When it came right down to it, it was exactly like they said: Blood was thicker than water. And Ethan and her pa had been close enough to consider each other blood. You didn't turn your back on blood.

And technically, Leah outclassed Chris, although it was only a formality. Ethan Montgomery had made her detective as a favor to her pa before he died, so that the station would be able to pay Leah more money in order to help raise her family. Then it became doubly important when she lost Billy.

Leah was just happy none of this mattered, as Chris seemed to come around now that he had arrived on the scene.

He searched the cat's body more closely than Leah had by using the various tools in the CSI kit and eventually gave up establishing a cause of death. It definitely wasn't anything external. It seemed like the cat had just simply dropped dead. "Maybe it had a heart attack?" he speculated.

"The cat was barely a year old," Leah said. "Seems a bit far-fetched to me."

"Well, somethin' might of scared it to death," Chris said. "But then, it's s'posed to have nine lives." He smiled at Leah, who didn't smile back. Chris's smile disappeared immediately. "Sorry, that was just a little joke to lighten the mood."

"We can use a little less lightenin', thanks," Leah replied.

Pulling the camera from the CSI kit, Chris took pictures of the body from all the different angles, exactly as he would a real human body at a real crime scene. *Good,* thought Leah. *Now he at least looks like he's taking this seriously.*

When he was finished taking pictures, he put the camera back in the case. "Well," he asked, "what do you want me to do with the cat now? I've pretty much done all I can."

"Bag it, I guess," Leah said. "Give it to Norm in the morning. He can probably tell us how it died and give us a rough time of death."

Chris looked up at her. "Seriously? You want me to get the coroner to give your dead cat an autopsy?"

Leah came in close and lowered her voice so Sylvie wouldn't hear. "I want to set this girl's mind at ease, Chris, and if that takes pulling some strings and getting Norman Crabtree to take a few minutes out of his day to examine this here body? Then, yes. That's exactly what I'm sayin'."

Chris just shook his head. "I think you're almost as crazy as she is."

"Chris, what if someone *did* do somethin' to this cat? I mean it didn't die of old age. There's no indication a coon or a coyote got it. *Somethin'* killed it, and we can't tell what after an hour of examinin' it? And *you* don't find that odd?"

"I reckon you've been readin' too many detective novels."

"I reckon you've been spendin' too much time behind your desk doin' too many crosswords."

With a huge sigh, Chris reached his gloved hand into the CSI kit and pulled out a bag big enough for the cat's body to go into. "Bagging the cat," he announced. "But I'm gonna have one problem."

"What's that?" Leah asked.

"I'm not really sure how I'm gonna attach the toe tag."

CHAPTER 8

Most nights when Sylvie suffered "incidents" she had trouble sleeping.

Tonight, she lay in bed with thoughts circling like a kaleidoscope inside her head. This happened often. Usually, it was always the same thoughts; she'd go through different parts of the past, trying to make sense of them. But making sense of some things was impossible. Sylvie knew that, but she couldn't do anything to stop the endless spinning. Sleep would come eventually, but before it did, she would have to succumb to the pain of reliving the memories of her childhood.

For a long while, she'd known she wasn't completely normal. When she saw her baby brother murdered that day something broke inside of her. Sylvie remembered it all so clearly: like a photograph, only one that went forward and backward in time with different pictures developing on it.

She'd known something inside her wasn't right back then, but she managed to hide a lot of it. After the initial shock wore off, and everyone grieved for Caleb, her folks appeared to somehow move on with their lives. It seemed they thought Sylvie had, too. The first indication her pa got that something was truly wrong with his daughter didn't actually happen until she was twelve. Until then, she'd done a good job of hiding her depression and her paranoia from the world. Sylvie would hear her folks refer to her as "a kid who likes to spend a lot of time in her room" and "someone who likes to go on long walks, alone."

That was back when she would still leave the house by herself. Now she couldn't imagine going on even a short walk alone.

But in her childhood, Sylvie helped around the house the way she was expected to, lending Mother a hand with cleaning, and making supper while her pa worked out on the farm.

"Can you wipe the dishes, hon?" Mother asked one particular night when Sylvie had been brooding. She brooded a lot, although much of the time she had no idea what she brooded over.

"Yes, Mother," Sylvie said.

With each wipe of a dish, she felt the thoughts of Caleb grow slightly more distant. Doing anything had a way of pushing the bad thoughts a little farther back.

"Is there anything else for me to do?" Sylvie asked when she was finished, hoping the answer would be yes.

"No, that's fine. Thank you. You really are a good little girl," Mother had said.

But Sylvie's motives weren't as selfless as Mother believed. She would have done anything to take even a tiny bit of those bad feelings away.

After the initial incident, it had taken Sylvie's pa a lot longer than her ma to get over Caleb's death. Sylvie would hear him crying some nights after everyone had gone to bed. She knew he was in his own bed being rocked gently by Mother, who was telling him that everything was going to be all right, and that Caleb was with the angels now.

"God called him early," she heard her tell him once. "He had plans for our little boy. We just don't understand them."

Sylvie would never understand plans from God that involved a three-year-old being shot all over her kitchen during supper. Especially such a happy three-year-old like her baby brother.

And that was how Sylvie remembered Caleb: happy. Maybe time had painted her memories, but Sylvie could not remember a time when little Caleb wasn't the perfect little brother.

Then Preacher Eli killed him.

Time is peculiar. It does change things.

Sylvie had come to understand this.

But she had hated Preacher Eli since that day. That thing hadn't changed. Time had left that one all alone.

And Sylvie had never been happy since that day. That was another thing that hadn't changed.

Not even when the baby was born. She *should've* been happy. It was *her* baby. But, somehow, Preacher Eli stole that, too.

Yet, before she was twelve, nobody really knew how much of a mess the inside of Sylvie Carson's head truly was.

Then came the day she saw her pa butcher the hog.

It was just before Easter, and Sylvie was coming back from one of her walks. She'd been out through their fields, past the horses and cattle, and well into the woods, which were full of mostly oak and birch. She remembered it like it was yesterday, but then she remembered every day of any importance in her life like it happened yesterday. It was that damn time-traveling photograph capable of developing a picture of anything in her past. The pictures were almost always ones she didn't want to see. But she couldn't control them. They just popped into her mind.

The morning had been wet and the grass full of dew. She had left for her walk around ten o'clock, just as the sky was beginning to clear. As usual, she walked to get away from everything. Mainly the farmhouse. Because getting away from the farmhouse was like getting away from the source of all the badness. It was like walking away from the tangled mess of nerves that her mind had become.

As she walked, she tried desperately to keep her thoughts clear—to just be in the moment with nature. She had found *that* was the key to feeling normal: to have no thoughts. Because without thoughts, you could have no feelings. Some days were less successful than others. Some days she got completely lost in her walks, and ended up deep in the forest when she realized the sun was falling and she'd better head for home.

This particular day, her thoughts refused to stop circling like sharks around a rowboat and, after an hour or so of plodding through the wet spring woods, she decided to head back and see if

Mother might have some work for her to do that might take her mind to other places. Lately, Sylvie had started to realize just how much Caleb's death had and continued to affect her, and she was beginning to see how much different it made her from other kids.

Sometimes the difference scared her. Sometimes it made her think thoughts that scared her even more. Thoughts of joining Caleb and his angels.

Looking back now, she wondered how she ever managed to make it through all that time without something like that ever happening. Especially given the years she would soon face alone. With absolutely nobody.

The sun was out when she made it clear of the tree line and she slipped through the fence into the cattle field. The day had grown warm, and the dew no longer clung to the grass. She climbed over the horse fences, giving Willow, her favorite of the six horses they kept, a quick pat down before continuing to the other side of the field to the barn where her pa was.

That's when she stumbled on him slaughtering the hog.

She saw the whole thing. And although she didn't want to see it, she couldn't look away.

First, her pa shot it in the head. And the moment that shot rang out, all Sylvie could see in her brain was Preacher Eli's handgun raised, and the trigger being pulled, and her little brother, Caleb, being blown apart.

Then, taking a knife, her pa cut the hog's throat. Blood gushed.

The kitchen full of Caleb's blood gushed into Sylvie's mind.

She stood there, ten feet away, staring. But what Sylvie didn't know was that she was also screaming. Screaming exactly like she was that day Caleb was shot. Only, on that day, she had just screamed in her mind. Today, she was screaming out loud.

Her pa raced over and tried desperately to calm her down. But Sylvie kept shouting, "Caleb! Caleb!" Pointing frantically, her arm trembled.

Picking her up, Tom Carson took her inside the house. Mother raced from the bedroom. Pa gestured for her to keep quiet.

They lay Sylvie down in her bed and put a damp cloth on her head. The screaming stopped, but she kept shaking uncontrollably.

Visions of her baby brother, as fresh as the dead hog outside, continued playing around and around her mind.

She got very little sleep that night. The next day, Sylvie's parents called for the doctor, who gave them a prescription for sleeping pills. If her folks had known how close Sylvie came to swallowing that entire bottle, they wouldn't have left it on her bed stand. But for some reason, she resisted.

But she never was the same again after that.

No longer did she leave the house to go for walks by herself. Her folks never again referred to her as "a kid who likes to spend a lot of time in her room," even though she rarely left it.

Now it wasn't just Sylvie who knew she was broken, but her whole family. At first Sylvie thought it might make things easier, but it didn't. It only seemed to affect Sylvie's pa, who relapsed into his nightly sobbing about his dead son. Sylvie would hear Mother telling him everything was going to be okay while she waited for the sleeping pills to kick in and take her to that one place where nothing ever hurt. That place she always hated waking up from.

Then, two years later, they lost Mother.

Her pa found the body, but Sylvie heard when he told the police how he came upon it. They must've made him tell the story at least three different times.

"I was walkin' into the barn and there were a bunch of flies buzzin' behind one of the horse stalls," he said. It had been less than an hour since he found her, and he could barely speak through his tears. He was seated on the chair in the living room. Three policemen were at the house. Well, two policemen and one woman. One of the men was taking his report. The woman wasn't wearing a uniform. She was out in the barn looking over the scene. The other man seemed to be interested in the inside of the house. Sylvie couldn't figure out why the house would be interesting to anybody when everything had happened in the barn.

Sylvie was sitting in the parlor just around the corner from the living room with her back to the wall so she could hear. She was crying, but not as much as she reckoned she should be, and it made her feel ashamed. Mainly, she just felt numb.

"I ain't never seen so many flies," her pa continued, " 'cept when somethin' like a dead coon or somethin' shows up on the property, so I looked round the stall expectin' to see somethin' like that." Sylvie heard her pa break down then and start sobbing.

"It's okay, sir. Take your time," one of the officers (probably the one taking the notes) said.

When her pa spoke again, it was hard to understand him. His nose was stuffed and his voice was full of tears. "And she was lyin' there. Covered in flies. I don't know how long she'd been there. I've been in town most of the day."

"What were you doin' in town?"

Sylvie's pa sniffled. "Buyin' feed and tack."

"You have receipts? People can verify you were there?"

There was a hesitation. Then, "What? Yeah, o' course. I was at Arnold's. And I talked to Pete for musta been twenty minutes. That's Pete at the tack shop."

"Where was the last place you was 'fore coming home?"

Another pause before Sylvie's pa answered. "Jim's," he said. "You know. The feed store. Why? You don't think I—"

"We just need to ask these questions. Standard procedure."

Then the other police officer asked, "Was anyone else home?"

"Yeah," Sylvie's pa answered. "My daughter. She was probably in her room." *Because she ain't been right since her brother died, and so that's the only place she ever is,* Sylvie thought, finishing his sentence in her head.

"We'll need to talk to her, too."

They asked Sylvie a bunch of questions she really didn't have very good answers to. She started feeling very accused, like they thought she killed her own mother. The fact was, there was no obvious cause of death, so a case file was opened and an autopsy was performed.

Turned out Mother had somehow ingested rat poison. After an investigation, the police arrested James Richard Cobbler, a radical member of Eli Brown's congregation. There was no evidence linking Eli Brown to the murder. Cobbler had acted alone and was, in his own words, "Acting in God's and Preacher Eli's best interest." He wound up being given the death penalty and died by electrocution.

Sylvie's pa never did get over it.

Now, no longer did Tom Carson have anyone to console him at night as he cried for the death of his three-year-old son. And he sobbed for the loss of his wife, too. The weight of having lost them both turned out to be too much for him. Ironically, in the end, he wasn't as strong as his daughter. Luckily, Sylvie hadn't been the one to find him. While she was at school one day, he'd gone out past the cattle fields, strung a rope over the bough of one of the oaks close to the outer edge of the woods, and hanged himself.

Once again, there was a police investigation and an autopsy. Tom Carson's death was determined to be a suicide.

Mother would've said, "God called them all early. He has plans for every one of us. You just don't understand them."

Sylvie would never understand plans from God that involved taking everyone in her family away from her before she even turned fifteen years old.

Besides, Sylvie had always wondered about the deaths of her folks. It had always nagged at her the way they both went: so close together, and so strangely. Why would her pa leave Sylvie all alone? Especially knowing she was the way she was? If Preacher Eli hadn't been in prison, her suspicions would have gone directly to him over her pa's "suicide."

Then part of her thought maybe *she* was the reason her pa did it. Because he couldn't deal with her without anybody else helping him. Part of her thought maybe it was her fault.

Sylvie not only suffered from what the doctors refer to as post-traumatic stress disorder (something Sylvie didn't really understand), but she had been extraordinarily lonely pretty near her whole life. Foster care didn't do anything but make her lonelier than ever. Even after meeting Orwin Thomas, she'd still felt lonely most of the time.

She wondered if this was how most other people felt.

All of these thoughts continued bouncing through Sylvie's head as she lay in bed staring at her ceiling until, finally, sleep took mercy on her. She either didn't dream or, thankfully, didn't remember what she dreamed after she awoke the next morning.

CHAPTER 9

The first thing Dewey had done once I showed him the swords was pull out his notebook and start jotting down a new invention. "What is it?" I asked, looking on.

He sketched a big circle with a smaller circle attached to the side. Then he wrote the word *rope* with an arrow pointing to the big circle and the words *wire tie* with an arrow pointing to the smaller circle. Then he said, "I'm a genius."

I still didn't know what it was. "How does this make you a genius?" His notebook was over half full of inventions. He'd been pretty busy considering summer wasn't even half finished yet.

He held out the pad for me to see more clearly, although I'd already seen pretty well what he'd drawn. "This will allow us to wear our swords on our hips like real knights. Like they is in, you know, scabbards."

I studied his diagram. "I'm assumin' the wire tie isn't pulled all the way tight?"

"No, we gotta keep 'em loose so the sword hangs down a bit. The cross guard will stop it from fallin' through."

So we went into my garage and started rummaging through my pa's stuff. Sure enough, we found some nice yellow rope that was flexible and perfect for wrapping around our waists and tying at the front. I thought we were going to have a problem coming up with wire ties, but Dewey even managed to find those in all that mess, too. I realized my pa sure did have a lot of garbage in that garage.

Within another ten minutes, both of us had our swords at our sides. Dewey's invention worked perfectly. I thought it was a much better idea than his satellite television reception with aluminum foil.

Me and Dewey had spent the last five days in my backyard playing with the swords me and Carry made in the garage on Monday, and I think they turned out pretty good. They didn't look as nice as the ones at Disney World, but after a minute or two of thrusting and parrying, our imaginations took over. After that, they may as well have been the real things. It was apparent very early on that I was a much better swordsman than Dewey, although he showed signs of improvement each time we fought.

Every day had been nice and sunny with just the odd cloud overhead to give us a slip of shade. Today there was a slight wind, which was a welcome break from the heat beaming down on us while our blades continued crashing. When they hit, they made a knocking sound like wooden blocks being banged together, but in my head I heard the clanging of solid steel forged by the finest of blacksmiths.

"Take that!" I said, with a thrust after blocking Dewey's slash. We were in my backyard, fighting between the two cherry trees. The sun was dancing in and out of the clouds that hung throughout the sky. Currently it was between them, beating straight down on us. I wiped sweat off my forehead with my left arm. It was getting hot.

Dewey stepped back. "Missed me!" he said and took another step back.

I kept coming forward, slicing as I approached.

"Hey, watch it!" Dewey's back came up against the narrow trunk of one of the cherries.

"You can't tell me to watch it," I said. "We're sword fighting. This is how you sword fight." I took another jab. He tried to block it with his sword but missed. The point of my weapon slid right down the edge of his and hit him square on the knuckles.

"Ow!" he yelled.

He dropped his sword to the grass and stuck his knuckle in his mouth. "That's the fourth time you've hit me there! Can you watch what you're doin'?" It was hard to understand what he was saying with his knuckle in his mouth.

"Dewey. We're sword fightin'. Fightin' sometimes involves gettin' hurt. Just be happy these aren't *real* swords. *You* wanted to use *real* ones, *remember?*"

"I never said I wanted you to scrape my fingers."

"No, just cut 'em off."

Dewey said nothing. Just stood there with his hand in his mouth.

"Pick up your sword," I said.

"No, I'm done playin'."

"C'mon," I said. "Don't be a baby. I hardly hit you."

"Abe, it hurt."

"You're a baby."

"Let me hit you."

"Go ahead. All you gotta do is get past my expert blocking technique."

"No, I mean just let me hit you so you can see what it feels like."

I put my hands on my hips, holding my sword at my waist with its tip facing the ground. "Do I look like an idiot?"

"Do *I?* Why would I keep playin' when all you do is whack my fingers?"

"Cuz it's fun?" I offered.

He just glared at me. I got the feeling it was less fun for him.

Just then my mother called me from the back door.

"What?" I called back.

"We're goin' out. Dewey has to go home. He can come back later."

"Where are we goin'?"

"Shoppin'."

"Where's Carry?"

"What does that have to do with anythin'?" she asked. The sun went behind a cloud. It was amazing how fast the temperature dropped.

"Can't I stay home with her?" I hated shopping. Especially the way my mother shopped. It was like she had to look at every single item in the store before making a decision about buying anything. You'd think my mother would let me stay home by myself, me being twelve and all. She sometimes did, but only on special occasions like when she didn't have any choice. But maybe because she worked as a police officer, she worried more than other parents about me being alone. Like she just expected someone to come to the house and snatch me away or something.

"No, she's goin' out," she said. "Besides, I wanna buy you a new pair of sneakers."

My head fell. I hung my arms from my sides. My sword went limp. "Do we have to go today?"

"Abe. Do as you're told. Do we need to have a talk about listenin'?"

I'd had enough talks with my mother about listening to last me the rest of my life. That wasn't the problem. I knew her point of view when it came to listening. "No."

"Good. Let's go. Dewey, thanks for comin' over."

"You're welcome, Miss Leah." He stood there, his hand still in his mouth. His words came out half mumbled.

Slowly, I wandered toward the back door. "What's wrong with his hand?" my mother asked.

"Abe tried to cut off my fingers with his sword," Dewey said, his mouth continuing to make the words near on impossible to understand.

"Abe," my mother said as I walked by her into the house, "do I need to take your new swords away?"

I stopped and looked up at her. "I barely scraped the edge of his hand. He's just being a baby. Look at this." I held up my sword, displaying both sides of it. "Carry even dulled the edges. I doubt I could kill a beetle with it."

"Just be more careful,"

"Thanks, Miss Leah," Dewey said. He was still standing in the backyard with his back against the cherry tree.

"Dewey?" my mother said. "Take your sword and go home now. I think your hand's gonna be fine."

"Yes, ma'am." He picked up his sword with the hand not in his mouth and headed around the house to the front where his bicycle was waiting.

"I'm not gonna get a call from his ma, am I?" my mother asked me.

"No," I said. "I barely touched him. Honest."

"Okay, cuz if I do, I'm tellin' her I had nothin' to do with it, and you were the mastermind behind the whole thing."

I searched her eyes to see what she meant by that and saw a sparkle there. She was kidding around. She knew Dewey was just as big a baby as I did.

Next thing I knew, me and my mother were in the car and going through town. About fifteen minutes into the drive, I realized we weren't headed anywhere we might be able to buy me a pair of sneakers. We were rumbling up Hunter Road, toward Blackberry Springs—away from downtown or anything even closely resembling a store of any sort. "Where are we goin'?" I asked. "There's nowhere to buy sneakers up here."

"I have an errand to run before we go shoppin'."

I had no idea what we could be doing going up in this part of town. There was nothing here except lonely houses spaced very far apart and a lot of forest. It was actually a rather pretty part of Alvin, with densely packed elm, hickory, oak, maple, and other trees lining the edges of the road. If you went up far enough, you came to the springs that ran between Cornflower Lake and Willet Lake. I had heard the springs were popular with teenagers who liked to drive up and park along the side of Hunter Road with their girlfriends.

Thinking of that brought back memories of me and my mother sneaking up on Carry and her boyfriend. That was last year when they were in his red car on the outskirts of town parked at the side of one of the old ranch roads. My mother actually pulled her gun on Carry's boyfriend and threatened to shoot him in his private parts. That memory brought a smile to my face. "What sort of errand is we goin' on?"

"I need to talk to someone. It won't take long."

I had no recollection of anyone we knew living up near Willet Lake. "Who do you need to talk to?" I narrowed my eyes. "Is this police work?" My mother had developed a habit of taking me with her on police-related matters.

She looked at me with a raised eyebrow. "Yes, it's police work. Why is it important to you *who* I need to talk to?"

I shrugged. "Just askin'. Since I'm comin', figured I should know."

A minute went by while it seemed like she was considering whether to tell me any more about it. Finally, she did. "I'm goin' to talk with Eli Brown. I promised Miss Sylvie I'd pay him a visit."

"Preacher Eli?" I asked, astonished. "Isn't he in jail?"

My mother took a deep breath. "He's done his prison time."

"And he's back *here?*" I asked. "In *Alvin?*" I found this exceptionally discomforting that a killer lived in my town.

"Yes, Abe. He's done his time. He's no longer a felon. He's a free man. He can live wherever he chooses."

"But he's a killer, Mom. He killed a kid!"

She sighed. It sounded like it came out through gritted teeth. "You don't understand the legal system, Abe. He killed a boy by accident. Eli Brown was committed to prison for doin' it and did all the time he was supposed to do. From the law's point of view, he's no longer a criminal."

"But he did kill Sylvie's brother."

She paused. "He did. But that was a long time ago. Time has forgiven him of his sin. So should *you,* Abe."

I didn't rightly understand what she meant. All I knew was that she was taking me to the house of a man who killed the last kid he ever got close to, and this didn't sit well with me. "Do you think bringin' me with you is the best idea, Mom? He *likes* killin' kids."

My mother hit the brakes, bringing the car to a stop on the side of Hunter Road. She turned and looked directly into my eyes. "Abe! I want to make sure we're perfectly clear on this subject.

First, Preacher Eli Brown doesn't *like* killin' kids. He killed Caleb Carson by accident. According to the court, he never meant to kill *anyone* that day, especially not poor little Caleb. Second, I would *never* put you in harm's way. If I thought there was even a hint of a chance that you comin' to his house was puttin' you in danger, I would *not* be bringin' you. Do you understand?"

I just watched her, not knowing if she actually wanted a response from me at this point.

"*Do* you understand?" she asked again.

I nodded.

"Good. Third, Eli Brown is *no longer* a criminal. *Do not* treat him like one. He is a member of society with the same rights as you and me. He is no better or worse in any way. Is that clear?"

Quickly, I nodded again.

"Good. Cuz you're comin' to the door with me, so you better be comfortable."

I swallowed. "Why? Why am I comin' to the door?" This made *no* sense to me.

"Cuz I want to see his reaction when I show up with you on the doorstep. I'm paying him a visit as an *assessment,* but I don't want him to know that's what I'm doin'. Please, Abe. Trust me. The man is old now. He was old when he went to prison. That was almost twenty years ago."

I thought all this over. After what I considered the proper length of time to consider it, I answered, "Okay, I trust you."

"Good." My mother started the car and pulled back out onto Hunter Road. She drove onto the small wooden bridge over the springs until we came to a small run-down house on the left side of the road about another quarter mile up. It was painted brown with a black roof and nestled in a small clearing surrounded by pine and fir trees. The ground around it was mostly dirt. There was a rusted truck trailer beside the house and a dented station wagon parked on an angle out front. Farther back in the woods, I could make out a small barn or maybe a garage that was stained a deep red. The siding, like the boards on the house, was aged and in need of refinishing.

"Come on," my mother said, opening her door.

I got out of my side. The air was thick with the smell of the pines, but a hint of an oil smell came along with it. I followed my mother's lead up to the door and watched a monarch butterfly float across the hard-packed ground beside the steps while she knocked.

Preacher Eli answered. A tall man, he was wearing a red-and-black-checkered shirt with sleeves that came down to his wrists. The sleeves were unbuttoned, but the shirt was done up to his neck and tucked into gray pants. He wore a black belt with a silver buckle. His pants went down into boots that looked remarkably similar to cowboy boots. He certainly didn't look much like a preacher to me.

His eyes went from my mother's to mine. It was obvious he had no idea who we were.

"Preacher Eli?" my mother asked.

Eli Brown rubbed his nose. "Now there's a name I haven't gone by in quite some time. Who might you two be?" His voice sounded like someone had taken a chisel to it. He asked the question in what I considered to be a most suspicious manner.

"My name's Leah Teal. This here's my son, Abe. I'm with the Alvin Police Department."

"You don't look like no police I've ever seen." His teeth were brown and crooked. There was a scar under his right eye as though he'd been slashed with a knife. It somehow reminded me of Dewey's hand being hit by my sword.

My mother pulled out her badge and flashed it. "I'm a detective."

Preacher Eli's eyes narrowed. He gave me a long look that made me very uncomfortable. "That so," he said, his eyes still lingering on me. "And what is it you is detectin', Detective Teal?" I was happy his gaze drifted back up to my mother.

My mother held up her palm. "I'm just here to ask you some routine questions, is all. Nothin' for you to worry 'bout."

"I think I'll decide what I should or shouldn't be worryin' 'bout if it's all the same to you." His eyes cut to my waist. I realized I was still wearing my sword on my hip. I'd grown so used to it, I hadn't even noticed it in the car. My hand automatically went to its handle.

He looked back up to my mother.

"Fine," she said. "I understand you was just released from the Birmingham Work Release Center a couple weeks ago."

The preacher's eyes narrowed again. "I don't hear a question in there. And what makes all this routine?"

"Just not very often we have someone like yourself return to the town where all their trouble started, is all. Just wanna make sure I understand your motivations."

Preacher Eli rubbed his chin. "I'm not so sure I'm obliged to discuss my motivations with the 'town detective,' to be right honest."

My mother swallowed. "No, you probably aren't obliged, but in the nature of goodwill, I think it might be a good idea. Especially since Sylvie Carson still lives in this very town."

Preacher Eli stared off between my mother and me at something distant and far away, as if lost in memories. "Sylvie . . . ," he said, more to himself than either of us. Then he glanced at me again. "That was the daughter, right?"

"That's right," my mother said.

"And how's she after all these years?"

"She's holdin' up."

"Good." He looked at my mother expectantly. "Is this what you came to talk to me 'bout? Sylvie Carson?"

"Have you been near her property since you got out of Birmingham, Mr. Brown?"

I tensed up. I figured if any question was going to set Preacher Eli off, it was going to be one like this. It almost sounded like an accusation to me. I wasn't all the way wrong, either. Only he didn't set off with quite the fireworks I anticipated. Something flashed in the man's eyes. I wondered if my mother saw it, too. "Hell no! Why would you ask me somethin' like that?"

Again, my mother's palm came up. "Just an honest question." She had her pad out and was taking notes. "Now you're absolutely certain? You didn't even happen to drive by one day?"

"I don't even know where the hell the girl lives!" Preacher Eli said. "What do you think? I got outta the joint just to finish a job I never meant to start in the first place? Have you even *read* the court

records? I didn't *know* that boy was sittin' there. I'd . . . I'd . . ."
He stopped, and for a second, I thought he was actually going to
start crying, although I got the feeling they weren't real tears. They
were them crocodile ones my mother was always keepin' on about.
"I don't need to talk to you about this."

He began closing the door, but my mother reached out and
held it open. "Preacher Eli?" she said softly. "Listen. I'm sorry I've
upset you. I just came here to make certain you're not a threat to
anyone."

His eyes were wet. He looked like a lamb the way he gazed
back at her. "A threat? Is *that* what you think? I have just spent
almost eighteen years repentin' every single day for the sins I have
done. If I could go back in time, don't you think I would give that
boy back his life? I have thought 'bout him constantly. 'Bout
birthdays missed. 'Bout graduations. 'Bout girlfriends. 'Bout him
not gettin' to have kids of his own. All missed. All cuz of me. And
you think I'm a *threat?*"

My mother looked down. "I'm sorry, Mr. Brown. I don't know
what I was thinkin'."

"The only thing I am a threat to is not bein' able to live my life
long enough to make up for the sins I committed eighteen years
ago." Now tears really did come to his eyes. I still didn't trust those
tears.

"Look," my mother said, "I really am sorry. I didn't come all
the way up here to upset you. How 'bout your family? How's that
boy of yours?"

Even through the tears, Preacher Eli managed a chuckle. "Boy.
He ain't no boy no more. He's forty-one. While I was gone, time
kept goin' and he went ahead and grew on me. I got some catchin'
up to do with him."

"He came and saw you while you were . . . inside, though?" my
mother asked.

"Yeah, he did. Even more so after my Louise passed."

"I'm so sorry to hear about the loss of your wife."

"She'd stopped comin' by so much anyway, after what
happened on that ranch."

"What do you mean?"

"After they found them Carson folks dead. Especially when Tom showed up swingin' from that tree . . ." He looked away and fell silent a moment. "She just stopped comin' by so much."

"How come?" my mother asked. I had no idea what either of them were talking about. I'd never heard of either of the Carson folks swinging from a tree. It sounded funny for someone to be described that way.

Eli shrugged. "Dunno. You'd have to ask her. But that won't be happenin' anytime soon."

My mother let this information digest. I didn't rightly know what it was that had her so lost in thought. "And . . . you have a grandson now, too, isn't that right?"

Another chuckle came through Eli's tears. I knew I shouldn't be trusting those tears. "What did you do, check up on everything you could about me 'fore comin' out?" he asked.

"Just bein' polite is all."

"Yeah, I got a grandson. Lives up north in Alabaster, 'bout twenty miles this side of Birmingham. Haven't seen him for a long time. I hope that changes soon."

"I hope so too, for your sake."

"Well," Preacher Eli said, "I'm gonna go now. I trust I've answered all your questions and you won't be back botherin' me no more?"

"Wait," my mother said as he was closing the door. "Can I ask you one more thing?"

"What?" he asked through the narrow space left between the door and the edge of the frame.

"Why did you return to Alvin?"

He didn't even think about that one. His answer came right away. "Because Alvin's where this all started and Alvin's where it has to be finished. I need to preach again and I need to preach from here. The only way I will ever find peace is through redemption and it's only here that I can find that. You can tell Sylvie Carson she is safe from the crazy preacher man. In fact, you can tell her he is so sorry for what he did to her brother and her life and that he knows he can never make up for it and for that reason he will not be in contact with her. Because any contact would just belittle such a thing. It would make it all seem too . . . what's the word? Trite, I guess. Now, please leave me alone."

With that, Preacher Eli clicked his front door closed. I felt relieved to have the conversation over. Something about the man didn't sit right in my soul. Whenever he had looked at me, I felt like a chicken on its way to the chopping block. I was very happy to be on our way back to my mother's car.

"Well, that settles that," my mother said as she backed her vehicle out of Preacher Eli's driveway and headed back south down Hunter Road.

"What settles what?"

"I can safely say Eli Brown is not a risk to Miss Sylvie or anyone else."

I didn't say a word, even though I wondered how my mother had arrived at that conclusion. To me, the whole encounter had been unsettling and, if anything, put Preacher Eli right on my radar of crazy people to watch out for. I couldn't believe this convicted killer was in my hometown, living right here in Blackberry Springs. Now, after meeting him, not only did I think Miss Sylvie might be unsafe, even *I* felt more unsafe on account of him knowing about *me*.

But then, my mother and I had a history of disagreeing over such things.

CHAPTER 10

One Saturday morning, once my mother had finished with breakfast and had all the pots and pans put away and the kitchen cleaned up, I finally asked her the question that had been bothering me for weeks. Well, actually, there were a number of questions nagging at me, but this one was especially bad, because to me it seemed like it shouldn't be a question at all.

"Aren't you gonna call that number?" I was still in my pajamas and my bare feet were cold on the kitchen floor, even though the rest of the room was hot—not only from breakfast but on account of the weather. It had been pounding down sunshine for well over a week now. And anyone can tell you, when the sun wants to fry up Alvin in late July, it can do a pretty darn good job of it. That's something Officer Jackson liked to say, although the way he said it was slightly different and contained a cuss word I wasn't allowed to use.

"What number?" my mother asked.

I couldn't believe she didn't know what I was talking about. "The number on the paper I gave you that belongs to my aunt." I turned my palms up in exasperation. "She told me to tell you to phone it. That was weeks ago."

My mother sat at the kitchen table, relaxing and enjoying a cup of coffee while reading the newest issue of *Cosmopolitan,* which I was almost sure belonged to Carry. When she heard my response, she hardly even looked up. She just slowly turned to the next page of her magazine and said, "We have no idea that woman is your aunt, Abe. I thought we've been through this."

From the living room, I could hear the television set. Carry had run in there as soon as breakfast was over and planted herself in front of it. If this was like most Saturday mornings, she wouldn't be moving until my mother demanded she go and get dressed and do something with the day. I think that girl could watch TV forever if nobody stopped her.

"I thought we got a background check spyin' on Pa that said she was my aunt," I told my mother.

Now she looked up. "First, we wasn't spyin' on nobody. And second, the background check simply said he had a sister. It doesn't necessarily mean the woman you met is her."

I raised one of my eyebrows. "You're scared of callin' her." I knew I was on shaky ground with this, but I felt it was the truth and my mother always told me I'd never get in trouble for telling the truth.

She laughed. "What would I possibly be scared of?"

"I dunno, but there's a reason you ain't callin', and it ain't because you don't think she's tellin' the truth. If that was all it was, you'd call just to check and see. You're scared she *is* tellin' the truth. You don't want to meet Pa's sister."

I saw her bite her lower lip and I wasn't sure if she was holding back yelling at me for something I said or if it was something else she was doing. But something I had told her made her go quiet. She didn't say anything for a long while. When she finally did, she actually surprised me.

"You know what?" she asked, closing the magazine and looking straight into my eyes. "I think you might be right. I think maybe I *am* scared. Maybe I *don't* want to meet your pa's family."

"Why?" I asked softly. This made no sense to me. I was overjoyed at having suddenly discovered new members of my family. I couldn't see why anyone wouldn't be.

"Because, Abe . . ." She started and then stopped. "It's . . . you wouldn't understand. There's just so many memories. Things I don't want to . . . things I would rather have stay in the past."

I frowned. "You're afraid of the past."

"What does that mean?"

"You never want to talk about Pa. You never want to think about him."

"Why would I want to think about what happened? It was horrible."

"Not about what happened. I mean about *anythin'*. It's like you would rather pretend he didn't exist than have to think about what happened to him. Well, that's not what *I* want. I want to know who my pa was." I realized I was starting to get loud and sounding like a baby. My mother was probably on the verge of sending me to my room.

"You don't even remember him," she said, almost as though she were talking to the walls. "You were so young. You can't possibly even remember what he looked like."

"I remember," I said, looking at the floor. "I have a picture of him I carry round with me."

Both our heads rose and our eyes met. It was the first time I'd told anyone about the picture, and the last person I thought I'd ever tell was my mother. After all, I sort of stole it from her. I searched her eyes. They were wet. Tears were coming to them. "Where did you—"

"Your closet," I said. "I found it in a shoe box. I hope you're not mad. I was lookin' for some wrappin' paper for somethin' I made you at school."

"My closet . . . ," she mouthed.

"Are you mad?"

"Where do you keep it?"

"The picture?" I asked. "In the drawer beside my bed. That's when it's not in my pocket. Usually it's in my pocket. It brings me good luck." Then, I repeated myself. "Are you mad?"

"Oh, no, Abe, I'm not mad. Come here." She opened her arms and I walked over and let her wrap me in a big hug. I felt her tears on the side of my cheek. "I've been so selfish," she said.

I didn't quite understand how she thought she'd been selfish, but I was sure glad she wasn't angry I took the picture from her closet. I was even gladder she wasn't going to make me give it back.

When she finally let go of me, she wiped her eyes and said, "Tell you what. I'll make that call. How does that sound?"

I beamed. "Really?"

"Really. But I'm not promisin' anythin' else will come of it."

"That's okay. I just want you to talk to her."

I saw my mother's chest heave as she took a deep breath and let out a big sigh. "Okay, well, I may as well get this over with."

I stood right beside my mother as she made the call from the kitchen telephone. Luckily for me, the woman I met on the street, Addison? She had one of those voices you could hear from the other end of the phone without even having your ear near it. I figured it probably had something to do with her being from Boston and all.

"Hi," my mother said after the call was answered. "I'm looking for Addison?"

"This is Addison." Right away, I recognized the accent. It was strange how people from different places talked in different ways. Even people from the same country.

"Hi, Addison, my name's Leah Teal. I got your number a while ago from my boy, Abe. Apparently—"

She didn't have to go any further, because Addison picked up the conversation right there. "Leah! I was wondering when you were gonna call. I was startin' to think you weren't, after all this time. I'm so glad that you did. I have so much to tell you. There's so much you and I have to talk about. I assume Abe has told you who I am?"

"Well," my mother said slowly, "he's told me who you *say* you are."

"Ah yes, you're a police detective. I mustn't forget that." I heard her laugh. "Trust me, I promise you I am exactly who I say I am. I have no reason to deceive you. I did not go all that way to just pretend to be Billy's sister."

"Yes," my mother said, ". . . about that. And I'd also like to know why you were followin' my little Abe round in your car. Seems a mite creepy to me."

"Let me guess," Addison said. "Billy never told you he had a sister?"

"Well, that would be a correct guess."

"Figured as much. I was sort of the black sheep of the family. Hard to believe, hey? Knowing Billy? But trust me, take all Billy's faults and multiply them by a hundred and you have a version of me back in those days. At least in my parents' eyes."

"I didn't really find too many faults in Billy," my mother said, a bit perturbed. I was getting the distinct impression she didn't rightly like this woman and it bothered me that they might be getting off on the wrong foot.

"Well, that's something!" Addison said. "Good for Billy. Maybe my memories are all mixed up. Wouldn't be the first time I got something wrong. Anyway, I did not call you to find fault with your poor dead husband, God rest his soul. And I am so sorry for your loss. Even though my condolences come at such a late date."

"Thank you," my mother said. "It was a very hard time for me and the kids."

"I can imagine," Addison said. Then she stopped and reevaluated. "Actually, I can't. I don't have children. But I can only hope that things have gotten better since Billy's passing."

"They get better. You know what they say," my mother said, "that time is the great healer. Why don't you tell me why it is you did contact my little boy, Miss Addison? And again, why were you followin' him like some sort of stalker?"

There was a hesitation on the other end of the phone as Addison took a breath so loud I had no problem hearing it from where I stood. My mother even pulled the receiver away from her ear.

"Well, first off, I was worried if I came straight to you, you might not believe me, or worse, you might just throw me out of your house. I had no idea what Billy had said to you 'bout me."

"He said nothin'," my mother said. "I already told you that."

"I didn't know that at the time. Anyway, I needed to give you some important news, and going through your boy seemed like the best way to go about it. You have to admit, it *worked*. We *are* talking on the phone. Maybe I made the wrong approach, I don't know."

"What news brought you round these parts then?" I could tell my mother was starting to get impatient.

"I wish I could say it was the good kind," Addison said. "But unfortunately, it is not. You see, my mother has been diagnosed with early-onset Alzheimer's and I would really like her to see her grandchildren while she is still in a state that she'll remember them. You know what I mean?"

"Grandchildren? You mean Abe and Carry?"

"Yes, of course. She still remembers seein' Abe."

"Where would she possibly remember him from? She's never met him."

There was a pause on the other end and then Addison said, "Actually, that's not true. Not exactly. She's met Abe. Once."

Now my mother was on full alert. I could tell her whole body went tense at this news. Even I wasn't quite sure what the heck Addison was talking about. I'd never met this grandmother. I'd surely remember something like that. But the idea of meeting them now made my skin tingle all over.

"I think you need to come back to Alvin and come on down to the station," my mother said. "Answer a few questions there for me."

"Wait," Addison said. "Let me explain before you freak out, okay? Your father brought Abe over to my parents' place once when Abe was a lot younger. He didn't stay long, but long enough that my parents got to meet him. They simply adored him. And they will love Carry too, although they've never met her. They've only watched her grow up through photographs."

"Photographs? What photographs?" My mother was trembling now, she was so panicked. None of this was making any sense to me and I was sure it was making no sense to her either.

"Leah, listen, please calm down. I can hear it in your voice that you are stressing about this. It's not so complicated. Your father met my parents at Billy's funeral, and ever since that day, until he became too sick to do it anymore, your dad had been sending my parents pictures of their grandchildren on a regular basis. And boy, did they ever love him for it. You know what I mean?"

My mother just stood there in silence, saying nothing in return. Behind her eyes it was like the gears of a clock were spinning. "But . . . but why? I don't understand. Why didn't he tell me?"

"For the answer to that, you would have had to have asked your father. And again, I am so sorry for your loss. He was a good man."

"You . . . you knew my pa?"

"I met him once, but my parents spoke very highly of him. They still do."

"Your folks, they was at Billy's funeral?" my mother asked.

"Yeah. Only they stayed out of sight because they didn't think you'd want them there. They assumed Billy would've told you nothing but bad things about them, given his past and everything."

"I . . . I don't understand," my mother said. "What past? Were you at the funeral, too?"

There was a hesitation and then Addison replied, "No, unfortunately, I had a more *pressing* engagement up in Boston. But that's another story and not one I want to get into right now over the phone. You know what I mean?"

"So your pa," my mother asked, "is *he* still alive then, too?"

"Yes, my father is alive and well, thank goodness. He looks after my mother. If he weren't here to do it, I don't know what would happen. Right now, my mother's not so bad, but she's going to get worse, you know what I mean, right? Anyway, they would both really appreciate it if you could find it in your heart to allow them to see Abe and Carry just once before my mother's condition worsens. Right now, most days, she's still pretty much normal. Lucid. You know what I mean."

"I . . ." My mother stumbled. "Listen, Addison, I appreciate that your ma is sick and I am sorry for that. But you have to understand, this is a lot comin' at me all at once. I need some time to come to terms with it. I gotta sort through it and make heads or tails out of it. I gotta figure out if I even *believe* it."

"I understand."

"Where are your folks now?"

"They live about twenty miles your side of Columbus up in Georgia. It's about a three-hour drive from Alvin. Of course, it would be much easier for my mother's sake if you could go see them, but if you would rather, I am sure they would make the trip out to you if it meant seeing Abe and Carry."

My mother took a deep breath and let it out slowly, trying to calm herself. "I'm gonna go now, Addison. I'll call you back when I've had a chance to digest this."

"Thank you, Leah. I appreciate you even considering it. You're a very nice person."

My mother put the receiver back in its cradle. She was white as a cotton sheet hung out to dry on a spring day. Her hands were still trembling. Turning, she slid her back down the cupboards until she was sitting on the floor staring straight ahead, looking way off into the distance the same way Preacher Eli had done that day we'd shown up at his house in Blackberry Springs.

"You okay?" I asked quietly.

"I'm not sure," she said. "You have grandparents alive on your pa's side. They want to see you."

I'd already heard, but hearing it again sent lightning bolts from the bottom of my feet surging up through my body. I had *new family*. Family I hadn't even *known* about.

"We gonna go?" I asked, trying to keep my excitement contained, although I'm certain my mother saw it in my eyes and heard it in my voice. It's hard to wrestle back that kind of energy.

"I dunno yet."

"Oh," I said.

Two houseflies were buzzing around the room, zigging and zagging, making complex patterns through the air. I stood and watched them. My mother kept staring at something way past that kitchen wall.

"Anythin' I can do for you?" I asked.

"Nothin'." Whatever she was fixated on was far, far away. "If this is all true, my daddy lied to me the last four years of his life." She turned toward me with the weirdest look in her eyes. "First I find out *your* pa lied to me, now I find out *my* pa lied to me. Has *anyone* told me the truth my entire life? Nothing makes any sense anymore, Abe."

"I tell you the truth," I said.

"I certainly hope you do."

"I do. I always do."

"Let's try to always keep it that way, okay?"

"Okay," I said. "How 'bout we pinky swear on it?"

But it turned out she didn't feel much like pinky swearing on anything.

CHAPTER 11

Leah showed up at work and gave a light rap on the office door of Police Chief Ethan Montgomery. She had already said hello to Chris and made a pit stop at the coffee machine to fill up her mug.

"Come in!" Ethan called out.

She opened the door and popped her head inside. "Got a sec?"

Ethan was sitting, as usual, in his large padded chair behind his big oak desk. He had his own cup of coffee, freshly poured, on the desktop in front of him. He motioned to the chair on the other side of his desk. "Sure. Come on in. What's on your mind?"

Leah closed the office door and took a seat.

"Well, as you know, that woman showed up and told Abe she was his 'aunt' and all." She took a sip of her coffee.

"I thought we straightened all that out with the background check on Billy. He had a sister. Her story's good." Ethan didn't touch his mug. It just sat there, pretty much dead center between his hands, steam rising from the top.

"Well . . . just cuz Billy had a sister don't mean this woman is her. This woman could be anyone."

Ethan Montgomery rolled his eyes, or came as close to it as Leah figured he dared do in front of her. He knew she had a temper. "Come on, Leah, you aren't that dumb. Now why would this woman show up on your doorstep claimin' to be Billy's sister? 'Specially after all this time? Ain't like there's any sort of inheritance or nothin' to be had. Least none that I know of."

Leah laughed. "None that I know of either." She held her mug in her lap with both hands. It was hot and she kept having to shift it from one hand to the other.

"Well . . . there ya go."

"It's just that—"

"It's just that you don't like anything drumming up memories of the past. I know. I've known you since you were just a bean sprout. You've always been the same way. Got that from your momma." Now Ethan grabbed his coffee and drank some. He put his mug right back down where it had been.

Leah took a few deep breaths. Suddenly, she wasn't sure why she was even in Ethan's office. She felt stupid for coming to him, like a little kid coming to her father for advice on something he couldn't possibly help her with, like when she first started liking boys in school. She glanced nervously around the room: at the law books stuffed along the shelves on the walls, at Ethan's big oak desk that barely fit width-wise in the room, at the floor, at the blinds hanging down the windows that looked out into the large room (they were always closed)—anywhere and everywhere but at him.

"What's really on your mind?" he finally asked, his chair squeaking as he leaned back, coffee cup in hand.

That chair had squeaked for as long as Leah could remember. Now it annoyed her that he hadn't bothered to fix it, or oil it, or do anything about it. Then she realized it was just her mind finding something to fill itself with other than answering the question he had just directed her way.

"Abe wants to meet this new family of his that's suddenly popped up out of nowhere." The windows behind Leah looked out on to the street. Through those windows, the sun peeked out from behind a cloud, its light breaking through the boughs of the fig tree that stood outside.

"You mean the aunt? I thought they met already?"

"There's more than just the aunt. There's grandparents, too. Billy's ma and pa. They live just outside of Columbus in Georgia."

Ethan leaned forward, putting his big forearms on his desk, bringing his hands almost as far forward as the pictures standing along the front. "Now how do you know that?"

Leah looked away again. Above her head, the large wooden ceiling fan slowly turned. "Cuz I called her. The aunt, I mean. Abe made me do it."

Ethan laughed. "Abe 'made you' do it? What did he do? Pull out your gun and hold it to your head?"

"No, he played a guilt card I wasn't ready for. Turns out he found a picture of Billy in my closet years ago and has been carryin' it around with him ever since. Never told a soul. Told me it's his good luck charm. Told me since nobody ever wanted to talk about his pa he had to just look at the picture and imagine what he was like."

Ethan turned sideways in his big chair and crossed one leg over the opposite knee. He looked out the long rectangular window beside the large bookcase. "Wow," he said. "That kid's good. Gotta give him credit."

"Made me feel horrible. Like I've hidden his father away from him all these years on purpose."

Ethan paused, then turned to her. He waited until she looked up and their eyes met. "Well, haven't you, Leah? Isn't that *exactly* what you done?"

Leah felt tears coming. "Oh, don't you go tellin' me stuff like that. I already feel bad enough." She took another sip of coffee, but barely tasted it. Her senses were all focused on her guilt.

"Well, if you came in here lookin' for sympathy, I think you picked the wrong guy."

"Actually, I came in here lookin' to make some sense outta things. See, turns out I got a few problems to reconcile."

Ethan's eyes narrowed. He was interested now. "What sorta problems?"

"Well, for starters, Billy lied to me throughout our entire relationship. Never once mentioned his sister and barely said a word 'bout his ma and pa. You'd think they'd all come up at least in passing."

"You didn't just assume he had a ma and a pa?"

"Oh, you know what I mean. And when I spoke to Miss Addison—that's the sister—she told me the reason he never talked 'bout her was on account of her bein' the black sheep of the family. But then she said something strange. That it was funny, her bein' the black sheep in a family with someone like Billy in it. She was tryin' to say Billy had to be pretty bad or somethin', I guess." Leah looked into Ethan's dark eyes. "What do you think she meant by that?"

Ethan took a big gulp of coffee. When he set his mug back down, it seemed almost empty. He slid it across the desk from one hand to the other. "I don't rightly know, to be perfectly honest. I didn't know the boy that well, but from what I did know, he seemed like a fine gentleman to me. Did well by you and those kids. And if there had been anything too bad, it'd shown up on that background check we done."

"That's what I keep thinkin'. But she made it sound like he was a bona fide hell-raiser. I tried to get something specific out of her, but she wouldn't give me any details. In fact, most of what she told me was vague. Especially when it came to her life and Billy's. She was more open about her folks."

"Some people are like that. You know that better than anyone."

"I know."

"So, what else?" Ethan asked her.

"What do you mean?"

"You said Billy lied to you, for starters. What's the rest?" Another big drink of coffee and this time Leah thought Ethan's mug was completely empty. His hands played with it on his desk, spinning it one way then the other.

She hesitated. This was the part she wasn't sure she wanted to talk about, especially with Ethan Montgomery, because of all the people she knew in Alvin, he might be able to actually tell her the truth. And she wasn't sure she really wanted to know the truth.

Above her that big fan continued to turn, always so slowly.

She let out a sigh.

"You're gonna tell me eventually," Ethan said. "May as well just get through it." He gave his mug another spin.

"All right then," Leah said. "According to this Addison woman, my pa knew her folks for the last four years of his life. She says they was at Billy's funeral, but stayed out of my way on account of they thought Billy would've told me things about them that would've made me not want them there. But they met Pa and he struck up a relationship with them."

She watched Ethan carefully while she said this, with the eyes she had developed during her dozen or so years working as a detective for the Alvin Police Department. And she was pretty sure in those eyes she saw something. Ethan had shifted in his seat uncomfortably during her little talk. He'd stopped playing with his mug, but he'd covered any other reaction well. Still, she thought she definitely saw something underneath his calm demeanor; she was certain he knew something and was weighing whether or not he was gonna tell her.

"You know anythin' 'bout this?" she asked him straight out.

"Your pa was a good man, Leah," he said flatly. He moved his chair back slightly from his desk, pushing himself away from her in the process, she noticed.

"My question was one with a 'yes' or 'no' answer, Ethan. I gotta know if my pa lied to me the entire four years before he died."

Ethan held up his hand. "You're startin' to get all riled up. Don't. And 'fore I answer your question—and I *will* answer it, I promise—I want to discuss your interpretation of the word *lying*. You have already convicted Billy of lying to you when really all he did was avoid tellin' you somethin'. Those are two different things." He pointed a thick forefinger at her.

"Ethan, come on. Failure to disclose is lyin'. You know that better than anyone, probably more so, to use your words right back at you." She was getting upset now. "Don't you read any of these law books you have on these shelves? If Billy didn't tell me 'bout his sister after five years of marriage, he *lied* to me. I don't care what you say. And if my pa was carryin' on a relationship with Billy's folks knowin' damn well I didn't know they even existed or anythin' 'bout 'em then he lied to me, too. And if you're gonna try to defend that position in any way then you're a goddamn liar yourself!" Her hands were trembling as she lifted her mug to her lips and finished her own coffee. It wasn't nearly so hot anymore.

Both Ethan's palms came up now. "Whoa, Leah, slow down. Seriously. Relax."

"Answer the question, Ethan!" she said, nearly shouting. Her mug swung down at her side. There was no question Chris sitting at his desk in the room outside the office could hear her yelling.

"Okay, okay," Ethan said. "Yes, your pa knew Billy's folks. He did meet them at Billy's funeral." He went back to sliding his mug from one hand to the other across the top of his desk.

"And *you* knew this, too? And you didn't tell me either?"

"Go ahead. Call me a liar. Might as well. Everyone's a liar. There's a reason you weren't told, Leah."

"Oh, yeah? And what's that?"

"Because," Ethan said. "Because you had enough on your plate with Billy's death. You had two kids to look after and you was refusin' to let anyone help you. You was still reeling from the Ruby Mae case, which nearly cost you your sanity. The last thing we all thought you needed was to have Billy's folks pop into your life."

Once again, he raised his forearm and pointed at her.

"Within a week of him dyin'," he said, "you took every picture of Billy down from the walls of your house. You basically packed your memories of him away. You didn't want anythin' to do with him no more. We was worried havin' his folks in your life would push you too far. As it was, we were all worried you was close to the edge." He picked up his mug and set it down hard on his desk with a thump. "And that's the God's honest truth."

Leah fell silent. Had she been that crazy after Billy's death? It was true, every photograph of him had been taken down and put away. To this day, she still hadn't looked at any of them. They were all in her closet. Her wedding ring came off the day after the funeral and was still in the shoe box with all the pictures Abe found. Every present and little gift Billy had ever given her she had taken out of sight and tucked away inside her closet. Some things she even threw away.

"Oh my God," she said quietly. "You're right. I packed Billy right up and tossed him out of my life the moment he died."

Ethan nodded. "Only you didn't really. You've never let him go inside of you. You've never gotten over his death. Part of you even hates him for what you think he did: You think he purposely left you to raise two young children on your own."

Her hand came to her mouth. "I'm . . . I'm an awful person. No wonder his folks didn't want to meet me."

"Oh, they wanted to meet you. They wanted to be part of your life so bad they was crazy 'bout it. They offered to support you and the kids. They wanted to be real grandparents to Abe and Carry, but Joe knew that couldn't happen, so he made them a deal and told them they had to settle for letters and photos that he'd send them on a regular basis."

"Apparently, he took Abe to visit them once."

"Is that so? Joe never told me about that. Good on him, I reckon. Does Abe remember?"

Leah shook her head. "No. He was too young."

"But at least they got to meet their grandson. What about Carry?"

"They only know her from pictures."

Putting his hands behind his head, Ethan interlaced his fingers and leaned back in his chair. It made another loud creak. "So I guess you got a decision to make."

"What's that?"

"Whether or not you try to make up for some lost time now and let these fine folks get a chance to play Grandma and Grandpa after all these years."

"I don't think I have much choice in the matter."

"Oh, it's entirely your choice."

Leah smiled. "You *have* met my son, right? He has his heart set on meeting them. When Abe sets his heart on somethin', it usually happens, one way or 'nother."

"Yes, I've had some experience with that myself," Ethan said. "I know his momma. Anyway, if it's any consolation, I think it's the right decision. As long as you can handle it."

Leah looked down at the floor. " 'Bout time I stopped runnin' away from ghosts."

"I think you'll find they ain't so much ghosts as imaginary monsters that are hauntin' you," Ethan said.

"Same thing."

"Not really."

Leah started to get up out of her chair. "Sorry for yellin' at you."

"It's okay," Ethan said. "Wouldn't feel like work if you didn't yell at me from time to time. But don't go so fast. Sit down for another minute or two." Pushing his mug out of the way, he pulled a file folder from a stack of papers he had on the top of his desk while Leah settled back into her chair.

Opening the folder, Ethan pulled out a few pages that were stapled together and flipped through them. "Am I to understand you asked for an autopsy for a *cat* last week?"

Oh Christ, Leah thought. *Here we go. Now I'm gonna get in trouble for wasting the department's resources.* "Yeah, I did, but I can explain. It was because Miss Sylvie was so—"

Ethan held up his palm again and Leah went quiet. "I'm not askin' you to explain. I just wanted to tell you the results are in. Thought you might like to know what caused the demise of your little kitty."

Leah tried not to look too surprised at this response. "Okay," she said. "What was it?"

"Well, first off let me read the note Norman attached to the front of his results here. It says, 'Thank you for giving me something other than heart attack victims to work on. This was quite refreshing.' " Ethan looked up at Leah. "I think that man needs to get out more."

Leah laughed.

Ethan flipped to the next page. "There was no physical signs of death, as you and Chris discerned at the crime scene, so our Mr. Crabtree did a pump of the animal's stomach as well as a toxicology analysis. It turns out your cat ingested common off-the-shelf brodifacoum. In other words, rat poison. What's surprising is the amount of poison Norm found in the animal's system. According to our coroner, there was enough to kill an elephant, or so it says here, although I reckon he may be exaggeratin' a mite." Ethan looked back up. "Norm figures there should be evidence of the cat bein' sick around the area. Find anythin' like that?"

Leah shook her head. "We searched the property pretty well, too."

"Any idea where that cat would find that amount of poison around Miss Sylvie's house? He couldn't have gone too far after consumin' it. Norm figures thirty minutes to an hour at most before he'd be dead. Probably sooner."

Again Leah shook her head. All she could think of was how dangerous it would be for the baby to have rat poison lying around. She hoped Sylvie wasn't that stupid. As far as Leah knew, Sylvie didn't have a rat problem, so why would she have brodifacoum lying around?

"Something about this is ringin' familiar to me," Leah said.

Ethan leaned forward and started playing with his mug again. "What's that?"

"Remember when Sylvie's ma was found in the barn?"

"Yeah, you investigated her death. Ruled it accidental."

"I did. With the help of some experts out of Mobile. It wasn't just my call."

"Right. What's your point?"

"She died from ingestin' brodifacoum, too," Leah said.

Ethan hesitated. "You're sayin' you reckon this cat's death and the death of Miss Sylvie's ma seven years ago are linked? Please tell me that's not what you're thinkin', because that's crazy talk. Besides, we caught the person behind Mrs. Carson's death. I should say *you* caught him. James Richard Cobbler. Crazier than a shit-house rat, that one. And I know *he's* gone. I watched him die. Up at Holman, in Atmore."

Leah remembered the look in Cobbler's eyes the last time she saw him on death row before his execution and shivered. That man had no emotion, just a cold, icy stare that pricked the bottom of her backbone and caused an electric shock to wind its way up. "I'm just sayin'," she said, "the whole thing has a familiar ring to it. Coincidence is all." Leah found herself lost in thought for a moment.

Ethan narrowed his eyes at her. "Coincidence *is* all. And don't you forget that. *Do not* try to link the death of a cat with the murder of someone seven years ago by one of Eli Brown's radical congregation members and turn them both into open murder cases. You'll have this entire department laughed out of town."

"What do I look like to you, Ethan?"

"It's not what you look like that's got me concerned," he said. "It's the way your mind works that *I'm* worried 'bout."

CHAPTER 12

The weird coincidence of Sylvie's cat dying from ingesting rat poison and Sylvie's ma going the same way settled itself into Leah's mind in a manner that wouldn't let itself go as Leah got into her car and headed for home. Only Police Chief Montgomery didn't have to worry, she wasn't thinking the cases were linked, but she did start thinking back about the investigation all them years ago when Sylvie's ma died. The court had decided James Richard Cobbler acted on his own volition and Eli Brown had no link to Mrs. Carson's murder. But what if that wasn't true? What if Preacher Eli's role in his land dispute hadn't ended with him going to jail? Everyone just assumed that had put an end to the whole contentious situation, but what if he kept connections with people on the outside and the whole thing had kept going? How much did the police and the courts really know about the land dispute, anyway?

Back when Eli Brown shot little Caleb, Leah's pa, Joe Fowler, had still been on the Alvin police force and he had been the lead on the case. Leah hadn't ever looked over her pa's files, so she didn't really know much about it other than what had been in the news since and local gossip. She had been the investigator for the death of both of Sylvie's parents ten years later, so she knew all about *those* cases, but she'd never pushed the idea that the murder of

Sylvie's ma might be linked to the earlier case her pa had handled involving Preacher Eli.

Now she couldn't help but wonder if it was.

So it turned out Ethan Montgomery did know Leah all too well. Her mind liked to make connections, only it wasn't the cat he had to worry about, but the digging up of old bones from the far-flung past. That's where Leah's brain was making links.

She decided it was time to review the old case files her pa had worked on and maybe pay a visit to the records office that was part of the Alvin Courthouse. Between the two of them, she might be able to come up with something pointing its way toward Sylvie Carson maybe not being quite so crazy after all. Because, like it or not, part of Leah was starting to believe the girl's calls weren't all false alarms. There were just too many things going on. Sure, some—probably even most—of her calls into the station were just cases of shadow jumping, but something in Leah's gut told her not to write Sylvie off as fast as everyone else had. Like she'd told herself a hundred times before, her daddy and Ethan had drilled it into Leah's head that she should listen to her gut. It was her biggest asset. And if she was perfectly honest with herself, she actually wasn't that comfortable calling the death of Snowflake accidental. It just seemed so odd that the cat would show up poisoned after all this time when she'd been going in and out of that house since the day Sylvie brought her home. And Ethan had raised a perfectly good question to which Leah didn't have an answer: Where did that cat find so much rat poison, anyway?

One thing being a detective had taught Leah was to not like unanswered questions. They never sat well in her stomach or any other part of her, for that matter.

Checking the clock on her dash, she realized she wouldn't be able to go to the records office until tomorrow. They likely closed at five and it was already half past. She would try to drop by work first thing in the morning even though she wasn't supposed to be on duty tomorrow. After looking through her daddy's old files about Preacher Eli and the Carson family (which she figured would make for some pretty interesting reading), she'd head on over to the courthouse and pay a visit to the records office.

But tonight she was going straight home for a nice relaxing bubble bath.

Or so she thought.

All too often, such thoughts turn out to be too good to be true. This turned out to be one of those times because, right at that instant, she got a call on her radio from the station. It was Chris telling her Miss Sylvie had just called in again with another disturbance. This time, he said, she'd seemed almost as frantic on the phone as she had when she'd found her cat lying dead on her back porch.

"What was she callin' 'bout now?" Leah asked.

"Hell if I know," Chris said uselessly. "She was so upset, I could barely understand a word that girl was sayin'. I finally just told her you'd be by as soon as you could get there."

Leah ground her teeth. She hated the fact that she'd become part of the protocol when it came to handling Sylvie. It pissed her off that nobody else would pick up the ball. She even found herself somewhat hoping it *did* turn out that her calls weren't completely benign just so everyone else would feel stupid. But that was a horrible way of thinking. She really didn't want it to turn out that Sylvie was in any actual danger.

"She said somethin' 'bout some door bein' open or somethin', I reckon," Chris said, after much prodding. "I'm not sure what door, or why it was open."

"You do know I was on my way home for the night, right?" Leah asked him. "I was off duty a half hour ago."

There was a long pause, then Chris said, "So you're not gonna show up?"

She wondered if Chris would go if she didn't. If he did, he wouldn't take anything Sylvie said seriously, so there'd be no point in him being there. He'd be as useless as udders on a Brahman bull. "No, Chris, I'll go. My kids can go hungry a little while longer. They're pretty well getting used to it."

This was a little white lie. Leah had started getting the kids to make their own meals on her workdays almost a year ago. She just figured that was fair. The last thing she ever felt like doing when she got home was cooking. On the odd day, she would break the rule by taking them out for a burger or something when she got home, but, for the most part, on workdays it was everyone for themselves. The rule hadn't worked out quite so bad, other than the fact that Abe seemed to eat a lot more macaroni and cheese than was probably healthy for a twelve-year-old boy to consume.

Leah could almost hear Chris sigh with relief on the other end of the phone. It just annoyed her. For the past month, there'd been really nothing else crime-wise going on in Alvin except Sylvie Carson's calls, and so he'd just sat behind his desk doing nothing while she worked unpaid overtime covering for his inability to be sympathetic.

"Okay, that's great," he said. "I appreciate ya doin' that. Montgomery said you would."

Oh, Leah thought. *That figures. He probably thinks I want to go investigate more of the cat murder scene, too.* "Yeah, yeah," she said. "Y'all better get me somethin' nice at the office Christmas party this year."

"We always do, don't we?"

"Chris, last year you got me nothin' and Ethan gave me a bottle of eight-dollar wine. I know hobos who drink better than that."

"Oh. Well, we'll try to do better this year."

"You got five months to think 'bout it."

"So, you're goin' to Miss Sylvie's now?"

"Yes, Chris," Leah said. "I've already turned my car round and I'm headin' back up Main Street. I'll be passin' the shop in 'bout two minutes. If she calls back, tell her I'll be there in less than ten."

"You're the best."

"I know it."

She hung up her radio, not bothering with the siren. She'd get to Sylvie's quick enough following traffic. Main Street cut an angle to Old Mill Road, making it less than a couple miles to her place.

On either side of Leah's vehicle, the shops along Main Street went by. Some were closing up for the night; others, like the restaurants, were just getting ready for the dinner crowd. Not that anything ever got that crowded in Alvin. Except maybe church.

She'd already gone back past the station. Now she came to a stop behind a Honda that was trying to parallel park in front of PJ

Party Pizza. Outside her window were the two most popular stores with local farmers, Superfeed and K's Bait & Tack—both of which were owned by rancher Jacob Tyne. Superfeed was already closed and Pete was taking the sign for K's in from the sidewalk, so it was shutting its doors for the night, too. A broad sassafras tree stood between them, its canopy of gray-green leaves extended from thick brown boughs that touched the sides of either building.

The Honda managed to make it to the curb and Leah continued driving, hoping Sylvie wouldn't be too agitated when she arrived.

She made it up past the courthouse, which pretty much marked the east end of Main Street. Most of the buildings and shops were flanked by the courthouse at this end and the library at the other, although the city had been doing recent development down past the library: mainly a small strip mall called Brookside that Carry and her friends hung out at. It was convenient because before it went in, Leah had to drive all the way into Satsuma to do most of her shopping.

Main Street didn't officially end until you continued past the courthouse and came to Hawk Tail Crossing where the road transformed into an iron bridge that went over the Old Mill River. After the bridge, Main Street became a highway that took you out of Alvin.

Leah drove over the bridge, hearing it rattle beneath her wheels. Under the bridge, the river ran low and slow. There hadn't been much rain lately. Some days, that river could be high and so fast you'd think it was going to wipe out everything in its path.

Right after Hawk Tail Crossing was the turn for Old Mill Road that led the short distance north up to Sylvie's place. Nobody lived between the turnoff and Sylvie's house—the area was just filled with forest on either side of the road. Mostly it was tall old oaks that cast the road in shadow. But among the oaks were lots of birch and maple, plus the odd elm and cedar. The woods broke tightly against the road, and if you stared into that dense forest you saw the trees quickly constricted and became closed very fast. They became full of thick, dark trunks wrapped with lichen. The boughs of most of the trees were covered in Spanish moss that hung like wild demon hair. Strangler fig and ivy wrapped around the bases of trees, and, in places, climbed up near the tops, choking everything off.

Leah didn't think the state of the woods probably helped much with Sylvie's mind—the way she was—living way out here by herself with just the baby to keep her company. Those woods conjured up all sorts of nightmarish images in Leah's mind even in the afternoon daylight. Once the sun went down, if you weren't careful, your brain could get away on you about it, Leah was sure.

The baby was lying in its bassinet, sound asleep when Leah arrived. She was glad to see that. She figured whatever emotional state Sylvie was in had to rub off on the child in some way, so if that baby was sleeping, things couldn't be that bad.

But she soon reassessed this idea. Sylvie seemed awfully upset as she escorted Leah outside to the backyard to show her what she found.

"Someone's been out here again," Sylvie said.

"Now what's happened?"

"Look."

Beneath Sylvie's house was a cellar, although to call it a cellar was really giving it more credit than it deserved. It was more like a crawl space. There couldn't have been more than two feet of room between the ground and the floor of the house.

It was enclosed, and to access it you had to enter through two tiny wooden doors that were made of what looked like tongue-and-groove cedar boards. They were constructed at an angle set between concrete sides. The doors weren't very large, maybe a little more than three-feet square each. A wooden block was attached to the center front of one door that swiveled through a notch built into the frame of the other to keep them closed. There was no other lock.

The left one was wide open. The right one (the one with the swivel-block attached to it) was closed.

"This is how I found 'em," Sylvie said shakily.

"Open, like this?" Leah asked.

Sylvie just nodded her head.

"Sylvie," Leah said. "This little piece of wood ain't much holdin' these shut. The wind could've blown this open, or even an animal could've swiveled that block of wood loose." Leah scanned the backyard, wondering where the brodifacoum that killed Snowflake might have come from. She also had her eyes out for any indication of where the cat may have gotten sick that she and Chris might've missed. "It's been pretty windy lately. I don't think this is any indication that anyone's been in your backyard."

Leah could hear the panic rise in Sylvie's voice. "They ain't never blown open before. Besides, that little piece of wood would've had to blow around off the other door. I don't think that's possible, do you? I think someone's been here."

Squatting down, Leah closed the open door and swiveled the block back into place. It was a pretty tight fit, she had to admit to herself. She wasn't about to say that to Sylvie. "Anythin's possible," she said instead. "I don't think anyone's been in your backyard. It's either the wind or some other simple explanation. Maybe you left it not quite closed all the way and all it took was a bit of wind to do the rest?"

"I ain't never been in that cellar in my life," Sylvie said adamantly. "I'm scared to death of what might be down there."

Leah looked up at her. "What you mean?"

"I dunno. It's just so . . . dark."

"Sylvie, there ain't nothin' in your crawl space 'cept maybe some mud." She opened the door back up again, took her pocket flashlight from her small-item pack, and shined it around inside the immediate area. It had a dirt floor that was pretty much level. She couldn't see anything other than dirt going back as far as her flashlight would allow her to see. "There's nothin' in here." She really should've probably gone under the house and taken a proper look, but truth be told, Leah had two fears in this life that she didn't tell nobody about. One of 'em happened to involve being stuck in tight, enclosed, dark spaces and the other was an irrational fear of spiders. Looking into this crawl space, even from outside, Leah was quite sure it fit both criteria all too well. It was dark and confining and probably the home of more than one spider. She didn't even like the view from the cellar doors. It gave her the creeps. She thought about Sylvie. *We all have our own monsters. Some of us just hide them better than others.*

She shined the light around a bit more. "There's nothin' here. It's clear."

"I still ain't ever goin' in there."

Leah stood up. "Nobody's askin' you to."

"Well, somebody went in there," Sylvie said.

Leah let out a long breath. "If there ain't nothin' in your crawl space, then why would someone want to go in there? It don't look like the most comfortable place in the world to me. I wouldn't go outta my way to be crawlin' round underneath your house in the muck." The dirt Leah could see from where she stood did show what could be scuff marks, but they really weren't indicative of anything positive, so Leah just wrote them off. They could've been made anytime. Orwin could have stored things under the house back before he left and they could still be from then.

"I think it was Preacher Eli," Sylvie said. "He's probably tryin' to figure out some way to kill me. Maybe he's gonna put a bomb under there."

Leah closed her eyes and thought happy thoughts. This was going to take all the patience she could muster. "Now, Sylvie, I went and saw Eli Brown just like I promised I would."

This got the girl's attention. Her eyes went wide and she moved closer to Leah. "What did he say? What happened? Did you mention me?"

"Slow down there, girl. Yes, I mentioned you. He told me in no uncertain terms that it would be a cold day in hell before he stepped anywhere near you. He said he deeply regrets what he done and that he can't possibly make amends to you so there's no point in even tryin' to apologize. So he won't be botherin' you. And he certainly ain't puttin' no bombs under your house."

Sylvie looked disappointed and dubious at the same time.

"Sylvie," Leah said, "the man is old. He's not the same as he used to be. He's done his time. He just wants to make peace with himself."

"He's foolin' you."

"No, he's foolin' *you*," Leah said. "And that's sad, cuz he ain't even doin' anythin', and you're lettin' him control your life. He's harmless."

"Then who opened my cellar door?"

"Nobody opened your goddamn door. The wind blew it open!" Leah stopped. She couldn't let herself get angry. "Listen," she said, much more quietly and calmly, "I'm sorry, but I can't let you go on thinkin' Eli Brown's out to get you. It ain't healthy for anybody. It definitely ain't helpin' you get on with your life. Now I went and talked to the man. I don't know what else I can possibly do to make you believe me."

"You honestly think the wind blew this door open? Even though it ain't ever blown open before?"

"I do," Leah said, although she wasn't quite certain she really did. "And there's no real discernable footprints or scuff marks that I can make out anywhere around here in the dirt."

"The dirt's hard packed here."

"You'd still think I'd see somethin'. All I see is your shoe prints goin' back and forth toward this area from the back door. They've made a track. Even if there had been footprints, they're lost now. I really think it was the wind, Sylvie."

"It hasn't been *that* windy. We've had windier times. It didn't blow open then."

Leah shrugged. "I can't explain that. All I can say is that it makes no sense that someone would come and open your cellar door. Ask yourself why would they do it, Sylvie? To go into your crawl space and get all dirty? And why would they leave it open? Why not close it if they're gonna do something sneaky? Why leave evidence?"

This one seemed to stump Sylvie. She looked deep in thought.

"You really have to start askin' yourself questions like these," Leah said. "Or you'll drive yourself crazy."

"What if someone's tryin' to *make* me crazy?"

Leah didn't think that would be much of a challenge. But then she chided herself for having a thought like that gallop around her mind. "Nobody's trying to make you crazy, Sylvie. Again, ask yourself: Why? Why would someone want to make you crazy?"

Again Sylvie looked deep in thought.

"Exactly," Leah said after a few seconds of silence. "There is no reason."

Sylvie let out a deep breath. "I guess . . ."

"You gonna be okay?"

"I guess so."

"How's the baby?"

"She's fine. Sleeps a lot."

"I noticed she was sleepin' when I came in. That's better than cryin', ain't it?"

Sylvie shrugged. "I dunno. I like it when she's awake. I like the company."

At that, Leah felt a twinge of pain in her heart for the girl. "Well, you just wait. Before you know it, she'll be fifteen and you'll wish she just kept quiet all the time. Trust me, I know." Leah smiled.

Sylvie smiled back, but it was a smile that didn't quite reach her eyes.

"Well, speakin' of which, I best be goin'. I have to get home and make sure my kids don't starve themselves."

Sylvie looked at the door still open where Leah had left it. "Okay."

"You want me to close that 'fore I go?"

"No, I can do it."

"Okay." Leah took one more look around the yard. Then, right before heading toward the back door, she turned and asked Sylvie, "By the way, have you ever had a problem with rats?"

Sylvie looked confused. "Rats? What do you mean?"

"You know, rats. Have you ever had them in your house or anythin' and had to get rid of 'em somehow?"

"No, why?"

Leah shook her head. "Just wonderin'. I'll talk to you soon. In the meantime, you take care of yourself and that baby. And find her a name, goddamn it."

Sylvie gave her a hint of a grin. "I'm tryin'."

"Well, try harder."

"Bye," Sylvie said. "Thanks for comin' out."

Leah walked into Sylvie's kitchen, hearing Sylvie swing the cellar door closed outside. Along with everything else, Leah now had a new unsettling feeling in her stomach because she really didn't like how tightly that wooden lock clasped between those two doors. Sylvie was right. It *was* very unlikely that the wind blew that door open.

CHAPTER 13

Just like when she found Snowflake dead on her back doorstep, Sylvie couldn't get to sleep after finding the cellar door open outside. She hated the fact that the police wouldn't believe her. She didn't blame Officer Leah. If she was honest with herself, Sylvie doubted she'd believe her stories either. And she had called the police so *much*, she was almost like that boy in that story about the wolf.

But she felt so vulnerable, especially it just being her and the baby way up here all by themselves out amid all the woods like they were. But then, Sylvie never really had felt like she had anyone. Not since Caleb died, anyway. It always felt like people could just be taken out of her life so easily. And they had been. First Caleb, then Mother, then Pa. One by one, they was gone.

That's partly why she jumped at dating Orwin Thomas when she had the chance. He was the first boy to show interest in her. Sylvie had a difficult time with relationships of any sort. She had no friends at school. So when Orwin Thomas, the number-one tight end for the Satsuma Westland Eagles, asked her out, she felt compelled to say yes.

Unfortunately, it was only a month after they started dating that Orwin tore out his anterior cruciate ligament.

It was during a rivalry game between Satsuma Westland High and Mobile Evercrest High. At the half, the score was tied at seventeen. It was right at the top of the third quarter that it happened. The Mobile Evercrest Panthers kicked off to the Westland Eagles.

Terrance Williams caught the ball on the fifteen-yard line and managed to run it to the thirty-five. The offensive team took the field, led by quarterback Barrett Mosley. Orwin Thomas had played tight end for Mosley for a year and a half and Mosley trusted him as much or more than any other player on the team. That's how good Orwin Thomas was. He would tell Sylvie all the time about how much he had *college* written all over him. There was even talk that he'd be able to write his own ticket, that he could go wherever he wanted after he graduated: Ole Miss, LSU, or Alabama. Football was the one thing in this whole big world that Orwin Thomas was good at.

Then came the next huddle. The call was a pass to Orwin, who would run out and down the edge of the field ten yards before cutting back in to make the catch. Mosley made the count and Orwin started his run. In the stands, as she pretty near always was, Sylvie sat watching her man. She was damn proud of him.

Orwin made his run down the field and cut in behind the Panthers' defenders just as the football was sailing straight into his open hands. The throw was slightly high, so he had to jump for it.

That's when it happened.

Two hits at near on the exact same time.

One came from the front, the other from the side. Both came low, both caught his knee. The side hit may have come slightly ahead of the one from the front. They tore his ACL completely to shreds, ripping apart his knee.

Remarkably, Orwin made the catch. But it would be the last catch he'd ever make. The doctors told him he'd never play organized football again. Certainly, all thoughts of college flew out the window with that catch, because a football scholarship was the only way Orwin was going to college. He didn't have the smarts to do it any other way.

It turned out, other than football, he didn't have much ambition either. He dropped out of twelfth grade fewer than two months later. Sylvie knew then that things were taking a turn for the worse, but in the back of her mind she wanted to stay hopeful. After all, Orwin was all she had.

Even though he had been in the twelfth grade, she was only in the eleventh. Yet, she was two years older than him on account of her missing school due to what had happened to her when she was younger. She had been set back three years of schooling. After her pa died, Sylvie had spent a couple of years in foster care, but was on her own when she met Orwin. She reckoned now that was half the attraction for him: that she lived on her own and was pretty easy pickings—something she now hated herself for.

Orwin Thomas was eighteen when Sylvie let him move into her place in Alvin. Everything about their relationship was like fireworks. When the romance clicked, it went off like hand grenades. Except, usually, it wasn't so much the romance but Orwin's temper going off like firecrackers on the Fourth of July.

"Where's the goddamn beer?" Orwin liked to yell when he came home from work. He did a lot of odd jobs around town, but mostly he pulled late-night shifts at Emmett's garage. One particular evening he seemed downright ornery.

"Maybe you drank it?" Sylvie offered.

"I didn't goddamn drink it! Have you been drinking my beer, bitch?"

Sylvie tried to laugh off his anger. "No. I don't like beer."

"Well, there was beer here last night, damn it!" He slammed the refrigerator door.

"Maybe we can go get some more?" Sylvie asked softly. She was always trying to keep his temper in check.

"With what? You think I'm goddamn made of money? I work and work and work my ass off and come home to this goddamn house and it's always a fucking pigsty."

Sylvie looked around the house. She had spent the day cleaning it because she knew Orwin liked it clean. There was nothing she could do when he was like this. But she did feel bad for him. She knew he was hurting about losing his football scholarship and he *was* the one bringing home the money.

"Is dinner at least ready?" he asked.

"It will be in ten minutes."

"What are we having?"

"Pork chops."

She knew he wouldn't argue with that. Orwin loved pork chops.

"How 'bout I go get you some more beer?" Sylvie asked.

This is the way it usually went. She tried to keep him appeased because, many nights, neighbors would call the police after hearing him yelling at her through the thin-paned glass of their small house, calling her all sorts of things before sometimes stomping out into the dead of night, occasionally not to be heard from for a day or two.

Even with all this, if truth be told, Sylvie was still upset when he disappeared that night, especially with him leaving her three months pregnant and all when it happened. She didn't much like being yelled at, but she took it. It was part of her lot in life. And she *did* love him. When he wasn't yelling and things were good, she was almost happy. As happy as she could be, given all that was going on inside that head of hers. She knew, deep in his heart, Orwin Thomas was a good man. He may have yelled a lot, but he did treat her well. In her heart back then, she figured he'd never hit her. And if any man ever had, she would pity him, for Orwin Thomas would hunt that man down and kill him to his last breath.

That, Sylvie Carson was certain of.

She suffered through these thoughts late into the night until the light outside her window began to grow to a light pink. Then she managed to fall asleep for a little bit until the baby woke her up just a short while later, wanting to be fed.

CHAPTER 14

My memory of visiting Preacher Eli that day with my mother continued to dig a great big hole in my stomach through the days that followed. I did not trust that man, nor did I like him living in my town. I decided something had to be done about it and, if my mother wasn't going to do anything, it was up to me and Dewey to.

I called Dewey on the phone and told him all about the meeting we had on the preacher man's doorstep and how he was crying those crocodile tears and all.

"I ain't never seen no croc cry," Dewey said.

"That's what I mean," I said. "I mean they wasn't real tears. He was just makin' 'em up to make my mom think he was sorry for everythin' he done."

"Then why don't you just say that?"

"It's an expression."

"I ain't never heard it before."

"You ain't never heard a lot of stuff before," I said.

"So you think he's up to no good?"

"No, I *know* he's up to no good."

There was silence for a second or two and then Dewey said something dumb. "You know, this reminds me of somethin'."

"What's that?"

"Your neighbor. Remember? You was sure he was up to no good. Turned out he wasn't."

"Dewey, you was sure too, remember? And this is completely different. Preacher Eli was in prison for near on twenty years for killin' a little kid. Mr. Wyatt Edward Farrow is just a carpenter."

"Still, parts of it feel the same to me."

"Well, it's different enough to me." I was getting frustrated, wrapping the telephone cord around my finger, wishing he'd let me get to the part where I told him my plan.

"So, what do you want to do?" he asked finally.

"I say we go watch his house."

"Again—" Dewey started, "this is soundin' like—"

"Dewey. The man was in *prison*."

"So you want to go spy on a man who killed a kid? What if he catches us?"

"He ain't gonna catch us," I said, now wrapping the telephone cord the other way.

"Why's that?"

"Cuz I'll have you with me."

"What's that supposed to mean?"

"Well, you're the great inventor," I said. "You're gonna invent a way for us not to be seen."

There was another pause on the other end of the phone until Dewey came back with, "Okay, give me a few minutes to think of somethin'. Then I'll ride my bike over to your place."

Dewey showed up about twenty minutes later on his bike with his inventor's notebook tucked in his pocket and a pair of garden shears and a roll of kite string in a small box in his carrier. "What are them for?" I asked. He had his rope scabbard tied around his waist and his wooden sword hung down his side from the wire tie.

He flipped open the notebook. "My brilliant design for hiding out. You told me there ain't nothin' but woods round where Preacher Eli lives."

"Yeah. So?"

"So, we're gonna become part of the woods."

In the notebook he'd drawn pictures of people with what

looked like wings. Actually, to call them people were giving them far too much credit. They looked more like stick figures. "I don't get it. Are they angels?"

"No, they ain't angels. Those are branches of leaves tied to their arms. And down their bodies."

"What's that on this one's head?"

"A branch."

I stared at him, my eyes wide with disbelief. "You really are brilliant," I said flatly.

He closed the book proudly and stuck out his chin. "I know. Let's go."

We took our bikes and rode the route down Cottonwood Lane, which was the road we both lived on. Then we turned up Hunter Road, which was the road Preacher Eli lived on. Cottonwood Lane is a nice ride. Before we left, I decided to bring my sword along, too. You never knew when a weapon might come in handy on a job like this, and we'd basically started taking our swords with us everywhere we went. Dewey's design actually worked out really well—it didn't even interfere with bike riding.

Cottonwood Lane was fairly flat, and on either side, pretty little houses were nestled among gardens and a wide assortment of trees that were planted on purpose, so they looked good. We rode past cherry trees, tulip trees, and magnolias Near the end of the road, we even passed an orange tree in the front yard of a small blue house.

The ride up Hunter Road was a different story completely. There were very few houses along the way, and the ones we did pass were spaced very far apart and surrounded by thick, quiet forest that seemed to close in on the road the farther up we went. Most of the ride was uphill, which was exhausting. There were a few flowering trees in the front of the woods that I didn't know the names of, but mostly the trees were tall and dense, filling the edges of the street with oak, fir, birch, and pine. It seemed the higher we got, the darker the forest appeared, until we finally made the wooden bridge that passed over Blackberry Springs.

We pulled our bikes to a stop on the bridge. The water gurgled and sputtered beneath us. It ran a curved path splashing over and around rocks and stones, some of which looked almost as big as me. The smell of the water filled the air where I stood, leaning over the bridge. It tasted like nickels and pennies in my mouth.

"Preacher Eli's place is only another block up," I told Dewey. "It's a shotgun shack on the left. There's no other houses around it."

"Then we'll have to be extra careful when we get close. We can dump our bikes in there right before we reach it." He indicated the deep ditch running along the right side of the road. "Then we'll dip into the woods and make the rest of the way on foot just behind the tree line."

Looking at the blackness of the forest made me swallow hard. The woods appeared ancient to me, like some evil thing out of a storybook filled with monstrous trees of every shape and size. I didn't really want to go traipsing through those towering giants.

But I followed Dewey's lead and, just before coming in sight of Preacher Eli's house, we threw our bikes into the ditch as he suggested (but not before he removed the kite string and shears from his carrier), and began our trek into the woods. At first, I jumped at every creak and crack of leaf and branch breaking beneath my or Dewey's feet, but soon I relaxed a little. After a while, it became not so bad. It really was just another forest, although this one hadn't been walked through in some time, if ever. We had to cut our own path through vines, strangler fig, brambles, and briar as we went. It took quite a while to make the short distance from our bikes to where we could see Preacher Eli's house peeking through the space between the massive tree trunks.

"Okay," Dewey said. "Now you have to climb one of the fir trees and start cutting off branches."

"I ain't climbin' no tree," I said. I was a terrible tree climber, for one thing. Even though I wasn't about to admit that.

"You have to. We need the branches."

"*You* climb the tree. I'll hold the string."

With a deep exhale, Dewey gave into the inevitable. "Fine. I'll need you to help me up to the first branch."

It took us a while to get him into the tree, but once he was there, Dewey turned out to be not a bad tree climber at all. Over the years I had noticed this about Dewey. He had strange abilities at some things and then at other, normal things, a complete lack of ability.

At any rate, he was doing a fine job of scaling the tree and shearing off big branches of fir with lots of leaves along the way. Up he went, his sword dangling from his side with its tip pointing straight down at me. As each bough fell, it brought with it the fresh smell of sap. I collected them as they came down, inhaling the deep aroma of the leaves. All my senses were alive to the woods. Now that my eyes had grown accustomed to the darkness, things no longer seemed so bleak and black. It all just looked very green. I placed all the boughs into a pile. Some did look like wings, much like the picture Dewey drew in his notebook. I wasn't about to tell *him* that, though.

"I think that's enough," he whispered.

"Okay."

He looked around beneath his feet. I immediately saw his problem. He'd cut off most of the branches he'd used to climb up the tree and now didn't have them to use to get down with. "Um, I'm kinda stuck."

"Can you slide down?" I asked.

He looked at me like I'd lost my mind. Somewhere off in the distance the sound of a woodpecker echoed through the trees. It sounded like someone knocking two blocks of wood together.

"No," he said. "Have you ever climbed a tree?"

"Not a lot. But I doubt if I did that I'd cut off my only way down as I went up. I think you'll have to jump."

"I'm way too high up to jump." I had to agree, he was quite high up.

"There are knots in the trunk sticking out along the way for a while below you. Can you use those to step on?"

Dewey kept looking around below him, as if some magical branches were about to appear. His lower lip twisted between his teeth. "You know, I have an invention in my book for just this very thing, but we don't have none of the stuff to build it."

"Ain't that always the way," I said.

Finally, he gave into the inevitable and used my idea. Slowly and deliberately, he came down, putting his feet on the knobs extending from the trunk. A few times his foot slipped off and my breath caught in my throat. I thought for sure he was going to fall and wind up stabbing himself in the side with his own sword, but somehow he managed to hang on. Then he got low enough that it wasn't so scary anymore.

"Okay, I think I can jump now. Can you catch me?"

"No."

"You have to."

"Okay," I lied.

He jumped and I stepped back out of the way. He landed on the soft forest floor, right on his rear end. Looking up at me, he asked, "What happened to catching me?"

"I told you I wasn't going to."

"Then you said you would."

"The second one's always a lie," I said.

He shook his head, wiping dirt from his shorts and his legs. "Whatever. Let's just get these branches tied on so we can start our stakeout. I'll tie yours on, then you tie mine."

It took another twenty minutes or so to dress up as fir trees. When we were done, Dewey looked remarkably like the stick man he'd drawn and I kind of felt bad about laughing at his sketches earlier. We both had big branches of fir leaves on our arms like wings, one coming down the front of our body, and one drooping over our head like some weird bird. I had to say, we did blend in much better with the green of the tree leaves and bushes around us than we had before we tied all the branches on.

Quietly, we crept to the front of the tree line right along the roadside that looked directly across at Preacher Eli's house. Both of us lay on the ground and propped up our heads with our hands on our elbows. We knew we were going to be here a long time, so we might as well get comfortable.

Well, as comfortable as we could be covered in itchy tree branches.

Leah felt odd pulling the Brown/Carson file from the archive drawer. She figured she must've been the first person to touch it since her pa put it there seventeen years or so ago. It made her remember her original days on the force, joining not because she wanted to, but because she *had* to. It was a year before she became pregnant with Abe and, with Billy's work being so sporadic, they needed the extra income.

She had been at her pa's house when he talked her into coming on board. It was right before his cancer got so bad. They had only gotten to spend barely two months working together before he had to quit.

"You'll come work for the department," he had said, but she'd only laughed.

"I ain't no cop," she'd said. "Remember that time you took me huntin'? It was the one and only time I ever shot a gun." She was sitting on the flowered sofa that was more the size of a loveseat. Like everything in her folks' home, it looked and felt brand-new. It was the way her ma had kept things, back while she was still here.

"You were bound to hit something. You were shakin' so bad you were aimin' at the entire forest," he said, and smiled. "But bein' a cop is different. We'll train you. This ain't a question, by the way." Pa sat at an angle across the small coffee table from her in the Queen Anne chair. He had his large elbows resting on the curled armrests, but they barely stayed there. He was a man who liked to conduct while he spoke.

"What makes you think Chief Montgomery would even *want* me?" she asked. "It would be complete favoritism."

"He's big on favoritism."

She rolled her eyes.

Her pa pointed at her. "I'll tell you one thing. He's big on you. And you can say this 'bout that man. If ever there was anyone whose heart was bigger than his brains, he's the one."

She threw a tasseled pillow at him. "You're not very nice. I happen to like Chief Montgomery."

"You won't. He's a son of a bitch when you work for him."

"I'm *not* comin' to work for the department. I ain't no cop."

Pa suddenly grew all concerned. He leaned forward, but before he could talk, Caroline went toddling down the hallway chasing her pa's Irish setter, Putter, with a squeal. Leah's pa waited for the noise to die down. "Leah, you have to start thinkin' 'bout your next move. You can't feed that kid on dreams, wishes, and stardust. I wish you could. Please. Take my offer."

"Don't you need to discuss this with Chief Montgomery?"

"Hang on."

Picking up the phone beside him, he made a call into the station and right then and there told (not asked) Ethan Montgomery that his daughter was coming on board to work as an officer at the Alvin Police Department. The call barely lasted a moment.

He hung up and smiled. "Done. You start tomorrow at eight."

"You're serious."

"Oh, honey, you're gonna find police work is *very* serious business." Six months later, she got her first big case when Ruby Mae Vickers disappeared from town and she discovered he hadn't lied. You couldn't get any more serious than that.

Shaking the memory from her mind, Leah laid the file folder on her desk. It was rather thick, thicker than most of the files she worked on. That usually meant the case wasn't as clear-cut as everyone would've liked. It meant there was lots of information that had to be kept. Extra information. Complications.

She wondered what kind of complications she was about to uncover about Preacher Eli Brown and Tom Carson's family.

Flipping the file open, the first thing she came to were the statements taken at the scene of the crime. They were in her pa's handwriting and, once again, she had to fight off old memories. If this didn't stop, she was never going to get anywhere with this case. She decided she had better strengthen her resolve and stop being so emotional. "Quit bein' such a goddamn girl," she said softly to herself.

"You? Bein' a girl?" said Chris from behind her, making her nearly jump clear out of the county. He had been in the restroom when she came inside.

"What you doin' sneakin' round?" she snapped.

"I wasn't sneakin' round . . . I was . . . well . . . that ain't no business of yours. What are *you* doin' is a better question. Ain't this supposed to be your day off?"

She sighed. "I came in to check on somethin'. Sort of a personal project for the time bein'."

Chris looked over her shoulder. "Preacher Eli Brown shootin' Caleb Carson has become your 'personal project'? I think you need to get out more. Miss Sylvie's really gettin' to you, huh?"

"I just want to check some things out."

"Suit yourself."

Grabbing a cup of coffee, Chris took his seat at his desk, picked up the newspaper, and began reading as though she wasn't there. She half expected his feet to come up on his desktop he looked so relaxed and at home.

"Oh, I'm sorry," Chris said, noticing her staring. "Did you want a cup?"

"No, I'm good."

"Okay."

She went back to the statements in the file. Tom Carson's account of the incident was this:

Eli Brown entered Carson house armed. He mentioned his and Tom's ongoing "land dispute" as to which Mr. Carson replied, "There is no dispute, the land is mine." Mr. Carson said Mr. Brown wanted the land to build some kind of "institution." To this, Eli Brown asked Mr. Carson to produce a deed. Mr. Carson said production of said deed was impossible as Mr. Brown had made sure the deed was disposed of. Unsure at this point what is meant by "disposed of" and why Mr. Carson cannot just get the government document reissued. Mr. Carson seemed unable to answer this when questioned. Mr. Carson went on to say his boy, Caleb Carson, had crawled under the supper table and into his lap before Eli Brown took a shot at Mr. Carson and because of that the shot hit the child and not Mr. Carson, as Mr. Carson believes Mr. Brown intended. It is noted that Mr. Carson's report is sketchy at best due to his understandable duress at the crime scene.

What her pa had written for Preacher Eli was somewhat different from Tom Carson's take on things:

Eli Brown was found in his church next door to the property assumed to belong to Tom Carson kneeling in front of his altar praying. It took a long while to calm him down, and, once we did, he would not talk about the murder right away. His initial concern was about the land Tom Carson lives on. Mr. Brown claims that Tom Carson stole it from him eight years ago. When questioned about how he stole it, Mr. Brown said he didn't know, but that the land belonged to his daddy and became his after his daddy passed. When questioned if he had documentation confirming this, Mr. Brown vaguely said there was no written will but a verbal agreement and everyone knew the land was church land. He further stated that for eight years he let Mr. Carson live on his land unmolested and only now wants it back in order to use it for a project. He claims to have told Mr. Carson he's willing to pay Mr. Carson the same price Mr. Carson paid for the land when he purchased it back in 1963, a sum he remembers as being nine thousand dollars.

(Mr. Carson later corroborated this sum, but stated that the land was worth at least ten times this much in today's market. When told this, Mr. Brown went on to state that the thievery committed by Mr. Carson didn't happen in today's market and therefore should not be held to its prices.)

When he finally talked about the murder, Mr. Brown confessed right away to the shooting of Caleb Carson so Officer Cody read him his rights. Mr.

> *Brown apparently waived his right to remain silent*
> *(Officer Cody had to ask him three times if he*
> *understood that he was doing so) because he kept*
> *talking anyway, saying that what happened was such*
> *a terrible shame and that he did not mean to pull*
> *the trigger and never planned on killing no one. Not*
> *Tom Carson, he said, and especially not that little*
> *boy. After that, he fell into tears and it was impossi-*
> *ble to get any more from him. So we cuffed him and*
> *brought him into the station.*

Leah had known the whole "Carson affair" was over some sort of land dispute; she just hadn't known the details until now. There was one more report, taken from Caleb's mother, but it didn't differ much from that of Tom Carson's. Strangely, Sylvie was never interviewed. Leah wondered why. There was hardly even any mention of her in the notes, just that she was there and had blood on her from the gunshot on account of where she'd been sitting. When that bullet got Caleb at such short range, it splattered pretty near the whole side of the kitchen.

Details of the land dispute were now high on Leah's list of things she wanted to know more about. Farther on in the file, she found an appraisal of the land. Tom Carson had estimated a bit high. The appraisal was dated June 15, 1971, and put the value of the land at forty-two thousand dollars. That was still a pretty nice gain from what he had purchased it for only eight years earlier. Still, back then land hadn't skyrocketed yet the way it did in the eighties. Leah couldn't even imagine what that ranch would be worth today. Probably over a quarter-million dollars.

Where had that money gone? Even if the ranch had been sold as part of Tom Carson's estate after his death, which Leah suspected it had, Sylvie should've gotten the money, but if she did, where was it? The girl showed no sign of having a pot to piss in.

There was only one way to find out what had happened, other than asking Sylvie directly, which might not really help at all. Lifting her phone, Leah put a call in for financial records to be delivered to the station for Tom Carson's ranch dating from the time of Caleb Carson's death up to the time Tom Carson was found hanging from the oak tree in his back field. She also made a call to order a copy of Tom Carson's tax returns during that time so she could get an idea of the ranch's profit and losses.

Meanwhile, Chris just went on reading his paper from his desk beside her.

Continuing with the file, Leah found the property deed that Tom Carson had apparently complained didn't exist. It was, in fact, his land, he owned it entirely, his being the only name on the certificate.

What was missing was any clarification as to what this "institution" or project was that the notes taken at the crime scene referred to. Leah found that strange, too.

"Chris?" Leah said, looking up at him. He actually *had* put his feet up on his desk. She could barely believe it.

Chris looked at her over the top of his paper. "Mm?"

"I need you to do me a favor."

"What's that?"

"I need you to go pay Preacher Eli a visit and ask him a question for me."

"Can't we just call 'im up on the phone?"

"I want you to look into his eyes and make sure he ain't lyin'."

"And you're askin' *me* because this is *your* pet project and . . . why?"

"Because last time *I* went, the man nearly threw me off his property, that's why. Come on, please? I think I found somethin' important."

"What do you want me to ask him?"

"Ask him what he planned to do with the land he wanted from Tom Carson eighteen years ago. It says in the report that he planned on buildin' some sorta 'institution.' I wanna know what it was."

"Now why would Preacher Eli tell me anythin'?" Chris asked.

"Cuz you're a police officer, goddamn it. Now get off your ass and go. And get your feet off your desk. You ain't at home."

Chris just laughed at her. He could tell she wasn't actually mad. "You really think Preacher Eli's up to no good?"

"I dunno. I didn't after I went and saw him, but now that I've read his file, I dunno. I just have a funny feelin' there's a lot more to the man than shows on the surface. Apparently, he has superpowers. He knows how to make things like property deeds disappear. At least until the police or the bank comes lookin' for 'em, that is."

Chris stared at her a long minute. "You're serious 'bout this."

"Somethin's up, Chris. Maybe it's all in the past, but there was definitely somethin' dirty 'bout him. I just wanna make sure the past stays in the past. As for the magic powers, I'm guessin' he had some inside help."

Chris laughed. "You mean like maybe God?"

"I don't think God would be the side I'd be choosin'," she said.

Chris might give the indication of not doing much at work, but the truth was he was a damn good cop. He noticed things most people missed and as he pulled into Eli Brown's yard, he noticed a new car parked on the right side of Eli's shack. Eli's station wagon was parked on the left.

Chris knew the car didn't belong to Eli for a number of reasons. First, it was too new. Eli had been in prison seventeen years and this Toyota was barely four years old. Second, the tire tracks leading through the dirt in front of Eli's house behind the car were fresh, so whoever drove it in did so recently. From what Leah told Chris about Preacher Eli, he wasn't getting out much these days. And lastly, what the hell would Eli Brown need two vehicles for? He wouldn't. His wife had been dead for four years. He lived alone.

So this meant he had company, which just complicated things for Chris. Chris hated complications. With a huff, he got out of his cruiser, put on his hat, and closed the car's door. He walked up the porch steps and knocked, expecting to see the aged face of the preacher man answer.

Instead, a young kid, probably in his late teens, swung the door open.

"Hey," he said.

"Hi," Chris said, trying not to appear too taken aback. "Is Eli Brown home?"

"Yeah, sure. Hang on."

The kid left the door open and walked off into the house. A minute later Eli Brown appeared in the doorway and things became much more the way Chris expected them to be.

"I already talked to you guys," Eli said, his voice thin and reedy.

"You haven't talked to me," Chris said. "I'm Officer Jackson." He held out his hand for Eli to shake. Eli studied it a moment before taking it in his own.

"What can I do for you, Officer? And is this gonna be a regular occurrence, the police showin' up on my porch like this?"

Chris laughed. "I hope not. It's a long drive and not a lot to look at but trees."

The preacher didn't return his laugh.

Growing serious, since the laughing didn't break the ice, Chris said, "I hope you don't mind me askin' you a few questions."

"I'm havin' a game of rummy with my grandson, who drove all the way down here from Alabaster just to see me. I'd really rather not waste his time answerin' your questions."

"They won't take but a few moments, I assure you."

"What are they 'bout?"

"Well, there's only one, really. And it concerns something we found in the report taken at the crime scene during the whole Carson incident."

Preacher Eli looked back into a room, presumably the room where his grandson was sitting waiting for him to return and play cards. Then he opened the door fully and stepped out onto the porch. Chris had to take a step back to accommodate him.

"Let me tell you somethin'," Eli Brown said in a clipped whisper. "I don't want any of that past bein' dredged up, you hear me? I done my time. I don't *need* this, and I certainly don't deserve it."

Chris held up a hand. "I assure you, you've got it all wrong. It's actually a question 'bout your intent."

Preacher Eli's eyes narrowed. He studied Chris's face. "My intent? What you mean?"

"Well . . . the report says you was gonna use the land to build some sorta 'institution,' but nowhere in the file does it explain what you meant by 'institution.' We was all just wonderin' if you could tell us what you had planned. We're all just interested, is all."

The preacher continued analyzing Chris, as if unsure as to whether to take him seriously or not. Finally, he said, "Okay, I'll play. I planned on buildin' an education complex."

"Education complex?"

"Yeah. You know, like a private school. Baptist. Alvin doesn't have a proper school that runs from kindergarten all the way to the twelfth grade so I was gonna give it one. I had the business plan, the blueprints, everythin'. I even had people ready to work on it. I was basically set to start diggin'. Then that whole fiasco happened."

Chris couldn't believe he'd just referred to killing a three-year-old boy as a "fiasco."

"I see," Chris said.

"That answer your question?" Eli Brown said, his eyes once again narrowing. He tilted back his head and looked down his nose at Chris.

"Yeah. That was it. Just the one."

"Good." With that Preacher Eli walked back into his house and closed the door behind him.

Chris angled into his squad car and backed out of Preacher Eli's yard onto Hunter Road. Just before he got to the bridge, he radioed Leah back at the office. "Well," he said, "his idea wasn't half bad. He wanted to build an education complex. Basically provide a private school for Alvin that went from kindergarten to twelfth grade. Save kids having to take the bus all the way to Satsuma for high school."

They talked a bit more about it. He told Leah about the grandson.

"What's the grandson's name?"

"No idea. You told me to ask about the institution he was buildin'. That's what I did. I ain't goin' back. The man gives me the willies."

"Fair enough."

When they were done talking, Chris added, "Oh, just before you go? There's somethin' you probably ought to know. Your son and his little friend are sittin' across the street in the woods from Eli's place with fir tree branches tied all over 'em with kite string. I think they're havin' a little stakeout."

Leah didn't say anything for a good couple of seconds. "You sure it's my son?"

"Oh, I'm sure."

"Dear God. Does Eli know they're there?"

"I don't think so. They actually did a pretty good job camouflagin' themselves."

He heard her frustration right through the radio. "Okay, I'm on it."

Chris set the radio back in its cradle and smiled. No, not much got past him.

CHAPTER 15

The most exciting thing me and Dewey had spotted so far on our watch of Preacher Eli's place was Officer Chris Jackson stopping by for some reason. We had no idea why he was there, but we did see Preacher Eli whisper something to Officer Jackson and then make a point of coming out on the porch to talk to him.

We figured this was on account of the fact that someone else was over at the preacher's house. Some guy who looked like a teenager who happened to answer the door when Officer Jackson knocked. I didn't have any idea who the guy was. Now that I knew he was there, I was guessing the silver car parked out front of the house might belong to him since I didn't remember seeing it when me and my mother came here. I figured this way of thinking was how detectives did their work. I was probably a natural detective.

Luckily, me and Dewey were dressed as trees and hiding in the forest, because if Officer Jackson had seen us he'd probably have told my mother and she would likely have not thought my idea of spying on Preacher Eli was a good one. We didn't see eye to eye on some things. I figured spying on people fell into the category of being one of those things.

But Officer Jackson had left maybe fifteen or twenty minutes ago (I'd forgotten to check my watch) and, of course, hadn't seen us. So we were in no danger of my mother finding out we were here. And Preacher Eli obviously didn't know either, or he'd have undoubtedly told Officer Jackson about us. That made me feel quite a bit better.

Since then, we hadn't seen any sign of Preacher Eli or the other guy in the house. Wherever they were or whatever they were doing they were doing it in a room away from the front windows.

"They're probably makin' plans," I told Dewey.

"What sorta plans?"

"Not good ones."

But still, it would've been better if we actually got to *see* them from time to time.

In fact, I was starting to get the feeling this whole idea might not have been my best idea. Worse yet, the only good part of it might turn out to have been Dewey's invention of creating a method of making us invisible to anyone who happened by.

That's when a car stopped on the road right in front of where we were lying. I didn't recognize the car right away because I wasn't really bothering to look at it. After all, we couldn't be seen, so the car must be doing its own business and was of no concern to us.

At least that's what I thought.

Then I studied the car a little more closely as I heard the driver's side door open. I actually *did* recognize this vehicle.

It was my mother.

I gulped. Had she come to see Preacher Eli again? What was *she* doing here? Why hadn't she parked in his driveway?

Then, as she came around the front of the car, I found out.

"Abraham Teal! Get out of those woods right this instant!" She was nearly screaming. I wanted to shush her. Tell her to keep it down on account of she was going to attract the attention of Preacher Eli, but there was no shushing her. "How dare you do something like this?"

I looked at Dewey. He looked at me. I still wasn't sure she

could see us, even though she seemed to be staring right at us. "You too, Dewey, get up! Come on! Now!"

Slowly, we stood from where we were lying, both of us covered in fir tree branches tied to our body with kite string. "Oh my God! You look ridiculous! What the *hell* are you doin'?"

"Watchin' Preacher Eli," I said quietly, still hoping not to be overheard across the street.

"Chris was right. You *are* on a stakeout. Well, guess what? Your stakeout just ended. Where's your bikes?"

Dewey pointed to the ditch, down a little ways.

"Nice," my mother said. "You threw your bikes in the ditch. Go get 'em!"

I started walking toward the ditch on the outside of the woods, but she stopped me.

"Take those things off you first," she said. "You look absolutely ridiculous."

I couldn't undo Dewey's knots. He had to take my branches off and then, using the garden shears, I had to take off his. Then we went and got our bikes. Dewey carried the shears. Halfway there, he turned around.

"What are you doin'?" my mother asked him.

"I left the roll of string in the woods," Dewey said. "I need to put it back in my dad's shed."

My mother let out a deep breath. "Go get it. But do it fast. You're ridin' home. I want you on your bike and down that hill in the next five minutes. Abe, you're comin' with me. Bring your bike up to the car. I'm throwin' it in the trunk."

"Why can't I go with Dewey?" I asked, climbing into the ditch. It was a very wide and deep ditch and getting my bike out wasn't easy. Luckily, there was no water in it on account of all the sun we'd had lately.

"Because I said so. Why do you have to spy on people?"

I thought this over, but before I could answer she told me it was a rhetorical question. Then she clarified: "That means I don't expect you to answer it. I expect you to *think* about it." I didn't really understand, but I knew when to keep my mouth shut.

After four or five attempts, Dewey got his bike out of the ditch. By then, mine was already in the trunk. "Bye, Abe," Dewey said with a wave. "Bye, Miss Leah." And with that, he kicked off and headed down the hill toward the Blackberry Springs Bridge and his home.

"Get in the car!" my mother snapped.

I got in the car. She got in her side and slammed her door. Turning the key to start the ignition, she told me, "If I ever catch you doin' somethin' like this again . . . so help me. Didn't we go through all this once before?"

I knew what she was talkin' 'bout. She was talkin' 'bout Mr. Wyatt Edward Farrow, just like Dewey had been on the phone this morning. But just like I'd told him, this was all different on account of Preacher Eli actually having shot a kid and gone to prison for it. I was about to tell her just that when she turned her face to me and I saw that look in her eyes that meant it was best to just keep my thoughts to myself. I'd learned that over the years you didn't mess around when she gave you that look.

So instead, I asked, "Where're we goin'? This isn't the way home." We'd just driven by the turnoff to Cottonwood Lane.

"I'm still workin'. Now you're stuck comin' with me."

"Comin' with you where?"

"Just mind your business."

She kept driving down Hunter Road, heading toward Main Street. Soon, the silence seemed to become too much for her because she broke it. "So. I decided to call that Addison woman back and tell her we'd drive into Georgia next time I had a day off. Meet these grandparents of yours. How do you feel about that?"

It was like dozens of lightning bugs suddenly swarmed up into my chest. "That's great!" I said.

We turned left onto Main Street and drove right past the library where me and Dewey had sat with my aunt Addison that morning it was so hot. The marble steps still looked bright white this afternoon, but a scattering of green leaves covered some. They'd blown from the maple trees planted beside them. "I'm hopin' your sister thinks it's great, too," my mother said with a slight worry in her voice.

I frowned. "You don't think Carry'll wanna meet her grandparents?" I found this a very odd thing to be figuring on. Surely, everyone wanted to meet their kin.

"It's tough to call how Carry will react to things sometimes. Your sister can be"—she searched for the word—"complicated."

"How do you mean—complicated?"

"She's just . . . never mind. She's a *girl*. You can't expect to understand 'em. Especially at your age."

I didn't say nothing, just watched the businesses sail by on either side of the road, while trying to guess what our destination was. Finally, I asked again. "Where are we goin', anyway? Seems like we're headin' all the way to the other end of Main Street."

"I *told* you," my mother said. "Mind your business."

I figured since I now seemed to be working with her it *was* my business to know where we were going, but I found out soon enough. It actually *did* turn out to be pretty near all the way down at the end of Main Street. She pulled her car to a stop right in front of the Alvin Courthouse. At first, I figured that was our destination, but it turned out we were headed to the public records office right beside the courthouse. I think the records office actually was part of the courthouse, but we entered through the front from the outside, so it seemed like a separate building. Compared to the courthouse it was small and squat.

Inside, it wasn't even as big as it looked from the outside. The room was filled with a musty smell, like the pages of old books. Sunlight shined through the three main windows along the front wall. The rest of the room was lit with fluorescent lights.

Bookshelves separated the room into sections, making it almost like a maze. Most were floor-to-ceiling shelves packed with spines of all sorts of books. There were also catalogs and files like we have in our school library explaining which books had what information in 'em so you could find what you were looking for. Maps and old photographs hung on the walls.

"I'm Detective Leah Teal from the Alvin Police Department,"

my mother told the clerk working behind the small pine desk tucked away in the back corner. "I'd like to check out your property records, if I may." The clerk's desk was stacked with papers, making it appear even smaller than it was, so it suited the room. The stacks were so high, some of them rose taller than the woman, who was a brunette with short, curly hair and large round glasses. The stacks made her appear even smaller than she turned out to be once she stood up.

"Oh, absolutely," she said, seemingly impressed with the fact that my mother was a detective. Her eyes fell to the sword at my side. Then they went back to my mother.

"This is my son, Abe," my mother said, explaining. "I reckon he believes he's Peter Pan."

The clerk laughed. I didn't find it very funny. My mother had just made a joke at my expense.

The clerk escorted us through the maze of shelves right across the room to the other side, where the thickest of the white-covered books packed a series of shelves on the back wall. I had never seen books so tall. Each one had to be nearly two feet in height. "You'll find all of the properties in Alvin and the outlying areas listed here. Each volume is categorized by location. You can refer to this map." She pointed out a map on the back wall that was broken out into squares.

My mother thanked her and set about tracing her finger up the map, northward. At first, I thought she was heading toward Eli Brown's new place, but she wasn't. She was following Fairview Drive, but instead of veering left like Fairview did, she let her finger curve off right and continue around the bend where it turned into Bogpine Way.

"Goin' frog huntin'?" I asked, with a laugh.

"Mind your business," my mother told me again, not taking her eyes off the map.

I thought I was being funny. Bogpine Way wraps around a dense forest that opens onto Beemer's Bog, a place known to get overrun with toads in late spring. Nobody goes near it on account of the smell and all the noise.

She stopped her finger about a third of the way up the Bogpine bend and tapped. "What street number do you reckon this is?"

I looked behind me to see if the lady clerk was still standing with us, but she wasn't, so I figured my mother must be talking to me. I didn't have a clue what she meant. "I don't know. How would you ever tell?"

"I guess you just estimate. This says one hundred down here and three hundred up here. That's about two inches between them. Would you say this is around another inch and a little bit? I'm looking for four-oh-five."

"I guess." I didn't rightly know an inch from an inchworm, to be quite honest. But I didn't want to sound dumb.

"Okay, that puts us in square zero-seven-C," she said, reading the numbers from the side and top of the map. "See if you can find that volume."

I started looking at the white books on the shelves. It took me a moment to realize they had numbers and letters on their spines. Unfortunately, it appeared the only ones low enough for me to see were from the letters E to T. "I reckon it's in one of the top rows," I said.

"I reckon you're right." My mother scanned the top three shelves. It took her a minute before she pulled one of the books from where it sat. It turned out to be even larger than I expected, at least half as wide as it was tall. These books were massive and thick with pages full of information.

My mother laid the book on a table under the map and carefully opened it to the back where an index listed the addresses by street number and page. She quickly flopped the pages back to the page she wanted. I found myself looking at a detailed map of a bit of road with some forest on the right of it. She flipped ahead the next five pages; every one showed a bit more of the road and the trees as it went farther up and curved right into the forest. I realized I was looking at one big parcel of land.

In the bottom right corner of each page was a square with writing inside it:

405 Bogpine Way, Alvin, AL 36573
$120,000.00
320 Acre Property (Cattle Ranch)
Owner: Unlisted.
Mon. 2 Mar. 1981 08:00:00

My mother stared at that square a long while.

"What is it?" I asked.

"I dunno," she said. "It don't make no sense to me."

"What don't?"

"The land's sat there this whole time untouched. Nobody's developed it. The old farmhouse and barn are just rotting away. I don't understand why there ain't no owner listed. I thought the state would be listed as owner, or at least the county."

"Owner of what?"

"The land Miss Sylvie's pa owned 'fore he died."

"Wouldn't Miss Sylvie own it? I thought kids got whatever their folks had when their folks died." That was my understanding of the whole thing.

"Miss Sylvie couldn't afford it."

"What do you mean?"

"Ranches cost money to upkeep, and Sylvie was only fourteen when her folks died. She was in no shape to look after the ranch alone, let alone worry about making the costs. She went into foster care."

"What's foster care?"

"Nothing you don't ever need to worry 'bout."

"Why would anyone want to live so close to Beemer's Bog?" I asked her, but she completely ignored me. She picked up the book and, leaving it open at one of the pages of the ranch Miss Sylvie's pa used to own, lugged it back to the desk where the clerk sat. "Mind if I bother you with somethin'?" my mother asked her.

The clerk smiled. "Of course not. That's why I'm here."

My mother came around to her side of the desk and bent down, showing her the page and the square with the writing in it.

"Right here," she said, "where it lists 'Owner.' Can you tell me what 'Unlisted' means?"

The clerk looked confused. "I ain't never seen that 'fore."

"Could it mean it's owned by the county? Because that's how I figure it *should* be. And the date of the record would be pretty near right."

The clerk continued to look at it in confusion. "No . . . if it's owned by the county, it always says 'Vacant,' not 'Unlisted.' Don't ask me why. 'County' would make more sense. But I don't know what 'Unlisted' means. It's almost as though the owner wasn't put in the records, but I don't see how that's possible. It's public information."

"That's what I thought," my mother said. "Would there be somewhere else I might be able to find out who this property belongs to?"

"We can run a title search on it. That will involve sending off a form to the Mobile County public records office, but it usually doesn't take long to get a response."

"And that will definitely have the owner listed?"

"It should. If *that* doesn't, something funny's goin' on. The next step would be to request a copy of the deed. That would list ownership for sure."

"What's this dollar amount?" my mother asked.

"That's the amount the land was appraised at when this survey map was made. We keep the actual assessment records separate, so if you wanted a recent assessment record, I could get you that. But it shows here that, on March 2, 1981, this property was worth one hundred and twenty thousand dollars."

My mother thought this over. "Is there any way we can tell if there is a lien on the property?"

"We can request that information as part of the title search. I'm sorry, Officer—"

"Detective," my mother corrected her. "Detective Teal."

"I'm sorry, Detective Teal, Alvin's just too small to have a records office that keeps much more than just basic records. Would you like me to help you fill out the request for the title search? We can do it right now and save you a lot of time."

"Sure."

And so my mother did that while I went back and looked at the big map of Alvin hanging on the wall. As I did, my eyes were constantly being drawn upward and westward to that little spot of land in Blackberry Springs where I knew, right at this very moment, Preacher Eli was planning his next move.

And I was willing to bet dollars to dingbats it had something to do with that teenager who drove that strange silver car me and Dewey had seen parked beside the house.

CHAPTER 16

The next day, me and Dewey rode our bikes down to Main Street just for something to do. We often did this—went for bike rides while we talked about this and that. It was nice having the wind on our faces and the sun on the tops of our heads, especially in the summer when it got so hot. We were in the middle of an especially hot spell, and sweat clung to my hair and occasionally ran down the sides of my face while we went along. Of course, both of us had our swords dangling from our hips. They'd become pretty much part of our standard wardrobe.

Today, Dewey had been doing most of the talking, going on about one of the inventions from his book. It was for an outboard motor he had developed (so far on paper only) that should work with the rubber dinghy he had in his dad's shed. "We can take the dinghy up to Willet Lake and I'll show you how it will work. That is, once we build it."

I wondered why he chose Willet Lake. It was a nice enough lake and all, but the only way to get there was by walking through a narrow path in the woods that opened on Hunter Road pretty near a half block up from Preacher Eli's place. Alvin had two other lakes to choose from, Cornflower Lake and Painted Lake, but Dewey had to pick the one that sat on the doorstep of a convicted murderer. Somehow it just figured.

"I don't really like boats," I said. What I really meant was that I didn't really like being shot to death in the middle of a lake by a crazy old preacher man.

"You'll like 'em when they have motors attached. Especially my motor. It'll go really fast. Did I tell you it uses a car battery and an electric egg beater?"

"No," I said. At that point, I started tuning him out as he went on about the intricacies of motor building using household appliances and common garden supplies.

Finally, I couldn't listen to him go on about ridiculous ideas for motors anymore so I casually changed the subject.

"Guess what my mom told me yesterday."

"Now how could I possibly guess something like that?" he asked.

"I didn't mean for you to really guess."

"Then why did you say it?"

I rolled my eyes. "It's just somethin' people say. Like 'Betcha don't know what I've been up to lately.' "

"I wouldn't know that either."

"I suspect you would have a better idea than anyone else would, though." We were getting off topic.

"Well, if I had to guess what you'd been up to," Dewey said, "I'd guess it would have somethin' to do with your ma bein' upset with you for catchin' you spyin' on Preacher Eli yesterday. She sure seemed mad."

"Aw, she wasn't so bad," I said. "I've had her much madder at me than that. Heck, all she did was force me to go to the records office with her."

"The records office? What the heck for?"

I pedaled backward slightly and slowed down my pace. We were coming up on Vera's Old West Grill on our left and the air was full of the smell of burgers sizzling on the grill. My mouth watered and my stomach gave a little rumble.

Dewey saw that I was braking and matched my speed. He

knew what I was about to say was important. "Now you can't tell nobody," I said, trying to keep my voice to a whisper, even though it's impossible to hear somebody whispering when you're riding a bike. So I ended up just talking as quietly as possible.

A group of three men came out of Vera's, laughing. They were all wearing golf shirts and dress pants. I figured they probably worked together—maybe at one of the office spaces that would soon be coming up on our right. Likely, they were on their lunch break.

Dewey knew I was serious. He waited until we were well past hearing distance of the men before he spoke. "I won't. You know you can trust me." Boy, did I have his interest now.

"My mom was checking out the land owned by Sylvie Carson's folks 'fore they died. I didn't know exactly what she was lookin' for, but from what I could catch, she seemed to think somethin' sneaky's goin' on. And all I could think of was that if there is anythin' weird, the obvious person behind it is Preacher Eli."

"Of course," Dewey said. "Did your ma agree?"

"I didn't ask her. But she did find out somethin' strange. Apparently, whoever owns the land isn't listed at the records office and the woman workin' there said that was quite unusual. She appeared rather concerned 'bout it, actually."

We came to a stop at the intersection where Sweetwater Drive runs through Main Street. On the corner across the street, Fast Gas looked deserted. There were no cars at the pumps and I didn't even see an attendant working there. Looking at the gas station made me think of my pa and how he used to work at a gas station farther down Main Street during nights and how, if he'd worked days, he'd probably still be alive. I was glad that gas station he worked at wasn't around no more and that they'd built the Brookside Mall where it used to be. Judging by Fast Gas, it certainly seemed like working the day shift was a much easier job than nights. You didn't even have to be out front. You could just hide somewhere inside if you wanted.

"So what did your ma do?" Dewey asked as we started riding again.

"She sent off for more records from the Mobile office that's a lot bigger and has more information. The woman said they'd know for sure who owns the land. My mom was really suspicious 'bout the whole thing and didn't seem to like it one bit that there wasn't no one listed. I really got the feelin' Preacher Eli's gonna turn out to be somehow involved."

"Wow," Dewey said. "That's somethin'. I can't wait to hear 'bout those records when they come."

The row of business centers came up on our right. There were three of them; each was a three-story cement building named after a hawk. There was Hawk Ridge, Hawk Point, and Hawk Landing. I didn't rightly know what hawks had to do with business. Each business center squatted back from the road surrounded by poplars and gardens full of rhododendrons and wild roses. The light wind picked up the sweet smell of the roses as we passed.

All three buildings had a sign saying OFFICE SPACE FOR LEASE out front. Ever since those structures went up over six years ago, they'd all had those signs in front of them. I doubted they'd ever find enough business folks in Alvin to lease three entire three-story buildings.

"Oh, and guess what else," I said to Dewey.

Dewey started to speak but I cut him off. "Again, I wasn't really askin' you to guess. Anyway, my mom told me she's gonna take me and Carry to Georgia to meet my new grandma and granddaddy that my aunt Addison told us 'bout."

I could see cogs spinning in Dewey's brain; he was thinking about something. "What?" I asked.

He brought his bike to a complete stop.

I stopped too, but had to walk it back to get alongside him. "What?" I asked again.

"It's just . . . I thought your ma was worried that Addison might not really be your aunt?"

"Oh, she doesn't think that no more. We got a background check on my pa and it showed he has a sister."

"Yeah, but you said she was still thinkin' this might not be *the* sister but someone else pretendin' to be her."

"That was 'fore she talked to her on the phone. Now she believes her."

"But . . . what if she *isn't* your aunt. And what if these other folks ain't really your grandparents? What if they ain't related at all?"

"Now why would anyone go and pretend they're my relations?"

"I dunno. What if they're after some sorta inheritance?"

I laughed. "Dewey, we ain't got nothin' to inherit."

"You got some things."

"Like what?"

"Access to information pertainin' to all the inventions I told you 'bout."

Laughing, I just shook my head. "You're 'bout as smart as a can of dew worms on a spring mornin' sometimes, you know that?"

Dewey got all indignant. "I'm only lookin' out for your best interests."

"Don't worry, my interests are all fine." I started pedaling again.

We were halfway up Main Street, just a little ways past the police department where my mother worked, when Dewey came up beside me again. "You know what? I got an idea."

"Yeah? What's that?"

"Why don't you and me go to the records office and check what kind of information they have about your grandparents? I bet they at least have their names. Maybe even their pictures."

I thought this over. It wasn't a bad idea. Not because I thought the people my mother wanted to take me to see weren't my grandparents, but because I would love to know as much about my family history as possible. It was the one thing I never really had in my life. Dewey now had me wondering exactly what kind of information they *did* keep at that records office about family stuff.

"Okay," I said. "That sounds like as good a way as any of spendin' the afternoon."

The same clerk was sitting behind the desk when we arrived at the records office. Neither her nor the desk looked so small today, as the piles of books and papers that had covered the top were gone. She had her hair the same and wore the same big glasses. Today she had on a blue shirt with frills around the collar. She recognized me right away. "You're that policewoman's son. Where's your momma?"

"At home." Once again I was overwhelmed by the odor of musty books. They actually tasted like old dust on your tongue, although the room was clean enough. It looked like it had just been washed up. The windows sparkled with the afternoon sun pouring in.

The woman looked a bit confused. "Oh, is there somethin' I can help *you* with, then?"

"I, um, want to find out 'bout my family. You know, my past family and all."

A wide smile spread across her face. "You mean your *genealogy*. Isn't that great! Is this something you're doin' for school?"

"No, ma'am," Dewey said. "School's out for the year. It's the summer."

Concern fell over her face. "Oh, that's right. So, this is just somethin' you're doin' on your own, then?"

I nodded. "Yep. Is that okay?"

"Absolutely. Although the only information you can get here is *public* information. Anything private, of course, isn't available from any of our records offices."

I didn't rightly know what she was talking about, but I just nodded anyway. "That's fine. I just wanna know about my . . . I can't think of the word."

"Ancestors?" she asked.

"That's right," I said, smiling. "About my ancestors. Find out who they were!"

"Or *are*," Dewey corrected. "That is, for the ones that are still livin'."

"Okay, let's see what we can pull out for you." She stood from the desk and it turned out she was wearing a black skirt as she came around. Once again she saw my and Dewey's swords.

"So are you *both* Peter Pan today? Or are *you* a Lost Boy?" she asked, turning her attention to Dewey.

Dewey looked at me. "What's she talkin' 'bout?"

I shook my head. "Forget it," I mouthed.

She led us to a different section of the room than she'd taken me and my mother to yesterday. "This is our genealogy section," she said. "Now, there's not a *lot* of information here. And it's pretty much confined to Alvin and the immediate outlying areas. We really don't go much farther out than Satsuma just because we don't have the room to store all the information. So, anybody in your family history who was born anywhere else might not show up. What's your last name?"

"Teal," I said. "T-E-A-L"

She wrote that down on a piece of paper.

"And what's your momma's maiden name?"

"You mean her name 'fore she married my pa?" I asked.

"Yes."

I had to think hard to remember. Finally, it came to me when I thought of Uncle Henry. His name was actually Henry Fowler, which was the name of my mother's dad. "Fowler."

"Okay. So far, so good. And your name is?"

"Abe," I said.

"And your ma's name?"

"Leah. L. E. A. H."

"And your pa's name?"

"Billy." I stumbled a bit. "He . . . died when I was two."

"Oh, I'm so sorry," she said. Then with her pen over her paper, she thought for a second. "I'll use William. He's probably in the archives as William. If nothin' comes up, we'll search for Bill or Billy. Okay, do you know your grandpa's name?"

Her questions kept going like this until I couldn't answer them anymore, which didn't take long. I knew my mom's dad was called Joe, but I couldn't remember the name of her ma. And I didn't know the name of my other grandparents on my pa's side of the family. Heck, I hadn't even met them yet. I told her about Uncle Henry, who was actually my *mother's* uncle, and Aunt Addison, but she didn't seem too concerned with uncles and aunts.

"Okay, that probably gives me enough to go on," she said. Pulling a large book from one of the shelves, she started turning pages. I watched from the side. Dewey tried to edge his way in and watch too, but I figured since we were looking up my family stuff, I should be the one who got to see what was going on. She kept flipping pages until she came to the F section and then found *Fowler*. Running her finger down the page, she came to the list of Joes. There were a lot of Joe Fowlers listed in that book.

"Do you know if your momma's pa was born in Alvin?" she asked me.

I shrugged. "I dunno."

She sighed. "Let's try Teal. We'll probably have better luck there. *You* were born here, right?"

"I was born in Satsuma."

"Okay, close enough. *You* should be in here." She pushed the volume she had out back onto the shelf and pulled out another one, this time opening it to the T section. "Oh, this is good," she said. "Teal is a much less common name than Fowler. Let's see. Oh, this is probably you right here, three from the top. There's only one Abraham on the list." Beside my name (if it really was me) were some reference numbers.

"What do those mean?" I asked.

"They tell us what book to go to next to get the real information from. These books are just sort of gigantic indexes."

"Wow," Dewey said.

She turned to the wall of shelves behind her and started studying the spines of those books. "Nope, not on this one." Then she walked around to the other side. Me and Dewey just stayed where we were beside the small table where the index book still lay opened to the T section.

"Found it!" she called out through the wall of books. She came around carrying a large binder with a blue cover. "Okay, according to this," she said, once more referring to the index, "your information is on page 125-A3."

She plopped the binder open on the table and began tossing pages, slowing as she got close to the right one. She ended up going a couple too far and had to turn back two. "Here we are: Abraham Teal. Let's see if this is you. Is your birthday March twenty-sixth, 1976?"

Suddenly, I got excited. "Yes! That *is* me! What else does it say?"

"Your momma's name is Leah Marie Fowler. Your pa's name is

William Robert Teal. Your grandma on your ma's side is Josephine Adeline Fowler." She looked at me. "There, see? Now you know."

"I guess my sister was named after her. My sister is called Caroline Josephine."

"You're probably right! Your grandpa on your ma's side as you know is Joseph Fowler, no middle name. Your grandma on your pa's side is Sara Lynn Teal, and your grandpa on your pa's side is Jeremiah Teal, no middle name."

Wow, did I ever feel important. I knew information about my family that my mother didn't even know yet. For once, it was *me* knowing stuff instead of everyone else.

"Does it say anythin' else? Does it talk 'bout what they did or anythin'?" Dewey asked.

"No, I'm afraid there isn't a lot of genealogy information kept."

"Can I write to Mobile for more, like my mom did?"

She frowned. "They don't keep much either. You'll probably get even less than we have. In fact, we've got more than most towns simply on account of Alvin bein' so small."

I frowned. This wasn't what I wanted to hear.

"I'm sorry," she said.

"That's okay." I examined my shoes.

Then she snapped her fingers. I looked up and she was beaming. "You know what you need?" And before I could answer she told me. "You need a historian. And I think I know *just* the person."

She walked quickly back to her desk and I followed behind her with Dewey on my tail, feeling the excitement rise like a trumpet blast in my chest. I wasn't certain what a historian was, but it sure sounded important. I supposed a historian was an expert on history. That made sense.

"I have a friend down in Chickasaw," she said, "who has been researching the genealogy of Alabama for years, but she especially knows *this* area. Let me give her a call for you."

I smiled. "Thanks!"

She dialed a number and waited for her friend to answer. Finally, she did.

"Hi, Dixie," the clerk said. "It's Mary Sue here. Yes, I know. Too long. Oh, you know. Yeah, still in Alvin. Still at the records office. Yeah . . ." I thought they were going to keep on chitchatting for days until finally Mary Sue, the apparent name of the clerk, interrupted. "Listen, Dixie, this is actually a business call of sorts. I have a young boy in my office. His mother is the detective of Alvin. Mmm-hmm. Anyway, he's trying to research his family history, and I showed him what we had, which was barely nothin', an' then I thought of you."

There was a long pause before Mary Sue spoke again. "Yes, he was born in Satsuma. I have some information about his daddy. He's passed away." She sort of whispered the words *passed away* as though saying them the same volume as the rest might have offended me. "Yes, I can give you the date of his birth and of his death."

She relayed all the pertinent information, including my grandparents and everything else, getting all of it from the book she'd pulled out. Then she asked me for my address, so I told it to her. "All right, I'll tell him to look forward to it. Thank you very much, Dixie. And I hope to see you soon."

She hung up the phone. "My, my, that woman can talk your ear off."

"Is she gettin' me information 'bout my family?" I asked with a big grin I couldn't hold back.

"She certainly is. She said to give her a couple days to compile it and then she'd put it in the mail for you. Her name is Dixie Spinner. You can watch for her package in your mailbox." Then she leaned over and whispered, "And you may want to write her a quick thank-you card after you get everything. She'd like that."

I thought that was a good idea, too.

I looked at Dewey. "This is great. I'm gonna finally learn 'bout my family."

"If there's anything to find out, she'll be the one to know 'bout it," Miss Mary Sue said. "And I can't guarantee she'll find any more information than we have here, but sometimes you get *real* lucky and she'll dig you up things like family crests and stuff like that."

"What's a family crest?" I asked.

"It's an insignia your family used way back to designate them from other families. It would appear on shields and flags and things."

That sounded pretty neat. I hoped I would get a copy of my family crest.

"Oh," she said, "and she won't find any real facts other than names, birthdays, cause of death, and that type of stuff 'bout anyone unless that person did something extraordinary or unusual. For instance, she told me she once dug up family history for this one feller who found out one of his grandfathers from way back was once wanted for seven train robberies. He turned out to be mighty proud of that."

I thought that sounded like a strange thing to be proud of. I wondered if maybe the "feller" she was talking about was Preacher Eli.

I thanked her again, a little concerned about my mother's reaction to the mail coming from this Miss Dixie in Chickasaw being delivered straight to my house. I wondered if this was something my mother would mind me doing. Oh, well, I'd have to make sure I was the one who checked the mail throughout the coming weeks.

"I think she was overanxious to help us on account of she knew your mother worked for the police," Dewey said on our way out.

"You know, it is possible she's just nice," I said.

"It's possible, I guess. But I think my theory's more likely."

CHAPTER 17

Over the following days, thoughts about the Brown and Carson land dispute circled inside Leah's head like hungry vultures over a cattle carcass. Likely, Leah thought, it was all spawned by what Abe had said at the records office. *"Wouldn't Miss Sylvie own it? I thought kids got whatever their folks had when their folks died."* At the time, Leah had told Abe that Sylvie couldn't have afforded the ranch, but was that so true? The ranch could've stayed in her name and been run without her. Besides, even if the ranch had been sold as part of Tom Carson's estate, the difference in value between what he originally paid for it in 1963 and what it was worth at the time of his death was well over a hundred thousand dollars. Even if it went for a rock-bottom price at auction, there would still be a substantial amount of equity left for Sylvie, one would think.

Leah received the financial statements and tax information she'd requested for Tom Carson. They arrived together at the station just as Leah was leaving for the day and she brought them home with her. Sitting on the sofa in the living room, she eagerly went through them, trying to discover the reason why Sylvie hadn't appeared to have gotten anything from the deal.

She examined Tom Carson's bank information first. There was a lot to it. It covered nine years of his life, and told an interesting story. That nine-thousand-dollar initial investment he had made slowly went wrong for some reason, and it was all laid out before Leah in black and white. Tom had taken out a line of credit with the Alvin First National Bank against the ranch almost immediately following the death of his son. At first, the line of credit only used a third of the equity he held in his ranch, but as time went by, he increased the amount of the LOC at higher and higher rates. The only thing that kept him afloat was the fact that the market grew as fast, if not faster, than the rate of his expanding line of credit.

One thing was for certain, though. Tom Carson got in way over his head financially due to *something* very early on. And even when the value of his ranch started to reach upward of a hundred thousand dollars, so did what he owed on it. Not only that, but according to the tax sheets Leah had requested, many years the ranch ran at a loss. That didn't help his situation one bit. But the losses in no way compensated for the amount of money actually being spent. Wherever that money went, there was no record of it.

It made no sense. From what she knew about the Carsons, they didn't go on lavish vacations or anything like that.

"What were you doin' with all your money, Tom?" Leah asked, continuing from page to page.

Because of the booming market, Tom was able to get away with defaulting payments on his LOC. Compound interest simply kept piling up higher and higher. It never got to the point where the bank threatened to foreclose, but if things hadn't turned around soon, Leah could tell that point was coming fast.

By the time of his death in 1980, Tom Carson owed the bank just under eighty-eight thousand dollars, an amount he could never pay back. Tom Carson must've known this—a fact that struck a nerve with Leah. *Could this have contributed to his suicide?*

There was indication that the bank called in the line of credit upon Tom Carson's death, which probably preceded the auctioning off of the property. Leah remembered quite distinctly that no will had turned up after his death, so an auction of the property was the most likely outcome. Still, even if the ranch *were* sold at auction, there was a good chance it would've gone for enough money to pay the bank debt and still have some left over as a nest egg for Sylvie. But Leah had no records of the land being sold. All she really had was the property survey map with the words *Owner: Unlisted,* and the original deed with Tom Carson's name on it in her daddy's police folder.

Could it be possible that the bank *hadn't* auctioned the ranch and that Sylvie Carson's name was the one that belonged on that title? Maybe all she needed to do to claim ownership was fill out some forms or make a court appearance.

The market had continued to boom since 1981, and Leah suspected the appraised value of one hundred and twenty thousand dollars they showed at the public records office was probably now at least double that. Surely, with the ranch not running and Tom Carson not spending his money on whatever it was he had been spending it on, there would be value in that ranch today. Maybe a *lot* of value.

The one thing that niggled at the back of her brain was the date on the survey map. It had been updated March 2, 1981, a date that, in Leah's eyes, seemed entirely too coincidental. It was fewer than four months after the "supposed" suicidal death of Tom Carson.

When had she started putting the word "supposed" in front of suicide with quotation marks around it when it came to Tom Carson? Leah wasn't sure. She knew these sorts of thoughts were exactly the kind Ethan Montgomery had warned her against having. He'd be mighty upset to learn she was doing such a thing now. Leah decided to wait for the title search she'd sent away to Mobile for before she decided how she would refer to Tom Carson's death to herself.

All of this also had Leah thinking about Sylvie Carson's present state of mind and whether or not her delusions were quite as delusional as people thought. Maybe she really was in danger. Maybe she always had been. If that land had even fifty thousand dollars in equity and Sylvie was the one entitled to it, her life suddenly did have reason to be threatened. A very good reason, in fact. In Leah's experience, money was always a good motive for any criminal act.

After an hour or so of being unable to set her worried mind at ease, Leah decided to go pay Sylvie an unscheduled visit. This would likely alarm the girl, as she wasn't used to the police showing up without her calling them first. On the other hand, maybe it would help ease her fears, knowing that Leah really did care about her and wasn't just coming because of her irrational phone calls.

This time Leah was going for selfish reasons: to clear her own mind. She had some questions she wanted to ask Sylvie, although she wasn't quite sure how to bring them up. There was a very good chance they were the types of questions that might set Sylvie off—questions about the past. Leah always avoided treading where memories lay when it came to Sylvie.

But today Leah was going to take Sylvie on a little trip down memory lane. Not because she wanted to, but because the detective inside her *had* to.

It was the first day of rain Alvin had seen in almost three weeks and even though it wasn't a hard rain, it came with a strong wind that made the raindrops fall at a slant. Grabbing her Crimson Tide sweatshirt, Leah pulled the hood up over her head and ran to her car, doing her best not to get soaked along the way. She drove through the bleak streets to Sylvie's house, trying to piece together how she would phrase her questions. It was important she did it right.

Above her, the sky was the color of asphalt and the clouds hung low and heavy. The rain started coming down harder as she turned up Old Mill Road, splattering off the hood of her car and the street. It was a miserable day.

By the time Leah pulled into Sylvie's, the dirt driveway had become a layer of mud. Leah's shoes became caked with it as she jogged to the front porch, her clothes getting drenched along the way. The raindrops were heavy and the wind hadn't let up. Her blond bangs hung limp in front of her face. She tucked them up out of the way.

Rapping on the door, she called out, "Sylvie! Sylvie, it's Detective Teal! Alvin Police!"

Nobody answered.

She knocked again, louder. She called out again, louder.

Still no answer.

Her heart sank. Where would Sylvie be on a day like today?

Around the yard, rain bounced and drizzled off everything in sight. If Sylvie was out with the baby and caught in all this it would be terrible. She didn't own a car. She would be on foot.

Leah tried knocking again, as hard as she could. This time she nearly screamed her name out. "Sylvie! It's Detective Teal! Open up!"

At last, she heard the dead bolts shoot, the chain slide. The door opened two inches. The blue eye of Sylvie Carson, usually wild and crazy, appeared welcoming and warm.

"Hey," Leah said, slightly out of breath from hollering. "It's me. I need to talk to you. Can I come in?"

Sylvie nodded through the crack. The door closed, the chain slid, the door opened, and Leah entered.

The house was warm and felt good. A sweet smell hung in the air. Sylvie had been cooking. "Are those cookies?" Leah asked, taking an exaggerated whiff.

Sylvie frowned. "A pie. It didn't turn out. Pecan. I make terrible pecan pie. I accidentally only put in a quarter the amount of sugar the recipe called for."

"Sure smells good."

Leah started taking off her shoes. "Leave 'em on," Sylvie said. "They're fine."

"No they're not," Leah said. "They're full of mud from your driveway." Finishing taking them off, she followed Sylvie into the living room. "Where's the baby?" Leah asked.

"In my room," Sylvie said. "Asleep. All she does is sleep."

"Be careful what you wish for. Things could be worse."

"I dunno. Sometimes I think she sleeps too much."

"It's healthy for her. It means she's growing . . ." A fruit fly buzzed around Leah's face. She clapped her hands at it, trying to squash it. ". . . And content."

"So *why* are you here?" Sylvie asked. Then she said timidly, "Sorry, that came out wrong. I don't mind you dropping by, I was just wonderin', is all."

"I need to ask you some questions. Can we sit somewhere?"

Sylvie nodded. "The kitchen? There's more light." Leah had to agree. The living room with its single yellow lamp looked particularly gloomy on this rainy afternoon.

They both sat at the kitchen table. "Are you sure that pie didn't turn out?" Leah asked. "It sure smells good."

"Oh, I'm sure. It's in my garbage."

Two more fruit flies buzzed around Leah. She killed them with one try. "You have a fruit fly problem, I see."

"Probably the pie."

"When did you make it?"

"An hour ago. Wasn't even cooled 'fore I threw it in the trash."

"Then I doubt it's the source of your fruit flies." The shotgun still hadn't moved from its place by the door. Four more fruit flies flew across the table.

Leah stood. "Where are they comin' from?" She checked the garbage under the sink. Sure enough, there was the pecan pie, not looking half bad. A little charred, but if it only had a quarter the sugar in it, it probably didn't taste near on as good as it looked. But there were no fruit flies around it. "It ain't the pie."

She checked the rest of the kitchen. "There's some here around the sink, but most seem to be comin' from your vents."

"Where do these vents go?" Sylvie asked.

"Outside." Leah opened the back door. The day had grown darker than ever. Her hand automatically went to the light switch. The outside light didn't come on. "I thought you was gonna replace this bulb."

"I did," Sylvie said, suddenly alarmed. "I replaced it a week ago."

"Well, it ain't workin' now." Leah tried the switch four or five times.

"It should be."

Standing up on her tippy-toes, Leah's fingertips touched the bottom of the bulb and slowly screwed it into the socket. After about two turns, it came right on. "It wasn't screwed in." Hesitantly, she looked at Sylvie.

Sylvie's eyes were wide. "I screwed it in. Believe me. I screwed it in all the way. Somebody unscrewed it!"

"I believe you."

"No you don't."

"Actually, I do."

Sylvie fell quiet. "Who would unscrew my lightbulb?"

"I don't know." A swarm of fruit flies were gathered around the back porch. "I also have no idea where these flies are comin' from, but you have a ton of 'em."

Obviously shaken up because of the bulb, Sylvie said, "Why don't you forget about the flies for now and come sit down and ask me whatever you want to ask me?"

"Okay."

Taking one last look at the bulb, Leah locked the door and turned off the light. She returned to her chair.

"Would you like a coffee?" Sylvie asked.

"No, I'm fine."

A moment went by while Leah gathered her thoughts.

"Well . . . ?" Sylvie asked.

"I don't know how to ask you these questions without potentially bringing up bad memories for you."

Sylvie looked at her. "Don't worry about my memories. They're always there and they're always bad."

"How do you deal with that?"

"I just *have* to. If not for me, then for the baby. Go ahead. Please? Especially if you think it will help figure out who's been in my backyard."

Leah took a deep breath and slowly let it out. "Okay. Here goes then. I need you to talk to me 'bout your pa. What do you remember 'bout him?"

The fingers of Sylvie's left hand began rubbing the fingers of her right. "You mean in general?"

"To start, sure."

"He was a good man. He made sure we had food and stuff. He loved my ma."

"What 'bout you? Did he love you?"

Something flashed in Sylvie's eyes. "Of course! What kind of question is that?"

"I'm only askin' cuz you left yourself out just now when you answered. And Caleb? He loved Caleb of course, too?"

Leah watched Sylvie's reaction and thought mentioning Caleb so early on may have been a bad idea. She thought Sylvie was about to break down, but somehow she managed to hold it together after a bit. "He took Caleb's death the worst. I think he would've rather seen anyone else go but his little boy." Her eyes refused to meet Leah's gaze.

"I don't think that's true," Leah said.

"What part?"

"All of it. First, I think *you* took your brother's death the worst. Look how it's still affectin' you. And second, I don't think he'd want to see any of his family die."

Finally, Sylvie looked up at Leah. "He killed himself because of what happened over Caleb. I didn't do that. I *couldn't* do that. I'd be too . . . scared."

Leah reached out and touched Sylvie's hand. "That's not fear, Sylvie. That's strength. Don't confuse the two."

"And he was the one always askin' me if I was okay. Kept askin' if I needed to talk to somebody about it."

"Talk to somebody? You mean like—"

"Like a professional. Like a shrink or somethin'. He told me that could really help."

"It probably could've," Leah said. "It probably *still* could."

"Well, I don't know about that. When he'd say it back then, I'd just get mad and ask him what the hell he knew about what helps with anythin' cuz all I hear at night is him cryin' himself to sleep cuz he lost his little boy." Her eyes grew wet.

"Have you ever *tried* talkin' to anybody?"

Sylvie hesitated. "Not really."

"Not really? Or not at all?"

"Well, I saw this psychologist for a while right before I met Orwin. I only saw him three or four times. I was goin' through a rough patch at school. He didn't help. He thought all my problems were cuz of Caleb when they were all cuz of school. All he wanted to talk 'bout was Caleb. I went to talk 'bout school."

Leah pulled out her pad. "Can you give me the name of the psychologist?"

"I can't remember. He was provided through assistance. Langwood or Langdon or somethin' like that. I was just comin' outta foster care at the time."

Leah wrote these names on her pad.

"You ain't gonna talk to him, are you?"

"Would it be okay if I did?"

Sylvie thought about it a moment then shrugged. "I guess. We didn't really talk 'bout nothin'."

"And he was here in Alvin?"

"No, Satsuma."

"Okay, thanks." Leah put her pad back in her pocket.

A silence fell over the table for a few moments, finally broken by Sylvie. Leah noticed she'd become more and more open with her. Probably, Leah thought, because she had grown to trust her. "You know, there were many times I wished it was me instead of Caleb that Preacher Eli shot that evenin'."

"I think that's normal."

"Sure didn't *feel* normal.

"Anyway," Sylvie said, "now that Pa's gone, I feel so bad 'bout all those mean things I said. I wish I had the chance to take 'em all back."

Leah locked fingers with Sylvie. "Oh, honey, I'm sure he understood. He was goin' through the same things you were."

Sylvie went quiet for a long while. When she spoke again, she said, "I guess in the end he proved I was right: He really didn't know how to make things easier. If he did, maybe he'd still be here."

"You can't think that way. You'll eat yourself up with the maybes and the guesses. Things are as they are. Everythin' happens for a reason."

"I don't believe that." Sylvie had let go of Leah's hand and was now looking at her fingers while they drummed on the table. "If you believe that, you have to believe God has a sick sense of humor. I want to believe God didn't play any part in what happened to my family. That He somehow managed to stay out of it, and I'll still find them one day when I leave this place and everything will make sense. But it's so hard to keep any faith sometimes."

"Do you go to church?"

Sylvie laughed. "Haven't done so in a long while."

"You should come with us sometime. We try to attend regularly." Truth be told, Leah's "regular" church attendance was more sporadic than she liked to admit. But she considered herself a God-fearing Christian woman just the same.

Sylvie laughed some more.

"I'm serious. Why are you laughing?"

"I have a baby. What would I do with her while I was in church?"

"Babies are allowed in church. There's lots of them there."

"Well, we'll have to see."

Leah gave her a warm smile. "Think 'bout it."

Sylvie looked into her lap and fell silent.

"Do you mind if I keep askin' questions?" Leah asked.

Sylvie shook her head silently.

"Did your pa ever do anythin' or act in any way that was unusual?"

Yet another laugh escaped Sylvie's lips. "He was the opposite of unusual. His world ran by his habits. He kept them up all the time. Out in the fields by six, Mother had breakfast on the table for him at eight; she had lunch ready at noon sharp. Twice a week he'd drive down to Mobile for supplies and things like that." She'd left out supper from her list of meals, and Leah figured, despite what she'd said about memories, there were some she really wanted to keep suppressed. Suppers were probably high on that list.

"Sounds like a good life."

"I don't know if he'd agree," Sylvie said. "Like I told you, he wasn't happy. He lost a lot. Then he finally gave up on it all, including me."

Leah sighed. She had no idea how to respond to something like that. There were some wounds that would just never heal, and nothing she could say was going to alter that.

She decided to change the subject. "Did he ever . . . *buy* things? For you and your family? Expensive things? Jewelry, maybe? Did you go on vacations? Anything like that?" Leah actually felt dumb even asking this question.

Sylvie laughed again. The girl could change her demeanor in a heartbeat. "Are you serious? Miss Teal, we lived a very simple life. We was farmers. We didn't ever go *nowhere*. I ain't never been on no vacation in all my life. I don't think I ever owned a piece of jewelry. No, my pa was a very sensible and practical man."

Leah knew in the back of her mind that there was some question to just how sensible he was. He had spent a lot of money on *something,* she just didn't know what, yet. From Sylvie's bedroom down the hall, she heard the baby wake up and start crying.

Sylvie looked at her. "I gotta go see to her."

"Okay, last question. Then I'll let you be. Do you know if your pa had a will?"

Sylvie mulled this over. "To be right honest, I never thought 'bout it. There never seemed to be any point in pursuin' somethin' like that and I'da thought if there had been one, someone woulda said somethin'. Ain't like we had nothin' anyway." Sylvie said most of this sentence as she walked away from Leah, leaving the kitchen and heading down the hall toward the cries of the baby.

Leah made a mental note to do a search for a will left by Tom Carson.

Sylvie returned with the baby on her breast, happily suckling away. Once again, Leah was impressed with how much of a good mother she'd become, given all the weaknesses she'd been handed in life. "You had a ranch, Sylvie," Leah said. "That was worth somethin'."

"Now what would I do with a ranch?"

She had a point, Leah guessed. "Listen, Sylvie. I want to thank you for takin' the time to talk to me."

Sylvie looked at her expectantly. "Will this help with anythin'?"

"I dunno yet. But I'm not givin' up until things make sense to *me*. So we're on the same team. Remember that, okay?"

"Okay."

Leah headed back out into the rain and got into her car. She drove toward home, both happy and frustrated. Happy that Sylvie was able to answer her questions without it causing her much undue duress, and frustrated because her answers hadn't seemed to answer anything. By Sylvie's account, Tom Carson was an ordinary man who had extraordinary things happen to him. If this turned out to be true, based on Leah's detective background, this would make him the exception to a very rigid rule.

CHAPTER 18

The property report Leah requested from the Mobile public records office finally arrived. Strangely, Abe had gotten the mail that day and had it sitting waiting for her on the kitchen table when she got home from work. For the past few days, Abe had been getting the mail every day. She was surprised at this new interest for him. Until now, he'd never paid much attention to the mail. Leah found his sudden concern over it weird, given that he didn't get any mail himself.

Oh, well, she thought, opening the manila envelope. *Kids go through phases. Be happy it's just mail he's interested in, Leah, and not something like setting fire to the house.*

She pulled the report from the envelope. There wasn't much there, just seven photocopied pages. One was a recent property assessment notice. The next five pages matched the survey maps she found in the Alvin records office exactly, right down to having "Unlisted" as the owner. She was starting to get very frustrated until she came to the final sheet.

This one was different. It wasn't a map. It was a page of information and history about the property, showing all the buying, selling, and any liens that were against it over the past thirty years.

Thirty years ago, the property was listed as vacant, which, the clerk at the records office had told Leah, is the usual way of saying it simply belonged to the county. "So there goes your poppa's claim 'bout ownin' it, Eli," Leah said quietly.

Then on July 8, 1963, the property was sold to Tom Carson for nine thousand dollars, which exactly matched what both Eli Brown and Tom Carson had reported to the police during their interviews after Caleb was killed.

For all Tom Carson's financial problems, the report showed no liens against the property the entire time it was in his possession. In fact, the report was strangely quiet until January 25, 1981. The ranch was then sold at auction by the Alvin First National Bank and purchased by a Mr. Argo Atkinson for $34,000 even.

Leah flipped back to the survey maps and checked the little box in the lower right corner. "Not a bad price for a ranch that would be assessed at one hundred and twenty thousand dollars barely a month later, Mr. Atkinson," she said. "Whoever you are."

How did he manage to buy it so low? Had nobody else been interested in it? Maybe the two strange back-to-back deaths of Sylvie's folks had everyone spooked about the place. People could be weird that way. Leah bet the bank was a bit peeved. They wouldn't have gotten back near the money Tom Carson had owed them from that sale.

She'd never heard the name Atkinson before, but a question still hung in Leah's mind. Why had he bought the place? Was it as an investment? Had he just planned to sit on it? He was paying tax every year on that land—at the *appraised* cost—and yet it just sat there. Nothing had been done to it in the eight years since Tom Carson died. Other than the ravages of time and storms, everything was exactly as it had been that day. Or at least it was last time Leah checked.

Surely this Argo Atkinson had some plan for the property when he initially bought it. Could his plans have somehow gone wrong?

She found the last value that the property was appraised at:

405 Bogpine Way, Alvin, AL 36573
$240,000.00
320 Acre Property (Cattle Ranch)
Owner: Mr. Argo Atkinson.
Mon. 4 Jan. 1988 08:00:00

It was the same parcel of land. Three hundred and twenty acres. It hadn't been broken up at all. And Argo Atkinson had made near on a quarter of a million dollars on his investment in eight years. That wasn't too bad, in Leah's eyes. So maybe it *was* just an investment.

But it had been a while since she'd been out to the ranch, so maybe things had changed since she was there last. Perhaps it was time for Leah to make another visit to 405 Bogpine Way. In the meantime, she was going to have Chris try to figure out who this Atkinson fellow was. She decided she'd radio him on her way out, and ask him to search the Alvin directory for anyone with that name. She doubted an outsider would be much interested in a ranch here in a small town like Alvin. Especially one, as her son had so eloquently put it, so close to a bog full o' stinky old toads.

The Carson Cattle Ranch (as it used to be known) was pretty much exactly as Leah expected to find it. At least it appeared that way from where she parked on the dirt drive leading up to the old farmhouse. Wildflowers and grass had taken over all of it that they could, but otherwise the place was just the way Tom Carson left it.

The steel gate at the street that ran between two wooden fence posts had broken from its hasp, so it was easy enough to swing out of the way so she could drive inside. The gate was flaked with dark red rust and squeaked as she pushed it open. Leah drove inside and parked at the end of the drive, staying close to Bogpine Way.

It had continued raining the past two days, although not nearly as hard as it had on that first day after the period of all the sunshine. Today there was a slight drizzle in the air and the cloud layer floated high in the sky, giving everything above the horizon a gunmetal-gray backdrop. The wind Leah had trudged through the other day when she drove out to Sylvie's was gone. Now it just felt wet and muggy with a slight mist that hung along the sloping ground.

Getting out of the car, Leah pulled the hood of her sweatshirt up and walked to the farmhouse.

The first thing she noticed was the smell. It was wafting down from Beemer's Bog like sulfuric acid. It was the sort of thing she doubted she could ever get used to. The second thing she noticed was the sounds of the toads. It wasn't even late spring when you expected a lot of toads. Beemer's Bog had to be a quarter mile from where she was and still all she could hear was them toads croaking. She couldn't imagine what the stench and sounds must be like if you went to the end of the property line where it came right up against the edge of the bog itself.

She was starting to see why there might not have been a lot of interest in purchasing this place at auction way back when this Argo Atkinson fellow basically stole it.

The farmhouse was built from timber that had weathered over time. It was gray, but then it had been gray even in Tom Carson's time—it had never been painted. She tried the front door and found it unlocked.

Stepping inside, she pulled off her hood as she came in through the living room, the same way Eli Brown must've entered on that fateful evening when everything changed for the Carson family. Leah could only imagine what it must've felt like sitting up at that kitchen table (which had long since been replaced by a new one, now covered with a layer of dust) while that old man trudged across the floor in his muddy boots with that gun in his hand.

Leah came up the short bank of stairs to the kitchen. Even though there was no blood left in that room, the shadows of death still remained. They ran through the cracks in the floorboards like Caleb's blood had that day Eli Brown had come. In Leah's head, his gunshot rang out, echoing through the kitchen, filling the darkened halls and winding its way up the stairs to the lonely bedrooms.

She saw the chair—not the same chair, mind you—but a chair in the same place Tom Carson had sat with his son in his lap when that bullet had left Eli's gun. She knew the scene by heart. She knew Sylvie had been seated to Tom's right, facing the doorway. She knew that Mother had been across the table from her husband, unable to do anything but look on in horror as her baby was taken away from her much too early.

Too many people knew about what had happened and, once again, Leah was beginning to see why Mr. Argo Atkinson got such a deal on this place. Who would buy a property with a farmhouse still full of the stench of death and its wicked memory? It lay everywhere she looked even though there were no physical signs of it at all. You could just *feel* it somehow. Something about the place wasn't right.

She suddenly wasn't sure she wanted to meet this Mr. Atkinson after all. She also wasn't sure she wanted to continue on through the rest of this house.

Strengthening her resolve, Leah stayed inside and began exploring the different rooms. The dust that had covered the kitchen table and countertops continued on, covering everything. She could taste it in the air. Corners were tangled with cobwebs. The farmhouse now belonged to nature and to its own past. It didn't feel like it had any place in time anymore.

At the top of a narrow staircase that led to the upper floor, Leah discovered Sylvie's room. It was exactly as Sylvie had left it when they'd found her pa hanged from the oak and put her into foster care. Most of Sylvie's things were still here. Her closet even had clothes hanging in it, unused for years. Little girls' clothes. Sundresses and pink and yellow things that were never to be worn again.

Leah found it all very sad. Something about the room just cried out loneliness. It was as though it was lost in its own shadows and engulfed in its own memories. Leah couldn't stay any longer in it and moved on through the house.

Next, she came upon the Carsons' bedroom and found it very stark and cold. It was a room that didn't feel like it could contain any love. She wondered if it ever had.

Caleb's room was a different story altogether. Like Sylvie's it still contained pieces of a childhood lost. There were toys in a toy box that would never again be played with. There were clothes in a chest that would never again be worn. But Caleb had died nine years before Tom Carson hanged himself.

So what did that mean?

This room had been kept as a living memory to a son the Carsons could never get back. They hadn't been able to let Caleb go, and now Leah wondered how much of this room was currently taking up Sylvie Carson's mind. Surely it couldn't have been easy living with this constant reminder of what had happened right beside where she slept every night. It had to take its toll. Sometimes, the best of intentions turn out to do the most damage. This was something Leah was learning all too well.

On top of the chest of drawers were dusty old photos of little Caleb in frames. Some of him playing with Sylvie, some of him out on the farm. In each one, he had a great big smile on his face.

Leah had noticed no such pictures in either of the other two bedrooms.

After seeing Caleb's room, Leah decided she'd been through enough of the farmhouse and went back outside. Deciding the rain had pretty much gone away, she opted to leave the hood of her sweatshirt down. The air still felt wet and, along with the scent of the bog, the gentle wind carried the smell of the woods.

She walked to the barn. She knew this area well. She had been called in when Tom Carson's wife was found dead in a horse stall. The stalls still looked the same to Leah as they had that day, only now there were no flies. There was nothing. Just a stillness. The hay still lay scattered across the wooden slatted floor. The white boards of the stalls still stood with marks where the horses' tack had run ridges into them. But no horses had been here for eight years.

She left the barn and walked out through the fields. First the horse field then on into the cattle field. Both fields and the entire property were surrounded by a white wooden fence made from three horizontal boards running between fence posts. The fence still stood, but much of it had fallen. Eight years of being ravaged by storms had taken its toll. In places, just individual boards were missing. In other places, entire sections had blown down, leaving gaps like missing teeth. Leah took advantage of these spaces to avoid any climbing. She kept going until she came to the woods on the other side of the cattle field.

And soon, there it was. The oak tree Tom Carson was found hanging from.

She remembered coming to the crime scene that day not really knowing what to expect and nearly getting sick at the sight of what awaited her. She could still see marks around the bough where the rope had been looped overtop. *Some marks never go away.*

The clouds overhead broke apart, revealing a watery afternoon sun. Leah stared at that oak for some time, not knowing what compelled her to keep looking at it. But it wasn't until the sun began dropping that she started back for her car. The whole time she'd been standing at that tree, she'd been lost in thoughts of things that hadn't crossed her mind for some time. Thoughts of her dead husband, Billy. Thoughts of her children. Thoughts of Sylvie and the baby. Thoughts of her own pa.

And strangely, while she had stood there, she had forgotten all about the terrible smell of the bog and hadn't heard the incessant croaking of toads.

Getting back into her car, she pulled out onto Bogpine Way and headed home. The road obviously got its name from the bog and the fact that tall, spindly pines lined either side of it. It was a curvy road that ran right up and out of Alvin if one kept going north past the Carson Cattle Ranch. But now she was headed south, back down toward town. Back toward life.

Her radio crackled. It was Chris. He was reporting back about his attempts to find this Argo Atkinson.

"Hey, Chris," Leah said. "Give me some good news."

"Afraid I can't. There's no Argo Atkinson living in Alvin or no Atkinson of any variety that I can find."

"What about other cities nearby? Can you try them?"

"Already have. Satsuma's a bust, and so is Atmore. I checked all the smaller directories. They came up blank. Conecuh County, though, they got Atkinsons, let me tell you. Got a Thelma Atkinson out in Castleberry, but I called her and she doesn't have any recollection of bein' related to nobody by the name of Argo. Same goes for Gus Atkinson in Evergreen. Ditto for Art Atkinson in McKenzie and Daisy Luanne Atkinson in Repton. No Argos. No relatives named Argo. Same story with Cliff—"

"Okay, Chris, I get your point."

"Ah, good. So, yeah, nothing on Argo Atkinson."

"All right, thanks for tryin' at least."

Leah hung up her radio wondering what her next move should be. Could someone be using the name Argo Atkinson as a pseudonym? Argo was a very uncommon name. You'd think somebody trying to disguise themselves would go for a more everyday-type name. The question she really should be asking herself was: Who would *want* the land? The obvious choice was a conclusion she didn't want to jump to, because it was too easy—and that was Preacher Eli.

Leah didn't want to automatically assume the worst of the man. Yet, Sylvie Carson thought Eli Brown was doing something sneaky and even Leah's own son thought the man was up to no good. Could Leah's gut feeling be wrong this time? Eli Brown had been in prison when Tom Carson died and the ranch was auctioned. Was it possible for the finger of someone like Eli Brown, who once had the power of an entire congregation on his side, to reach beyond the bars of his cell?

Leah Teal was starting to do something she didn't like much at all: She was starting to second guess herself and mistrust her gut.

One thing was certain: This wasn't a good sign.

CHAPTER 19

Leah had just pulled into her driveway back home when her radio went off again. Of course, it was Chris. He was the only one whoever called her on her radio, other than Police Chief Montgomery the odd time.

"Yeah, Chris? What is it? Please tell me you've uncovered Argo Atkinson."

"Nope. But I got another call from Sylvie Carson. This one actually sounded serious."

This got Leah's attention. Outside the car window on her way home, dark, pregnant clouds had rolled in beneath the high ones. The sunset apparently brought them along with it. Dusk looked foreboding, as though the sky was preparing for thundershowers. "What? What did she say?"

"That someone's been in her house."

"*Inside* it?" Sylvie asked. "Are you sure she said *inside*?"

Chris chuckled, but it was a grave chuckle. "Oh, I'm sure, all right. She must've said it ten times in the two-minute phone call. Said somethin' 'bout a shotgun bein' monkeyed with or somethin'. As usual, she was too frantic for me to catch most of it."

The shotgun. The last thing Leah wanted to hear about was that shotgun. She pictured it in her mind, leaning up against the back door, loaded and ready to shoot.

"Okay, I'm on my way," she said.

Leah considered using the siren this time, but traffic wasn't bad at all so there was really no point. Even so, she broke most of the posted speed limits and made it to Sylvie's in what was probably record time. When she pulled up in front she got out of her car and looked up at the sky. The clouds were literally roiling right above her. Black, thick clouds that looked like harbingers of evil.

She hoped they didn't portend that anything horrible was going to be found inside Sylvie's house. Leah still had no idea really what was going on. Just that it had to do with the shotgun and somebody being inside. "Oh dear God," she said quietly. "Please don't let her have shot someone."

The first flash of lightning lit up the western sky somewhere over the ranches on the other side of Alvin just as Leah reached the porch steps. Leah knocked on Sylvie's door. "Sylvie!" she called out. "It's me! Leah! Open up!"

She hadn't bothered with all the formalities this time. She hadn't even thought to bother with them. She was too concerned about that shotgun and what might've happened. And she was concerned about that baby. Obviously, Sylvie was okay. Or, okay enough to make the call into the station, at least.

The door swung open without Sylvie checking through the latch first. "That was quick," she said. Her face had a forced-calm yet panicked look to it that Leah hadn't quite seen before.

"What's happened?" Leah asked. Just as she did, the low rumble of thunder swept across the sky. It sounded quite a ways off.

Lightning flashed across the sky three times.

"Gonna be a helluva storm," Sylvie said, her voice matching her face.

"Sylvie?" Leah asked. "What happened? You told Chris someone's been inside your house."

She nodded. "Someone has been. Come in."

Leah came in. She went to take off her shoes but Sylvie stopped her. "Don't. I don't care 'bout a little mud. This is too important. You have to see this while it's still here."

What did she mean by that? *While it's still here?* "Okay . . . ," Leah said. She followed Sylvie into the kitchen where the shotgun still leaned against the door like it always did. Leah was just about to ask her what the hell she was supposed to be looking at, when she saw it: five 12-gauge shotgun shells lined up in a straight row along the top of the kitchen table.

Leah's eyes quickly went straight to Sylvie's. "Where did they come from?"

"They was in the shotgun."

"Who took 'em out?"

"Whoever was in my house."

Sylvie's eyes were still locked on Leah's. If the girl had blinked, Leah missed it.

"Okay, you need to tell me more. What the hell's goin' on?"

"Me and the baby were out shoppin'. We just went down to Finnegan's at Finley's."

Finnegan's at Finley's was Finnegan's Five and Dime. It was located at Finley's Crossing about a half mile from where Sylvie lived, so it got the nickname Finnegan's at Finley's. "You walk down?" Leah asked.

"Yeah, I ain't got no car."

"You carry the baby?"

"No, I brought the stroller."

"Didn't know you had one."

"I got one. Salvation Army donated it. It ain't the greatest, but it works well enough."

"Okay, so you walked to Finnegan's. Then what? Wait, did you lock the door before you left?"

Frustration flickered in Sylvie's eyes. "Of course I locked the door 'fore I left. I always lock my door. And my windows. I checked every one an' they was all locked. An' when I got home, they was *still* all locked. Every door and every window."

Concern fell over Leah. "Okay, so you walked to Finnegan's. Continue your story."

"I bought some milk and some juice and some eggs. Then we walked back."

A pocket of silence followed. "And then . . . ?" Leah asked.

"And then I came home and found the shells sittin' here just like this. I was careful not to touch nothin'. I called the police station right away."

"You *sure* you didn't touch anything?"

"I searched the goddamn house and made sure nobody was still here. That's what I did as soon as I hung up. I'm not stayin' in no house with my baby that might have some killer in it!"

Leah held up her hand. "Good," she said calmly. "That's good. You did the right thing. Now I want you to think back. Are you absolutely *sure* you didn't touch any of these shells or the gun or the table or nothin'?"

"Yeah," Sylvie said. "Of course I'm sure. Why? You think I did this and I'm lyin' 'bout it?"

"No, Sylvie. Not at all. I think we might be able to get prints off the shells."

"Oh." Sylvie finally broke her stare and looked away. "As long as you don't think I'm lyin'."

"Where *is* the baby?" Leah asked.

"Still in the stroller. She's in the bedroom. I checked the window. It's locked with a stick in it. Nobody is comin' in there. She was up all mornin'. Just fell asleep on the way home. She needs to nap."

"Go check on her."

"Why?" Sylvie asked, suddenly losing any trace of calmness from her face.

"Just to make me happy."

While she was gone, Leah took the opportunity to look around the rest of the house, making sure that Sylvie was right, and if anyone had been inside they weren't here any longer. She checked the pantry in the kitchen and the closet in the hall. Everything looked deserted. The rooms were all empty. The back door was locked.

Sylvie came back a few minutes later. "She's still sleepin'. You had me scared outta my wits."

"Sorry. Just my mother's instinct kickin' in. I have to go out to my car and radio Chris to come with the fingerprintin' kit. You okay here by yourself a few minutes?"

"Yeah. Don't you think I am?"

"I think you are. I just did a search of the premises. There ain't nobody here no more."

"I know. I already told you, I checked."

Outside, the storm had grown. Fork lightning cracked open the sky above Leah's head just as her foot hit the top step leading down the porch. It was followed quickly by the clap of thunder before she even made it to the car. Then the sky opened up and rain began washing down in one big wave. She pulled the hood of her sweatshirt up tight, but it was already too late. She could feel how wet her hair was underneath.

Inside her car, she radioed Chris back at the station and told him what she'd found at the scene.

"Are you serious?" Chris asked. "Is there any chance Sylvie did this and just doesn't remember?"

"Chris, she's never done things and not remembered before. I think we have to take this seriously. I want you to bring the printing kit. She says she hasn't touched anything. We might be able to lift somethin' from those shells."

"All right. Have you looked outside? It's crazy."

"I'm out in it now."

"All hell's breaking loose."

"Don't I know it."

CHAPTER 20

Back in the house, Leah did remove her shoes this time. They were completely covered in mud dredged up from all the rain splatter. Lightning spiked so brightly, Leah would catch it out of the corner of her eye, illuminating things in an iridescent glow. Thunder continued booming, at times so loud it felt like the house would shake apart.

Sylvie's hands trembled. She was pacing. Leah hoped this incident wasn't going to set her back years of development. She wondered how fragile the girl really was. Sometimes she seemed as breakable as a ceramic doll.

"You okay?" Leah asked her.

Sylvie nodded, and then said quietly, "It's just the storm. I've never liked lightning storms ever since what happened."

"I understand," Leah said. She could imagine that each time that thunder boomed it echoed in Sylvie's mind the way that gunshot had rung out in her kitchen right before supper that evening. Leah needed to take Sylvie's mind off the storm. Luckily, she still had some questions that needed answering.

"So, how did they get in?" Leah asked.

"Who?"

"Whoever emptied the shotgun."

"I'm assumin' through the door."

"You said you locked it when you left."

"I always lock my doors. And my windows. But there were no windows busted when I got home, so I assume they somehow got in through a door."

"Was the door still locked when you came back?"

"Yeah. I already told you that, too."

Leah thought about this. "Get your locks changed tomorrow. If you need some money, I can lend it to you." But her thoughts continued lingering on who could get into a locked building. Picking locks seemed like the sort of skill you might learn after seventeen-odd years in prison.

"How's that gonna help if they didn't need keys this time?"

"I dunno," Leah said honestly, "but it certainly won't hurt."

"I don't feel safe," Sylvie said. Her eyes had widened. Leah could now see that fear had replaced most of the panic.

Leah gave Sylvie a hug. "Listen. So far, it's all been harassment. If they can get into the house, then they could've already hurt you if they wanted to, so obviously they don't want to. Someone's just out to scare you."

"Well, they're doin' a fine job o' it."

Sylvie began to quietly sob into Leah's shoulder. Leah considered what she had just told her and wondered how true it was. The harassment (if it all *had* been harassment) was ramping up. Was she *really* not in any danger? Leah didn't honestly know. "Is there . . . do you have anywhere you and the baby could go? A friend's place, maybe? The home of a relative? Just until things simmer down a bit for you?"

Panic rose in Sylvie's eyes. "You really think I'm in danger."

"No, I'm just tryin' to err on the side of caution, is all," Leah lied.

Sylvie scanned the floor. "I ain't got no place to go. All my relatives are dead, and I ain't got no friends."

Once again, Sylvie had managed to break Leah's heart. It seemed to happen more often than not lately. And as much as Leah hated to admit it, her gut feeling was starting to shift. Things were beginning to feel more and more like Eli Brown might be behind something after all.

* * *

Chris showed up at the door carrying the fingerprinting kit and looking like a drowned rat. His eyes were glued skyward when Sylvie opened the door. Thunder rattled the house as he came inside. Leah showed him the shells lined up on the kitchen table.

"That's so weird," he said.

"Wanna hear somethin' weirder?" Leah asked. "No sign of forcible entry. No broken windows. Doors were locked when Miss Sylvie left and they was still locked when she returned."

He looked at her. "So the lock was picked?"

"That's what I'm thinkin'."

"Who would go to all the trouble of pickin' her lock just to empty her shotgun and leave the shells all tidy like this on the table?"

Leah let out a big sigh. "When we get back to the station I want you to get as much information on Preacher Eli Brown as you can. If that man so much as took an unscheduled crap in the woods while he was in prison, I want to know 'bout it."

Lightning lit up the backyard as, right behind it, another thunderous roar shook the world.

"Shouldn't we try to lift any prints before jumpin' to conclusions like that?" Chris asked.

"You're right. Get the prints. But I have serious doubts anything's gonna show up."

Turned out Officer Chris Jackson was able to lift a set of prints from the shells on Sylvie Carson's table. Each shell had one and only one set of prints on it and the same ones were on each shell—and they all belonged to Miss Sylvie.

"Figured as much," Leah said. Her and Chris were back at the station. "Anyone knowin' enough to get in and out of that house without showin' any sign of physical entry ain't 'bout to leave behind stupid evidence like fingerprints."

"Guess you were right," Chris said. "I suppose it's time for plan B?"

"If plan B involves seeing how Eli Brown fits into all this, then you're absolutely right in tune with my way of thinking," Leah said.

CHAPTER 21

I had been checking the mail before my mother could get to it every single day since me and Dewey went to the records office on our own and the lady made the call to her friend for more information about my family's history records. Mainly I was doing it on account of I didn't know how my mother would react to me going there behind her back. Her temper could be a mite unpredictable at times.

It wasn't always easy getting to the mail first. There were days the mail lady practically drove up and handed the mail right to my mother because my mother happened to be outside in the driveway. In fact, on two occasions when that happened I just braced myself and prayed that those weren't the days my information decided to arrive.

I got lucky. They weren't.

When my records finally did come, they turned up on a day my mother was at work. This made everything really simple and allowed me lots of time. As soon as I saw it, I knew the big yellow envelope was for me. Stuffed in our mailbox, it didn't even fit without the mail lady having to nearly bend it in half to get it in.

Sure enough, when I pulled it out, there was my name right on the front: *Abe Teal*. And, in the top left corner, was the name and address of the historian lady: *Miss Dixie Spinner* with an address in Chickasaw, Alabama. Excited, I rushed inside, happy my mother would be at work at least another four hours. This gave me a *ton* of time to go through all the information without even having to be sneaky about it.

I carefully opened the envelope using the silver letter opener my mother got as a gift from my uncle Henry one year for Christmas. She rarely used it, but I wanted to be sure not to rip any of the papers inside.

I pulled out a bundle of pages. There were some loose sheets on top and then some stapled together. I looked at the top one. On a small card, paper-clipped to the corner, was a note:

> *Dear Abe,*
> *I hope you find this information useful.*
> *It's nice to know young people are taking*
> *an interest in their family histories.*
> *If there's anything else I can do for you,*
> *please give me a call.*
> *Miss Dixie Spinner*

She even gave me her phone number. I couldn't believe how nice some people could be. Historians seemed especially nice to me.

Unclipping the card, I set it aside and started looking through the top sheets that were not stapled together. They had been put in separate. There were quite a few. At least a half a dozen.

I got really excited then. I wondered what kind of information I was about to find out. Obviously, there was a lot more here than just the names and birthdays of my parents and my grandparents like they had at the records office downtown.

The first page was more or less all about me. It said *Vital Statistics* at the top and listed things like my birthday and exactly where I was born and even had the time of my birth. I wondered if my *mother* even remembered that. I thought it was pretty neat that I now knew exactly when I was born right down to the minute.

Farther on, it showed that I'd lived in Alvin in this same house all my life and it showed the address. I began to realize that if they showed this much information for everyone, there might not be any more people listed in this package other than my parents and grandparents on all these pages after all.

Then it displayed my immediate family. Unlike the records office on Main Street, it had Carry (along with her birth date) included, and my mother and my pa. It not only showed my pa's birthday, but also said *Deceased* after his name and had the date he died and a small explanation: *Death due to motor vehicle accident.*

Then, at the bottom of the page, it said: *Teal and Fowler references supplied under separate cover.*

I didn't quite know what that meant, but I put down the first page and was surprised by the second. It was a listing of all the Teals, going back about one hundred and fifty years. And each one had extra information, like children and birthdays and how they died, and anything else pertinent. Right at the top of the list was me!

Teal, Abe
 Born: March 26, 1976
 Sister: Caroline Josephine
 Mother: Leah Marie Fowler

Teal, William Robert
 Born: May 7, 1955
 Sister: Addison May
 Mother: Sara Lynn Harris
 Deceased: July 3, 1978
 Death due to motor vehicle accident.

Teal, Jeremiah
 Born: September 1, 1936
 Son: William Robert (Deceased)
 Mother: Rebekah Davis (Deceased. *Heart failure*)

Teal, John Owen
 Born: February 24, 1912

Son:	Jeremiah
Daughter:	Francine (Deceased)
Brother(s):	Mark Lee (Deceased)
	Paul Adam (Deceased)
Sister:	Lily Jude (Deceased)
Mother:	Lily Anne Kendricks (Deceased)

And so the list went on, going back to 1842. Everyone from John Owen Teal down was dead. Some had up to nine brothers and sisters, and some had none. I read them all, fascinated to find out I was related to so many people I had known nothing about.

And this was just on my daddy's side.

I came to the last one, right at the bottom:

Teal, Isaac Jacob Lee

Born:	June 12, 1842
Son:	Jacob Lee (Deceased)
Brother:	Joseph Matthew Isaiah (Deceased)
Mother:	Martha Christina Franklin (Deceased)

Then it had two words beneath that, before several paragraphs of stuff. And those two words were:

<CHART, cont.>
Historical Significance.

It turns out I was related to somebody really important after all! My great-great-great-great-great-grandpa won a major Medal of Honor for freeing a bunch of slaves during the Civil War.

I had to call Dewey and tell him.

"What did he do?" Dewey asked after answering the phone. He only seemed half interested, which bothered the heck out of me.

"He freed *slaves,* Dewey. There ain't much that's more important than that. Remember all that stuff my mom told us about racism? My great-great-great-great-great-grandpa fought against racism a hundred an' fifty years ago."

"What'd he do?"

"Well, accordin' to this paper in front of me he did lots. There's so much information 'bout it that it runs onto the next page. You want me to read it to you?"

"Can you just give me the general idea?"

"Well, it happened up in Georgia, right after the Union navy took over some port."

"Which port?"

"Doesn't say, but some port close to Fort Pulaski."

"What's that?"

"A fort, Dewey. What do you think it is?"

"What kind of fort?"

"The kind you fight from. This was during the Civil War."

"Oh, you didn't tell me that part."

"I reckoned you could figure that out for yourself. Anyway, I guess Fort Pulaski was an important target, but the Union hadn't hit it yet; they'd only taken the port. That's when my great-great-great-great-great-"—I was running out of breath sayin' all them greats—"grandpa walked right up to the door of one of those old plantations. He was carryin' nothin' but a couple of pistols and, I suppose, he just let himself in."

"You mean the door was unlocked?"

"I don't rightly know, Dewey. It don't actually say. Maybe he knocked. I dunno. Whatever happened, he demanded that the owner free all the black folk he'd been keepin' as slaves."

"What did the owner say?" Now Dewey sounded more interested.

"He said he didn't like people tellin' him what to do, is my guess," I said. "All it says here is that a gunfight broke out inside that plantation between my grandpa from a hundred fifty years back and a half dozen other folk who either owned the plantation or worked for the guy who did."

"So your however many greats grandpa was a Union soldier?"

"No, that's just it. He was a Confederate. I suppose he just didn't agree with slavery. That's the part that makes him a hero."

"Did he die?"

"No. In the end, it says, and I'm reading it straight off the paper now, Isaac Jacob Lee Teal won his battle and walked out the front door of that big white house with one hundred and ten black men jumpin' up and down around and behind him, all hootin' and a-hollerin'." I actually embellished that a little for Dewey's sake.

"That's what it says in the records you got?"

"Well," I admitted, "not quite. I made it more dramatic."

"So what happened next?"

"The next day the same Union navy that took the port attacked Fort Pulaski. They had more soldiers and better guns and the fort surrendered within a day. But word 'bout my ancestral grandpa must've spread because he came marching toward the captured fort, over the hills and through the trees with all the black men still following him."

"Why was they still followin' him?"

"Guess they didn't know where else to go. Will you quit interruptin'?"

"Okay."

"Anyway, the Union navy captain didn't arrest my great-great-great-great-great-grandpa. Instead they allowed him on board their ships and made him an honorary Union soldier. He was even given a medal for what he done and everythin'."

There was a bit of a pause, then Dewey said, "So your great-great-great-great-great-grandpa was a bit of a traitor, you're sayin'."

I got real mad. "No, Dewey. He was a good man who believed everyone should be free."

Dewey laughed. "I'm just kiddin'. I think that's a neat story."

"Me too. I'm real happy I got these records. I can't wait to meet my new grandparents now."

After hanging up the phone, I leafed through the rest of the document. There were other pages listing the line of daughters for the Teals, then these were followed by similar pages for the Fowler lines. All of them went back approximately the same number of years as the first one I had examined.

There were also cross-reference pages showing who married who and things like that, and even a tree structure that kind of explained how all my uncles and aunts and great-uncles and -aunts all connected. A lot of it I couldn't understand very well, but I still found it all very interesting and exciting.

But absolutely none of it compared to the story I'd found about my great-great-great-great-great-grandpa Isaac Jacob Lee Teal.

That man was a true hero.

That's when my sister, Carry, walked into the house, carrying a small plastic shopping bag. I guessed she'd been down at the mall with her friends where she usually hung out. I was about to tell her about Grandpa Isaac Jacob Lee (who was *her* ancestral grandfather, too), but she spoke before I had a chance.

"Come on, ass face, follow me."

"Mom *told* you not to call me that!" I said.

"Whatever." She walked into the living room and turned on the television.

I sat there, thinking I should really go see what she wanted, but then part of me thought I should just stay put, her being so rude and all.

"I told you to come here!" she demanded from the other room.

"Why should I do anything you tell me?" I shouted from the kitchen.

I had forgotten that there actually *was* a reason. The devil pact I'd signed with my sister the day we made the swords had somehow completely slipped my mind. Now it was about to come back and bite me in places it turned out I really didn't like being bitten in.

"Because we have a deal, remember? When we made the swords? Time to pay up."

Curious, I wandered into the living room.

Carry was sitting on the sofa with her socks off and one foot up on the coffee table. In her hand she had a bottle of brand-new purple nail polish. "Today," she said, "you learn how to paint toenails! Aren't you the lucky boy?"

"Uh-uh." I shook my head, slowly backing out of the room.

"Yep. You said *anythin'*. And this falls under anythin'. Now get over here and pay up."

It was horrible, demeaning work, painting Carry's cheesy toes. I kept asking myself: *What would Dewey think if he could see me now?* Every time I tried to speed up the process, she'd slow me down and tell me to make sure I did a good job. When I was finally done with both feet, it was like someone had stopped sticking me with a hot poker. I was so glad to be finished.

I quickly bottled up the polish and handed it to her.

She twisted her foot in the sunlight falling in through the window behind her, looking at her toes gleaming purple in the afternoon light. I had to admit, they didn't look half bad.

"You did all right," she said.

"I'm just happy I'm done."

Then she said something that froze me to my core: "For now."

"What do you mean?" My eyes went wide. My hand trembled.

"You're doin' this every week for the rest of the summer."

"Am not."

"Am too."

"You can't make me."

"You gave me your word. What's Abe Teal's word worth?"

She had me there. My mother had drilled it into my head that you're only as good as your word. I consoled myself with the fact that she'd at least cut the job off at the end of summer.

With a hung head, I slunk back into the kitchen, leaving the smell of fresh nail polish and the sound of canned laughter from the television set in the living room behind me.

CHAPTER 22

The next day, Chris was holding out a report in his hand as Leah took her seat at her desk. "Ask and thou shalt receive," he said.

She looked at him. "Eli?"

He nodded. "Yup."

"Anythin' incriminatin'?"

He gave a little shrug. "I dunno. It just came in 'bout ten minutes ago. I skimmed it. Nothin' stood out at me as bein' particularly nasty. Other than shootin' a three-year-old, but we already knew 'bout that one."

Leah scanned the first page of the report. There were notes from all Eli's parole board hearings. They spilled on to the second and third sheets. "No wonder he got out early," she said. "He was like teacher's pet in prison. I've never seen such nice things said about anyone in one of these things."

Chris had his elbow on his desk with his hand supporting his head. "Maybe our preacher man really done gone an' changed his ways."

Leah flickered her eyes at him above the page she was reading. "Nobody's this nice in prison. Eli was up to somethin'. That's what it tells me."

"Why, Detective Teal, ain't we a mite cynical?"

"No, I'd say I'm a mite realistic. This ain't my first bull ride." She quoted from the page: " 'A strong influence on his peer group with an attitude that's a welcome diversion from the normal dreary and contemptuous one that seems to infiltrate this establishment.' " She laughed. "Of course they're dreary and contemptuous! They're in goddamn prison! What the hell do they expect?"

"Apparently, what they like is someone who is a welcome diversion from that," Chris said. "Someone like Eli Brown."

"I've been to his house. The man was pretty contemptuous to me."

"Actually, he wasn't far off of contemptuous with me, either. Hmm."

"I think we definitely have a suspect," Leah said. She turned the stapled page over and found a page full of basic background information, including priors, education, family records, basic stuff.

She quickly looked it over. Other than the murder of Caleb Carson, it contained nothing unusual, but then she hadn't expected it to. She already knew Eli Brown had no prior run-ins with the law, and the rest of the information was basically useless to her.

Then something caught her eye.

"Whoa, Nelly," she said. "I think we just got ourselves a *Bingo!*"

Chris pulled his chair in close and looked at the page from the side. "What's that?"

"Look under family records," she said. "Check out the name of his deceased wife."

Chris found the part on the page she was referring to and gave a low whistle. "Well, I'll be damned."

There it was, typed right there in black and white:

**Wife: Catherine Anna Brown nee Atkinson (Deceased).
Died 1984 of stroke.**

"I think we just found our link between Sylvie and Eli Brown," Leah said. "I mean other than through little Caleb."

* * *

It took one call to the Alvin public records office to find out that Argo Atkinson was the father of Catherine Atkinson and another call to the Mobile public records office to discover that he was alive and well and living up in Tuscaloosa.

"So, Eli Brown's father-in-law purchased the property as quickly as he could snatch it up after Tom Carson hanged himself," Leah said to Chris after putting down the phone. "It all seems a little too convenient to me."

"Definitely something fishy goin' on."

"I think the reason we haven't seen no development on it is on account of Eli's been in prison up until now. I think he plans to go ahead with that little 'project' of his."

"Could be."

"And you said his grandson was down from Alabaster? I bet that ain't no coincidence either. Did he seem like the business type to you?"

"Hard to tell. He was just wearin' a T-shirt and jeans, but he could be. Probably just got out of college or might still be in college, I dunno."

"I bet he's here to help Eli throw this thing together."

There was a silent spell between them. Outside the window, two yellowhammers dipped in and out of sight.

"Still doesn't tell us why this would amount to Sylvie bein' harassed," Leah finally said.

"That's what I was thinkin'."

"Unless . . ."

"What?"

"Unless they was worried she still had claim to the land."

"That would be impossible. You said the bank put it up for auction. And that was eight *years* ago," Chris said.

"Maybe Eli thinks different."

"Still, what's the point in harassin' her?"

Leah thought this over and shrugged. "Well, if he could get her to the point that she went off the deep end and actually became hospitalized she'd be much less of a threat to anyone. You gotta reckon, if what we's sayin's true, she's gonna have some kinda reaction when he starts buildin' on her daddy's plot of land."

"You reckon?"

"I reckon so. She hates Eli Brown more than anyone. And she probably has every right in the world to."

"So . . . ," Chris said. "What do we do next?"

"That's a good question." Leah drummed her fingers on the desk. Outside a monarch butterfly fluttered among the tops of the hydrangea bushes that barely came up to the bottom of the window. "I suppose we have another talk with our favorite old preacher."

"I was afraid you'd say that. You or me?"

She smiled with a bit of a wicked grin. "Oh, you ain't gettin' this one."

CHAPTER 23

Me and Dewey rode our bikes down Hunter Road and over to Church Street where the Full Gospel Church was. Full Gospel was Alvin's black church, and we'd been there before. I knew Reverend Starks quite well and he always seemed happy to see us when me and Dewey dropped by. Today being a Thursday, I didn't know whether or not he'd be around. Church services were normally held on Wednesdays and Sundays, but I thought Reverend Starks lived in the church so I suspected we might catch him there if we were lucky.

My mother had told me she had asked Sylvie Carson to come to church with us next time we went on account of all the troubles she'd been going through lately. My mother thought it might bring her some comfort. Well, last time I was at Full Gospel, it was during the end of one of their services, and there was so much singing and happiness I couldn't imagine a place more comfortable than that. Certainly not Clover Creek First Baptist where we usually went. I had nothing against Reverend Matthew, but his sermons could put a gerbil with a sugar rush to sleep.

So, even though it was a black church, I was going to ask Reverend Starks if it was okay for us to come. Especially given what my great-great-great-great-great-granddaddy did for him and his people.

I hadn't mentioned any of this to my mother yet. I figured I'd wait and see if I could get permission from Reverend Starks first and then surprise her with it. This didn't seem like the sort of surprise that I'd get reprimanded for. Although, when I thought it through now, I realized if I included the part about my ancestry it was going to cause some complications to the story.

The church was an old wooden building painted white and had square stained-glass windows. It looked similar to Clover Creek First Baptist where we normally went, only Full Gospel was an older building and wasn't taken care of as well as Clover Creek. I don't think it was because anyone purposely neglected it, I think it was more on account of they didn't have the money to paint it as often or to put in as many gardens around it, and stuff like that. The paint on the boards was starting to come off. It definitely could use a new coat.

The church door was closed as me and Dewey rode our bikes into the churchyard and up to the entrance.

"So what do we do?" Dewey asked. "Knock? Or just see if it's unlocked and go inside?"

"I dunno," I said. I had no idea of the etiquette of what to do at church when it wasn't in service. "I suppose knocking can't hurt."

We set our bikes down on the ground and, with swords at our sides, climbed the steps to the church doors and knocked on them. Because they were made of thick, heavy wood, our knocks were not very loud.

We waited for a while, but nobody answered.

"I don't think he heard us. Try the door," Dewey said.

"You try it," I said.

Slowly, he reached out his hand and grabbed the handle and pulled. Nothing happened. I saw him let out a breath he'd been holding. "They're locked." He sounded relieved.

We tried knocking again, but again our knocks weren't very loud and again nobody came.

"We could try kicking it," Dewey suggested.

I stared at him. "We ain't gonna boot the church door."

"Why not?"

"It's a place of God, Dewey."

"Oh."

He didn't mention kicking it again, so I suppose that was explanation enough.

We stood there another minute until finally I came up with an idea. "You know, if Reverend Starks lives here, he doesn't live in the actual main part of the church. I mean, where would he sleep? In the pews? I bet there's another door in the back. One that goes into the part he lives in."

"That makes sense," Dewey said.

We walked around the church to where four large willows grew, their long branches draping like huge umbrellas with tiny flowers that shook gently in the breeze. One of the willows was close enough that it touched the side of the church.

I'd never noticed before, but the church was actually shaped in an ell. You couldn't really tell from the other side, but another building came off the main one. This building didn't have the stained-glass windows or any of the decorative religious look that the other did. It was just a normal houselike building, with small windows and a small porch. It was white, like the rest of the church, only the trim back here was all done in forest green. If this was where Reverend Starks lived, he had a very small house.

We walked up the two steps to the porch and knocked on the door. This time our knocks sounded like real knocks.

"Coming!" a deep voice called out from somewhere on the other side of the door.

"I hope it's him," Dewey said nervously.

"Who else could it be?" I asked.

A half moment later, Reverend Starks answered the door. Only, he wasn't dressed the way I was accustomed to seeing him. He was dressed like a normal person in dark green pants and a striped shirt. I nearly didn't recognize him until he smiled and I saw his gold-capped tooth. Then I knew it was him. There was no mistaking Reverend Starks's smile or that tooth.

"Abe! What a delightful surprise!" He took my hand in both of his and shook it. "And Dewey . . . right?"

"Yes, sir!" Dewey said, shaking his hand, too.

"What brings you boys round these parts? Been a while since I've seen you."

"I wanted to talk to you 'bout somethin'," I said.

"And he wants to ask you somethin', too," Dewey added.

I glared at him.

"Is that right?" Reverend Starks said. His voice was deep and full. "Well, why don't y'all come inside?" He looked around the yard. The sun glittered off his eyeglasses. "Nice to see the rain's stopped again."

"Yeah," I said.

"Let's hope we get back to that sunny spell we had a week ago," the reverend said. "I was quite enjoyin' that."

"So was we," Dewey said.

Reverend Starks led us through a small kitchen that was very neat and tidy, down a narrow hallway, and into a small parlor that contained a little divan with a floral pattern and two chairs, both upholstered in burgundy, situated around a low cherry table.

"Go ahead, sit wherever you like," Reverend Starks said.

Dewey and I sat beside each other on the divan. "Can I get you boys anything?" the reverend asked from the entranceway into the parlor.

"I'll have some sweet tea," Dewey said.

I glared at him again.

"What 'bout you, Abe?"

"I guess," I said. "Since you're gettin' some anyway."

Reverend Starks went back to the kitchen.

"Why are you askin' him for stuff?" I whispered harshly to Dewey.

"Because he offered."

"He was just bein' polite."

"I really want some tea."

"He didn't *really* want to get you some."

"Actually, I wouldn't have offered if I didn't want to get it," the reverend said, coming back into the room with two glasses of tea. Each had a slice of lemon floating in it. He set them on the table in front of us.

"Thanks," we both said, almost in unison.

Reverend Starks took a seat in the burgundy chair closest to me. "So, what is it exactly you wished to speak with me 'bout, Abe?"

I hesitated. Now that I was here, I wasn't sure how to begin.

"Well . . ." I stumbled. "I . . . um . . ."

"Abe's grandfather from way back freed a bunch of black slaves and he wants to tell you 'bout it," Dewey said after taking a gulp of tea. Then he quickly followed with, "This tea's really good. You make it yourself?"

The reverend laughed. "Yes, I did. So, what's this about your grandfather?"

"Well," I started again after glaring at Dewey for the third time, "my great-great-great-great-great-grandfather was a Confederate soldier who I suppose was actually *against* slavery. And one day after the Union navy took over a port up in Georgia, he marched into a plantation with just two pistols and, after winning a gunfight against six men who I reckon must've owned the plantation, he walked out with a hundred and ten slaves that he'd set free. He brought them to a fort that the Union navy had moved on and defeated and the Yanks made him an honorary Union soldier and even gave him a medal."

Reverend Starks sat back in his chair and interlaced his fingers. "How do you know all this?"

"I went to the records office here in Alvin and they connected me with this historian woman from Chickasaw who got information on my family history for me."

"Well now," the reverend said. "That's pretty interestin'. Sounds like you've got some pretty great blood in you."

I smiled. I knew, of all people, Reverend Starks would be impressed. "I reckon he was a hero," I said.

"Sounds like a hero to me." The reverend glanced down at the sword at my waist. "Is that what you're tryin' to become carryin' that sword?"

I felt my cheeks redden with embarrassment. "Oh. These are just pretend."

"I see."

Dewey was looking around the room. "How come you ain't got no TV?"

I couldn't believe how rude he was being.

Reverend Starks laughed. "Because the Lord keeps me busy enough without me needin' no television, that's for sure."

"I think it's weird not having a TV," Dewey said.

"Dewey!" I said, through gritted teeth.

The reverend leaned forward. "Abe, there was something you wanted to ask me?"

"Yeah. I was wonderin' . . . I mean, I know your church is for black folks and all . . . but—"

"Full Gospel is for everyone, Abe," he said, cutting me off.

I brightened. "So then it might be okay if some white folks attended? Just one time?"

"Abe, as I said, all folk are welcome in this house of the Lord. And not just one time but any time and all times. Why are you askin' me this?"

"On account of I wanted to know if it would be all right—that is, if my mom agrees—if we could come along one day to your services."

"I would absolutely love it if you did!" The reverend slapped his knees.

I hesitated. "Would it be okay if we brought Miss Sylvie? She's this girl—well, she's sort of a lady, I guess. She's older than me—my mom works with her and she's got quite a few problems and my mom promised to take her to church next time we went cuz her spirits need upliftin'. And I think her spirits would get way more uplifted here than at Clover Creek First Baptist where we usually attend. Not that I don't appreciate Reverend Matthew . . . it's just that . . . well . . . anyway . . . so, would it be okay if she came along?"

Reverend Starks just looked at me a long minute. "You're not listenin' to me, boy. All folks are welcome, all the time. You don't need to ask permission. And it sounds like she needs the Lord's help as much as anyone, maybe even more so. And I reckon my congregation would just love to see some new faces." The reverend's face lit up with a creased smile.

I didn't rightly know what my mother would say about attending church at Full Gospel, but I knew I was going to ask her first chance I got. From what I knew about God, He viewed all people the same, black or white. It was my mother who had spent a good deal of time teaching me that, so she should not be disagreeable to the idea. I didn't mind church at Clover Creek where we regularly attended (not that we attended quite so regularly), but I thought we could use a change for once. And I definitely thought bringing Miss Sylvie along was a good idea given all she was going through.

I told Reverend Starks I would do my best to see him next Sunday.

"That would be grand, Abe." He held out his hand for me to shake it. His brown fingers were huge with pink fingertips. They wrapped right around mine as we shook.

"Oh, and I want to say sorry," I said.

"Sorry? For what?"

"For the swords. I forgot we was wearin' them."

"Why are you sorry?"

"On account of I doubt Jesus would be very appreciative of swords, especially in the house of the Lord."

"Well, this isn't the church, this is my house. And Jesus doesn't have a problem with swords, Abe. In Matthew 10:34, Jesus says, 'Think not that I am come to send peace on earth: I came not to send peace, but a sword.' "

I couldn't *believe* he knew all this stuff by heart.

"So Jesus wanted people to fight?" Dewey asked. I was kind of wondering the same thing.

"Jesus was a warrior," Reverend Starks answered. "The word of God is represented by a sword. If we take two passages a little further on, it might make more sense to you. Matthew 10:38 and 10:39 where Jesus says, 'And he that taketh not his cross, and followeth after me, is not worth of me. He that findeth his life shall lose it: and he that loseth his life for my sake shall find it.' "

"I still don't get it," Dewey said. "And how come you don't have a cross on any of your walls?"

I could not believe how rude he was being.

"We don't need crosses to be reminded of Jesus, Dewey. Remembering the Word is enough." He shifted in his chair. "And I *do* have a cross. A very simple one. It hangs in my bedroom."

"And you have a cross in your church," Dewey said. "Two of 'em. They're small ones, though. Compared to Clover Creek, at least."

"Dewey!" I hissed. He was completely out of line.

"What? I'm just tryin' to figure things out."

"Dewey," Reverend Starks said, "big crosses isn't what the Lord Jesus is about. This—" He tapped his chest where his heart was. "*This* is what the Lord Jesus is all about. Keeping Him in your heart and keeping your faith strong."

"So is *that* why He's sayin' we should follow him with our own cross or else we will lose our life or whatever it was you said?"

Reverend Starks pushed his lips together into a thin line, looking away in thought for a second or two. "Dewey, Jesus is sayin' that to be a warrior one must be brave, and if you are not brave enough to face your own fears, you do not deserve his love. And if you discover a way to live without his love, you shall lose all that is dear to you. It is only by being brave enough to give up everything you have that you will really find what's important, and it will all come through the love of the Lord Jesus." Reverend Starks turned his head and stared straight into my eyes. "This is the true strength of the warrior, Abe. The true test of the sword. Although, always remember the true test of a warrior is not *raising* that sword—it's knowing that even though you have the power to take a life, you also have the power to spare it; and there's always more power in mercy than in dealin' out death." The reverend's eyes drifted back to Dewey. "Is that clearer now?"

Dewey didn't answer right away, so I took advantage of the silent spot and jumped in. "I think so," I said. "My great-great-great-great-great-granddaddy was brave like that. He risked everythin' he had in order to free them slaves. I bet he didn't like shootin' those people at that plantation, but he probably reckoned he had to in order to get them people free. I'd hope that if I were in his shoes, I might do the same."

A smile came to Reverend Starks's face. "Abe," he said, "I reckon you just might have the heart of a warrior."

CHAPTER 24

Leah didn't like the expression on Eli Brown's face when he opened his door to find her on the porch. "I thought I made it clear that I was to be left alone," he told her in a commanding yet still somehow brittle voice.

"That ain't yours to command, I'm afraid," Leah said. "I'm here on police business."

"I ain't got no business with no police."

"That again ain't your call to make."

A young man dressed in a button-down white shirt tucked into a pair of dress pants came into the room behind Eli. "Is it the police again?" he asked.

"Never you mind, Leland," Eli said. "I'll take care of this."

"No," the boy—Leland (who couldn't have been much older than twenty)—said. "Let me." He came up beside Eli and told Leah, "My grandfather is old. Can't you see he's been through enough? Why do you people insist on botherin' him? He's done his time. Far as I know, that makes him a free man. Surely you have better things to do than bother old men who are repentin' their deeds 'fore the Lord."

Leah nearly laughed. Judging by the way the boy was dressed, which was much different from how Chris had described finding him that day he came out, she thought her guess that he was involved was probably on target. "First off," she said, her voice growing loud and stern, "you make your granddaddy sound like some decrepit ancient hermit. He ain't much a day over sixty. Secondly, I have reason to believe he might be involved in some illegal activity that requires my attention. In fact, the only reason I'm *telling* you this instead of telling you to go out and play is because I think you may be involved, too." She shifted her gaze to Eli. "Now we have a choice. We can do this here, or we can do it at the station. Personally, I'd prefer the station. I'm more prepared to back up everythin' I have to tell you with documentation down there. But I don't think we'll need those documents, on account of I don't think you'll be tellin' me I'm wrong."

Eli looked her up and down as though trying to decide how seriously he should take her. "What's this 'bout?"

"The Carson Cattle Ranch."

"And what of it?"

"And it's connection to Argo Atkinson." Her eyes locked on Leland. His own eyes suddenly widened.

Eli looked around the yard, as if checking the weather. It had grown windy and a few clouds had gathered overhead since Leah left the station. "All right," he said. "You may as well come in. I don't relish a trip to your police station." His voice no longer held the commanding tone of the preacher part of him it had a few minutes ago.

"Fair enough," Leah said, and followed him inside.

Ahead of her she heard the boy whisper to Eli, "Are you sure this is a good idea?"

"It was gonna come out sooner or later," Eli replied to him. "It's just happenin' a bit sooner than we expected."

Eli led them to a little room just past the door where a settee stood along with a chair and an oval coffee table. None of the furniture matched in color. The settee was a dark green, the chair was made of oak, and the table pine. The floor of the room was rough-hewn knotty pine. A small, shiny cross hung on one wall. The rest of the walls were bare.

Pulling her notepad from her pocket, Leah took a chair as Eli and his grandson took a seat beside each other on the settee. They had to move a couple of blankets out of the way to do so; this was obviously where the boy had been sleeping.

"Before we start," Leah said to the grandson. "Your name's Leland? Leland . . . Brown?"

He just nodded.

"You have to say 'yes' or 'no,' son," Leah said.

"Yes," he said angrily.

"And you live in Alabaster?"

His face snapped to Eli's. "How . . . ?" He looked back to Leah. "How did you know that?"

Eli's hand came down on Leland's knee. "Because I told her," he said. "Now relax. You're actin' guilty. You haven't *done* anythin'."

"Why are you here, Leland?" Leah asked.

Eli interrupted. "I thought you wanted to question *me*."

"I'll get round to you, don't you worry 'bout that." Her gaze fell back on Leland. "Why are you here?"

Leland glanced across to Eli and back to Leah. "Just . . . vistin' my grandpa. Haven't seen him in so long." He grinned, but Leah could tell it was a fake smile even if she'd been standin' five acres away. This kid may have been the worst liar in the history of scam artists.

"That all? Nothin' else?"

He shook his head. "Nope."

"Eli," Leah said. "Who is Argo Atkinson?"

"My father-in-law."

"And are you aware that his name is on the title of the Carson Cattle Ranch property?"

"Yes." The boy kept looking from Leah to Eli and back to Leah like he was watching a tennis game.

"Can I ask why you hadn't told me this before?"

"Lots of reasons," Eli said. "The main one bein' I don't see how it's any of your damn business. Another bein' that I was never asked."

"I came here and inquired specifically 'bout Sylvie Carson."

"And I told you the truth, that I ain't been near her property or her. Nor do I have any plans to be. That has got nothing to do with land purchased by my father-in-law. In fact, the land really isn't my business at all. It's his. Perhaps he's the one you should be questionin'."

Leah wrote down everything they said. Taking statements was something she'd had lots of practice at. And interviewing Argo Atkinson was something she had already planned on doing. Only, Eli came first because she had a sneaking suspicion that Argo hadn't bought the land for himself.

"Do you know what Mr. Atkinson plans to do with the ranch?"

There was a brief hesitation, during which Leland looked to Eli expectantly for an answer. Finally, Eli broke the silence. "I think," he said slowly, "that he plans on developing on it."

"What sort of development?"

"A religious educational institution."

"Grandpa . . . ," Leland whispered, loud enough for Leah to hear.

Again Eli's hand came down on his grandson's knee. Eli turned to the boy and said, "It can't be kept a secret, Leland. Once the tractors start diggin', folks are gonna know what's goin' on. Better to get this out in the open now. It ain't like we're doin' anythin' wrong."

"So," Leah said, "Argo bought this land for you, on account of you was in prison?"

"Argo made an *investment*," Eli said. "Do you have any idea how much he's already gained on that property since buyin' it? It turned out to be a very shrewd investment."

Leah knew exactly how much he'd already gained. She even had the paperwork to back it up. She looked to the kid. "I have a hunch, Leland," she said.

He just stared back, like a goldfish in one of them round glass bowls.

"Call it a gut feelin'," she said, "but it's definitely there."

"What's that?" he asked.

"That you's lyin' to me."

He shook his head. "No I ain't."

"I think you are. I think your granddaddy might be tellin' mostly the truth, but I think you lied to me earlier."

"No, ma'am, I did not." She could see his back coming up while simultaneously fear rose in his eyes.

"I think you are down here to help your grandpa Eli start workin' on his institution. In fact, I bet if I ran a check on you, I'd discover that you're either in college or just graduated with some sort of degree in business management."

She saw him swallow. She definitely wasn't far from the mark.

"Did you know I can arrest you for lying to a police officer?"

"Give the kid a break," Eli said. "He's not used to havin' questions fired at him. He's only twenty-two, damn it."

Twenty-two? Damn, he looked young for his age. "I'll tell you what," Leah said. "I'll give you another chance, Leland. Tell me again: Why are you down here?"

He looked at Eli. Eli nodded slightly.

When Leland spoke again, his voice was shaky. "I'm here to help find investors for Grandpa Eli's institution and help reorganize his congregation. We need to get his church back up and runnin' 'fore anythin' else can proceed. Then we need money."

"Surely the property has enough equity to move ahead with your project?"

Eli answered that one. "My father-in-law don't wanna risk his investment any more than he has to. He didn't buy the property *for* me. It will remain his, at least until he dies. If we have to mortgage the property for some of the funding then I suppose that's a route we'll have to take. But he won't mortgage more than half of it. He's already made that clear. And building this facility is gonna cost more than that."

"We're eager to move ahead as quick as possible," Leland said. "Now that Grandpa Eli's back home."

"Hmm," Leah said. "I see a few complications in your plans."

"What's that?" Leland asked.

"I reckon that even though the sale went through eight years ago, there's still a chance Sylvie Carson might be able to have it overturned given the state she was in at the time of the sale and the matters surroundin' it. We need to follow that up with the courts. This is especially true with the new evidence I'll be presentin' on account of I'm reopenin' the case files for the deaths of Tom Carson and his wife. Something 'bout it all don't sit right with me. I'm startin' to think Tom Carson's hangin' wasn't suicide at all. I've been thinkin' maybe more people than just James Richard Cobbler were possibly responsible for Tom's wife's death."

"This could stall the project," Eli said, his voice rising. "You could hold up the question of land title for the property in the courts for years."

Leah shrugged.

"Listen," Eli said, trying to remain calm. "We've done nothin' wrong. We waited 'til the property was available then bought it at auction. We was lucky enough to get it at a low price. There ain't no funny business happenin' in anythin' we're doin' despite what you may reckon. It's all fair an' square."

"I don't reckon it either way, Mr. Brown. Like I said, those deaths just don't sit well with me. And I want Sylvie to have a chance at gettin' a piece of any inheritance she might have comin' to her if she deserves one. That's all. There ain't no 'funny business happenin' in anythin' *I'm* doin' either. It's all fair an' square." She did say that last bit a mite sarcastically, she had to admit, but she wasn't prepared for the reaction that followed.

Leland lowered his eyes at her and, in a menacing voice no longer filled with any sort of shakiness, said, "You'd better stay out of our way, or I reckon I wouldn't want to be in those shoes of yours." Eli's hand once again fell onto Leland's knee. This time with an obvious squeeze.

"Is that a threat, Leland?" Leah asked.

"Take it any way you want to."

"You don't want me to take it as a threat. Trust me."

"You accuse us of all sorts of things, and then tell me what I can and cannot do? In my granddaddy's house, no less. I reckon you should leave now." Leah started wondering if the whole "shaken up from talking to the policewoman" thing was an act. This young man didn't seem to really be too shaken up at all. He appeared completely in command. And a little scary.

One thing was for certain, though: They'd gone for her bluff. That made her happy.

"Yes, it's 'bout that time," she said, standing and tucking her notebook away. "Oh, just one last thing. If I catch either of you anywhere *near* Sylvie Carson, I won't be askin' no more questions. I'll be shootin' first. And I'm a better shot than even you are, Preacher Eli." As soon as she said that, even Leah thought she'd overstepped the boundary of good taste.

"Get out!" Eli Brown roared.

CHAPTER 25

"I don't know 'bout this, Abe," my mother said as she pulled off Church Street and into the Full Gospel parking lot. She was watching all the black folks driving in and getting out of their cars. A whole bunch of them was walking up to the church's door where Reverend Starks was greeting each one of them.

"What don't you know?" I asked. "We was invited."

"We don't really . . . fit in."

"I thought you said there ain't no difference between black and white, especially in the eyes of the Lord."

She sighed. "I did say that, didn't I?" Pulling the car to a stop, she threw it into PARK. "Okay, I guess we're really doin' this."

I was sitting in the backseat with Miss Sylvie and the baby. The baby had been crying something awful when we picked her up. That crying continued through the first half of the drive. Then I suppose the car ride put her to sleep because she wasn't crying anymore. I was glad about that. Crying babies weren't something I much liked listening to.

"Seriously, Mom?" Carry asked from the front seat. Neither my mother nor my sister had taken off their seat belts yet. Me and Miss Sylvie had. My mother and Carry just kept watching the people funneling to the front door of the church. There wasn't a single white folk in the bunch. I thought it was exciting. "This is ridiculous," Carry said to my mother. "It's bad enough you make me go to *normal* church."

My mother shot Carry a look. "Just for that, I'm glad we're here. You need to learn more tolerance, both for religion and for differences in people. Now, I promised Abe we'd come here and try it one time, and so here we are. We was invited. It ain't like we're showin' up unexpected." Then, hesitantly, as though she weren't quite sure I actually told her the truth about being invited, she asked me, "Is it, Abe?"

"It most certainly is not," I said.

"How do you feel about it, Miss Sylvie?" my mother asked.

"It's fine," Miss Sylvie said. Her voice was soft and quiet, as though she didn't really care what we did. I don't think she really wanted to be here or anywhere. I wondered if Miss Sylvie ever got excited about anything.

"Okay," my mother said, taking a deep breath. "Let's go." She finally undid her seat belt.

The church's open front door where Reverend Starks was standing was at the top of three large concrete steps that were cracked. There was a hand railing running up the side of the stairs, but it was busted near the top and so it didn't look very safe.

I tried not to look at everyone else as we approached the door, but I couldn't help but get the feeling that people were looking at us. I was happy when Reverend Starks spotted us and a wide grin immediately spread across his face. "Abe!" he said, after finishing up welcoming the couple entering in front of us. "I see you decided to take me up on my offer! What a great surprise!"

He squatted down and shook my hand. When he stood back up again, his knees popped. He shook his head. "Indications of gettin' old," he said, turning his attention to my mother.

The morning sunlight reflected off his eyeglasses and he pushed them up on his nose. "Ms. Teal," he said, taking her hand in both of his. "It's been a long time. How have you been?" His voice was low and soothing and full of what sounded to me like genuine concern.

"Good . . ."

He smiled. "You've done such an amazing job raising two wonderful children." Still holding my mother's hand, his gaze swept to Carry. "Caroline, right? I haven't seen you since you were about a foot or two shorter than you are now." He laughed. "You're still as pretty as I remember."

Carry blushed and said thank you.

Reverend Starks let go of my mother's hand and turned his attention to Miss Sylvie. "And you must be Miss Sylvie," he said. I couldn't believe he remembered her name just from the discussion me and him had the other day. "It is a pleasure to meet you." He lowered his voice while talking to Miss Sylvie, obviously in an effort not to wake the baby she had on her shoulder. He shook her hand.

"Pleasure," Miss Sylvie said. "I'm Sylvie Carson."

"It's a *genuine* pleasure, Miss Sylvie Carson." The reverend looked the baby over. "And who do we have here?" he asked in a whisper. "Someone who obviously enjoys a good nap, I see. We have somethin' in common." He smiled at Miss Sylvie. I saw the light reflect off the gold of his capped tooth.

Miss Sylvie looked awkwardly to my mother. "Um," she stammered, "she's my daughter. She . . . she doesn't have a name yet."

Reverend Starks's smile never flinched. "I see. Well, the Lord loves all babies, whether they be called by names or be nameless."

Relief flooded across Miss Sylvie's face and, for the first time since we'd picked her up, she actually smiled. It wasn't that big, but at least it was a smile.

"I'm so sorry to hear you're suffering through some hard times right now," the reverend told her. "Just keep your faith in the Lord Jesus. Remember that God is light and in Him there can be no darkness."

Miss Sylvie seemed a bit taken aback, but she just nodded. "Th . . . thank you," she said shakily. She probably wondered how Reverend Starks knew so much about her.

"Would it be all right if I ask my congregation to offer a special prayer for you today?" Reverend Starks asked her.

Once again Miss Sylvie looked to my mother, who didn't seem to have any response for her. "I guess so." Miss Sylvie's voice still quivered.

That big smile once again spread across Reverend Starks's face. "That's fine, then. Welcome to my church." He held out his arm in a gesture for us to enter.

It had been a long while since I'd been in the Full Gospel, and I'd forgotten how it looked. Inside, the church wasn't a lot different from Clover Creek. From the outside, I could have sworn it was a smaller building, but now that I was inside it actually felt larger. Or maybe it was just that the pews were closer together and there were more of them. Like Clover Creek, everything was made of wood (probably pine), although the wood here at Full Gospel didn't shine the way it did at Clover Creek. There were holes where knots had fallen out and gouges in some of the boards.

We were about three quarters from the front where the pulpit stood, which was as close as we could get. I wondered if the church would fill up completely. If so, that would be a lot of people, probably more than the congregation we usually had at Clover Creek. Considerably more.

The walls left and right of the pulpit were angled and each had a large stained-glass window set in the top. There were four other stained-glass windows along the main side walls. On the angled wall right of the pulpit stood a choir of twenty-six people. I counted them twice, so I knew. They formed three rows, each row standing on a higher bench. The back row stood above the rest. I think they were all teenagers. Mostly, they were girls, but six of them were boys. A white cross hung above them, just below the stained-glass window.

We didn't have a choir at Clover Creek. We did a lot of singing, but just by ourselves.

I knew services always ran longer here at Full Gospel than at Clover Creek on account of all the extra singing they did. They were really big on singing and the singing was the part I was most excited about.

The light shining through that window above the choir cast down on the pulpit, lighting it in an array of reds and yellows. It gave it an unearthly glow. Behind the pulpit was another cross, bigger than the one by the choir and very similar to the one that hung behind Reverend Matthew. Only this cross wasn't nearly as big as the one at Clover Creek.

Spaced along the main side walls every few feet were candles that weren't lit. I guessed they were used for special occasions. The sunlight coming through the stained glass was the only light inside the church, making everything feel as though I was in a dream.

Miss Sylvie shuffled in first, the baby still on her left shoulder, asleep. I went in next, followed by my mother and then Carry, who I could still hear complaining under her breath.

My mother kept shushing her.

The pews weren't padded like the ones at Clover Creek, they were just wooden, but they weren't that uncomfortable. They were old and the row we sat on wasn't attached to the floor very well. It rocked back and forth a bit as we took our seats.

About fifteen or twenty minutes later, Reverend Starks closed the front door and the light from the colored glass in the windows suddenly really made everything magical. I looked back over my shoulder, amazed to find every pew full. There were even some people standing behind the last one. I didn't know exactly how many people had shown up for church today, but it was a lot more than we ever got at Clover Creek.

And every single one of them except us was black.

Reverend Starks walked slowly up the center aisle and stepped up to his pulpit.

"First," he said, in his low voice that now grew as he used it to preach. "I would like you all to welcome some guests today. Y'all may have seen them as you came in. They are sittin' there." He pointed us out. "They are the Teals, Ms. Leah Teal, from the Alvin Police Department; her son, Abe Teal; her daughter, Caroline Teal; and their friend Miss Sylvie Carson."

All around us people began to clap. In front of me, people looked over their shoulders and smiled. A woman wearing a pink lacy hat gave me a little wave. I felt a mite embarrassed, but I did feel welcomed just the same.

"Now, Miss Sylvie is goin' through some tough times right

now, so I promised her we'd all give a little prayer for her. So before I get started with our regular service, I'd like to do just that."

And he went right into his prayer for Miss Sylvie, asking the Lord Jesus to please help her find her way. He called her one of His flock and said she had lost her way and needed guidance and a road map. I was pretty amazed he was able to give such a detailed prayer about Miss Sylvie based on what little I'd said about her. He even made mention of the baby, who I hadn't even talked about and he'd only just met outside for the first time.

The fact that he had even remembered her name had been a miracle in my eyes. Then I remembered him quoting those Bible passages to me and Dewey off the top of his head. He was really something.

As he spoke each line, everyone in the congregation (who were sitting holding hands with their heads bowed and their eyes closed) repeated the line. When he was finished, he said, "Amen." And everyone followed with one loud "Amen" in unison.

Miss Sylvie looked as though she had no idea what to make of everything or how she was supposed to react. The baby continued sleeping. To me, that was yet another miracle.

After that, Reverend Starks started the service with three songs from the hymnal. The choir led the way, bellowing out the words so loud and fine it sent a shiver through me. Everyone sang along, including me. At least I tried to, following with the hymnbook I found in the back of the pew in front of me. After the three hymns, Reverend Starks went into a pretty standard sermon, much like Reverend Matthew would give at Clover Creek First Baptist. Like I usually did, I tried to keep up but couldn't quite understand everything he was saying. Normally, it didn't bother me so much, but today I was trying extra hard to stay on top of things. I really wanted to know what Reverend Starks was talking about.

He went on for probably thirty minutes until finally coming to what sounded like the conclusion. Usually the conclusion was when you got the real important stuff.

"I would like you to recall Psalm Thirty-four, versus sixteen through nineteen," he said. " 'The face of the Lord is against them that do evil, to cut off the remembrance of them from the earth. The righteous cry, and the Lord heareth, and delivereth them out of all their troubles.' " Reverend Stark shifted his hands on the pulpit as he read the next verse. I couldn't see it, but I assumed he had an open Bible in front of him. I didn't think he could possibly have *all* this Bible stuff memorized. " 'The Lord is nigh unto them that are of a broken heart; and saveth such as be of a contrite spirit. And many are the afflictions of the righteous; but the Lord delivereth him out of them all.' "

He looked up and scanned the congregation in silence. I got the feeling this was the end of his sermon and, as I said, usually the end was pretty important so I really wanted to figure this part out.

I didn't rightly know if I understood completely what he had said, but it sounded to me like Lord Jesus was going to protect everyone who was good from evil and that even good people had problems and cried and stuff. I whispered to my mother if that was what he meant by what he said.

She shushed me.

"I'm only tryin' to understand church," I said quietly. "You should be happy." I never really took that much of an interest in church usually. I mean, I always listened to what Reverend Matthew said at Clover Creek First Baptist, but I didn't much understand what he went on about most of the time and didn't bother following up like this. Today I felt like I should really try to clarify things. I'm not sure why, but for some reason, today church felt kind of special. Maybe just because we were at Full Gospel. Maybe I didn't want to let Reverend Starks down by not being able to figure out what he was preaching about.

My mother whispered back, "He's sayin' God is close to the broken hearted."

Miss Sylvie sat there with the baby on her shoulder. If ever anyone looked broken hearted, she certainly did. I suddenly felt a whole lot better for her. I wondered if Reverend Starks had written this sermon special just for Miss Sylvie, but then I remembered he didn't know for sure that we were coming today or not.

There actually was more to the sermon after that, but the rest didn't last too long. Unlike at Clover Creek, the sermon ended early so that a lot of the time could be spent doing more singing, which really did turn out to be the best part. This was different singing from the hymns we sang at the beginning of the service. It was much more powerful. It seemed to hit me right in the heart.

The choir led every song and the singers had incredibly loud voices. Actually, so did the congregation. It seemed as though everyone attending Full Gospel knew how to carry a tune better than anyone I ever met in my life.

Their voices were beautiful and they rose up until they filled that entire building, which suddenly didn't seem very big at all. It felt so small, in fact, it seemed like the voices were going to shatter the stained glass. Then, the choir grew even louder and it felt like the whole church might burst with the joyousness of song.

I tried to sing along following the words in the hymnal, but I wasn't a very good singer. My mother also mouthed words, but she didn't seem to be actually singing anything. It didn't matter. There were more than enough people singing already. I was downright amazed how loud that group of people and that choir could sing. I was sure most people up and down Main Street could hear them right now.

And then it felt as though the song somehow did break through the small building and lifted it up into the sky where it shone in the heavens like a bright star.

Miss Sylvie held the baby tightly against her chest. Amazingly, the baby still appeared to be asleep. Miss Sylvie had her head tucked against the baby's cheek and tears spilled from her eyes. At first, I couldn't figure out why she was so upset. Then I realized she was overwhelmed by all the singing. I came to this conclusion on account of I felt the very same way, only not quite to the point of tears. But there was something very emotional about it all.

The tall black woman wearing a yellow summer dress standing in the pew behind her leaned ahead and put her lips close to Miss Sylvie's ear. The woman had black curly hair and wore glasses. Raising her voice loud enough for Miss Sylvie (and me) to hear her over the singing, she said, "Go ahead, child, it's okay. Cry. Cry, and let the blessed sing for you."

That moment felt almost magical to me. Time seemed to stop as something caught in my throat, and for an instant I did feel something like tears stinging the back of my eyes.

I thought later that maybe God really had been there in that church that day with all of us. At least in that moment He was.

CHAPTER 26

Me and Dewey were out in my backyard again, thrusting and parrying and swinging and blocking with our swords. We were sure getting a lot of fun from these wooden toys me and Carry had so simply constructed. I was so glad I had come up with the idea to make them now. And Dewey's invention for holding them around our waists had turned out to be brilliant. We virtually took them with us everywhere we went. Folks around town were getting used to seeing us with swords dangling from our hips. It was like we were real knights.

Today was particularly fun. The day was sunny, but not too hot, and there was a sweet smell in the air; I think it was the neighbor's magnolias from next door. The scent just made everything that much more perfect. And Dewey had yet to whine even once about me hurting his hand or anything.

Truth was, he had gotten so much better with his sword that I didn't hit his hand anymore. He had a good block and was able to see my moves coming and counter them or step out of their way before they could do any damage. It made me wonder how good we'd be with real swords. I hoped one day in the future, when I had money of my own, I might go back to Disney World so I could buy myself one of them real swords. Then I wouldn't need to go through my mother at all. Lots of things would be much easier when I got older.

Dewey had just come at me with a series of slashes and swings that had forced me almost all the way across the yard when Carry stepped out the back door and stopped us mid-play. I didn't realize right away what was about to happen, but when I did, a darkness passed over my heart. For I suddenly recognized what she had in her outstretched hand. She wiggled it at me from the porch: a brand-new bottle of bright pink nail polish that glistened even brighter and looked even sharper than it should have under all this sunlight.

"Oh, Abe," she sang out with chimes in her voice. "It's time to come inside for a bit."

I stared at her, my heart jackhammering like the foot of a rabbit thumping the ground. Then I looked at Dewey. I didn't know what to do. This was the last position I wanted to be stuck in. Dewey could *not* find out what terrible fate had befallen me. He would never let me forget this as long as we both were still alive.

"Abe," she sang out again. "Remember your word? It's been a week . . ."

I let out a deep breath. "Dewey . . . I have to go inside for a while." I wanted to get in the house before Carry said too much. I jogged over to the porch where she stood and carefully placed my sword up against the outside wall of the house.

"What's goin' on?" Dewey asked from the backyard, his sword pointing at the ground, his hand shielding his eyes from the sun. "You paintin' your sister's nails, Abe?"

There was a question I wasn't about to answer straight out. "I just have to go inside."

"But why?"

"To do something . . . chores."

"What kind of chores?"

"Not very fun ones."

"How long will you be? Should I just wait out here?"

I took off my shoes and followed my sister into the house.

"Yes," I called out over my shoulder. "Wait for me. I'll only be fifteen minutes!"

"More like twenty-five!" Carry shouted from the living room. "He's doin' a *proper* job!"

I felt my face cycle through ten shades of red. I wished Carry would just shut up. She'd already done enough damage. There was no way I would ever live this down. My only hope was that somehow Dewey was simple enough that I could cover up the truth. But if Carry kept on talking, that would be near on impossible.

Chapter 27

Leah sat at her desk making phone call after phone call to different psychologist offices in and around Satsuma, looking for anybody who knew anything about a psychologist with the last name of Langdon or Langwood or anything sounding like it. She wasn't having much luck. She was beginning to wonder if Sylvie had made the name up.

Truth was, she didn't rightly know what help some psychologist Sylvie saw while still back in school might be to her anyway, especially given that Sylvie said she'd only seen the man three or four times over a handful of months. Leah wished she was seeing somebody now. Somebody a lot more often than just three or four times in as many months. The girl needed someone to help her, someone who knew what he was doing.

Obviously, Tom Carson had known that too, despite Sylvie not taking him seriously on account of what he did to himself.

Leah started pondering that. From what she'd heard about Tom Carson he was a very proud man. It would've taken a lot for him to admit his daughter was in so much trouble she might need professional help. And professional help would require money. There was no way, being a cattle farmer and all, that Tom Carson had a medical plan. So, him telling Sylvie she should go see someone meant he must've had plans to further mortgage the farm just to pay for her expenses. Takes a mighty strong man to do something like that.

Or someone who could directly identify with her situation.

The thought struck Leah like lightning hitting an oak tree. What if *that* was where Tom Carson's money had been going? What if all that time since his son had been killed, Tom Carson had been seeing some sort of therapist and paying the bills by mortgaging the property?

It made sense. And it was easy to find out.

She made a quick call down to the station in Mobile. Officer Mindy Wright answered the phone.

"Hi, Mindy, it's Leah Teal, up here in Alvin." Leah had met Mindy quite a few times. The Mobile department often threw summer functions and invited all the officers from the small outlying towns to bring their families down and participate. It was a highlight of Abe's summer. The last one had only been just over a month or so ago, around the end of June. "I need medical records for a Mr. Tom Carson. Used to live up here. He passed away in 1980. Owned the Carson Cattle Ranch."

Mindy said she'd have to get them from the public records office, but it shouldn't take more than a phone call.

"That's why I'm callin' you." Leah laughed. "I have to write letters and jump through hoops for anythin' out of there. Then I gotta wait a week."

"That's crazy," Mindy said. "I can have 'em for you probably within the hour. I'll just fax 'em on up to you."

"Thanks. Oh, but . . . we don't have a fax right now. We *had* one, but it kinda broke. So can you just call me with the information? I only want a few items."

"Sure. What's your number?"

Leah gave her the number.

She hung up the phone and started remembering exactly what it was that Sylvie told her that her pa had said:

He was the one always askin' me if I was okay. Kept askin' if I needed to talk to somebody about it. Like a professional. Like a shrink or somethin'. He told me that could really help.

Now that she played it back in her mind, Leah thought it was an odd thing for Tom Carson to say unless he *knew* from his own experience how much it could help. No, the more she thought about it, the more this made sense. It fit with the money being spent. Medical bills weren't cheap, especially if medication was involved.

It had been just forty minutes since Leah called down to the station in Mobile when her phone rang. It was Mindy Wright with Tom Carson's medical records.

"Okay, what do you want to know?" she asked.

"Did the man ever go see a psychologist or a therapist of any kind on a regular basis?"

"Leah, he saw the same doctor every Tuesday and Thursday week in and week out from the fall of seventy-one right up until he died. It doesn't look here like he missed too many days at all."

"Where was that doctor?"

"It was a Dr. Lisa May Turner. She was right down here, in Mobile."

"Does the report show if he was on any medication?"

"Yep. She prescribed an assortment of different things, none of which I can pronounce. Looks like she changed it up every six months or so at the beginning and then every few years later on."

"I don't suppose you got an address for this Dr. Turner?"

"One sec, let me see if she's still doin' business here in Mobile." Leah could hear Mindy typing on her computer. They had a much bigger database then the Alvin department. It was controlled by something called a mainframe. "She is. Dr. Lisa May Turner, psychiatrist. You got a pen handy? I got a phone number and an address for you."

"Yep, shoot." Leah jotted down the information as Mindy relayed it. When she was done, Leah said, "Thanks a million. I owe you one."

"You owe me a sack race next year. You bowed out this time round."

"That was on account of my daughter and them boys, remember?"

"Oh, I remember," Mindy said. "Have a great day, Leah."

Leah lifted the phone and dialed the number she'd written down on the paper in front of her. A young woman answered. "Dr. Turner's office."

"Hi, this is Detective Leah Teal. I'm with the police force up here in Alvin. I was wonderin' if it would be possible to speak with Dr. Turner."

"I'm afraid she's with a patient right now. Can I get her to call you back?"

Leah left three numbers before hanging up: her office number, her home number, and her car phone number.

Hopefully, she'd be able to convince the doctor she was who she said she was over the phone, otherwise she would have to drive down and show her badge to get any information due to doctor/patient privileges. She figured worst case she could always just get Mindy to go question the doctor for her. She'd actually pretty near got all the information she really wanted to know anyway, other than the actual cost of each of Tom Carson's visits and the price of his medication.

The only other thing Dr. Turner would be able to tell her about the man was that he suffered from depression, but Leah had already figured that out in 1980 when she found his dead body swinging from the bough of that oak tree in his back ninety. After all, despite her recent suspicions, they *had* ruled it a suicide.

CHAPTER 28

Leah didn't hear back from the psychiatrist until after she got home from work that night. It was a pleasant enough evening. The sky was still a nice dark blue, just beginning to get a touch of color in the gloaming, and the weather was pleasant.

Caroline was out with friends, but due home sometime in the next hour. Leah's daughter had been much better lately about coming home when she said she would. This made Leah happy. Leah's plan was to fix her kids a decent meal tonight—something they didn't get nearly often enough. On the menu was chicken-fried steak, potato salad, and greens, a favorite of both Abe and Caroline.

Abe and Dewey were out in the front yard playing with their swords, making all sorts of racket. Leah closed the door when the phone rang.

"Hi, this is Dr. Lisa Turner," the woman said. She didn't sound as Southern as most folk down in Mobile. "I'm looking for Detective Teal."

"This is Leah Teal. Thank you for takin' the time to call me back."

"Absolutely no problem at all. What can I do for you, Detective?"

"I'm hopin' you can give me information on a patient you had from late 1971 until 1980. A man by the name of Tom Carson."

"Tom Carson. Let me think. You're asking me to remember a long way back. Let me check my files; can you hold on a sec?"

"Certainly."

She came back on the line momentarily. "Oh, yes. Mr. Carson. I remember now. What, exactly, did you want to know?"

"Can you tell me what you were treatin' him for?"

There was a silence on the other end. "Normally, Detective Teal, this would fall under privileged information. But—am I to assume this is a criminal investigation?"

"Yes, it is."

"And the man *did* commit suicide."

"Yes, he did. I handled the case."

"Then I think I can make an exception. I treated him for depression. He was actually diagnosed in 1973 with major depressive disorder."

"What medications was he taking?"

"Oh, let's see. A number of things. We kept trying different combinations of tricyclic antidepressants and MAO inhibitors. There's always a lot of guesswork with psychotropic drugs until you find things that work for patients. Generally, it's not one single drug but a combination that does the trick. Once Prozac came on to the market, he went straight on to that."

The medications didn't mean much to Leah. She only wanted to know one thing about them. "Were they expensive?"

"I'm a doctor, Detective, not a pharmacist. But I can't imagine they were cheap, especially not back in those days."

"So . . . around twenty-five dollars a month?"

The psychiatrist laughed. "Probably closer to two hundred. And like everything else they would've gone up in price as time went by."

"Can I ask you how much your rates were back when Mr. Carson started seeing you?"

"Um, let me check if I have that on file. Yes, it's right here. Two hundred and fifty dollars an hour."

"And he saw you an hour every Tuesday and an hour every Thursday?" Leah was astounded by the amount of money they were talking about.

"No, he came for two-hour sessions on each of those days."

"And, like everything else, did your rates also go up in price?"

"That's very likely."

"I see. Thank you, Dr. Turner, I think that's all the information I need."

Leah hung up the phone thinking, *Become a doctor, Abe. Geez. Did I ever go into the wrong field.*

Me and Dewey were outside in my front yard, battling away with our swords as we usually were these days. The evening was getting on, and I figured in a few more hours there'd be swarms of lightning bugs out here flying between the bushes that were planted around my bedroom window. They always seemed to gather there on nights like tonight—nights when the sky had those red streaks through it, like it was beginning to get now.

"I'm gonna slice your hand off," Dewey said, stepping and swiping at me with his blade.

Normally, I'd have stepped back, but lately I'd gotten better at blocking his blows. Both of us were getting mighty good with our swords. Pretty soon we'd be as good as real knights, we were sure.

The big floppy flowers from the neighbor's magnolias next door filled the evening air with their sugary aroma. They always smelled stronger at night, but tonight they seemed unusually strong, for some reason. Bits of fluff from the cottonwood trees floated in the sky around us as we parried. It was certainly a good thing I didn't have hay fever like Luke Dempsey at school. Luke couldn't go out of doors from most of the late spring months right through to October on account of all the cotton in the air.

Just then, a beat-up old station wagon turned off the road and into my drive. I turned to look at it just as Dewey came in with another swing. Because I wasn't looking, he got me on the back of the hand.

"Ow, Dewey! For cripes' sake! I wasn't even lookin'!"

"Sorry," he said.

I held my hand up over my eyes and squinted into the windshield of the station wagon where the low sun was reflecting off the glass. My heart nearly leaped out of my body. "Do you know who that is?" I whispered to Dewey.

He came up beside me, lowering his sword. "No, who?"

"Preacher Eli!"

"Are you absolutely certain?"

We waited, watching as the car door opened and, sure enough, out stepped Preacher Eli in his cowboy boots.

"It is!" Dewey whispered.

I shushed him.

Preacher Eli was wearing a white dress shirt with a vest over the top and had his hair combed nice and neat. It looked like he'd just shaved his face. Walking right past, he gave us barely a glance before heading up the porch steps to the door and knocking.

My mother opened it. From the look on her face, she was obviously just as surprised as we were to see Preacher Eli show up at our house. I didn't even like knowing that he knew where I lived, him being a killer and all. My mother didn't look like she wanted to invite him in, but he seemed determined. Finally, she did. To me, she looked frightened.

"See?" I said to Dewey after the door was closed. "My mom's startin' to see things my way. I knew she would. I *told* her that man was up to no good. Did you see her face? She don't trust him."

Dewey shrugged. "Looked to me like she just invited him into your house. I don't think she looked untrusting."

"You don't know my mom."

He didn't have a reply to that.

After a while of staring at the house, we went back to our sword fighting.

Leah brought Eli Brown into the kitchen; looking at the steak sitting on a plate waiting to hit the frying pan, she wondered how late her dinner was going to wind up being. "So, Mr. Brown," she said after showing him to one of the kitchen chairs and taking the one beside it. "Where's that grandson of yours? What's his name? Leland?"

"That's right," Eli said. "He drove back to Alabaster to his daddy's for a while. Ain't nothin' more for him to do on the project 'til we get the permit to start workin' on the church."

"You're talkin' 'bout your old church? Beside the Carson property?"

"Beside my father-in-law's property," Eli corrected. "That's right. The town had it condemned. We want to fix it up so it's usable once more. Need to start up my congregation again."

"So you can raise money."

"That's right," Eli said again. "Nothin' illegal 'bout that, is there?"

"No, Mr. Brown, there isn't."

"Leland'll be coming back in a couple weeks. 'Sides, I wouldn't have brought him here anyway. That boy ain't levelheaded enough for adult conversation like the type we need to have. He's fine for business stuff. Just not . . ." He trailed off.

"Emotional stuff?"

"Yeah, I guess," he said. "Goes in like a bull moose. I tell him that's not the way to approach things. You want to soothe a bear, it takes honey. It certainly don't take no shotgun."

Interesting choice of words, Leah thought.

"To be right honest, the boy's just got a lot of passion." He laughed. "And you certainly bring the passion out in him, Miss Teal."

"I'd prefer if you called me *Detective* Teal," Leah said. "And to be right honest, I reckon I bring the bullshit out in him. No offense."

"None taken, ma'am."

"So why don't you tell me why you're here, Mr. Brown?"

"I came here on friendly terms, hopin' we can work things out like civilized folk."

"I already see a problem with that, Mr. Brown. So far, there don't seem nothin' civilized 'bout the way you conduct yourself."

"Now hold on there just a sec, Miss—*Detective Teal,* that sounds like an accusation."

"No, I'm just statin' a fact."

"I ain't done nothin' wrong since goin' off to prison seventeen years ago."

"Your wife's daddy bought the Carson Cattle Ranch."

"Fair and square."

Their voices were rising. Both of them were getting their backs up, but Leah wasn't about to be the one to lower hers down.

"Just seems a mite suspicious to me," she said. "And he got it at such a low price. Now, how did he swing that?"

Eli Brown stood from his chair. "I don't see how my wife's daddy's business deals are any business of yours. The bank accepted the deal. The deed is in his name. Everythin' 'bout it is legitimate!"

"That's somethin' we'll have to see 'bout."

"Well, I don't need you stickin' your nose in my business and tryin' to mess things up for me. I finally have a shot at doin' somethin' good!" They were practically hollering now. There was no question Abe and Dewey could hear them from the front yard outside.

"Somethin' good?" Leah asked, her voice still loud. "Somethin' like tormentin' a poor girl after killin' her baby brother?"

Eli stamped his foot. "I told you! I don't even know where the girl lives, goddamn it!"

Leah cut him off. "Now that don't sound too preacherlike to me, using the Lord's name in vain. I'm startin' to think just maybe you had somethin' to do with what happened to Sylvie's folks so your wife's daddy could buy their land."

Something appeared in Eli Brown's eyes then. It passed by quickly, but it was dark and evil. It scared Leah. It must've been the same thing Tom Carson saw that afternoon, right before the man's finger pulled the trigger of that gun and forever changed the lives of his innocent family. The volume of Eli Brown's voice lowered and so did the tone. When he spoke, the words came out one at a time, very precise and methodical. "If you're gonna go round makin' accusations like that, you better have an arrest warrant backin' them up, you hear me? Or else—" He stopped himself.

"Or else what, preacher man?"

"Just watch yourself."

They both stared at each other in silence, the hatred in Eli Brown's eyes palpable.

Then the telephone rang and Leah nearly leaped onto the kitchen ceiling.

Breaking their stare, she answered it. It was Miss Sylvie. Once again, she was in turmoil.

"Slow down, girl," Leah said. "Tell me again."

"It's the backyard," Sylvie said on the other end. "Someone's been out there again."

"And you know this how?"

"The cellar door's open again."

"Same one?" Leah started suspecting there was something wrong with the latch after all.

But what Sylvie said blew that theory right out of the sky. "*Both* of 'em. And there ain't no wind, Officer Teal." Leah eyed Eli Brown, wondering if he could pick up who she was talking to. "Go outside and check. And there hasn't been any wind in the last thirty minutes, and this happened in the last thirty minutes."

She was talking so fast, Leah could barely understand her.

"Just calm down, Sylvie, please? I'm trying to keep up."

"There ain't no goddamn wind!"

"How do you know it happened in the past thirty minutes?"

"On account of I was outside sittin' with the baby in the sun, watching it go down. Then I got tired of breast-feedin' and went inside to fix her a bottle of milk that I'd pumped so I could put her down. When I came back out to get her blanket and stuff I found the doors open."

"Are you sure they weren't open when you were outside earlier, and you just didn't notice?" Leah asked.

Sylvie practically screamed into the phone. "They weren't goddamn open!"

Leah had to move the receiver away from her ear. She was getting tired of people yelling. "Okay, okay," she said calmly.

"Whoever done it must've been watchin' me. I'm afraid, Miss Leah!"

"Okay, Sylvie? It's all okay. You're fine, right?"

She heard Sylvie breathing hard on the other end.

"Y—yeah."

"Whoever did it is gone now. You're fine and your baby's fine, right?"

"Yeah, she's here with me."

"Good. I'll be there as soon as I can. Try to remain calm, okay?"

"Okay."

Leah hung up the phone and stared at it a few seconds. This basically just exonerated Eli Brown. He couldn't have been at Sylvie's in the past thirty minutes on account of he'd been here at her place during that time. "Your grandson really up in Alabaster?" she asked Eli, her eyes still glued to the phone.

"Yeah," Eli Brown said calmly. "No reason to lie 'bout that. You can check it out with his pa if you want. Let me give you the number."

He gave her the number.

"Sorry," Eli said, "but I couldn't help but overhear some of that. Miss Sylvie, I presume?"

Leah nodded.

"And she's had troubles in the past thirty minutes?"

Another nod.

"So you know it's not me doin' it, now?"

"Looks like on the surface that would be the case."

Eli rubbed his chin. "How 'bout we just say I accept your apology and move on? I came here tryin' to repair broken bridges, not blow 'em all to hell and high water."

Leah kept staring at the phone. If it weren't Eli, then she had no suspects.

"And I trust," Eli said, "that your little threat 'bout Sylvie disputin' the land deal was just a ruse?"

When Leah didn't react, Eli continued: "Yeah, I didn't think she had any argument for it. I just didn't want things held up."

With a laugh, he shook his head. "You certainly put Leland in a panic, though. Think 'bout it, Detective. I'm tryin' to build a *school*. Why would I be harassin' and, hell, *murderin'* folk to do somethin' that, in the eyes of the Lord, will be such a blessing to this community? It don't make no sense."

He pushed his chair in, getting ready to leave. He laughed and shook his head again. Leah met the preacher man's eyes. The corners of his mouth creased into a small smile as he held out his hand. "Can we at least *try* to exist in the same town without tearin' each other's throats out?"

"I—I guess we can try," Leah stammered and actually, to her own surprise, shook his hand.

"I'd appreciate that."

One thing she could say about Eli Brown. Whatever charisma he had had as a preacher all them years ago still lurked underneath his scruffy demeanor. She had no doubt he'd be successful at raising the money he needed to build his school. That charm was all just hidden away a bit beneath years of being worn through from spending so much time in the state prison system. Being on the inside can change a man. Leah knew that. She'd seen it happen on many occasions. Usually, the changes weren't good. They manifested at the worst times, and in the worst ways.

She wondered what sorts of things she'd see manifesting from Eli Brown.

"I've gotta go get supper on," he said, heading through her kitchen for the living room. "And I suspect you've gotta go pay Miss Sylvie a visit. Thank you for your time, Detective."

Ever since we heard my mother hollering, me and Dewey had stopped playing with our swords and had come as close as we dared to the picture window at the front of the house and tried to listen to what was going on inside.

"You *still* think she trusts him?" I asked.

"I have to admit," Dewey said, "that's a lot of yellin'. I reckon you might be right."

"Of course I'm right. I'm a good judge of character."

The yelling calmed down and then we heard the telephone. My mother was quiet while she talked on the phone, so we couldn't hear any of her conversation through the front window. We were also at least a room away on account of we couldn't see anyone in the living room, which meant my mother and Preacher Eli had probably gone into the kitchen.

I pointed this fact out to Dewey.

"She sure must've been yellin' awfully loud, then."

I smiled. "See? Told you."

A little bit later we did see my mother and Preacher Eli come around the corner into the living room and we quickly ducked down and crab-walked back to our places in the front yard where we'd been sword fighting. Assuming our positions, we went back to battling, although our attention was really on the front porch where the door was being opened. My mother said good-bye to Preacher Eli.

"I'll get to the bottom of this," she told him.

"I reckon you will," Preacher Eli said. "And I hope you do, soon. Have a fine evenin', Miss Teal." He caught himself. "Sorry. I mean *Detective Teal*."

"You too, Mr. Brown."

Once again, Preacher Eli gave us the slightest of acknowledgments as he trudged past and got into his car. Me and Dewey had stopped fighting completely as he backed out and headed down the street toward Hunter Road, probably bound for his little shotgun shack sitting up in Blackberry Springs like a command post.

Back at the door my mother had slipped on her shoes and was coming outside, too. "So, I s'pose I was right after all," I said, pushing my chest out slightly.

" 'Bout what?" she asked.

"Preacher Eli. I told you he is not to be trusted. He already done and killed once. You can't trust killers. I bet you feel a bit silly now for getting so mad about me and Dewey having our stakeout."

My mother came down the steps staring at me. Something flashed across her face. "That man ain't up to nothin'."

"What do you mean?" I felt my own face begin to get warm. I was tired of having to explain the same things over and over when I was always right and everyone else seemed to always be wrong.

"Eli Brown's innocent."

I wondered if my face was getting red. It was definitely growing hot. "But—" I stammered. "We heard you yellin'."

"You should mind your business," she said, pointing at me.

That did it. Now I got really upset. I was tired of minding my business. I was tired of not being taken seriously. "I'm so sick of you not listenin' to me!" I snapped, my voice rising in volume and speed. "Preacher Eli is guilty!"

"Abe! Calm down right now!"

But I didn't calm down, and Dewey's face grew ashen and his eyes looked like saucers as he watched. They filled up with fear.

"Preacher Eli is the one who's been upsetting Miss Sylvie! You just refuse to listen on account of it's me tellin' you! If it were anyone else, you'd listen! You never listen to me!" My voice had grown to hollering. Tears stung the back of my eyes. "You didn't listen to me 'bout my aunt Addison and you ain't listenin' to me 'bout this!"

"Abe!" my mother yelled back. "Drop your tone, right now!"

"I will not! I'm so sick of bein' ignored! So sick of mindin' my own business! So sick of—" My face felt like it was on fire. As I screamed, I waved my sword in the air. With a frustrated wail, I held it out horizontally in front of me and lifted my knee. With one hard yank, I brought it down and with a loud *crack!* I split it in two, practically breaking it right at the hilt.

Dewey hadn't moved. His expression hadn't changed.

I felt a tear run down the cheek of my burning face.

"Dewey," my mother said calmly, "go home."

"Yes, ma'am." His voice trembled.

"Abe, go to your room. I have to go see Miss Sylvie. You'll stay in your room until I get back home, understood?"

Not another word was spoken as Dewey picked up his bike

and rode off down Cottonwood Lane beneath that red-streaked sky, and I slowly stumbled up the front steps of my house, crying. Cotton floated in the air behind me as I went inside, kicked off my shoes, and went to my room.

Collapsing on my bed, I let the tears run from my eyes, over the bridge of my nose, and on to my pillow, unsure of what had come over me.

CHAPTER 29

On the ride over to Sylvie's, Leah forgot all about Abe's outburst, and began to unwind all the theories that had been building up in her head. She had done exactly what Ethan Montgomery warned her not to: She'd let her imagination run amok. Preacher Eli wasn't guilty of harassing Sylvie Carson. Why would the man get out on parole and then risk that freedom just to barnstorm the sister of the boy he'd accidentally killed? When she thought of it now, it so obviously made no sense; she chided herself for falling so easily into believing it. She had *wanted* to believe it.

Then there were the "mysterious" deaths of Sylvie's parents, which weren't so mysterious at all. Sylvie's mother's death had been a mystery for a few weeks when it happened all them years ago. Then Leah and those experts from Mobile had pieced together a perfectly fine working plot and followed a few leads that brought them straight to a suspect. One of Eli Brown's parishioners had gone out on his own and done the deed, thinking he was working in the name of God. Eli Brown tended to attract the extremists, and nobody was as extreme as James Richard Cobbler. Even on his way to the chair (known as Yellow Mama in these parts), the man still held that he'd done nothing wrong. He'd been working in the name of the Lord. Well, that was a Lord Leah was happy not to call her own, thank you very much.

Despite how torn up he'd been about losing his wife, even Tom Carson had seemed satisfied with how justice had prevailed once the actual sentence was carried out. The case had been solved, damn it. Shame on Leah for dredging up old memories that were in no need of dredging up.

And Tom Carson's case had never been anything but a suicide. Leah had no idea what made her suddenly decide to turn it into something else. The man had been so depressed he'd spent his life savings on a therapist. He'd even waited until Sylvie wasn't home to kill himself and made sure she wouldn't be the one who found his body; that responsibility fell to a farmhand.

No, so far, all Leah's theories had been mirages. In some ways, she was worse than Sylvie. She'd been jumping at shadows.

She was thinking about all this as she pulled into Sylvie's drive to discover, just as Sylvie had said she would, both cellar doors wide open around the back of the house. And just as Sylvie said, there wasn't any wind, or at least not enough to make that a credible excuse. Besides, last time she was here, Leah felt the way that clasp had tightened. There wasn't any way those doors were blowing open unless Alvin was hit by a twister.

So that meant someone really was coming into Miss Sylvie's backyard. This was hardly any surprise given that the last time Leah was called out someone had obviously been inside her actual house. Leah still found it disquieting how they'd somehow left the place completely locked up behind them. The strange part was the complete lack of any evidence of potential danger. Well, she supposed that mucking around with Sylvie's shotgun showed some disturbing signs—but whoever it was had *dis*armed it. They had made the place safer, not more hazardous.

This time it really seemed as though someone was trying to make Sylvie look like (or think that) she was going crazier than everyone thought she was. Because, if she really did only go inside for a half hour, this whole incident was set up to make it look like she was paranoid and delusional. And, possibly, to make people think she was doing these incidents to herself (which, of course, *had* crossed Leah's mind).

Like before, Leah got down on her hands and knees, and this time she forced back her fears and went partially into the crawl space with her flashlight. The dirt ground was uneven, but there was nothing and nobody down there. Just a bunch of dirt. Again she saw marks in the dirt, but she couldn't tell if they were any different than they had been before. Just like last time, Leah felt a little ashamed for not searching the crawl space properly, but she couldn't bring herself to go in any farther. As it was, her pulse was up. Besides, there didn't appear to be anything down here but probably some spiders stuck in this tight, dark space.

"Well, we've definitely found the source of your fruit-fly problem," Leah said to Sylvie. "They're all comin' from down here in your crawl space." There were flies everywhere beneath the house.

"Why would there be fruit flies in my crawl space if there ain't no fruit down there?" Sylvie asked. She'd calmed down considerably since Leah had arrived. Leah got the feeling both of them were getting a little too used to this same routine.

Sylvie's question was one Leah couldn't answer. "I don't know, but there ain't no fruit that I can see. Not even a dead possum or anythin' like that. Could be a stray banana peel or somethin' tucked away in one of the corners, maybe."

Just like every other time she showed up at Sylvie's, Leah pulled out her pad and took down an official statement from Sylvie. And just like every other time, Sylvie added in her own editorial comment, this time using Preacher Eli's name in place of "the suspect" or "whoever did it."

"I wasn't gone for not even thirty minutes," Sylvie said. "And Preacher Eli came and opened these doors. God only knows what else the man did."

Leah didn't bother trying to explain that Eli Brown had been with her. Instead, she calmly said, "You don't know for sure *who* is responsible for this, Sylvie. Just remember that. Everyone is innocent until proven guilty."

"I know it's Preacher Eli. *You* might not, but I do." Sylvie was holding the baby, who was sucking on a soother.

Leah let out a breath. "I'm leavin' that out of the statement."

With a shrug, Sylvie said, "Suit yourself."

After she'd taken the report, Leah stood back and examined the doors one more time, wondering who really did it.

The baby started getting fussy and Sylvie said, "I have to go inside and give her the rest of her bottle. I spent all night pumpin' it, so she's gonna drink it. Is that okay? Or do you still need me?"

"No, go ahead. I'm just going to have a look around."

As Sylvie walked back inside, Leah started thinking about all of the different times she'd been called out to Sylvie's lately. First it was for the flowerpots. That one she wrote off as paranoia. Even if it turned out to be someone messing with Sylvie, it was so benign, it wasn't worth putting on the list. But then there were the big ones: the single cellar door being opened; the shotgun being unloaded, and the shells being lined up on the table; the dead cat on the porch; and now both cellar doors being opened.

She squatted back down and swept the cellar again with her flashlight. *Was* there something down here she wasn't seeing? And if there was, why would someone draw attention to it by leaving the doors open, unless they *wanted* it found? That made no sense. What *did* make sense was using the doors to make Sylvie *think* she was going nuts.

But who would want to do that?

Part of Leah was disappointed Eli Brown was no longer on the suspect list. He'd fit so well, in so many different ways. Maybe it could still be him. She had called Leland's dad in Alabaster from her car phone on the way over and he had been able to put Leland on the line, so Eli's story about his grandson going home checked out. Could there be a *third* partner?

What about the shotgun? How had they gotten into the house and back out again without any evidence of breaking and entering? There was no way in Leah's mind that she could see Sylvie accidentally leaving a door or a window unlocked, or not noticing if a door was not locked when she got back home. The girl was far too paranoid.

It had to be someone good at picking dead bolts. But in a town of fewer than two thousand people, how many potential suspects do you actually *have?* Again, that's why Eli Brown had been such a great suspect. It was a skill he could've picked up in prison during the past seventeen years.

Unless . . .

Unless it was someone who didn't have to use a door or a window.

Leah stepped back and took in the back of the house. How else could somebody get in?

There were ducts, but they were much too small to crawl in through. There was no fireplace and, besides, was she seriously considering someone coming down the chimney?

No, it had to be a door or a window.

And then it came to her.

And when it did, she had no idea why it had taken this long before she thought of it.

What if the person who broke in had used the door but didn't need to know how to pick locks?

Because, what if the person breaking in *already had a key?*

Now the question was: How many people might have keys to Sylvie Carson's house?

Leah walked in the back door where Sylvie was breast-feeding the baby. "Sylvie?" she asked. "Who has keys to your house?"

"Nobody," Sylvie answered. "I just changed the locks."

"I mean before that."

"Nobody."

"Are you sure?"

"Positive. Why would I give out any keys?"

"What about Orwin?"

There was a long silence while Sylvie considered this. "Actually, I don't know what happened to his key. I doubt he still has it."

Leah had her pad out again and was back to taking notes. "Can I ask you some questions about your relationship? With Orwin?"

Sylvie shrugged, rubbing the back of the baby's neck. "Sure."

"How would you describe it?"

"It was fine. I mean it wasn't perfect, but whose is, right? We had our good days and our bad days."

"Describe a bad day."

"He'd come home from work in a mood or it would be a day when he couldn't find work."

"And . . . ?"

"And he'd usually get drunk and loud. You know."

"Pretend I don't."

"Well, he'd call me names and stuff."

"So he'd get verbally abusive?" Leah asked.

"I guess. Not sure if I'd call it abusive."

"Did he ever get physical with you?"

"What do you mean?"

"Did he ever *hit* you?"

Sylvie looked away.

"I'll take that as a yes."

Sylvie looked back at Leah. "Not very often. And it was usually on account of me doin' somethin' dumb."

"And I'll ignore that completely." Leah jotted down a few more notes on her pad. "Do you know where Orwin is now?"

Sylvie shook her head.

"No idea at all?"

"None."

"Do you know anyone who *might* know? Close friends? Relatives?"

Sylvie looked at the ceiling while she moved the baby higher onto her shoulder so she could burp her. "Well, Orwin does have this aunt he was close to. She lives somewhere in . . . oh, I can't remember."

"He's close to her?"

"Yeah."

"How close?"

"Well, we were short money once and needed rent and he called her and she drove all the way down to lend it to us. She lives, like, four hundred miles away. Somewhere in Arkansas, I think."

"Wow, that's a long way to come to lend someone money. Do you remember her name?"

"His aunt . . . um . . . Jolayne. That's it. Jolayne."

"Did you pay the money back?"

Sylvie finished burping the baby and put her back into cradle position. "What?"

"The money Jolayne lent you. Did you ever pay it back?"

"Yeah. About three weeks later. Orwin drove it back to her."

"You didn't go?"

"No, I stayed here."

"How come?"

Sylvie shrugged. "I dunno. He just told me I didn't have to come and that he'd be fine goin' alone."

Leah put her pad back in her pocket. "Okay, thanks."

"Why are you askin' 'bout Orwin? You gonna try and find him?"

"I might."

"Think you can?"

"Shouldn't be too hard," Leah said. "After all, he still has your car, doesn't he?"

On her way home, Leah's thoughts wandered away from Orwin Thomas and Sylvie Carson and back to her son probably still lying in his bed back home. Leah wasn't mad about his outburst, but she was concerned. She was pretty sure she knew what had driven him to it, and, the truth was, she was going through a similar emotional conflict herself.

It was this whole new family popping up in their lives that was digging up memories of Billy. For Leah, those memories came mixed with anger, guilt, and blame.

He'd been gone ten years, but it'd only been very recently she'd realized she still hadn't gotten over his death. When he died, she took down all his pictures and put them away along with anything else that reminded her of him. Just thinking about him was too painful to bear, so she hid those thoughts away as best she could.

One of the best hiding spots turned out to be behind a big heap of blame. She blamed him for leaving her alone. Blamed him for dying. And that made her angry.

In the first couple years, she had gone to grief counseling, so she knew the drill: five steps of grieving and you have to go through it before you're out of it. Only she couldn't stand to get through the first step. So she stopped the cycle before it even had a chance to start.

It turns out there's a funny thing about grief. It won't be stopped. The cycle will keep going all by itself if you try to keep it bottled up too long.

And the part she hadn't realized was that by hiding Billy's death away from herself, she had taken a daddy away from her children. Especially from Abe. She saw that now, and it was that realization that allowed her to come to terms with needing to resolve Billy's death in her own mind.

Funny, but the therapist said first comes denial, then anger, then bargaining, then depression, and finally acceptance. Somehow that therapist had missed the one thing Leah needed to work out the most. And, in her mind, that was forgiveness. She needed to forgive her husband for dying on her.

But tonight, she had a little boy at home who needed her to push all of this aside and be there for him as his mother and, even if it killed her on the inside, to show him that she accepted his pa's death.

Because her boy wanted nothing more than to know about his pa. And he had every right in the world to get his wish.

CHAPTER 30

By the time my mother returned from Miss Sylvie's, I had stopped crying. I still didn't know why I had flipped out in my front yard. I was starting to think I might have some emotional problems or something like people on TV were always talking about. The worst part was I knew I was in for it the minute I heard her car pull in the driveway. Normally, I couldn't even give my mother the slightest "tone" (a word she used a lot that I didn't rightly understand), and this time, I outright screamed at her for five whole minutes. I didn't know what was going to happen, but I had never wished I was Dewey so bad in all my life.

I heard every detail as she walked into the house. I listened to her take off her shoes and put away her keys. Then she checked the fridge. She was supposed to make chicken-fried steak and potato salad tonight, but I didn't think she still would. It was getting on quite dark and when I heard Carry come home at least an hour or two ago, I was sure I heard her fixing something to eat before she headed to the living room to watch television.

She never once wondered where I was or, if she knew, why I was in my room. My sister didn't really pay much attention to my life. We got along okay. We still did things together, like the day we made the swords, but I had found that more and more it required a lot of begging on my part to get her to be an active participant.

Or I wound up having to paint her toenails once a week for an entire month. Things like that.

Finally, after what sounded like my mother going through the mail, she left the kitchen and came down the hall. She didn't come right to my room; she went to her own first. I started thinking that maybe she'd forgotten what had happened.

But then I realized nobody could forget all that.

And she hadn't. She was in her room about ten minutes before she came in and sat on the edge of my bed. I was facing away from her, toward the wall with my window. I didn't turn around.

"Abe?" she asked. "You awake?"

Her voice was very calm, which can sometimes be even worse than when she sounds upset, so I've learned not to trust it. I've also learned never to lie to her, so I said, "Yes."

"Will you turn around?"

I turned over in my bed, leaving my head on my pillow. I could feel the stains from my tears still on my face even though it had been at least an hour since I stopped crying.

I expected to see her looking full of anger.

Only she wasn't.

"Are you okay now?" she asked.

Her question confused me. "I—" I started, then answered with, "Yeah."

"Do you know what happened outside?"

I just shook my head. It was the truth.

"I think I do. I think you got a little overwhelmed by everything that's been going on lately."

I hesitated. Was I not going to get in trouble? "What do you mean?"

"Well, first, I think I made a mistake taking you to Eli Brown's that day. Second, this whole thing with your new grandparents and that woman who's your aunt—I reckon it's got you thinkin' 'bout your pa and that's drummed up a bunch of feelin's you just don't know how to handle. And I've been very selfish, not tellin' you things 'bout him. So that's gonna stop. Right here. Right now."

There was something on the bed beside her. She'd brought it in with her. It was something I'd seen before, but not for many years: the shoe box from her closet that I "stole" the picture of my pa from, the one I kept in the drawer beside my bed and carried around in my pocket for good luck.

Seeing it now made my heart start hammering against my chest. What was she going to do?

Slowly, she lifted the top off the box. It was exactly as I remembered it: full of scattered photos of different sizes.

"I want to go through some of these with you, and tell you 'bout them. Tell you how old your pa was when they was taken and where we was and stuff we were doin'. That is, if you want to hear 'bout it?"

I gave her a big smile. "Boy, do I!" Then my throat went dry and felt too tight to get any more words out.

"And then I want you to have them."

I blinked, stunned. "Have what?" I managed to ask.

"The pictures."

"All of them?"

"Yes. As long as you'll take good care of them."

"Yes. I will." I couldn't believe it.

So we went through the pictures one at a time. Some we skipped on account of them being similar to others, but she told me stories about how my pa used to play football with his friends in the afternoons and how they used to go camping and hiking and then after Carry came along how they would take her down to the beach in Mobile and then they'd take me after I came along and how much I loved the waves and the sand. I listened to every word as though it were coming from the Gospels.

Then she reached into the box and stopped talking.

Her face fell sort of flat of emotion. She looked like somebody had just told her some very bad news.

"What is it?"

"Just—I forgot this was here," she said, pulling out a gold ring.

"What is it?"

"My wedding ring. I put it in here when I put the pictures away."

I watched her face, waiting to see if she was going to get angry the way she used to when I would bring up my pa. Or maybe she'd start crying, the way I remembered her doing a long time ago when things would remind her of him.

But she didn't do either. Instead, she just put the ring in her shirt pocket.

"What are you gonna do with it?" I asked.

"I'm not certain," she said. "But you certainly don't need it."

I laughed. "No. I'm happy with the pictures."

"I'm sure I'll find some use for it." Her voice sounded very far away.

"Mom?" I asked after a moment of silence.

She sort of jerked back to my room. "Yeah?"

"You okay?"

She reached down and hugged me. "Yes, I'm fine."

"Mom, when am I gonna meet my new grandma and granddaddy? You said we was going."

Sitting up, she replied, "Whenever I can get time away from work to drive to Georgia. We'll need a whole day. Right now Miss Sylvie's takin' all my time."

I frowned. "Does she have to call the station constantly?"

"Hey!" my mother snapped. "Sometimes people really *do* need the police to help them."

"Does Miss Sylvie?"

She thought that over. "Let's just say I don't think Miss Sylvie's as crazy as other people do." From the way she said it, it was obvious the topic was to be left at that.

It didn't matter; I was more interested in getting back to the photographs, anyway.

We continued going through pictures another thirty minutes or so. Then she asked me if I felt like eating anything. I told her I hadn't had any supper on account of she told me to go straight to my room and stay here until she got back from Miss Sylvie's.

"Well, I have potato salad already made," she said. "Let me quickly fry you up some steak Then I think it's bedtime."

"Okay," I said and got out of bed and followed her to the kitchen with the shoe box full of photos underneath my arm.

While she cooked, I kept looking through the pictures, feeling closer and closer to my pa. I was happy my mother was able to talk about him without getting angry or sad. It seemed to me that must be a definite improvement in the way she was handling him being gone. But then, I was just a kid, so what the heck did I know?

Well, I knew I loved chicken-fried steak and potato salad, which I had two helpings of before putting the pictures safely away in my own bedroom closet and going to bed for the night.

Not much later, Leah decided to go to bed early. During the summer she always went to bed before her daughter, Caroline, who didn't really have a bedtime through the summer break. But tonight Leah retired even earlier than usual.

It was around ten when she walked into her bedroom and turned on the lamp beside her bed. She began undressing so she could get into her pajamas when she remembered the wedding ring she'd put into her pocket earlier on.

Pulling it out now, she stared at it a long while under the soft glow of her bedroom lamp. It brought up strange emotions. A year ago, she wouldn't have been able to hold it in her hands without throwing it. Now, she just felt oddly empty looking at the big O it made.

When Billy died, she could very well have pawned it out. She threw out a lot of things with his memory attached to them, but something had made her keep this ring. There must've been a reason. She had hidden it away, but she'd kept it nonetheless.

Now the ring more intrigued her than upset her.

She had no idea what to do with it now that she'd given the shoe box to Abe. So, gingerly, she placed it on the table beside her bed right beneath her lamp where it continued to sparkle in the warmth of the golden glow.

By the time she woke up the next day, she'd forgotten it was even there.

CHAPTER 31

The first thing Leah did after getting back to work was call directory assistance up in Arkansas and ask for all the numbers they had matching any Jolayne Thomases. She was given five.

She dialed the first one and nobody answered.

She called the second, asked to speak to Orwin, and was told, "I don't know no Orwin."

On the third try, she got lucky.

"He's out of town," the woman on the other end said. Her voice was deep and gruff. "Who is this, anyway? If you one of his ex-girlfriends you ain't got no business callin' here. How'd you get this number?"

Leah just hung up. "Yeah, he's not in town," she said to herself, "on account of him bein' here in Alvin."

"You say somethin'?" Chris asked from the desk beside her. He was doing the crossword in the newspaper.

"Nothin' important."

Using her computer, she looked up the area code of the telephone number she'd just called and discovered it was in Pine Bluff. That was another good use for the computer; it could do reverse phone numbers for most telephone listings in and around Alabama and had information for every area code in the country.

Putting in another call to the Pine Bluff sheriff's office, she told them who she was, gave them her badge and station number, and asked if she could acquire information on Jolayne Thomas.

"You got more than just a name for us to go on?" the officer at the other end asked. He sounded a bit put out by her request.

"I got her telephone number." She gave it to him.

"So, what sorta stuff you lookin' for?"

Leah had learned from what happened with Tom Carson. *Don't overlook anything.* "Everything," she said. "Financial records, medical records, a background check, the works."

"You wanna know what size of panties she wears?"

Leah didn't laugh. "I'd really appreciate the favor if you could do this for me."

"This information *that* important to you?"

"Yes," she said. "I think it may be."

She heard him sigh. "All right. Let me see what I can do. What's your fax number?"

Luckily, Ethan had gone out and replaced the busted fax machine last week so she had a number to give him that would work.

"Some of this stuff is gonna take some time," the officer said. "I'm gonna have to make some calls. It's gonna take a while. You want me to send everythin' at once after I get it all, or would you rather have it in bits and drabs as it comes in?"

"I'll take it as it comes, if that's all right with you."

Another sigh. "Doesn't matter to me either way."

Leah thanked him again for his time and hung up, hoping the officer would actually do what he said he was going to do.

After the call into the sheriff's office, Leah wasted no time in getting on to her next task: running a background check on Orwin Thomas. Opening the cabinet containing the five hundred or so gray five-and-a-quarter-inch floppy discs that made up their station's computer database, she found the one listed in the T section between Ta and Tm. If they had any data on the computer for Orwin Thomas, this would be where she'd uncover it.

Returning to her desk, she slipped the disk into the drive and waited while the computer read it. It chunked and whirred like it always did. Pulling up data on the computers wasn't fast, but it was a helluva lot faster than going through drawers of file folders. She only hoped someone had entered the information from the file folder onto the disc.

While she waited, she chided herself for not considering Orwin a suspect immediately.

The goddamn house was still locked when Sylvie came home, Leah, she thought. *Why didn't you think of him right away? Why did it take so long to consider it might just be someone with a key?*

She knew the answer. It was because she had Eli Brown on the brain. And Sylvie was partially to blame for that, and so was Leah's son. But that was no excuse. *It shouldn't have mattered; you're a goddamn detective. Do your job.*

Eli Brown was an innocent man in all this whose father-in-law managed to finangle a ranch at such low cost there wasn't any chance of even a dime being left over for anything even remotely resembling an inheritance for Sylvie. The bank wouldn't even have got half of what was owed to them on the place.

When the background check finally loaded, it was full of surprises and yet, at the same time, none of them really surprised Leah at all.

The first surprise was how much information on Orwin Thomas was available on the computer. Someone (likely Chris) had gone through all his files and entered everything into the system. That made things a lot easier. As an adult, Orwin Thomas's record was absolutely clean, but his record as an adolescent was another story. It showed three counts of theft, one with aggravated assault, one count of possession, and "a noted history of fighting."

Unfortunately, because he was a minor, it was a juvenile record, and it was frustratingly vague.

"Chris?" Leah asked.

"Yeah." Chris had just returned from using the "facilities" and swung around in his chair so he was facing her. He had back-straddled it.

"I need you to work some magic for me."

"What kind?"

"That thing you can do with juvey records?"

"You mean get all the dirt?"

"Yeah, I need you to do that."

"Just give me a name," he said.

"Orwin Thomas."

"Orwin Thomas? Star tight end? Torn ACL?"

"That'd be the one."

"You suspect the superstar might not be so shiny?"

"Well, his adult record looks like it's been Turtle Waxed it's so clean, but from what I can see, there are hints that his juvey one might show a different picture."

"I'm on it." Chris grabbed a handful of floppy discs from the database cabinet and began inserting them into his computer one after another while madly typing away. Soon, he began making telephone calls, receiving calls, and receiving faxes. This was something the man truly had a gift for. Leah had no idea how he did it. He must have connections in all the right places because, literally, less than an hour later, he put a compiled report in Leah's hands.

"Okay," she said. "Sometimes you really do astound me."

"Oh, I bet you say that to all the boys."

"Warn me now, anything I'm not gonna like in here?"

"Depends on whether you're lookin' to nail him to the wall or to a cross."

"Okay . . . that sounds interesting. I'll leave it as a surprise."

The reports outlined everything and more.

Orwin Thomas got caught twice stealing from Applesmart's Grocery, and he once walked into Fast Gas with a tire iron and asked the person behind the register to empty it into a bag. He also got caught for possession. It was just a small amount of marijuana, but it was enough to almost get him tried in adult court (he'd been seventeen years old at the time).

There were also five separate incidents of fighting where police were called to the scene, although no arrests were made. Still, the report definitely showed a notable history of violence in his teen years. And these were only the fights where the police showed up. Leah was certain there were probably many more that went unreported.

The first happened when Orwin was fourteen and the last was

when he was eighteen. Even at eighteen, no legal action had been taken against him.

Twice when he was brought in on the other charges he was evaluated by a psychologist, a different doctor each time. The first one said Orwin showed violent outbreaks throughout their discussion and acted angrily toward some of the questions being asked. The report said the doctor found this pattern "disturbing" and that Orwin displayed an inherent distrust of authority figures.

The second psychologist suggested that Orwin showed signs of mental illness and even went so far as to say, at times, his behavior was borderline psychopathic in nature. The report stated, if left untended, Orwin's mental condition could grow into a potential risk to himself or others.

Orwin had been seventeen when that second assessment had been made. He'd managed to stay out of trouble ever since.

This fact did little to comfort the empty hollow expanding inside Leah's gut as she read.

She paged down to a list of Orwin's known associates and saw the usual suspects. Even for being a small town, Alvin had its share of troubled teens, just like everywhere else. And they tended to flock together like black sheep.

Then her eyes settled on one name in particular: Darius "Dee Bee" Baylor. Leah wasn't sure what it was, but something about that name was setting off alarm bells in her head.

"Chris?"

"Mmm?"

"Where have I heard the name Darius Baylor 'fore?"

"Dee Bee? He was part of that takedown I made. Remember? *The Biggest Bust in Dixie?* I think that's what the *Alerter* called it." He smiled smugly.

"Oh, right. Now I remember."

Leaning back in his chair, Chris interlaced his fingers, pushed out his arms, and cracked his knuckles. "Yep," he said. "Four of *them. One* of me. *Incredible* odds."

"So I heard," Leah said, as disinterestedly as possible. "Like I said, you're a superhero."

The fax machine began slowly rolling out a thin sheet of paper.

Chris got up out of his chair and, with an arrogant sashay to his step that made Leah wish she'd never asked about Darius Baylor, he strutted over and patiently watched each page crawl out and curl onto the gray carpet.

Picking up the cover sheet, he said, "Financial records for someone named Jolayne Thomas livin' in Pine Bluff, Arkansas? This for you?"

"That was quick," she said. "And you were sittin' right here beside me just over an hour ago when I made the call askin' for the records. Didn't you hear me?"

He shrugged. "Guess I wasn't listenin'."

Chris continued watching as each separate page crept from the machine and curled up onto the floor.

"You know watchin' it don't make it go any faster," Leah said.

"I know. I just find technology fascinatin' is all."

Finally, when it was all finished, Chris brought all the sheets to Leah's desk and handed them to her. She scanned them and quickly concluded things weren't exactly right with Jolayne Thomas.

At one time, near on a year ago, the woman had a fair amount of money in the bank—just over a hundred grand.

But since then, she had drawn almost all of it out. And it came out in just three lump sums. The first happened pretty near ten months ago and was for the curious round number of seventy-five thousand dollars. The other two were for amounts around fifteen thousand dollars each, and both happened in the past six months.

There was another interesting tidbit of information inside these pages. Jolayne Thomas had two credit cards, but they were both attached to the same account. One was in her own name, and the other was in the name of Orwin James Thomas.

"Well, that answers *that* question," Leah said.

"What question?" Chris asked. He was back at his desk, more interested in what Leah was doing than his crossword.

Instead of answering him, Leah focused on that seventy-five-thousand-dollar withdrawal. She jotted down the date and did a quick calculation in her head. Despite what she'd wanted to tell Chris, she remembered his coke bust well. She knew exactly when it had happened. And this withdrawal took place within a week before that time. *And* now that she thought about it (and again, this was something she couldn't believe she was only thinking of now), Orwin Thomas had disappeared from Sylvie's life the day after Chris brought in those four guys and all them drugs.

Her brain quickly put two and two together. Orwin Thomas had once been a pretty big high school football superstar. He'd have connections. She was willing to bet one of those connections offered him an investment he couldn't turn down. Buy low, sell high. Easy money for Orwin, who was in need of some easy money. He just needed to find the funding for the deal.

That would be where Miss Jolayne came into the picture.

"When you, you know," she asked Chris, "single-handedly caught them guys with those drugs, you found money on them too, right?"

"Sure did," he said. "About sixty-three thousand dollars. Them DEA guys that come up from Mobile figured they musta sold some of that coke 'fore I managed to nail 'em."

"Hmm."

"Hmm, what?" Chris asked.

She searched his eyes. "What would you say if I told you I think I know who bought it?"

Chris gave a little laugh. "I'd say I wish you woulda known that ten months ago so I coulda caught him with it and put him away, too."

Leah mulled this over. Orwin was back in Alvin, and there had to be a reason he was back, and it wasn't just to get Sylvie all riled up. No, that part was a distraction, Leah figured. Orwin probably thought that if Sylvie called the police enough times with false alarms that the police would stop coming out and that would make her place a lot safer to get in and out of.

Leah turned her attention back to Chris. "I think he still has them. The drugs, I mean."

Chris gave another little laugh. "Now you're just teasin'."

"I reckon it was Orwin Thomas who bought 'em and when you made them arrests he got scared that one of them guys you put behind bars was gonna go on and tell you who they sold it to, so he hid the stuff and left town. And now, I think he's come back to get 'em."

"Why now?"

That was a good question. Leah considered it. "I don't rightly know. Maybe enough time has gone by that he no longer feels afraid that someone's gonna squeal on him." The dwindling balance left on the financial records sitting in front of her popped off the page. "Maybe he needs the money, so he needs to sell 'em."

"Okay, so where did he hide them?"

This one didn't take much thought. Orwin had come and checked to make sure his stash was still there once and not closed the crawl space door properly behind him. That's why the wind had blown it open.

"Under Sylvie's house. In the cellar," she said. Then she remembered the last time Sylvie had called her out to show her both doors thrown wide open. That hadn't been because of Orwin checking anything and not closing something properly. "Only," she said, "I think we're too late. I think he's already got them."

"Because he left those cellar doors open?" Chris asked.

"Mmm-hmm."

"Why wouldn't he close them on his way out?"

"Two reasons, I reckon," Leah answered. "One, he didn't need to. He got what he was after. But the second is more disturbin' to me. For one reason or another, Orwin Thomas is tryin' to make Sylvie Carson look crazier than she is. Or make her more paranoid than she is." And the scariest part about that to Leah was that the man knew she had a loaded shotgun leaning up beside her back door.

Chris was already halfway out of his chair, grabbing his keys and heading for the door by the time Leah finished her sentence. "Well, we're damn well gonna check and make sure those drugs ain't still there," he said. "Come on. You can come with me in the cruiser."

It was midmorning when they arrived at Sylvie's. They found her home, running around like a dog chasing its own tail. For once, the baby wasn't sleeping. In fact, it was downright cranky, and didn't seem to want to eat, or be burped, or be held, or be put down. Or nothing. Even Leah gave it a try.

"Well, I don't know what she wants," Leah said, handing her back to Sylvie.

"Let's go check that cellar," Chris said, walking past.

Leah followed him outside. Sylvie trailed behind, baby wailing in her arms.

"So, which of us is goin' under?" Leah asked nervously.

Chris gave a small chuckle as he opened the cellar doors and shined his flashlight inside. "It's just dirt. Doesn't even look wet. It does look like someone's been under here recently, though. What are you 'fraid of, spiders?"

"I ain't afraid of nothin'," Leah said, not wanting to admit he'd hit half the equation directly on the bull's-eye. "I just don't relish the thought of bein' squashed up in that two-foot-high space while I wiggle round like a snake searchin' out the area."

"That's okay, I wanna go anyway. If the coke *is* down here, this is still part of my bust."

Leah let that one go by. Far as she could tell, she'd done all the work.

"It's all yours," she said.

Chris started to go in stomach first. He made it in about as far as his feet, then turned around and came back out.

"What's wrong?" Sylvie asked from the porch.

"Nothin'. I think it would be better to go in on my back."

He went at it again, on his back this time. It did seem to give him more leverage with his feet. Soon he was out of sight. Leah squatted down and watched through the doors, but all she could make out was the occasional sweep of his flashlight. Then, from beneath the house came a loud, "Eww!"

"What is it?" Leah called out, a little worried.

"Found the cat puke!"

More time passed while his light went from one side of the house to the next. After about fifteen minutes, he finally yelled, "I found something!"

"What?"

"Looks like . . . bags of coffee. Twelve of 'em. All stuffed around in a circle. The middle of the circle is empty, but it looks like it used to have somethin' in it. I'm guessing that's where the coke was. There's a white powder sprinkled all around the outside of the ring of coffee bags."

"Is it coke?"

A pause and then, "No. I think it's brodifacoum. Orwin was probably worried about rats getting into his drugs. It was a good thing to be worried 'bout too, on account of it looks like they got into at least two of the sacks of coffee. There's fruit flies everywhere."

"Well, that explains why they're under your house," Leah said to Sylvie.

"I think that's it," Chris said. "There ain't nothing else under here."

"Okay," Leah said, "You may as well come out then."

"I don't understand," Sylvie said. "Why is there sacks of coffee in my cellar?"

"Because your ex-boyfriend is a dumb shit," said Chris, pulling himself through the crawl space doors. Standing up, he brushed dirt off his uniform. He turned and let Leah get the dirt off the back. Most of it cleared away, but there was some that would stay until his uniform was properly washed. "Sometimes drug traffickers pack cocaine in coffee to throw drug dogs off the scent in airports."

"Does that work?"

"Hell if I know. But I have no idea why he thought using coffee under your house was a good idea. I guess he suspected we might come round with some airport drug dogs and send them into your cellar lookin' for coke. Unfortunately, the closest thing to that happening was your cat goin' in when that door was left open and eatin' some of that brodifacoum."

Sylvie looked about ready to cry. "That bastard killed my cat. He killed my goddamn cat."

Leah came up and gave her a hug. "Hey, at least you don't have to worry 'bout him comin' round here no more. He'll be gettin' outta Dodge as quick as a cat with its tail on fire. If he even suspects we're onto him, he won't hang round Alvin a minute longer than he has to, and I got a hunch Orwin's a pretty suspicious guy. When we made all them arrests last year, he was gone before the sun came up." She looked Sylvie straight in the eyes. "You're safe now. This is the last place he'll turn up again."

"Yeah," Chris said. "If he's smart, he'll stay as far away from Alvin as he can possibly get." He thought for a moment, and then turned to Leah. "Which reminds me. I better call the DEA in Arkansas and give them a heads-up on what's goin' on. He probably won't be stupid enough to keep the stuff at his house, but I bet they'll put him under surveillance and, sooner or later, catch him tryin' to push it."

"What 'bout the guys you arrested?" Leah asked. "Can't you get one of them to swear to selling it to him? Might be enough to take him in on. Then I've got Jolayne's financial records . . ."

"Maybe. They'd want a deal, though. I'd have to talk to the DA. Right now, we need all the states between here and Arkansas to issue an APB on the plates to Sylvie's Skylark he's driving."

"I'll get that done," Leah said. "Although, he took the stuff out of here. He's gone. No question 'bout it."

CHAPTER 32

Leah decided to take the kids out for supper at Vera's Old West Grill at the west end of Main Street. It had been a while since they'd been out together as a family. Two days ago, all the stress of the Orwin Thomas case she'd been working on had come to a rather unsatisfying end. Sure, the law would probably eventually catch up to Orwin Thomas, but Leah wanted it to happen here and she wanted to be part of it. She wanted to show Sylvie that the bad guys don't always get away. She thought it might help with the girl's paranoia. At any rate, Leah thought the next best thing was to spend some quality family time and just get out of the house for a nice meal and unwind a bit.

The weather was horrible. Rain washed through the town, and black clouds hung so low and heavy in the sky they seemed like they might almost touch the tops of some buildings.

At dinner, the kids appeared to enjoy themselves. At least they weren't arguing—not *really* arguing, anyway—which was a welcome change. They did banter back and forth a lot, but that was something they always did, whether they were happy or not.

Abe had ordered a hamburger and fries, and Caroline had gotten barbecued ribs with coleslaw and white bread. Leah ordered a sirloin steak, medium well.

"So are you kids enjoyin' your summer?"

"I was," Abe said.

"Not anymore?" Leah asked.

"Not so much. I ain't got my sword."

"That's cuz you broke it," Caroline said. She had barbecue sauce all around her lips. Her fingers were covered in it, too.

"How do *you* know I broke it?" Abe asked her.

"Dewey told me. He was outside in our backyard having a sword fight by himself and I asked him where the heck you were, and he said he didn't know and that it didn't matter anyway on account of you broke your sword over your knee cuz you threw a little fit."

"It wasn't a fit."

"What was it then? Dewey said it was a fit. He called you a girl."

I was surprised my sister didn't consider that a sexist remark. "Dewey says lotsa stuff that ain't true. You know, he thinks he's a genius." Abe took such a big bite of his burger, Leah was worried he might choke on it.

"Maybe he is," Caroline said. "Ever thought of that?"

Abe laughed. "You've *met* Dewey, right? He tried to get satellite TV by using up all our aluminum foil."

"At least he *tries* stuff. He's smart for tryin'. Don't you think so, Mother?" Caroline put a rib in her mouth and pulled out a clean bone and set it upon her plate.

"Leave me out of this."

"Mom don't like Dewey," Abe said. "She thinks he's weird."

"I never said that."

"You have too. Lotsa times."

Leah cut off a piece of steak and had it ready on her fork to go into her mouth. "Well, he's a bit *different* at times," she said. "But I've never said I don't like him." She put the steak in her mouth.

"Well, I *like* Dewey," Caroline said. "I find him quite interestin' and entertainin'."

"I like Dewey well enough," Abe said. "If I didn't, why would I hang round with him?"

"On account of you only have one friend?" Caroline laughed.

"That's not true."

"It's not? Name two more."

"I can name lots more. I just don't wanna."

"You're so full of shit your eyes are brown."

"Hey!" Leah snapped. "Language."

" 'Sides," Abe said, "my eyes are blue. Just like my pa's were, ain't that right, Mom?" He took another bite of burger. He was definitely starting to grow up. There was a time not so long ago when Leah could remember Abe not being able to get through half a Vera's Texas Burger. Now tonight it looked like he might finish this one entirely.

"That's right," Leah said.

Caroline studied Leah as if her hair had turned into rattlesnakes. "You're talking 'bout Pa now?"

Leah smiled. "We're testin' the waters."

"Huh," Caroline said. "That's new. It's a nice change. I miss him sometimes."

"I do too, honey," Leah said sadly.

"I wish I could," Abe said. "You guys are lucky to have known him good enough to miss him."

Leah's heart almost broke then. "I'm sorry."

On that note, they all went back to finishing up their food.

The rain was coming down like marbles being poured out of a bucket from somewhere in heaven when they walked outside of the restaurant. Luckily, they weren't parked far away, or they'd all have been soaked by the time Leah quickly unlocked the car doors and everyone piled inside. As usual, Caroline got the front seat and Abe got in the back.

"Boy, am I full," he said, lying across the cushions as if the entire backseat were a sofa.

But Leah shushed him. As soon as she opened her door, she immediately heard Chris on her radio trying to reach her. Quickly, she picked it up and answered it. "Chris. It's me. What's up?"

"Leah! I've been trying to reach you for half an hour."

"Sorry, I was out for dinner with the kids. What's up?"

"Well, it was one thing, then it became two things, and now it's three things."

"Uh-oh. Sounds like a disaster. Go ahead." Leah didn't start the car, she just sat there, parked, talking on the radio. The rain continued pelting the windshield. It made a ruckus, splattering on the roof of the car.

"First, we got a credit card transaction flag for Orwin Thomas for a purchase he made *yesterday*."

"Okay."

"Ask me where he made it."

"Where?"

"Fast Gas. In *Alvin*."

"In *Alvin*? Why the hell is he still *here*?"

"Well, we don't know if he's *still* here. It looks like he filled his tank, so he may have been heading back to Pine Bluff. But he was here yesterday."

"Why would he have hung round all this time? He got them drugs *days* ago."

"I can't answer that."

Leah's mind raced. It made no sense. He should have left town immediately upon getting what he came for. It was the only logical thing to do. *And people always do the most logical thing, unless there are other variables at play you don't know about.* Now *that* was the detective in her thinking.

"What's the second thing?"

"About fifteen or twenty minutes ago Miss Sylvie called."

"What did she want?" *This is new,* Leah thought. *Chris calling her* Miss *Sylvie.*

"She said she reckoned she saw the shadow of someone outside her house lookin' in her window."

"Was she panicky?"

"She sounded a little upset."

"Did you go check it out?"

"Er—" Chris stumbled. "No."

"Did Ethan go?"

"No."

"Why didn't anyone go? If you can't get hold of me, it's your responsibility to go."

"I just, um, figured since you've always gone before that you'd want to be the one to go this time." He sounded fumbly and embarrassed and Leah was glad. He deserved to be embarrassed.

"Okay, I'll stop in there on my way home. Now, what's the third thing? Your things are gettin' me progressively more and more irked, by the way."

"Not my intention."

"I know."

"Third thing is you got another fax. This one is the medical records for Jolayne Thomas in Pine Bluff, Arkansas."

"Do you mind givin' me the highlights? Go from most recent events first and head backward please."

"That's easy. This year there's only two things of note, really, an' they're both the same thing."

"What's that?"

"She had two visits to some place in Little Rock called Forever Fertility. The last one was just shy of two months ago and the time before that was around four months ago."

"Sounds like a fertility clinic. That explains the two fifteen-thousand-dollar withdrawals from her account. So Miss Jolayne's tryin' to have herself a baby."

"Yeah, but by the looks of this, it don't seem like she's havin' much success." Chris laughed.

A thought suddenly struck Leah like a brick bein' dropped on her from a fourth-story window. "Oh dear God," she said.

"What is it?"

"Chris, I gotta go. I'll radio back when I can."

"Um . . . okay."

Cutting off their conversation, Leah clipped the radio back into its holder and started the car. "Buckle up, kids."

"Aw," Abe complained from the backseat. "But I'm so full."

Reaching down beneath her console, Leah pulled out her blue-and-red light and plunked it on the dash. It lit up the street around them. The falling rain reflected the light like colored sheets. She hit the siren. "I don't care," she told Abe. "This might be a bumpy ride."

"You ain't takin' us to a crime scene, are you?" Caroline asked from beside her, quickly clipping her seat belt on while Leah peeled out off the curb and did a U-turn right in the middle of the street.

"I dunno yet," Leah said. "I just might be."

"Do you really think that's a good idea?"

"Oh, trust me," Abe said. "After a while, you get used to it."

Leah picked up the big telephone that sat in the console of her vehicle and dialed Sylvie Carson's home number. "Please don't let me be too late," she said under her breath as she heard it ring on the other end. "Please, God, don't let me be too late."

Leah had realized during her talk with Chris that Orwin had indeed come back for his drugs, but he'd also come back for something else. There was a reason he'd been trying to make Sylvie look insane. He'd been trying to make her look like an unfit mother, but it hadn't happened fast enough for him. He'd tried pushing her over the edge, but what he hadn't realized was that Sylvie was already so far over the edge there wasn't much farther for her to go. She was used to living over the edge, if that was even possible. So used to it, Orwin Thomas had failed to make her any crazier.

But now, Leah knew, with a full tank of gas, Orwin was ready to finish the job he'd come down from Arkansas for and then truly get out of town. And the real job hadn't just been to get his drugs. That had been *half* of it. The other half was to get something else. Something much more precious than seventy-five-thousand-dollars' worth of cocaine. Something Joylane wanted for her very own but couldn't have, and so Orwin Thomas was going to provide her with one.

And that thing was Sylvie's three-month-old baby girl.

CHAPTER 33

Thank the Lord Jesus Sylvie Carson not only had a telephone in her bedroom, but she answered it. As soon as she did, Leah heard more panic in the girl's voice than she ever had before. Sylvie was scared practically to the brink of her last breath of life.

"Sylvie, it's Leah. Listen to me, now. I think you and the baby are in danger." Leah was driving as fast as she could. Her siren wailed and her red and blue lights danced in the darkness. Still, it was a treacherous night to be driving fast and she had to be careful. The last thing she needed was to get into a crash. That would only guarantee she didn't make it to Sylvie's on time. Plus she had her kids in the car with her.

"Leah!" Sylvie said, nearly screaming into the phone. Her voice was quivering. The baby wailed in the background. "I—I've been trying to call the station, but I—I left the phone number in the kitchen . . . I—I'm locked in my bedroom. It's . . . it's Preacher Eli! He's at the door! He's—" Her words cut off. She was too panicked to talk.

Goddamn it, Leah was too late.

"What's goin' on, Sylvie?" Leah asked. "Talk to me. Slow down."

"He's tryin' to get in! He's comin' at it with an ax or somethin'!" Sylvie yelled. "The door. My goddamn front door!"

Shit. Leah had seen that door enough times. *That door ain't gonna stand up to an ax very long.*

"Listen to me, Sylvie. I might not get there in time. It's not Eli. It's Orwin. He's come for your baby." Rain pounded the windshield of Leah's car, making it hard to see and forcing her to drive more slowly than she wanted to. Everything outside was awash in rain and went by in streaks.

"Orwin? He's come back?" Suddenly, Sylvie's entire demeanor changed. This wasn't good. Leah needed her to stay scared.

"Yes," Leah said. "But he's come back to hurt you and take your baby. Sylvie! Listen to me. You say you're in your bedroom?"

"Y—yes." Good. At least the panic was back.

"With the door locked?"

"Of . . . of course."

"You have the baby?"

"Yes."

"And . . . Sylvie?" Leah asked. "Do you have your shotgun?"

A hesitation. Then, "Yes. Do you think Orwin has a gun?"

"I don't know," Leah said. She was about to say that if Orwin had a gun he'd probably have already used it to shoot the lock out of the door, but she decided not to. Thank God Sylvie had had her locks changed.

Leah passed a road marker, her dashboard flasher lighting it up blue and red on this horrible night. She remembered the kids in the car and cursed under her breath. She still had near on two miles to go. She wasn't going to make it in time at this rate. But it was going to be close.

Leah decided she had to tell Sylvie something important, just in case. Something she actually couldn't believe she was about to say. "Listen to me carefully, Sylvie," Leah said. "I may not make it there in time. Do you understand?"

"Oh God . . . ," Sylvie said.

"Sylvie, listen. If I don't get there, it's up to you. You've *got* to protect that baby, understand? You have to save your child, and her mother. *At whatever cost it takes.*"

"I don't know if I can." Sylvie's voice cracked in a loud whisper. "My hands are shaking something fierce. I can hear him pounding on the outside door. It ain't gonna stand up much longer."

Damn it.

"You *have* to," Leah said. In the darkness, trees whipped past both sides of the car. The heavy dark clouds made everything nearly impossible to see on this dark rain-soaked night; all Leah made out was just what reflected back in red and blue. Occasionally, a streetlamp roared by, its light blurred because of the rainwater on the car's windows. There wasn't a lot of other traffic on the roads. For that, Leah was thankful.

"I don't know *how*," Sylvie said. "I keep thinkin' about what happened to Caleb."

"What happened to your brother is *why* you have to do this."

Silence. And then, "I'm scared."

"I know you are," Leah said. "So am I. I'm coming as fast as I can."

Leah knew she had to take a break from this call and contact the station for backup, but she didn't know how to do it without causing Sylvie to completely break down. "Listen, Sylvie? I need to radio the station. I'm not gonna hang up, but I need you to just sit tight one minute. Can you do that?"

"No! Don't go!"

"Okay, okay." Leah thought hard. Then she said to her daughter, "Caroline, pick up the radio and get Chris on the line. Tell him I need backup at Sylvie's house. Him *and* Ethan. Tell him it's a ten thirty-five."

"What?"

"Just do it!"

"Okay." Caroline picked up the radio. As Leah continued to fumble through her pep talk with Sylvie she heard her daughter convince Chris she was who she said she was and that she wasn't kidding around. Part of Leah became very proud of her in that moment.

"I hear him," Sylvie said. "Now he's bootin' the door."

"Sylvie?" Leah asked. She could tell the girl was on the verge of breaking down.

There was no response.

"Sylvie!"

"Yeah," she finally answered. She was out of breath. The night around Leah's car seemed to close in and grow even darker as she approached the edge of town.

"You can do this."

"I can do this."

Leah was coming up fast on the end of Main Street where the railroad tracks were, right before the turnoff to Old Mill Road, which was only a few minutes from Sylvie's house. But a train was coming. In fact, it was almost at the road.

Leah's brain scrambled to make a decision. The rain streaming down made it look like Leah had more clearance than she actually did, and she slammed her foot heavy on the gas pedal.

For a moment, all she saw was Caroline silhouetted in the train engine's white light. "Mom!" Caroline screamed.

Leah's heart felt like a wet bag trying to beat its way free from her rib cage. With barely a foot to spare, the car bolted over the tracks as the train rumbled past behind them. She'd made it, but the train would definitely slow down Chris and Ethan. They would be at least five to ten minutes behind her.

Cranking the wheel sharply to the left, Leah fishtailed onto Old Mill Road and flew up the curvy, wet street. Leah's pulse slowed a touch as she tried to catch her breath.

"Oh my God!" Caroline said, breathing hard. "That was crazily close."

Abe just sat in the backseat. If he'd noticed the train at all, he didn't let on.

"Sylvie?" Leah said, the phone still to her ear. "You can save your baby. Your brother would want you to."

Leah heard a loud *crack!* Sylvie cried, "He's broken down the front door!"

Now all that was left between Sylvie and her baby and Sylvie's psychopathic ex was a locked bedroom door not nearly as thick as the one he'd just made it through.

And still the rain continued to hammer Leah's car. Her

headlights barely lit up the road ten feet in front of her. The rest was showered away into darkness by the deluge of rain.

"Oh my God!" Sylvie shrieked. "He's coming!" Her fear flooded through the line as Leah heard Sylvie's phone drop to the floor. Leah listened hard. She heard Sylvie say Orwin's name, but after that, all she heard was the sound of Orwin yelling. It crackled in her car phone's speaker and didn't stop until . . .

One gunshot.

Then . . .

Then there was nothing else.

Just silence.

The phone went dead.

CHAPTER 34

Leah's car bounced into Sylvie's driveway, her red-and-blue light giving the house and surrounding trees a surrealistic glow. She'd passed Sylvie's old Skylark that Orwin had taken off in parked about a half mile down the road, positioned discreetly off to the side—barely visible in this torrent of rain. She already had her seat belt undone and her door partially open as she threw her vehicle into PARK and raced to the front door of the house, pulling out her gun along the way. "You kids stay down on the floor of the car!" she shouted back. "You hear me? I'm talking specifically to *you*, Abe. And in the name of *Jesus,* do not get out of that car!"

The rain had turned the dirt drive to muck. From somewhere inside the house came the wailing of the baby, nearly screaming at the top of its lungs. Leah so rarely heard that baby cry that she immediately took it as a bad sign.

This was not a time to wait for backup. She was going in alone.

The front door of the house was swung partially open. In its center was a huge hole full of wooden splinters where Orwin obviously came through with the ax. On the side of the porch, there was just enough room for Leah to stand with her back against the siding along the edge of the door without being in the doorway.

She stood there, feet at shoulder width apart, with her gun pointed down at a forty-five-degree angle, ready to be raised and fired.

"Alvin Police!" she called out as loudly and commandingly as she possibly could. "Whoever's inside, identify yourself!" Then, for good measure, she added, "The house is surrounded."

She didn't expect an answer. What she expected was a gunfight, but she knew Orwin was young and probably working alone. She was experienced and a pretty good shot. She liked the odds.

There was no answer, just like she figured. Just the continued screaming of the baby. At least *she* was okay and sounded as though she was still in the back bedroom. Leah decided to give Orwin one more chance before she turned and started shooting into the house. "Alvin Police!" she hollered again. "This is your last chance!"

Then she heard it. And it wasn't what she expected at all. It was the gentle sobbing of a girl. Leah could barely make it out over the noise of the baby shrieking. From the sobs, she heard Sylvie's voice nervously call out, "I—it's me, Miss Leah. Sylvie. I—I'm in the bedroom."

"Where's Orwin?" Leah yelled back.

"Lyin' beside me. I—I shot him. I think he's dead."

"Where's his gun?"

"I—I don't know. I never saw no gun. J—just the ax."

"Where's the ax?"

"Lyin' beside him."

"Throw the ax down the hall toward the living room," Leah called back.

There was a pause and some stumbling then a loud clump. It didn't sound like Sylvie had managed to toss the ax very far.

"Was there anyone with Orwin?"

"I—I don't think so."

"Okay. Sylvie? I'm comin' in." In the distance, over the cries of the baby, Leah heard Chris's and Ethan's sirens getting closer.

Leah turned into the open doorway and braced to take a shot. With her left arm, she gently pushed the door open so she could see more of the living room. She took a step into the house, making a circle with her gun ready. The living room was clear.

She got to the kitchen and did the same. The kitchen was clear.

She saw the ax laying a third of the way down the hall from Sylvie's bedroom. Slowly making her way toward it, Leah got to the ax and lifted it up. She tossed it the rest of the way to the living room. It landed with a very loud *thunk!*

Unlike the front door, Sylvie's bedroom door looked like it only took one or two swings of the ax to get through. It had popped open at the latch. Leah gently pushed it all the way open, keeping her gun ready in case she was looking at a hostage situation, and Sylvie had just been answering what Orwin had been wanting her to answer.

But that wasn't the case.

Leah found Sylvie crouching in the corner, the crying baby held tightly in her arms. Lying on the floor about six feet from her, at the foot of the bed, was Orwin's body, faceup, his arms outstretched between the bed and the wall, a hole in his chest where the shot from the shotgun entered his body.

Squatting beside him, Leah felt for a pulse, even though from the looks of the body there was no need. She could see the carpet of Sylvie's bedroom floor through the hole the shell left behind. Nobody could look like that and be alive.

"Is he dead?" Sylvie asked softly, still cowering in the corner.

Leah nodded. "Very." She went over and knelt beside Sylvie and the baby. "How are you? Are you okay?"

Sylvie nodded.

"And the baby?" The baby was still crying.

"She's okay." Sylvie was cradling her, rocking her gently. The baby's crying slowed down and she grew quieter.

Sylvie stared at Orwin's body, wide-eyed and terrified.

Leah wrapped her arms around Sylvie and the baby, rocking them both together. "It's okay, honey. It's over. He can't hurt you now."

"I know."

Leah pulled away and looked in Sylvie's speckled blue eyes. "You *sure* you're okay?"

She just nodded quickly, biting her lower lip.

"Absolutely sure?"

"I *will* be."

Leah's lips formed a thin smile. "You *will* be." It was the most positive thing she'd ever heard the girl say.

"So it wasn't Preacher Eli after all? All this time?" Sylvie asked.

Leah shook her head. They were pressed up against the white heating radiator that stood along the bedroom wall. "No, hon. That man wants only one thing," she said. "Forgiveness."

Sylvie's voice quivered. "I—I can't give him that. I don't think I'll ever be able to."

Leah began rocking her again. "That's okay, honey," she said. "It's not *you* he wants it from."

Sylvia stayed quiet a moment then said, "Guess what?"

"What?" For a moment, Leah thought the girl's face was bleeding, but when she touched the spot where the blood was, she found it wasn't Sylvie's blood. It was Orwin's, just smeared on Sylvie's body. Probably from when Sylvie crawled across the floor to get the ax.

Sylvie smiled sadly. "I picked out a name for the baby."

Leah brightened. Outside, she heard two police cruisers pull into Sylvie's yard. "You did? Well, it's about time. This baby deserves a name." They spoke almost in a whisper. The baby had stopped crying completely. "What're you gonna call her?"

Sylvie gazed down at the tiny girl cradled in her arms. "Hope," she said, and gave Leah a great big smile. "I think it fits. How 'bout you?"

Leah returned the smile. "I reckon it's near on perfect."

CHAPTER 35

Two days after my mother solved the Sylvie Carson incident, Ethan Montgomery gave her a week off work. She decided we would use the first day of this time off to finally make the trip up to Georgia to meet my new grandparents. In the end, my mother didn't have to worry: Carry was just as excited about meeting them as I was.

At least at *first* she appeared to be. Then the long drive got to Carry and, about an hour and a half in, she started complaining about her legs being cramped and having to go to the bathroom. We must've stopped four times on account of things wrong with Carry, but eventually we got to Columbus.

My new grandparents lived in a pretty, one-level house with a nice lawn and well-kept gardens. The windows all had boxes full of flowers. Everything was blossoming or full bloom, making it not only look like the kind of house you see in fairy tales, but it also made the air sweet, too.

It was late afternoon when we arrived and the sun was slamming down like a hammer striking an anvil. I don't know that I ever felt the sun as hot as I did that day. It reflected so brightly off the yellow siding of my grandparents' house that it looked like they lived on the sun.

Their door was white, and under the afternoon sky, it was the brightest white I could ever imagine. The grass was trimmed perfectly and felt lush and green beneath my new sneakers as we walked to the door. I couldn't believe how excited I was to be meeting blood relatives I didn't know I even had barely a month and a half ago. Especially relatives on my pa's side.

My mother opened the screen door and knocked on the white wooden one behind it. I examined the house, wondering how often they painted it, on account of everything looking so brand-new. A few seconds later, a tall man with thinning white hair and black-rimmed glasses answered.

The minute he saw us, a big, toothy smile came to his mouth. "Why, I know you. You're Abe! And you're Carry! I'd know you two anywhere!" he said. And then to my mother, he held out his hand. "And you must be Miss Leah. It's a pleasure to meet you and I sincerely want to thank you for taking the time to make the trip out." The sun glittered in his glasses.

My mother shook his hand. She smiled back, but not with nearly as big a smile as my granddaddy was beaming at her. I wished hers was bigger.

"Come in! Come in! Sure is nice outside, though. But the air is so dry. It's drier today than happy hour at the Betty Ford Clinic."

I looked at my mom to see what he meant.

"Just go inside," she whispered.

We piled into the house and began taking off our shoes when he stopped us. "Leave 'em on. Everybody does round here. Come on, your grandma's anxious to meet you!" He took us through the living room and down a hallway into a smaller room that reminded me of the parlor at Reverend Starks's house, only this room was bigger and had a television. A woman sat in a rocking chair in the corner knitting. The minute we walked in she beamed at all of us. Then she stood and gave us all hugs. "Oh, I'm so glad you came! Little Abe! And Carry! And Miss Leah!"

She took a step back. "Well, let me take a look at you."

Awkwardly, me and Carry stood there, not certain what we were supposed to do. I felt like maybe I should do a twirl for her or something. Then she said, "I'm your grandma Sara. That there is your grandpa Jeremiah." She shook her head at me. "Oh, boy, do you ever look like your daddy. Don't you think he looks like his daddy, Jer?"

I gave a broad smile back. Nobody'd ever told me I looked like my pa before. That made me very happy. "Have a seat," my grandma Sara said, gesturing to the davenport and chairs around the room. She sat back in her rocker. "Grandpa Jer will put on a pot of coffee."

Looking to my mother, I got the slightest of nods from her. I was allowed to drink coffee, but only on special occasions. I guessed this must've counted as one of those special occasions.

Me and Carry sat on the davenport. My mother appeared very uncomfortable, looking at all the pictures in the room. "Are you hungry?" Grandma Sara asked us. When she spoke, she did so louder than she should've, almost like she was yelling everything at us.

"No," I said back. "Carry made us stop for lunch." I paused and added, "Almost twice." Then, after another pause, I said, "And two more times so she could go to the toilet."

Grandma Sara laughed and slapped her knee. Carry just glared at me. She was keeping remarkably quiet.

Grandpa Jeremiah came back in and told us the coffee'd be ready soon. "The pot's on the blink," he said. "You gotta work with it. I had to go round my elbow to get to my thumb."

I had no idea what he was talking about. I looked at Carry, but she just looked back blankly.

"We were so surprised when Addison told us you'd talked to her," Grandpa Jeremiah told my mother. "We had no idea she had planned to come down and set this up. It was one of the nicest things she's ever done for us."

"Can I ask you somethin'?" my mother asked him.

"Certainly."

"Well, you two were at Billy's funeral—that's where you apparently met my pa—how come Addison never came to the funeral?"

I saw Grandpa Jeremiah cast a nervous glance at Grandma Sara. "Well . . . that's a bit of a story."

"We have time," my mother said, which I thought was quite rude of her. He obviously didn't want to talk about it.

"She was up in Boston."

"I know. That was gonna be my next question: How come she lives in Boston and y'all is way down here in Georgia?"

Grandpa Jeremiah's gaze dropped to the floor. "We sent her to Boston when she was seventeen on account of she got involved with a bad group of kids. Got hooked on all kinds of things. You know—drugs and that. So, when Billy passed away, she was up there in one of them rehabilitation clinics. We was too worried if we let her out for the funeral she might have one of them relapses."

My mother was clearly taken aback by this news. "Oh, I'm so sorry. I shouldn't have pried."

"No, it's fine. It's probably best that you know."

"Is she still . . . ?"

"No, she's been clean now goin' on . . . well, Abe's what? Eleven?"

"I'm twelve," I said.

"Oh, I'm sorry. Of course, you are twelve. And you was two when Billy died. So she's been clean near on eleven years."

"That's fantastic!" my mother said. "Good for her. You must be very proud. She stays up in Boston because she likes it up there, then?"

"She's built herself a life up there. She's got friends and a husband. She's workin' on startin' a family of her own. She comes down to see us often enough, I suppose. Calls at least twice a week."

"I see." My mother fell silent again. She still hadn't sat down. She seemed captivated by some pictures they had displayed in frames, sitting on top of the cabinet that held the television. I looked harder and realized they were pictures of me and Carry. "You got these from my pa?" she asked.

Grandpa Jeremiah gave Grandma Sara another quick glance before answering. "That's right. Your pa was a good man. He sent us lots of pictures so we could see our grandchildren grow. Sure missed him when he went."

My mother picked up a picture of a young man in a T-shirt. He had blond hair and did sort of look a bit like me, so I figured it must be my pa. "Yeah," she said, sounding very far away. "Me too."

Grandpa Jeremiah came up behind her. He looked over the top of his glasses at the photograph. "Billy'd have been 'bout, oh, fifteen or so when that was taken, I reckon," he said. "Always wanted to be a rock star."

Grandma Sara laughed. "A singer!" she said. "Can you believe it? That boy couldn't carry a tune if he had it in a bucket with a lid on it! But oh, he tried."

"Did he ever sing for you, Mom?" Carry asked.

"He tried."

I wished I could have heard him sing.

My mother picked up another picture of my pa. This time it was one of him and a girl. The girl didn't look like my mother. Grandpa Jeremiah lifted his glasses above his eyes and got a better look at it. "Oh, I remember her. Girl was a few crayons short of a complete rainbow, if you ask me." He laughed. When he laughed his voice broke up and he sounded much older than when he spoke.

"Better go check on the coffee, dear," Grandma Sara said.

Grandpa Jeremiah left and she added, "Good thing that man has me. He couldn't find his own ass with both hands stuck inside his pockets." Her eyes cut to me and she quickly covered her mouth. "Oh, I'm sorry. I guess I should've said rear end."

"It's okay," I said. "I know the word *ass*."

"Hey," my mother said. "Language."

"I was just pointin' somethin' out."

"I don't care."

Grandpa Jeremiah returned with the coffee. By the time he'd poured five mugs and we'd started drinking it, everyone seemed much more relaxed, even my mother. She'd stopped curiously looking at pictures and taken a seat in one of the chairs. I discovered my grandpa Jeremiah had a fondness for talking about his son, and, in the next hour, I learned more about my pa then I ever knew the entire time I'd been alive. I was even getting used to the funny way both my grandparents talked.

We found out that my pa used to like to sneak out and then make up stories to cover his tracks, but my grandpa always found out the truth. "I'd tell him, 'That dog don't hunt,' " he said. "But he'd try it again and again, thinkin' each time he could pull the wool down over my eyes." He turned to me. "Back then his elevator was stuck on the second floor."

"Yeah," my grandmother said, "but he had a knack for fallin' into a barrel full of crap and comin' out smellin' just like a rose."

"That's only on account of you let him get away with so much."

"I most certainly did not," my grandma said. "He would get into one of his angry moods and I'd tell him, 'Well, you can just go and get glad the same way you got mad or you can just die.' "

When she said that, the room went silent. She brought her hand to her mouth. "Oh, I'm sorry . . . ," she said, trailing off. "I didn't mean . . ."

Everyone looked at my mother, who seemed to not even notice what had been said. Then she realized everyone was looking at her. "Oh, hey, it's fine. Seriously." She laughed. "It's just a figure of speech, right?"

My grandpa pointed at her. "See? This is why I've always liked you. You were always best for my Billy. You kept him out of trouble. You were the one who'd say, 'My cow died last night, mister, so I don't need your bull.' "

There was a pocket of silence, finally broken by my mother.

"How do you know what I would say?"

"What's that?" Grandpa Jeremiah asked.

"How do you know what I would say? Billy never saw you after him and me started goin' out."

Grandma Sara laughed. "Of course he did. He kept dropping by right up until a few weeks before your weddin'. Then Jeremiah and him had that fight. We should've seen it comin'. After Billy met you, it was like he was a new man. He used to fight with us constantly. Wasn't a week went by that Billy and his daddy didn't almost come to fisticuffs. I think once they actually did, but Jeremiah refuses to tell me the truth."

"I've told you the truth," Jeremiah mumbled. "You just refuse to believe it."

"But then you came along and everythin' seemed to change." She paused and then asked my mother quietly, "Didn't you know this?"

My mother shook her head. "Until Addison met my boy in the street, I didn't really know y'all existed. Billy hardly ever talked 'bout you."

Both my new grandparents just shook their heads slowly and sipped their coffee. "Ain't that just like Billy," my grandpa Jeremiah finally said.

"What do you mean?" my mother asked.

"Ain't nobody gonna mess all over him and call it apple butter," my grandma answered.

"I—I don't understand."

"Billy blamed me," my grandpa said. "For the way he was. On account of he could get violent. In fact, it's amazing he never had no run-ins with the police, but he got lucky."

"I never knew Billy to be violent," my mother said.

"That's probably why you never heard 'bout his family. In Billy's mind, his family was the cause of his violent tendencies. If he don't tell you 'bout them and leaves 'em out of your relationship, the violence stays away, too."

My mother looked like she was a deer caught in a trucker's headlamps. "But—if that's true . . . then . . . it worked."

"The mind is a funny thing," my grandpa said.

"And a tragic one," my grandma added. She kept studying me and Carry sitting on the davenport. I realized Carry hadn't spoken much at all, even though I hadn't really either. "And we've missed so much."

"Thank the Lord Jesus we met your daddy," Grandpa Jeremiah said to my mother.

There was more conversation, most of it filled with funny phrases from my new grandparents, and there was a lot of laughs. Even my mother laughed. It had been a long time since I'd heard her laugh, and I was happy to witness it again. We wound up staying for homemade jambalaya that was really good and for dessert Grandma Sara pulled a freshly baked pecan pie out of the oven. Nothing ever tasted as good as that pie.

When we finally said good night and headed home, it was nearly nighttime. The first stars had begun to peek out of the sky around a full moon that was rising low in the east.

"We're awfully glad you came out to see us," Grandpa Jeremiah said at the porch, after hugging each of us and shaking my hand.

Grandma Sara hugged us all, too. "Please come by anytime. Or maybe we can make the trip out your way. We'll see you again, good Lord willin', and the creek don't rise."

"We'll have to see, dear," my grandpa said, and a stillness fell over everyone that I didn't rightly understand. I caught my mother sharing a knowing look with my grandpa Jeremiah.

After our good-byes, we got into our car. Of course, Carry took the front seat and I was relegated to the back. It wasn't so bad; at least I had it all to myself.

On the way home, Carry wasn't nearly as annoying as she had been on the way there. She only made us stop twice and both times were for her to use a restroom. One of those times my mother was stopping for gas anyway, so it wasn't a wasted stop.

We talked about my new grandparents during the drive home, each of us agreeing we had a very enjoyable time and that they were good people. "It was a nice visit," my mother said.

"It certainly was," I agreed. "I just wish we'd have done it a lot sooner."

To this, there was no reply, and my mother seemed to get lost in her thoughts for a long while. In fact, she pretty near stayed silent all the way back to Alvin.

When we hit the city limits, I decided it was time that silence was broken. "I guess my pa came from good blood."

"I guess he did," my mother agreed.

"I'm happy that I look like him."

"You *do* look a *lot* like him sometimes."

"How come you never tell me that?"

"I will. From now on. I'll make a point of it."

I beamed a great big smile in the darkness.

"They sure talk funny," Carry said. "Half the time, I was still tryin' to figure out what they'd just said while they went on to sayin' the next thing."

When she said this, we all laughed and laughed as the last of the stars popped out of the night sky. Above us, the moon, big, full, and round, shone brightly, reflecting off the hood of our car, and lighting the road for the rest of our way home.

CHAPTER 36

It was late by the time Leah and the kids arrived back home in Alvin.

Leah saw the kids quickly to bed and had a feeling Abe was asleep before she even left his room after tucking him in. The purple light of early evening had darkened to an almost-black through his thick curtains, and his bedroom was cast in shadows.

In Caroline's room, Leah's daughter had some odd points to make about meeting her grandparents earlier. Leah didn't normally see Caroline to bed. Usually (especially during the summer months) Caroline stayed up well past Leah's bedtime. But tonight she'd headed straight to her room, something unprecedented. So Leah had just sort of popped in to say good night before going to bed herself.

It had been a long day, undoubtedly for everyone.

"Mom?" Caroline asked, getting under the covers. She'd already slipped on her pajamas and brushed her teeth while Leah was tucking Abe in.

"Yes?"

"Am I ever as bad as Grandpa Jeremiah and Grandma Sara said Pa was when they were talkin' 'bout him bein' so disobedient and all?"

Leah let out a small laugh. "You have your moments."

Frowning, Caroline said, "I don't mean to be, you know."

"I know. And I also know you'll grow up into a fine young woman." She paused and said, "You *have* been makin' your brother paint your toes every week, though. I'd say that classifies as bein' a tiny bit mean."

"Did *he* tell you that?"

Leah shook her head.

"Then how do you know?"

"Honey, I *am* a police detective *and* a mother. We have our ways. Not much gets past us. I reckoned by now you'd have figured that out."

Caroline turned and looked out her window. Leah followed her gaze. The drapes were open and a few stars twinkled around the full moon hanging outside.

"Think maybe it's time you let him off the hook?" Leah asked.

Caroline pulled her covers up to her chin. The moon and stars lit up her face as though it had a spotlight on it. "Yeah, I s'pose. Gonna miss havin' such nice toes, though. He really did do a good job."

"That's your brother. He don't do nothin' without puttin' his heart into it. But you're doin' the right thing for lettin' him off the hook. And as far as me and you go, you're just a bit tricky when it comes to my part in it all."

"How so?"

"Well . . ." Leah sighed. "I'm realizin' I need to start spendin' more time with you. And, as your grandparents would probably say, 'Sometimes I find myself busier than a cat tryin' to cover its crap on a marble floor.' "

Caroline laughed.

Leah kissed her daughter's forehead.

"Go to sleep," Leah said. "Don't worry 'bout the way you are. You're perfect. You an' Abe both are. I wouldn't change an ounce of you even if I was able to. You're my perfect daughter."

Leah got up and left Caroline's bedroom, pulling her door closed behind her. She went into her own room and collapsed onto the bed. It had been a long day with a lot of driving, and a lot of emotions had been tossed up inside her from meeting Billy's parents.

She couldn't believe what they'd said about Billy having anger and violence issues. She'd never seen it. Not once. Not even an indication of it.

Could someone really change that much?

The lamp on the table beside Leah's bed was still on and its light caught the edge of something gold on the doily beneath it. It was the wedding band she'd placed there just over a week ago. Leah picked it up.

Lying on her back with her head against her pillow, she held it up toward the ceiling, examining it in her fingers—a circular band of gold; an unbreakable symbol that went around and around, without a beginning and without an end. A symbol of eternity.

Only, there had been a beginning, and there had been an end.

A very abrupt end.

Billy had been taken from her one morning when Abe was just two years old and Caroline five, and Leah had been left all by herself to raise both their children. And for that, until now, she had never been able to forgive him. And she'd felt guilty about that selfishness ever since. She's hated herself for hating him. Even when she had pulled this ring out of the shoe box before giving the rest of the contents to Abe, she wasn't sure why she had done it. The ring only reminded her of what had happened, and that had always made her angry.

Except tonight, there was no anger. No guilt.

Nothing but acceptance and relief.

For the first time since she could remember, she knew her kids were going to be okay.

She knew *she* was going to be okay.

Sometime between placing this ring on her nightstand and this moment right now, something inside Leah had changed, and she'd found something that had been hidden from her for ten long years.

Forgiveness.

She wasn't even sure who, exactly, or even what, she had forgiven.

But that didn't matter.

The important part was that she'd found what she'd been unable to find all these years.

Slipping the ring onto her finger, she reached up and switched off the lamp. Turning over, she pulled her blankets up over her body, wrapping her hands around them. A tired heaviness sank her deeper into her pillow.

A soft smile came to her lips. She felt it in the starlit darkness as she closed her eyes and gently fell into a quiet sleep. And, for the first time in ten years, she happily dreamed of being Mrs. Billy Bob Teal once again.

Tomorrow would be another day.

Tomorrow, there'd still be lots more time to play detective.

Close to the Broken Hearted

Michael Hiebert

ABOUT THIS GUIDE

The suggested questions are included to enhance
your group's reading of Michael Hiebert's
Close to the Broken Hearted.

Discussion Questions

1. Do you think Preacher Eli meant to pull the trigger on the gun that killed Caleb Carson? Do you agree with the conviction of manslaughter he was given for the crime?

2. The night Sylvie discovers Preacher Eli is being released from prison, Leah goes to visit her. For the first time, she arrives to find Sylvie acting almost normal. Why does this scare Leah so much?

3. Abe seems to lack an inherent trust in people, especially strangers. In this book, he immediately sentenced Preacher Eli as guilty in his head as soon as he met the man. In *Dream with Little Angels,* he does the same thing with Mr. Wyatt Edward Farrow, his new neighbor. How much of this distrust do you think comes from him having spent his life as the son of the only detective in town? How much does Leah's habit of bringing Abe with her on police matters affect him?

4. Why is family so important to Abe? And not just his immediate family either. Why is learning about his ancestry such a huge event for him?

5. Why do you think Sylvie chooses to live in one of the most desolate places in town, where there's nothing but a narrow road lined tightly with a dark forest? Does this behavior seem to go with or against the way she acts toward the rest of the world?

6. Why do you think Preacher Eli's father-in-law was able to purchase the Carson property for such a low price when it was sold at auction? Do you think Eli's reputation came into play? How much did the fact that three people had died on the property affect the price, do you think?

7. Do you think Leah was right when she immediately jumped at Preacher Eli being the prime suspect when Sylvie came home and found the five shotgun shells lined up neatly on her table?

8. Abe's religious point of view is very much that of a child and yet it seems to be fully functional. Where do you think he acquired such a point of view and, given his upbringing, why do you think it is so important (or maybe better put as unimportant) that his family went to the all-black Full Gospel Church for services?

9. What do you think was the true cause of Tom Carson's suicide, or was it a number of different factors? If the latter, what were they?

10. The wooden swords are a major symbol throughout the book. What do they stand for? What is the significance of Abe breaking his sword when he does? What is happening in his life at this point in time?

11. Do you think Leah makes the right decision in bringing her children to the crime scene when she finds out Orwin is in the process of breaking down Sylvie's door? Do you think she tends to put them in needless harm, or is the opposite true and she's actually overprotective?

12. Ultimately, Sylvie having the loaded shotgun in her house turns out to possibly save her life. Do you agree that it was a good idea to keep it loaded and ready all that time?

13. Is taking Abe and Carry to see their new grandparents a good idea, given the health of Grandma Sara? Leah hints early on that when Abe lost his grandpa on her side, it devastated him. Isn't she just setting things up for that to happen again? Do you think they'll visit again, or will this be a one-time occurrence?